Perfect Together

KRISTEN ASHLEY

ROCK CHICK
PRESS

Cover Image: Pixel Mischief Design

Perfect
TOGETHER

KRISTEN

NEW YORK TIMES BESTSELLING AUTHOR

ASHLEY

Prologue

I KNOW

Wyn

"You...have a place?"

"Apartment, yeah," he grunted.

"You've rented an apartment."

It was a statement, and the pain in it was not veiled.

Hearing it was why my husband of nineteen years looked from placing some of his folded T-shirts into one of his Tumi cases, to me.

His next wasn't a grunt, it was gentle and sweet, and butchering when he repeated, "Yeah."

"So, we're done," I said tonelessly.

He straightened from his packing, "Wyn—"

"Like so much else in our lives, *you* have decided we're done."

His beautiful, full lips thinned.

But he didn't answer.

The suitcase on our bed that he was packing, the leather bag he used for weekenders already crammed full, zipped shut and sitting on the floor, his workout bag the same, the Tumi carry-on the same, his empty part of the closet and currently emptying drawers...

These were his answer.

"There's no talking about this? Working this out?" I asked.

"We've talked ad nauseam. We've—"

I leaned his way and grated out, "Nineteen *fucking* years, Remy. You're just throwing that away?"

I could see immediately he was getting angry (I mean, it was actually *twenty-one* fucking years, including dating, engagement, so of course I would).

"I'm not throwing dick away, Wyn."

I glanced pointedly at each bag that told a different tale.

"You never took a goddamn thing I said seriously," he noted.

Okay, now *I* was getting angry.

"Are you insane?" I demanded.

"Were you in California last weekend?" he asked.

I felt my hair sway as my back went ramrod straight.

"I asked you not to go, you went," he bit out.

"You *told* me not to go, and it was work, I couldn't *not* go. So yes, I went."

"You can do whatever the fuck you want, Wyn, you own the goddamned company. That includes saying no and sending someone else."

"And how, precisely, do I say no to Fiona Remington?"

"You open your mouth and form the letters n and o."

I stood there, staring at the man I'd shared a bed with for decades, the father of my three children, and I felt cold creep over my skin.

"I'm on the cover of the top magazine in my business, for fuck's sake," he stated. "On it for winning that award this weekend, and my daughter was my date because my wife was kissing ass in Hollywood."

That cold grew icy.

"You don't want to do this, Remy," I warned. "There's no coming back from this."

"Of course I don't want to do this, Wyn," he spat. "But you've given me no choice."

Oh no, he did *not*.

I swung an arm out to the Tumi. "So this is on me?"

"The city of fucking *Phoenix* gave me an award, Wyn, and you were not *here*."

"The highest-paid, most critically acclaimed actor in Hollywood asked me to style her for awards season, Remy, and she had this one window to sit down for a consultation before she's off to Algiers to begin a punishing three-month shoot, and she won't step foot on American soil until two days before the award shows begin. So I needed to be *there*."

"Yeah," he said, the finality in that syllable like a crush of stones landing on my head. "You did."

After he spoke those words, he walked back to the dresser and emptied the drawer.

As he shoved the tees in with the others, I whispered, "There's no coming back from this, Remy."

He didn't look at me as he flipped the suitcase shut, zipped it, and then tugged it from the bed.

Only when he had both bags over his shoulders, the suitcases tipped to their wheels—strong and fit, my rugby-playing husband, he didn't seem weighed down at all with a representation of our entire life hanging off his shoulders—did his eyes find mine so he could give me an answer.

And that answer was not his words.

"I know."

That answer was my tall, strong, handsome husband walking out our bedroom door.

CHAPTER 1
Walgreens

Wyn

T*hree years later...*

"Typical alphahole bullshit. Typical Remy, yanking your chain like this."

I was in my car.

My friend Bea's voice was sounding from the speakers.

And my heart just stopped beating.

This situation was obviously acute, so I made the first right turn I could, into a Walgreens parking lot.

I parked.

And I tried to get my heart beating again.

Though, this was hard since my mind was working triple-time.

"I mean, what in *the* fuck? You just cannot shake this jackoff loose," Bea kept ranting.

I stared at my windshield, deep breathing.

"I mean," she carried on, as I was just then realizing she was wont to do, "he walked out on you and three kids. He couldn't let that be his Dick of the Century finale?"

"Sabre called this family meeting, Bea. Remy didn't," I told her something I'd already told her.

"Why does it have to be at Remy's house?" she shot back.

Why did she care?

"I don't know," I replied. "I didn't quiz Sabre on the whys and wherefores. My eldest son has never asked us all to get together. I'm more preoccupied with Sabre calling a meeting at all, and it being so important he's driving up from Tucson with Manon, and what that might mean, than nagging him about why he picked his dad's house."

"Well, I know why," she declared.

And she did.

This was why my heart had stopped beating.

Because she knew everything about everything.

And when this skill she had came down to me, it was everything about Remy and why he was always behaving one step up from caveman.

Or one step below dick.

Or jackoff.

Or motherfucker.

Or asshole/alphahole (that second one was her favorite).

There was no denying Remy was an alpha. There was also no denying he was hypermasculine. And last, there was no denying these things had an effect on our marriage.

But there was further no denying they were both part of the reason why I fell in love with and married him in the first place.

Bea went on to tell me why Sabre had called the meeting at his dad's.

"Because he wants that bitch there."

Okay.

I was not a big fan of Remy's live-in girlfriend, Myrna. She and I didn't often have opportunities to be in each other's space, but when we were, we avoided each other like the plague. And I (quietly) did not like her due to some of the things Manon, my daughter, told me about her. (Suffice it to say, Manon didn't like Myrna either—it wasn't hate, but there was not a lot of love lost between the two.)

But I wasn't hip on calling another woman a bitch unless she was categorically, well...a bitch.

And as far as I knew, Myrna wasn't that.

At least not categorically.

"If he does, wouldn't it make sense that he'd call the meeting at Remy's?" I asked, the words coming out of my mouth even as I wondered why in the heck

I was explaining family things to Bea in a manner I was actually *defending* them. "He'd hardly ask Remy and Myrna to my house."

"Remy has no problem showing up at your house," she pointed out, but I wasn't sure why.

Though, it did get me to thinking, because no, he didn't have a problem with this.

Even if we barely had anything to discuss anymore. All the important decisions had been made, and now our kids were old enough to make their own.

Yves, a senior in high school, was the only one home, but he had a car. He stayed where he wanted when he wanted, and he spent just as much time with Remy as he did with me.

As for Sabre and Manon, they were both down in Tucson at the University of Arizona, but like Yves, they had cars, and when they were home, they stayed where they wanted, when they wanted.

And the truth of that was that Manon was often with me, not only because she wasn't a fan of Myrna's, and Sabre stayed with his dad, because he and Remy (along with Yves), were two (three) peas in a pod.

It was just that Yves was at a time in his life where he still needed Mom *and* Dad.

Manon was sallying forth in this world as a young woman, and therefore, she needed me.

And Sabre was at a time where it appeared he needed to be around his dad.

I found this all entirely natural and had no qualms with it.

Of course, I'd like to see my first son more. But even if he slept at his father's house, he was like Manon: his life was so busy, sleep was mostly all he did there.

We had our mother/son times. It wasn't like he ignored me. Just as Manon spent quality time with her dad.

But Remy did often show at my house to "discuss things."

I didn't have a chance to get a lock on remembering what those things were in my present moment.

Bea was, as I was just then noting was her usual, on a roll.

"So *you* have to be around *her* during a *family meeting*, which is a *slap in the face*."

"I honest to God don't know why we're having this conversation. It's none of your business what Sabre wants or what I decide to do about it."

Those words came out mostly because I was ticked, and I had the tendency to get ticked at the drop of hat. As such, I didn't tend to allow myself a second to think on that emotion before I did something about it.

And in that second, I considered how that might have affected a number of things in my life, and...

Damn.

"Did you just say that to me?" she asked, sounding deeply wounded.

"Bea, you phoned and asked me over for wine, pizza and Netflix, and I told you I couldn't because I had this meeting then I had to get to the warehouse. It's kickoff night. You know we have a ritual on kickoff night. Then you started in on Remy, and Sabre, and Myrna, and really, I must say that I don't know where this vitriol comes from. But I'm worried my son is going to tell me he got some girl pregnant, or he's decided to change his major even though he's graduating in May, or something like that. And you're spewing loathing for Remy when our divorce has been final for two years and we've both moved on."

"First, if you remember, *he* divorced *you*, and *you did not want that*," she retorted. "And second, ask yourself, Wyn, have you moved on? Have you *really* moved on?"

Okay, now I wasn't ticked.

I was mad.

I was also freaked at her second point.

And those, for me, were not a good mix.

"I can't even begin to imagine why you'd remind me Remy was the one who divorced me," I stated coolly.

"Because it's like you forgot he ripped your heart out and crushed it under his boot, this after he'd kicked it around for ten years."

"And as a friend you feel it's your job to remind me of that?" I asked.

"Well, *yeah*," she answered.

"I think we need to stop talking," I told her.

"I disagree, since you're driving over to his house because Sabre is growing up to be a chip off the old block."

Oh no.

Hell no.

"Think about what you just said to me," I whispered.

But I wasn't done.

Boy, was I *so* not done.

"Now, I listened to you verbally abuse my husband for ten years," I continued. "And I'm going to have to have a think about that. But do not mistake me and do not miss this message, Bea. Listen carefully. Never...*ever*...speak badly about my son, to me or *anyone*."

With that, I hung up and I stared at my dash, fuming.

Bea rang right back.

I refused the call.

Okay.

Okay, okay, okay.

Heck, now my mind was working quadruple-time.

Put this aside, Wyn, I cut into my own raging thoughts to tell myself. *Get it together. Get to Remy's. You're running late. You always run late. He hates that.*

He did.

He'd tease me about it in the beginning. The first three, four, five, ten (okay, fifteen) years of our marriage.

Then, it annoyed him, and he let that show.

Not long later, around about the time he left, it pissed him off, and he let me know.

My response?

I took it as my tall, dark, gorgeous husband still being tall, dark and gorgeous, and I was the mom of three babies. I still carried baby weight even after they were nowhere near being babies. He was no longer doing the appreciative up-and-down that told me the extra fifteen minutes were *so* worth it, and he was going to show me just how much when we got home.

No, I was no longer his hot wife he couldn't keep his hands off.

I was the fat mother of his kids he didn't have any patience for.

I was also the starting-her-own-business woman who suddenly needed ten more hours in the day to continue to fold his laundry, get the grocery shopping done and look decent for his client dinners.

The interior of my Range Rover rang again, and as it was Bea, I didn't accept the call.

But I made one to someone else in our posse, top spot bestie shared with my other top spot, Bernice.

The call was to Kara.

She picked up on ring three.

"Oh hell, a call before Sabre's meeting," she said as greeting. "Are you okay?"

That was Kara.

It would be Bernice too.

Are you okay?

Not, *Typical Remy bullshit.*

"Do you think I haven't moved on from Remy?" I blurted.

"Uhhhhh," she drew that out then asked, "Let me guess, Bea phoned."

I blinked.

"She's blowing up mine, by the way," she said.

"I just told her off," I shared.

9

Kara said nothing.

"She was ranting about Remy," I continued.

"How am I not surprised?" she muttered.

"Right?" I stated. "Is she like, *unhealthily* committed to bitching about my ex-husband?"

"She is not a card-carrying member of the Remy Gastineau fan club, no."

I forged ahead, even if it was tentatively, "And has she not been that for a very long time?"

Kara again was silent.

"She hates him," I said softly. "Things fell apart with him and that's bad enough for me. I don't need her being really mean about it."

"Bea is a woman who has no issues speaking her mind," Kara noted.

"Yes, and that should be encouraged, but filters also should be in place. For instance, not bitching about my ex then rolling that into priming herself to begin bitching about my son who you think is acting like my ex."

"She didn't," Kara breathed.

"She did," I confirmed. "It wasn't overt, but considering she can't stand Remy, calling Sabre a chip off the old block, I got the gist."

"Holy crap."

"Yeah," I agreed.

"Sabre *is* a chip off the old block, so is Yves, but in very good ways because you and Remy didn't work out, but..."

She hesitated.

It felt like my ears might start bleeding, I was listening so hard.

"When he wasn't being up his own ass, Remy was a really good guy," she finished carefully.

I stared at the building that sat in front of my car.

"I'm gonna call Bernice," Kara said gently. "I think we need a Cock and Snacktails night."

Bernice, in a previous incarnation, had been a flight attendant. And she'd been on a flight where one of her colleagues had screwed up the cabin announcement once they'd leveled off, not stating the attendants would be serving "snacks and cocktails," but instead that they'd be serving "cock and snacktails."

This was already hilarious.

It got better when Bernice started serving, and she asked some little old lady what she wanted, and the lady pointed in the air to indicate the announcement and ordered, "What she said."

Since that flight, and Bernice relating this story, any night where we got together and had cocktails and munchies, we called Cock and Snacktails night.

But outside of the night we had them two days after Remy left me, the night after Remy served me with papers, the night after Bernice's husband confessed to cheating on her (not whole hog, he'd just kissed another woman, but, trust me, that was almost a worse betrayal than taking it to the limit), I felt right now I needed Cock and Snacktails more than ever.

"I let him come over and we bicker about stupid shit, Kara," I admitted softly, even though she knew this. "Manon going over her monthly budget and how much of that goes to Starbucks, and how my then twenty-year-old son really wasn't old enough to do a cross country drive with his buds, though he was. It's like we make up shit to bicker about."

All Kara said was, "Cock and Snacktails," which set my gut to twisting.

Because I knew she didn't want to get into it then, since there was a lot to get into because she agreed with me.

"I'm holding on to him," I said in horror. "He's moved on. Has the bachelor pad he's always wanted. The petite, beautiful, free-spirited, younger woman. And I'm holding on to him, giving Manon extra money, defending her right to copiously caffeinate, forbidding Sabre to have something he really wants, and my son is mature, smart, it is something he should have without me making it a headache and a huge discussion with his dad."

"Cock," Kara said slowly, "and Snacktails, sister."

I looked down to my dash again and saw the time.

I was supposed to be at Remy's house in five minutes and I was, in the current traffic, a good fifteen, twenty minutes away.

Even noting this, I could not get past the epiphany that was assaulting my head.

"I told him when he walked out on me, he couldn't come back, and he was good with that," I shared. "But even if those words came out, I never let him go."

"Wyn, honey, go see what's up with Sabre. And then it's kickoff night, yeah?"

Of course, she remembered.

Bea didn't.

Kara did.

"Yes," I confirmed.

"Be with your staff, open that champagne, toast the latest box of fabulousness your twenty thousand subscribers are going to love that you curated for them as the preeminent stylist of Hollywood, Bollywood, and everything in between. In the meantime, I'll get with Bernice, and we'll set a time to have girl time. Is there any night you can't do it? Or should I call Noel?"

Noel was my assistant.

11

Noel had decided he wanted to live the life of *Devil Wears Prada* without (I hoped) the devil part. Therefore, Noel had a self-imposed duty of being on twenty-four, seven.

And I could be dramatic. But I once picked up my own dry cleaning on a Saturday because I was in the same strip mall, and he'd lost his mind in a way we did not want a repeat.

Truth?

It was no skin off my nose my PA felt picking up my dry cleaning was his sacred duty.

So I let him.

In other words, I answered the only way I could, considering the last time I put something in my own schedule was two weeks into Noel's employment (and we didn't want a repeat of that either).

"You better call Noel."

Kara started laughing.

I felt my lips tip up, because I adored her, and Noel and his foibles meant he made it his mission to take care of me.

But I had, at most, twenty minutes to come to terms with something earth-shattering.

I had, at most, twenty minutes to finally let go of the love of my life.

"I gotta go, I'm going to be late to the meeting," I said to Kara.

She read my tone, which wasn't exactly beaten, but it wasn't far from it.

"I'll tell Noel it's emergency planning, okay?" she asked.

"Okay. Thanks for listening."

"Anytime and every time. Love you, babe."

"Love you back, babe."

We hung up and the instant I saw her call fade from the screen on my dash, I saw something else.

And heard something.

"Hang on a second, baby."

I turned and looked at the big, amazing-looking guy sitting on the barstool. The guy who had been smiling at me as I walked to and by him.

"You did not just walk by me."

I had.

Even as he'd smiled at me, I'd walked right by Remy, never thinking once that gorgeous man was smiling at me that way because he wanted me to stop.

But he didn't let me walk away from him without giving him my number.

He was so confident, so sure of himself, I'd never met a man like him.

From the second he spoke to me, I was drunk on his attention.

We'd had our first date the very next night.

I'd slept with him on our third date, which was three nights later, a Friday, and I hadn't left all weekend.

Over the next two years I'd moved in with him, got engaged to him and married him.

After that, I'd given him babies.

After that, we'd raised them.

In the beginning, it was heaven.

In every way, we were perfect.

Perfect together.

But eventually, we did not drift apart. We broke apart.

And then he shattered us.

Ever since, I'd been sitting among the pieces trying to figure out how to start the process of gluing us back together.

While Remy had bought his mid-century pad, kitted it out with a personal style only an award-winning architect could pull off, and gone on with his life, falling in love with and introducing our family to another woman.

And I had to come to grips with that. Right now.

So it was going to make me later, but I checked the clock.

And I did what I did when I had to do something that didn't fit into my life, my schedule, the load I carried.

I gave myself five full minutes to feel it.

This meant I sobbed in the parking lot for two minutes.

I struggled with pulling my shit together for two minutes.

I dried my tears and did my best to fix my face for a minute.

Then I pulled out of the parking lot and left Walgreens—and the love of my life—behind.

CHAPTER 2

Hugh Hefner

Wyn

P ulling up to the curb in front of Remy's house, it was not the first
time I considered how deeply it sucked that his house was so cool.

Once Manon left for school, I did things to the home Remy and I
had raised the kids in. Things that gave me the world's best bathroom and
closet, but it usurped two bedrooms.

Even if her room was one of them, Manon was all over it.

She helped me with the design and was perfectly okay staying in the "guest"
bedroom (because I let her redecorate, so it was mostly all her, just a more
sophisticated, mature her). An additional carrot on that stick was that it had an
en suite.

Sabre bunked with Yves whenever he stayed with me, something Yves was
down with, but Sabre was upset I'd destroyed his bedroom even though he'd
said, "I'm never moving back home," approximately five hundred times in the
months before, and then the years after he'd gone to school.

Not to mention, when he wasn't cross-countrying it with his bros, he was
camping with them, in Rocky Point with them, playing rugby with his league,
interning at different firms (including his father's), dating copious "babes", or
staying with his father.

Oh yeah, and when Remy heard about the renovations, he came over and
we didn't bicker about it.

He'd lost his damned mind and nearly shouted the house down about how

14

"irrational" it was to take a house from a five-bedroom to a three-bedroom, and "...in this neighborhood, you're flushing a hundred thousand dollars right down the toilet, Wyn."

"Considering I'm *dying* in this house, Remy, what do I care?" I'd shot back. "The kids will bury me, sell it, and put their children through college with the proceeds. It's a win for them in a time hopefully they'll be so full of grief, they won't give a damn about a hundred thousand dollars."

"Bullshit, woman..." (And by the by, we'll just say I was never, *ever* a fan of when the word "woman" came out of my ex-husband's mouth, pre-divorce, but definitely not when he was yelling at me after it), "...when Yves is out, you're either going direct to a high-rise with a concierge and a valet that parks your fucking car for you or you're moving to LA. You intend to die in this house, my ass."

As long as even one of my children was in Phoenix, *my* ass was in the Valley of the Damned Sun.

However, he might not be wrong, because I'd never considered it until he mentioned it, but someone valeting my car when I came home sounded heavenly.

I did not share that.

I said, "Considering I bought you out of this property and it's only my name on the title, darling, what on earth does it matter to you?"

"Stop fucking calling me 'darling.' You know I hate it. It's fucked-up New York Fashion Week bullshit."

"I know it is," I confirmed. "I also know how much you detest it, *darling*, so clue in. I use it to *piss you off* when you're *pissing me off* in hopes you'll get so pissed off, you'll *take off*."

Oh yes.

We had a very healthy divorce, Remy and me.

We won't get into the argument we had when Sabre told him I was changing back to my maiden name.

My business name was still simply *Wyn Gastineau*, it had an "Inc." behind it officially, but not as it was known in the biz. It was my name, the end.

But I legally went back to Wyn Byrne personally.

I did this after Myrna moved in with Remy.

Okay, since it was on my mind, we'll get into it.

It went like this.

Remy: "So, you're punishing me for being with someone else?"

I was, of a sort.

Me (in denial, not only to him): "The world doesn't revolve around you, darling."

Yes.

I'd thrown in the "darling."

Remy: "Bullshit, Wyn. Has it occurred to you that we might not be together, but we're still a family?"

Me: "I haven't *disowned* our children. I've *changed my name*. And frankly, what my name is, is no longer any of your business."

Remy: "You dumping my name and our history and every memory we've ever made is none of my business?"

Seriously?

And *he* called *me* "prone to drama" (which he had, numerous times)?

Me (at the same time trying not to let my head explode): "*I* wasn't the one who walked out on *you*, and *I* wasn't the one who filed divorce from *you*. You want to talk about a memory, Remy? Let's talk about *that* one."

For those scores, it was a stalemate on my house reno (only because he still thought he was right; I still knew it was none of his business).

But I'd sure won that last one.

I knew this because it'd bought me three whole Remy-free weeks while he seethed.

And damn it all to hell, while he did that, I'd missed him.

These were my thoughts as I walked from my car to his house, which was set deep into a big lot on a curve in a street in the historic neighborhood of Encanto.

Ranch-style. L-shaped. With lush, tropical landscaping that was so old and established, it was a beautiful, cultivated jungle. This surrounding a small front courtyard with a fountain that you could see through the wall of windows that made up the front of the house.

Although I'd been there several times, I had never been given a full tour, but I knew to one side Remy had a home office and Sabre had a bedroom, which should be the guest suite, but it was a private young-adult-man space now (another reason Sabre stayed with Remy).

Down the longer side, the end of which was Remy and Myrna's master suite that had a sunken bed area I had a secret longing to see, there were also Jack and Jill bedrooms for Yves and Manon, and a poker room.

Yes, a room dedicated to freaking *poker*.

Because Remy was that guy.

The man's man.

He did not sit and watch football on Sundays because those were the days he played rugby. And after he played rugby, he drank beer and ate steak with his rugby buddies. He'd had a spell where he'd been a triathlete, and he'd moved on from this to dedicate time to snowboarding (something he already did, and he still did it) and mountain bike riding (and luckily for him, we lived in Arizona, so he could do that year-round).

Obviously, he played poker the entire time I knew him.

He was further an ace at pool (and had a pool table in his family room, a room that also had a wet bar, not kidding, *a wet bar*).

His house included a somewhat formal sunken living room, which was what you walked into from the front door.

This room had a grand piano (Remy and all the kids played because his mother decreed that "gentlemen understand the finer arts by *participating in them, cher*") and two walls of windows.

One that looked to the front courtyard.

One that looked to a backyard, which showcased a rectangular mid-century pool and patio replete with perfectly placed barrel cacti, boxy furniture with bright turquoise cushions, and shade provided by specially designed "umbrellas" made of turquoise fabric stretched between three wide and tight white circles attached at an angle to a white pole, and they looked like they belonged in Tomorrowland.

In other words, they were fabulous.

Remy's house further included a one-lane kitchen that managed to have a remarkable amount of counterspace because it was so long. It also had excellent and unexpected lighting, and cabinets suspended by short rods over the outside counter that faced the pool-table-wet-bar-bedecked family room. Milky, sliding glass panels covered the fronts of the overhead cabinets. Minimalistic handles on the lower. Stainless steel appliances that, I noted every time I was there, were miraculously fingerprint free.

It really was magnificent.

The whole home.

Or at least what I'd seen.

And luckily for Remy, he'd found a woman who would move into his massive, four-thousand-square-foot mancave and not change a thing.

Not put her stamp or personality on an inch of it (at least, any of it I'd seen).

Except, of course, the framed nude photograph of herself she'd given Remy for Christmas last year.

In front of my children.

I had to hand it to Remy. By Manon's report, although this portrait hung in their bedroom, he'd not been best pleased, and he hadn't hidden it when he'd received something so personal without warning in front of his kids (her excuse, also according to Manon, "But, baby, they're *all grown*," and no, the woman had no children of her own, which might explain that).

17

But it was on display in his house where his children lived.

Perhaps not in the living room...but still.

"I never go into their room because...gross," Manon had said about it. This had genuinely made me sad.

Because Remy and Manon used to cuddle up in our bed all the time, watching romcoms (they were both suckers for a good romcom, or a bad one) or reading (they were big readers and we hadn't had any furniture where dad and daughter could snuggle and lose themselves in books, except our big bed).

One could say, if you wanted to stake your territory in your man's house that you had to share with his kids, that was a good way to do it.

And that was how I took it.

With all things *Remy!* spilling all over his home, including his kids being there a lot of the time, Myrna had to stake her claim somewhere.

So she did.

But honestly, though I'd never utter these words out loud to anyone (not even Kara and Bernice, definitely not Bea), I would be happy in that house.

Absolutely, my huge kitchen with its acres of marble countertops (Remy's reno, almost upon us moving in, in fact our entire house had been reno'ed and decorated by him—not a surprise, since projects he worked on now, he designed everything from the building to the furniture and carpeting) and my new master suite that was most women's dream, would be hard to walk away from.

But his house was just that awesome.

And if that was what he'd wanted (and I knew it was, he'd talked about it often enough), once the kids were all gone or close to it (say, *now*) I would have given it to him.

Which would cue Bea getting in my face about it, like she did anytime I "gave into" Remy.

This was all on my mind as I walked from my car to his front door and pressed the button for the doorbell.

It wasn't a surprise when he opened it almost immediately.

And he did it with a face like thunder (again, no surprise).

Still, that face was unbelievable.

He was ridiculously attractive, had been when we met, and was even more so now.

Tall (six foot three). Built solid and bulky with thighs that could spawn their own religion. He had messy, dark, always overlong hair that now had threads of silver in it, and classic French male features. Strong, distinctive nose. Heavy brow. Thick eyebrows. Wide forehead. Perfectly formed mouth that had a tendency to rest in a delicious male pout or a distressingly outstanding smirk.

He was, as I stared up at him glowering down at me, cool.

That was Remy.

Cool.

Effortlessly so.

He was who Hugh Hefner wanted to be, standing there in his fabulous doorway with his distinctive home behind him wearing a pair of jeans that were soft as velvet (I knew because I'd washed them) and faded almost white. They hung loose but hinted at a superior ass (the hint was true) and could bunch in mysterious, delicious ways around a promising package (and it lived up to that promise).

Up top, a pale-yellow button-up shirt that opened to give a generous visual of a strong, tanned column of throat and the cut of his muscled collarbone and hung off his shoulders in a casual, "I don't give a shit" way that was so attractive, you could taste it on your tongue.

His feet were bare, the front hems of his jeans draped over his ankles, and the back hems were raw ends because he'd been walking on them for years.

He was top-to-toe beautiful.

And he was no longer mine.

"You're late," he bit, his rich voice edged with barbs, like molasses tinged with serrano. "No fuckin' surprise."

"I'm sorry," I replied. "I am. Yes. I've no excuse. But I truly am sorry."

His head ticked with surprise at my response because I was always late, and I always had an excuse, and at our end, this always bugged him, the being-late part, *and* the excuse part.

Then his eyes narrowed.

"Have you been crying?"

Guess I should have allotted another minute to fixing my makeup.

"I'm good. I'm fine. I'm here. I really am sorry that—"

"Why have you been crying?"

There was no use denying I had. First, I couldn't really hide it. Second, I knew this man, every inch of his body, every mood he could have, every expression that could pass over his face, all of it like the back of my hand.

He knew me the same.

So there was no point.

I locked eyes with him and said, "Honestly, Remy, I'm okay. But Sabre probably—"

"Why have you been crying, Wyn?"

"It really isn't that big of a deal."

Lie: I'm crying because I finally came to terms with the fact that we're over.

"I'm good. Honestly."

19

Lie: You were the love of my life and I let us fail.

"I'm okay now. Let's do this with Sabre."

Lie: I wasn't. But I was determined I would be. Eventually.

He didn't move out of the door to let me in.

"Remy—" I started.

"Why have you been crying, Wyn?"

It was an unexpected blow, but man, did it sock me right in the chest.

I drew in breath to recover from the warm concern in his tone, the soft worry on his face, the intense scrutiny of those caramel eyes.

I opened my mouth, and I had no idea what was about to come out, particularly since his gaze dropped to my lips, and I felt that familiar, lovely heat hit other parts of me when it did, before a call came from inside the house.

"Is it Wyn?"

Myrna.

I swallowed, closed my eyes, dropped my head, shifted my chin to the side and gave it a second before I opened my eyes and looked at Remy again.

Mistake.

Huge.

Because I just did all of that. And he'd just watched me do it.

Another expression was on his face now, and apparently, I'd lied before.

Because he was studying me in a way he never had.

Though the warmth and concern were not gone.

"Come in," he murmured, finally stepping out of the way.

I tucked my clutch closer under my arm and stepped my Louboutin-shod foot over the threshold.

One thing my profession had insured I had not lost the ability to do: walk around in four-inch heels like they were sneakers.

And this was the only thing I had going for me when I looked down into the sunken living room and saw my children not there, so I moved right, toward the kitchen and family room that sat in the point of the L of the house to see my kids lounging there.

And to be confronted with Myrna in the kitchen.

Remy was six-three. Sabre was six-four. Yves was his dad's exact height. Manon was five-eight.

I was five-nine.

Myrna was at most, five-four, probably more like five-three.

I knew everything about clothes, shoes, handbags, makeup and accessories, and every designer in the world (not exaggerating) sent me freebies. For my clients. And for me.

And I used them.

All the time.

Myrna was a granola, boho, throw-on-some-mascara (maybe), pick-up-your-multi-colored-woven-fringed-crossbody-and-go desert rat.

She mountain biked with Remy.

My ass had tried a spin class once and I detested it, so that had never happened again. But the kids had bought me a pink Schwinn with a cute basket, which I occasionally rode to the grocery store or a coffee shop, and by "occasionally," I meant this happened maybe five times a year.

I was blonde, my hair ranging from shades of gold to butterscotch (not really, I had no idea what my natural hair color was anymore, and I didn't allow myself to come even close to finding out, and I never would, *until the day I died*).

She was a brunette, her long, wild, perfectly tousled hair falling near to her waist when it wasn't wrapped in some slapdash knot or twisted into twin braids.

Mine went to my bra-strap and I had it professionally blown out once a week, the other two times I did it myself, and I was (almost) a master.

She was busty, but otherwise thin.

I had tits and ass for days, never in my life had I had a flat stomach, and right then was no exception.

I was (if pushed to define it at all, never my favorite thing to do) what I preferred to consider "seasoned."

She was thirteen years younger than me.

At that moment, she was in cutoff shorts, a slouchy mustard-colored three-quarter-sleeve top that had some kind of metallic bits sewn in and some tassels dangling. Worn Birkenstocks were on her feet and a scarf thing was happening in her hair. Her exposed limbs were tanned.

I was in green houndstooth, wide-legged pants, a severe black blouse buttoned up to my neck, red suede pumps with a thin ankle strap, and sun had not touched my skin unless it was carefully sunblocked since Remy and I moved from New York to Phoenix so he could take the job in a cutting-edge firm that had handpicked him from college.

"Mom, you think you could not be late sometime in one of the millennia you've lived in?" Sabre asked.

And I hoped it went without saying that I loved my son more than breath.

But his saying that in that moment when I was facing off with Myrna hurt.

Badly.

I tore my eyes from her and looked to him.

He was not the spitting image of his dad. He got my eyes and there was a lot that was all Sabre. But he got his dad's body and mouth.

He was also looking beyond me, to who I assumed was his father, and Sabre might not be hanging his head, but he was close to it. Thus, I assumed Remy was giving him a look that shared how he felt about the millennia comment.

Yes, Remy could shout in my face, but he did not (ever) allow any of our children to disrespect their mother.

My gaze moved to Manon, who had Remy's coloring, my skin, and some of my features, the rest was all her.

It was Yves who looked most like one of his parents, that parent being his father. Yves moved like Remy, with that big cat's prowl. They even had a similar sounding deep, rich voice.

And they were all hanging about the family room like it was their home.

Which it was.

"I'm sorry. No excuses. Something happened, I should have ignored it, and didn't and—" I started.

I didn't finish because Yves interrupted me, wearing the same exact expression his father had only moments before while his eyes moved over my face.

"You all right?" he asked.

"I'm fine, honey."

"Wyn is here."

I twisted at the waist and looked back at Remy, who said these words.

And from where his attention was focused, I saw he said them to Myrna.

I just didn't know why he said them since I was there, the woman could see, we'd both stared at each other not a minute ago, so my arrival didn't need to be announced.

"Yes, sorry," I put in, attempting to interpret what was going on with him and rectifying what I thought he was noting was my mistake. "Hello, Myrna."

"Wyn," she pushed out like she'd done it after sucking a lemon.

"Wyn is here," Remy repeated.

My gaze went back to him.

His face was bland.

Oh boy.

Trouble was definitely flirting with paradise.

"Remy—" Myrna started.

"What'd I say?" he asked like he really didn't care if she remembered, but regardless, what she was not doing that he wanted her to do, she needed to do it...*immediately*.

Yikes!

Trying not to call attention to myself, I walked into the family room thinking at least I'd never had *that* Remy.

I'd seen that Remy, when he was around people he did not care for, they annoyed him or frustrated him, or were simply of an ilk he didn't have any fucks to give them.

His deep freeze was chilly, believe you me.

But his bland indifference seemed worse.

I used to tease him about both.

For my part, I might get the deep freeze on the most intense of our occasions.

Predominantly, though, I got the hothead, shout-the-roof-down, never-say-die, duke-it-out-verbally until someone either slammed out of the room or you attacked each other and fucked it out.

I had honestly thought it was all going to be okay when I got back from California those three years ago because, before I went, we'd gone at it but ended fucking it out.

But when I came home, he'd been packing.

And he'd already had a furnished apartment to go to. So even before that, he'd been planning.

So I'd obviously been wrong.

"She can stay, Dad," Sabre put in.

Remy cut his eyes to his son, and I was about to hug Yves, but I went still and stiff, like I had to be prepared to throw myself between them to protect my boy with the way Remy did it.

Sabre clamped his mouth shut.

I didn't hug Yves, or Manon, and definitely not Sabre, as I watched with perhaps inappropriate fascination as Remy turned back to Myrna and lifted his brows.

My gaze shifted to her, and I saw her face get red with embarrassment, anger or hurt, I had no idea.

Though it was probably all three that made her stomp loudly in her Birks toward Remy, grab her multi-colored woven crossbody (I wasn't lying) from the counter, then turn and stomp the other direction to the door to the garage where her old pickup rested beside Remy's Tesla.

She slammed the door behind her.

She did not say goodbye.

"Can we do this?" Yves asked impatiently, but there was a pitch to his voice that had me belatedly studying him closely.

He was ill-at-ease, for certain.

I read this as the fact he knew what this was about.

And I was seeing with the way my youngest was being, and also taking in the demeanor of my middle, not to mention my eldest, that my thought processes needed to shift to dealing with something like Sabre having gotten some girl pregnant and now, I not only had to get over being a divorcée, I had to come to terms with becoming a grandmother.

We were a touchy, affectionate family. We'd started that way because of me (Remy's mother was an overbearing, snobbish, horrendous Southern woman —the exact opposite of every single Southerner I'd ever met—and his French father was largely absent, and when he wasn't, he was indulgent of his wife, so we could say hugs weren't *de rigueur* in the Gastineau household). And our open affection had never died.

But so this could get started, then be over for my son, I didn't do the physical greetings I usually would.

I took a seat in an upholstered armchair with a low, double-buttoned back and short legs, and tucked my clutch in my lap.

Once down, I watched, morbidly enthralled, as my kids sat one-two-three on Remy's couch, with Yves sandwiched in the middle.

Yes, Yves.

Not Sabre.

Yves.

What was going on?

Remy strolled in, cutting across the room with long-legged purpose, coming to my chair.

I thought he'd stand beside it, since there was no other furniture he could sit on around me. The matching armchair to the one I was in was at the opposite side.

But no.

I watched with lips parted as he parked his ass on the *arm of my chair*.

The.

Arm.

Of.

My chair.

Like he did back in the day.

Like he did and I loved him to do. Complete with leaning back, resting a hand in the top of the chair, close to me, my protector, his long bulk ready to spring forward on attack or to defend should some rabid dog suddenly enter the room, or someone came close to landing a drop of martini on me.

He was studying our children while I had my head tipped back studying him.

And since he continued studying our children, slowly, I turned their way to see Sabre scowling at his father, Yves looking fidgety and not focused on much of anything, and Manon staring at me.

The second I caught my daughter's eyes, she mouthed, "*What... is...happening?*"

She meant her dad and the chair.

I wished I knew.

But it would take a while to find out.

Because right then, the evening took two sharp and exceptionally unexpected turns.

And not a member of our family was going to be the same after them.

CHAPTER 3
Come to Terms

Wyn

"All we ask is for you to just be cool and let Yves say what he has to say and then think about it for a second before you say anything."

This was Sabre's opening.

And there weren't a lot of words, but there was a lot there.

First, whatever this was about, it wasn't about Sabre.

It was about Yves.

Second, whatever it was, Yves was so uncomfortable about it, he'd leaned on his big brother to instigate the meeting and then start the proceedings.

Third, Sabre was brash, brave, aggressive (the good kind, says his mother), a risk-taker, called them as he saw them, and rarely (okay, maybe not-so-rarely) he could be too honest for his own good.

Like his dad.

Manon devoured life. If there was an invitation, and she could physically or legally (I hoped) do it, she said yes. She was a wee bit of a Daddy's Girl (okay, she was a lot of that). She was hyper-social, loyal, dependable, creative, highly-strung (just a little bit, says her mother) and hilarious.

Like her mom.

Yves was a mix of Remy and I both.

Except he only got the good parts.

Yves listened before he spoke. Yves walked into a kitchen someone was cooking in and asked what he could do. Yves noted a wineglass getting low and filled it. Yves did his homework without you begging him to do it. Yves kept his room clean.

In other words...

Yves was the perfect child.

Therefore, the fact this was about Yves significantly increased my anxiety.

And last, it was crystal clear our children had not missed both their parents had quick tempers.

This had me letting my clutch slide off my lap as I moved to the edge of my seat and mindlessly reached out, curling my fingers around the muscles above Remy's knee.

It also had my mind racing through a memory.

That memory being a time, post-argument between Remy and me.

After we'd fucked it out.

"We need to be quieter," I whispered to him, tangled in his long limbs and our soft sheets. "Kids don't like to hear their parents fight."

"We need to be ourselves," Remy retorted. "We need them to understand they should express themselves and their emotions. We need them to learn that you wouldn't fight if you didn't care. We need them to go into their relationships knowing they shouldn't back down from their point of view if they really believe in it. And we need them to understand that fighting, in the end, is healthy. And they'll understand that, baby. Because they'll see, even if we do it, we always come out of it stronger, but more importantly, together."

We had always come out of it stronger and together.

Until we hadn't.

And what had that taught our kids?

"Yves?"

Remy's voice calling his son's name called my focus to my baby boy.

To all my children.

Manon was holding Yves's hand.

As I watched, Sabre was running his hand up Yves's spine and then he gripped the back of Yves's neck.

Okay.

What was going on?

My fingers tightened on Remy's thigh, and nothing occurred to me but to feel the warmth of connection when his hand covered mine.

"Okay, I've thought a million times about how I was going to say this," Yves started.

He swallowed.

My body tensed so deeply I thought every muscle would snap.

Remy's fingers curled around mine.

"And the only thing I could come up with was just to say it straight out. So that's what I'm going to do," Yves went on.

He went silent.

The room went silent with him.

Remy and I sat on edge—literally on our perches, and figuratively in our emotions—waiting.

Yves's eyes were on me, they flicked up to his dad, then they settled on me.

"I'm gay," he declared.

I blinked.

Remy didn't move.

Was that all?

And more importantly, was drama a genetic trait?

"I know that—" Yves started to go on.

He didn't finish.

"*What do you know?*" Remy barked.

I jumped in surprise at his tone.

Yves's gaze sliced up to his dad.

I looked up at Remy too, and saw he was far from bland.

His jaw was set, his cheekbones were flushed.

I knew that look.

He was furious.

Oh God.

"Remy," I whispered.

"What do you know?" Remy repeated, aiming these angry words Yves's way.

Wait a minute...

How was this happening?

Remy was not that man.

It was part of being a *true* man's man. It was one of the myriad reasons I'd loved him as deeply as I'd loved him.

This kind of thing had never, not ever, been an issue with him.

I'd worked at Bergdorf when we met. I had every intention, twenty some years ago, of being what I eventually became. I'd gone from sales associate to personal shopper and had just started to cherry pick my own clients when Remy and I decided to start a family. We'd also decided I'd stay at home when they were little, but I'd go back to it when our last entered kindergarten.

This I'd done.

Remy worked in the design world. He was at a big firm at first and then struck out on his own. He'd had lots of clients and part of his job was to be in the right places at the right times to find more.

We were active. Social. Had a wide range of friends.

We still did, and for the most part (outside Kara, Bernice, and obviously Bea, as well as Remy's childhood friends back home, Beau and Jason), we'd managed not to make them pick sides in the divorce.

We had people from every walk of life in our spheres.

This was never an issue for him.

Nothing was ever an issue for him.

If it was, it would have been an issue with me.

We'd also never discussed it, but we didn't because of just that. It was never an issue, which was one of the reasons, for me, why it was so attractive about Remy.

He didn't have to play cool.

It was just who he was, and he expected others to be the same.

And that was it.

Yves didn't answer his father's question, but I could see my son's throat ripple with another swallow.

It was Manon who was staring daggers at her father, and Sabre's face was getting red with anger.

"How about you, Sah?" Remy asked his eldest. "You into guys?"

"No, Dad," Sabre spat. "Don't be a—"

"You're into girls?" Remy cut him off.

I started pumping his hand.

He ignored it as Sabre answered, "Yeah, but what does it—?"

"So, when's the family meeting for you to announce that?" Remy demanded.

I stopped pumping his hand and started thinking.

Fast.

"Manon, what are you into?" Remy asked as I did that.

"Dad, you've made your point," she said softly.

"Have I?" Remy returned. "Have I made my fucking point?"

Okay.

Oh God.

Oh hell.

"Remy," I whispered urgently.

He let my hand go, stood, leaned forward and roared at his youngest, "*You know your mother is all good, but you staged this fucking show because you thought I*"—he pounded on his chest— "*wouldn't be?*"

Yves stood too. "Dad—"

"Are you fucking joking about that shit?" Remy asked.

Sabre also stood and shouted, "Dad, this isn't about you!"

Remy turned to him. "It isn't? Seems to me it is. You knew, Manon knew, your mother doesn't give a shit and you knew that too. So this isn't about me?"

I hated, especially when I thought he was out of line or acting irrationally, when he asserted things, and he was right.

Remy's attention shot back to Yves.

"Is that the kind of man you think I am?" He shook his head sharply. "No. Strike that. Is that the kind of *father* I am to you? And if it is, *how* is it that? Tell me. How? When did I *ever*, Yves, *ever* give you the impression my love would come with conditions?"

I felt that slice me wide open.

Because there it was.

And the vein of open, oozing hurt threading through his words underlined it.

Remy's mother was vain and cosseted, a social butterfly born in the wrong era, though there was no era that would make it all right for your narcissism to trump motherhood.

Her love of her only son had conditions, boy did it ever. When she wasn't treating him as an accessory, he was tested by her from the moment he could cogitate. And when he failed, which was often (in Colette's estimation), her punishment was masterful in its cruelty.

Remy's father ignored this entirely, but his love came with conditions too.

Remy was going to be the man Guillaume wanted him to be, that being a man just like Guillaume, and he put a great deal of effort into it. This happened when Guillaume was around, which wasn't that often, considering he was off making scads of money or attending one of the mistresses he hid from Colette, but not from his son.

So it was a steady shift with Remy's dad between iron control, which was a form of mental abuse, and casual neglect, which was not at odds with what Remy got from his mother, also iron control in the form of emotional abuse, mingled with casual neglect.

Although some words had been shared with our kids about Remy's history while they were growing up, once they started maturing, not much had to be said. Guillaume and Colette didn't hide from their grandchildren how they were with their son, and in Colette's case, she treated them all exactly as she did her own child.

Truth be told, that was the same with me. Remy didn't talk about his parents much to the point of actively avoiding the discussion. There were words shared, but they were the bare minimum.

However, they were enough, because I didn't miss it either and I felt there was no need for him to have to go through it again by dredging it all out for me. Not if he didn't want to.

And although Guillaume treated me (and eventually Manon) like he treated his wife, with urbane adoration, Colette abhorred me and put very little effort into hiding that.

So, the three of our children had been told of their father's less-than-loving upbringing, they'd witnessed it and they'd been given a taste of it.

Therefore, when I took in my kids and all three of them looked like they'd been slapped, I knew they were belatedly realizing their mistake.

Because there was one thing Remy Jacques Gastineau had never fallen down on in his life.

Being the loving, supportive, attentive, kind, funny, protective parent he'd never had.

I stood too, touched the back of his hand and whispered, "Honey."

He looked down at me and I drew in a sharp breath at the pain in his eyes.

"Dad," Yves called.

Remy's head jerked that way, and he growled, "Get over here."

Without hesitation, Yves moved toward his father, and when he was in reach, Remy's arm shot out, he cupped the back of his son's head and yanked him the rest of the way.

Their bodies collided. I swallowed a sob. Manon let one loose. Sabre grunted. Yves wrapped his arms around his dad and Remy kept his hand on Yves's head, pushing it into his neck as he curled his other arm tight around his son's upper back.

"I will love you always, Yves. Always," I heard him say.

"'Kay," Yves pushed out, that syllable thick, and now he was clutching at his father's shirt, the material bunched in his fists.

A tear slid down my face.

"Get this, son, there is never anything you can do and definitely never anyone you could be that would make me love you any less," Remy stressed.

"I'm sorry I thought—" Yves began, voice still hoarse.

Remy cut him off. "No, Yves, I'm sorry I lost it like that. That wasn't cool."

"I get it," Yves said.

"I know you do. It still wasn't cool."

He was kinda right, he was kinda wrong, and I was far from just kinda crying.

"Love you, Dad."

"I'd step in front of a bullet for you, Yves."

Yves's back hitched powerfully.

Remy held on.

Okay, no, I was sobbing.

I then found myself caught at the waist by my daughter, who immediately pushed us into the two-man huddle that equally immediately accommodated to fit us in, and within moments, Sabre shoved in on the other side.

We were all holding together tightly, our heads touching and our arms around each other like we were in a scrum. Yves's breath was loud and coming fast and difficult. Manon was whimpering. I was holding my baby boy's gaze and trying to smile at him through my emotion. Remy was holding us all together with his long arms.

It was Sabre who broke the moment.

"We are such huge-ass dorks."

"Don't be stupid," Manon shot back.

"We *are* dorks," Yves agreed and tore his gaze from mine to look at his father. "Dad, I'm so sorry."

"Not another word, kid," Remy returned.

Yves shut up.

"It has to be said, Dad, we totally blew this," Manon pushed it.

"Baby girl," Remy replied.

It was gentle and sweet.

It was also a command to stop talking.

She did as her father not-quite told her.

"Okay, so what do you need from this, honey?" I asked Yves. "Should we go out and buy champagne or something?"

"Do I get a party because I'm hetero?" Sabre asked.

"Sure," I answered.

"Me too?" Manon queried.

"Of course," I said.

"Can I ask for a Nordy's gift certificate instead?" she inquired.

I smiled at her.

Then I said, "No."

She rolled her eyes.

We started to edge back, because we were close, touchy and affectionate, but we weren't weird, and that was when the next strange thing came from Remy.

He stopped us from completely disengaging by clamping down hard on my hip and keeping me tucked to his side.

The kids did move back, not far.

But I couldn't move away, at all.

And the way this was, I was stuck with my arm also around him.

Like we were holding each other.

Uh...

"We have one more thing to talk about before I hit the wine fridge to grab a bottle," he stated.

All our kids looked to their dad.

I tested his hold on me.

It tightened.

I stopped testing.

"Myrna is moving out."

I went completely still at his announcement.

"Oh my God," Manon breathed, and then she let slip a quiet, "Yay."

Yves emitted a noncommittal, thus hiding his real reaction (he didn't say much about her, but my sense was that he wasn't big on Myrna either), "Erm."

Sabre demanded, "Are you serious?"

I examined my oldest and something hit me that I hadn't noticed, or it was something he'd never let show.

He had a crush on his dad's girlfriend.

Ulk.

"I am serious," Remy confirmed. "She was supposed to be out today... before this meeting. I'm uncertain why that didn't happen. She will be out by the end of the week."

I had no idea why I had to be there, and attached to Remy, while he shared this information that was none of my business with our kids.

But although I wouldn't mind a glass of champagne to toast my youngest having the courage to share his truth and us moving on from that as close as ever (as such, with their mom and dad split up), I was acutely uncomfortable in my current situation because I was entirely comfortable and familiar with it.

Manon was too, as well as more, which she was giving me indication of as I stood in the curve of her father's arm. She did this with a rapid up and down of my position and repeat before bugging her eyes out at me.

I clenched my teeth.

"You're dumping her?" Sabre asked.

"Myrna and I are moving on with our lives not together," Remy answered at the same time didn't.

"What the fuck?" Sabre's voice was rising.

Remy's patience instantly slipped.

"Do we speak like that in front of women?" he growled.

That was another part of my ex that I'd loved, and it sucked not because he had it, but because the reason he did was that both his mother and father drilled it into him.

He was a thoroughly modern man.

But there were things that were old-fashioned about him.

One of them being that he was and never lost being a traditional Southern gentleman.

This was communicated as well in his voice, which was the part that wasn't the same as Yves's (alas). Remy had a faint, upper-crust, New Orleans accent that was tinged with the melodic purr of French.

This was because Guillaume and Colette lived mostly in New Orleans, but they owned an apartment in Paris and a villa in Toulouse, and outside other occasions they went to France, without fail they spent every Christmas in Paris and every summer in Toulouse and that had rubbed off on their boy.

There were, of course, caveats to this particular rule, as Remy had recently demonstrated when he blew his stack. And Remy let loose however when he was around me.

But this rule for his boys wasn't just about that.

It was couched in an overarching rule about respect for women.

That respect was both practical (when they were younger, he'd given them The Talk which included him telling them he'd provide them with condoms whenever they needed them, taking them to get HPV vaccinations and explaining to them that they got clear consent before even kissing a girl, and if he ever heard word they'd taken advantage of a woman who was in no state, he'd lose his mind). As well as traditional (you opened doors, picked up the tab, gave the girl the seat with the best view and pulled it out for them, made certain their food and beverage were served before yours and didn't use foul language in their presence).

So, yes.

It sucked, but I had to admit, outside his fantastic looks and the fact he existed at all, Guillaume and Colette gave Remy something beautiful.

"I'm telling you not simply because you'll wonder where Myrna's gone when she's no longer here," Remy continued. "But also so you can have whatever words you want to have with her should you want to keep in touch. I know you two care about each other, Sabre, so do what you feel is right."

Manon said nothing.

Yves was studying his trainers.

Myrna was probably not going to get any texts from those two asking to meet up for coffee.

Sabre was glowering at his father. "So she's just in your life one second, then she's out the next?"

"It wasn't like that, and no offense, son, but it really isn't your business what it was like," Remy replied.

"Seems like that," Sabre fired back. "You two have always been good. You never fought once. Not that I heard."

"Think about that," Remy returned.

Sabre shut up.

My eyes got big as I pressed my lips together.

Remy gave my waist a squeeze and I knew what that meant so, out of sheer habit, I did what it meant.

I tipped my head back to look at him.

"What do you think? Dom?" he asked casually after what kind of champagne he should uncork.

Okay.

What the hell was going on here?

"Mom, don't you have a kickoff tonight?" Manon put in.

"Oh shit, Mom, I didn't remember. Shit, I'm so sorry," Yves said.

"It's okay, honey," I replied to Yves. "You know you're always more important than anything."

Remy grunted.

I turned to look at him, my brows coming together.

"You disagree?" I asked.

"I didn't say a word," he answered.

"Not an intelligible one, but you very much spoke," I retorted, and yes, there was some heat in it.

That was when he grinned at me.

I stared at him grinning, but I felt that grin somewhere very specific.

Okay!

WHAT THE HELL WAS GOING ON HERE?

"Is there something you two have to tell us?" Sabre asked, finally letting his parents' position sink in.

"No." I pulled forcefully out of Remy's hold. "There absolutely is not. Now, are we having champagne or what?"

"I don't actually need you guys to toast the fact that I'm gay," Yves remarked.

"We aren't toasting that. We're toasting courage and truth, having the former and standing for the latter," I informed him.

"You are so extra, Mom," Yves teased.

"Excuse me," I began. "But when you have children, and you watch them stick by each other as you three did today, navigating what should have been certain, but what society and media and every coming-out movie, and let us please be done with them and just have gays being gays or whatever, the LBGTQ experience has many faceted and nuanced experiences than just the coming out bit, as David Rose on *Schitt's Creek* so brilliantly portrayed." I realized I was digressing into sermonizing and pulled it together. "But you felt like they were uncertain waters, so you navigated them close to each other's sides, then you can talk to me about extra."

Manon leaned toward her younger brother and stage-whispered, "And again with more extra."

I looked to the ceiling and huffed out a breath.

"Go to your kickoff, Mom," Yves urged. "We'll have a celebration about courage and truth when Noel has the chance to have it catered."

"Catered," Sabre said. "How did they not know you were gay?"

"Dude," Yves shot back. "It's you who loses it over Lucie's crab cakes. I'm doing you a solid."

"He just loses it over Lucie," Manon decreed.

"She's too old for him," Yves said.

"Who says a man has to date a younger woman?" Manon asked.

"Right, who says?" Sabre put in.

Please, God, let that be about Lucie, who did make amazing crab cakes, and not about Myrna, who was far too old for my son.

Though, Lucie, at a guess, was in her mid-to-late-twenties so she was not.

Hmm.

"You talk to Noel, I'll provide the booze. Family celebration at the old house," Remy decreed. "Sunday, after league." He looked down at me. "Six o'clock."

By the by, "the old house" referred to *my house*.

I...

Uh.

What?

Absolutely not!

"Works for me." Yves.

"Me too, I don't have a class Monday until the afternoon. I can leave Monday morning and make it, no sweat." Manon.

"If it's crab cakes, I'll get up early to drive down Monday and make class. So I'm in too." Sabre.

Remy smiled at me.

I narrowed my eyes on it in order not to land my fist in it.

Then I shook it off and took the short trek to the armchair to retrieve my clutch.

Once I'd done that, I turned to my children and demanded, "Hugs."

They came to me one by one, and I took my time over them, especially with Yves.

"Love you forever and ever," I whispered in his ear.

"Love you too, Mom," he grunted in mine.

We broke apart, I cupped his face a second, he shook his head and smirked at me—so like his father's—then I dropped my hand, turned to his dad and dipped my chin.

"Remy," I said as farewell, intent to exit *tout de suite*.

"I'll walk you to your car."

For fuck's sake.

Since our divorce, the man had not once walked me to my car.

In order not to make a deal of it, I nodded, smiled at each of my kids in turn, then preceded Remy through his house, out his door, down his walk and to my car.

I'd rounded the hood and was in the process of opening the door when it shut because Remy's hand was on it.

I turned to him.

"What are you—?"

"Why were you crying earlier, Wyn?"

Ugh.

We were back here.

"I have kickoff to get to," I reminded him. "And as usual, I'm late."

"Won't ask again," he warned.

"Remy," I snapped.

"Answer me this, are you okay?"

No, I was not.

Because not an hour ago, I'd let him go.

Now, he was being strange and maneuvering a family celebration at my house that he was attending.

And all the other.

Including the fact he was breaking up with his girlfriend.

I did not want to be the broken-hearted ex *and* the rebound.

I mean, *blech*.

"I told you, I'm fine."

There came the smirk, and it did what it rarely failed to do.

It wet my panties.

"You have always been a shit liar," he said.

Right.

Enough.

"I had it out with Bea before I showed," I shared, his face went hard, and suffice it to say, Bea wasn't his biggest fan, he wasn't hers either and I knew he only put up with her because she was my friend. "I think I'm coming to terms

37

with a few things about her and it's no excuse to be late to something as important as what just happened, but that was why I was late."

"Good you're coming to terms with some things about that woman, so maybe you'll come to terms with the fact that she played a role in breaking us up."

I stared at him.

"And yeah, babe, it'd be super fucking good you finally came to terms with that," he concluded, no longer warm, concerned and slightly flirtatious, he was annoyed.

Also, he was done.

He communicated that last by leaving me at my car and walking away.

CHAPTER 4
Poison

Remy

"I think we have more to talk about."

"We disagree on that."

"You need to give this more time."

"We disagree on that too. What we didn't disagree on, at least that was how I remember we left it when we spoke two weeks ago when I started sleeping on the couch, was that you would be out by this afternoon. And you were not."

Remy stood in his bedroom with Myrna, who had returned.

Manon and Sabre were heading back to Tucson after the family meet.

Yves was at his mom's.

So this could finally be done.

He fucking hoped.

"Remy, we hit a rough patch."

Jesus Christ.

Was she serious?

"Myrna, that's quite an understatement."

"We can talk through it."

"We cannot. And I'll add at this juncture, I was never at one with watching you compete for my affection with my daughter, and I shared that. And you didn't stop. I told you not once, but repeatedly, in that game, you would not win. You didn't stop playing that game. But that isn't the only reason you lose because that wasn't the only game you were playing, and you know it. Now, you told me you needed two weeks to sort things to move out. You've had those two weeks. It's Wednesday. I'm giving you an extension. You're out by Saturday afternoon. But between now and then, it's you who'll be sleeping on the couch."

She jerked up her chin in an annoyed way. "And what if I'm not? What if I intend to do what you seem like you *don't* intend to do? Fight for us?"

Us?

After all her shit, she thought there was an us?

"There is no us. We're done," he stated. "I told you that. I told you why that is, even if you couldn't possibly mistake it. And there's no coming back from it, Myrna, and you know that too. But if you're not out, I'll move your things myself. And if it goes beyond that, I'll inform the police."

Her mouth dropped open before she used it to ask, "Are you being serious?"

"What, in our discussions about this, are you not understanding?" he asked.

That was when she lost it.

"How I could give you a year of my fucking life and you're just *done* with me!" she shouted.

"All right," he said, trying not to sound bored, which he fucking was and had been for too goddamned long. Until, obviously, recently. But his boredom had not gone in the right direction for Myrna. "I'll count this down."

"Do not—"

"One, when you brought it up, I told you straight when we met, I did not want more kids. You told me you didn't want any either. Therefore, imagine my surprise when, one month after you moved in with me, you started on about kids. I reminded you of my views on that, which were unshakable, something else I reminded you about. Regardless, three weeks ago, you shared you thought you were pregnant. Even though, since we started, we've had multiple conversations about contraception, and you can't have missed how committed I was to this considering we have not had unprotected sex by, as you promised, us both seeing to that, as you told me you were on the Pill and I never failed to wear a condom. And although both of those are not infallible, using them together and a possible pregnancy coming from that, means it's highly likely someone isn't covering their end. And that was not me."

"I missed a few pills and—"

"Myrna, if that was the case, you should have told me, and we shouldn't have had sex."

"I couldn't know the condom would break."

He wasn't going to allow her to try to pull that shit again.

He'd seen the fucking evidence, for fuck's sake.

"It didn't break," he bit out.

Her neck started getting pink.

Yeah.

He sounded like a fucking bull when he breathed out hard through his nose.

Then he said softly, "You tampered with them."

"Remy," she whispered.

Yeah.

She fucking tampered with them.

"And then you had a pregnancy scare, which, fortunately, was only a scare. And equally fortunately, it made me investigate things, and that, Myrna, as I've explained before, is what you cannot ever come back from. And I cannot even begin to imagine how you think you could."

"Okay, but really, there's more to talk about."

She could not be sane.

"I'm fifty-four goddamn years old and you were trying to trap me with a kid by poking holes in fucking condoms and skipping pills. There is not anything more to talk about."

"I'm thirty-nine and my time is nearly up, and I wasted a year of that time with you," she spat.

"And well before you did that, I told you I didn't want more kids," he returned. "So if that was important to you, *you* should have left *me*."

"I was in love with you!" she yelled.

"If you were, then why the fuck would you betray me that way?"

"Because maybe, if I gave you a kid, like *she* did, you'd love me as much as you love her," she shot back.

Remy said nothing.

Myrna did.

"And maybe, if we had a kid, you'd give them and *me* some of the attention you shower on *Manon*."

"Listen to yourself, Myrna. You're jealous of my daughter."

"Tell me I don't disappear when your precious Manon is around."

His gut twisted in a foul way.

"This is actually repulsive," he told her.

"Think of it from my perspective," she begged.

"I am, and what I think is that somehow, to my disgust, after successfully managing not to do this exact thing for thirty years, I got involved with my fucking mother."

Her head jerked like he'd hit her.

"Oh, but *Wyn* isn't like Colette," she baited.

Remy shook his head. "We're not doing this."

"Did you think of her when you fucked me?"

"You've got the couch until Saturday, Myrna."

"Impossible," she said like he didn't speak. "You couldn't think of her. She's fat, I'm not. I cannot even *begin to imagine*," she mimicked his words, "how she got as far as she did in fashion with the way she is. Talk about Colette. All of that type are just like your mother. All they give a shit about is appearances. Including *Wyn*."

Remy said nothing, just crossed his arms on his chest, but she was finally doing something she'd never really done, even when she'd told him she thought she was pregnant, and he found out how that might occur.

She was pissing him off.

Myrna wasn't finished, though.

"You are an incredibly fit man, you take your health seriously, what you do is important, lasting, it'll leave a legacy, you have actual talent. Tons of it. What do you see in her?"

"She's the most beautiful woman I've ever laid eyes on, she always was, and she is to this day, not only because she physically just is because she's fucking gorgeous and has amazing style, but also because her heart is big, and her first thought is not for herself, but for kindness. Even with that, she's driven, ambitious, focused. She's the best mother I've ever seen and she's an insanely good lay. And yes, before you ask, she's so much better than you, I wonder how we got to the point of you living with me. No wait, I remember. You asked to move in due to your situation with your old place, and you needed some time to save up to find something better, so you weren't supposed to be here this long in the first fucking place."

"I cannot believe you just said that to me," she hissed.

"Unlike you, Myrna, I have never not told you the truth."

"*Fuck you!*" she screamed.

"Friday," he returned. "Out by Friday. Or honest to God, Myrna, I'll put you out."

"You're going back to her, aren't you?" she demanded.

And again, Remy told her the truth.

"Yes, Myrna, I am. As fast as I can get her to forgive me and let me back in because leaving her was the biggest mistake I've made in my life, and I've been paying for it from the moment I picked up my suitcases and walked away."

She scored a point with, "And still, you got involved with me."

Remy nodded. "Yes, I did, and I'm sorry for that, because I swear to Christ,

I was always honest with you. But I can't say the same about how I was with myself."

"What's that supposed to mean?"

"You don't want to know."

"Actually," she flicked out a hand, "I do."

"All right then, what it means is, until Wyn walked up to the house today and I knew someone had upset her, it cut me to the bone not only because she was upset, but because I'd made it so I couldn't do dick about it. Only then did I realize what a colossal mistake I'd made. But you exposing what you are, us being done, you eventually being gone, Wyn being upset, Yves sharing what he shared and how he shared it, I've come to terms with a number of things I should have come to terms with a long time ago. And you know me. I don't fuck around."

"So you're telling me, just today you've figured out you're still in love with her?" she asked sarcastically.

"Yes," he answered.

"That is such horseshit," she returned. "Newsflash, Remy, I wasn't just competing with your beloved daughter. You took every opportunity you could find to spend time with Wyn, so I was also competing with your ex-fucking-*wife*."

"Yes," he agreed. "That's what I came to terms with and that's what I just apologized for."

"So you fucked me over but it's me who has to live with it?"

"I was absolutely not as honest as I should have been about my feelings for Wyn, mostly because I didn't understand them, until today. But it was not me who made moves behind your back to tie you to me when, without a doubt, Myrna, I would have figured out how I felt about my wife eventually. And as such, you still would have been out, and if you'd done what you wanted to do and we'd made a child, that child, who I would love and care for, but it would not negate the fact that I didn't want it, would be sharing time between a mother and father who had wholly no emotional ties to each other whatsoever."

Her voice was small, and he wanted to give a shit, but after what she'd done, he just didn't, when she asked, "So you also didn't love me?"

"Did I ever tell you I loved you?" he asked in return, being cold and remote not only because she'd killed anything he'd felt for her, but because the woman had to *get this* and then *go*. "When you asked if you could move in, what did I say?"

"Remy—"

"What did I say, Myrna?"

She shut her mouth.

So he reminded her of something he knew she didn't need the reminder.

"I said I enjoyed spending time with you. But I warned you I'd ended a long relationship that would never really be over since we'd made a family. I also said, although I cared about you, I was concerned your feelings went deeper for me than mine did for you. I further warned you I wasn't certain I'd grow to reciprocate that."

"But you let me move in anyway."

"Your lease was up, and they were raising your rent without increasing services. You weren't down with that, decided at your age it was time for you to live somewhere nicer, and asked if you could move in for a couple of months in order to cover it. That turned into a year because I wasn't paying attention."

"So this was just a trial phase and I failed, now you're done with me?"

"I never lied to you, and I never led you on. Most importantly, and I can't believe I need to keep driving this point home, I didn't make moves to change the course of your life by making you pregnant when that was something you did not want."

She was a dog with a bone and proved it by stating, "But you knew what I'd think if I moved in."

"I'm not in your head, Myrna."

"You knew I was in love with you."

"So this is on me?" he asked.

"You knew I was in love with you!" she nearly shouted.

"You took a chance, and it didn't pan out," he returned.

"So you could have an easy fuck waiting for you in bed every night, you let me move in with you knowing you'd eventually go back to your wife and break my heart."

This was the second time that day when someone gravely mistook the man he was.

The first, he couldn't abide.

This one wasn't as important. But it was the same.

He couldn't abide it.

Because it was bullshit.

"You need to find someplace else to stay tonight and come get your things tomorrow," he told her.

Her eyes got big. "Are you serious?"

"You've had weeks to figure this out, Myrna."

"So now you're done with me, you chuck me out like garbage?"

No.

Now, she'd forgotten that he told her two weeks ago they were irrevocably over, and if she wanted a family, that was what she needed as much as he did. And he'd asked her how long it would take her to find a place, get her shit from storage, and sort herself out, and she'd asked in return that he give her two weeks.

He'd slept on his own fucking couch for those two weeks.

And she was still playing games.

"You know, I didn't treat you like an easy fuck, Myrna," he stated. "You just were one."

She gasped in outrage.

"And if you can't own that, when there's absolutely not one fucking thing wrong with it, it isn't on me," he finished. "You came into my home with designs. You knew where I was, but you wanted more, and you thought you could make that so. You couldn't. And now you're throwing a tantrum because you haven't gotten what you wanted. But it's not going to change anything, except precipitating it being finished. Now you need to leave and text me tomorrow with when to meet you here so you can come and get your things."

"And that's it?" she asked.

He didn't know how he could be clearer.

"That's it."

"You think you're everything, Remy Gastineau, but you're nothing but a piece of shit."

Good she found that out before she forced a kid on him.

He didn't answer.

She ran into the closet, and he shifted to watch what she did in there, but she only grabbed one of her million tote bags, shoved some clothes in it, then she stormed out.

She flipped him the bird as she passed him.

He sighed.

But he followed her.

And he only got close when she opened the door to her truck. But he did this to reach beyond her and nab the garage door opener.

He then moved to stand in the door to the house to watch her pull out.

When she cleared the garage, he hit the button for the door to go down.

He then pulled out his phone and found a twenty-four-hour locksmith.

He called.

And he didn't go to bed until all the locks in the house and the code for the security alarm were changed.

And when Remy went to bed, he didn't think of his son being gay (mostly because he didn't care about that, at least not that way).

He didn't think of Myrna.

He thought of that toxic, negative, man-hating woman, Bea, upsetting Wyn.

And he was thrilled beyond belief Wyn might finally be opening her eyes to that poison.

And he was pissed as all fuck she'd upset Wyn enough to make her cry.

CHAPTER 5

Over

Wyn

*O*h my God! If it was me, I would have left that alphahole years ago. Honest to God, Wyn, I do not know how you put up with his shit!

"Earth to fashion queen, come in fashion queen."

I jerked in my chair, Bea's remembered words fading from my mind, and blinked up at Noel, who was not only standing beside my desk, holding a coffee I knew was for me, he was snapping his fingers in my face.

"My *gawd*, gurl, you were so far away, I was worried I'd have to call Chris Pine and request he board his spaceship to go get you. And by the way, shame on you for coming back into the room. Now I can't call Chris."

"I have a lot on my mind," I mumbled.

"Mm-hmm," he said, putting my coffee down, leaning a hip against my desk, putting his index finger to the skin under his soul patch, and watching me. "I know. Cock and Snacktails, sister. On Saturday night. That is *before* that hunka hunka burnin' *looooove* shows at your house on Sunday with your three love children in attendance for Lucie's crab cakes and lobster rolls."

"Please tell me you didn't order the lobster rolls."

"Wyn, you're *rolling* in money. *Stawp* with the poor girl syndrome already. You can afford lobster."

"It isn't about the money, Noel. It's the way they're cooked." I gave a shiver.

"How do you think they cook crab?" he asked.

"Yes, well, my son asked for crab cakes," I reminded him.

He did an exaggerated eyeroll that had me squinting at him. "Oh, how you spoil those children."

"They're grown, and what's with the I'm-gayer-than-gay act?"

His vibe took on an aura of excitement.

"I'm honing it because I'm pitching our YouTube show again, and I have to *flame* for *ratings*, guuuurrrrrl." He lifted both hands and spread them out while saying. "*Wyn Gastineau, Stylist to the Stars, and Her Plucky PA Noel* has a nice ring to it."

He dropped his hands and I stated (again), "We're not doing a YouTube channel."

"You give good style, *hunnee*, and the fact Fiona Remington's assistant called yours truly not five minutes ago to share Fiona's in town next week and your two asses better be at the bar at Durant's or she's firing you, isn't the only thing that proves it. And bee tee dub, you're having drinks with Fiona next Tuesday. But you're Insta numbers are not *oh...tee...dee...see* only because of you."

"OTDC?"

"Off the damn charts, hun."

I drew in breath and released it.

Noel spoke through this.

"I flame all *over* your Insta." He did a fall back snap to punctuate that, something I'd seen him do exactly two times before in our acquaintance when he wasn't doing it for social media. "I'm like a one-man Queer Eye inserting my gems of wisdom in between your fabuloso fashion suggestions, and so I claim at least a quarter of your millions of followers."

He was not wrong about this.

"Now, tell mother what has your mind so far away," he urged.

"Yves is gay."

Noel snapped straight (or at least his body did, away from my desk).

"What?" he whispered.

"He came out to us yesterday."

"The family meet wasn't about Sabre becoming a baby daddy?"

Although (after I got through Sunday) I decided I'd give Remy a wide berth (it was September and I was thinking the next time I saw him should be Sabre's graduation in May), I was rethinking that, since all thoughts went to baby daddy when they considered Sah calling a family meeting. And perhaps Remy and I should discuss it.

(Sah was his nickname because his full name was pronounced the French way, "sah-bru," soft u, rather than the English way, "say-brr," and because

Manon couldn't say it when she was little, she called him Sah-Sah, and a version of that stuck).

"No, Sabre stepped up for Yves as an effort at deflection," I explained to Noel.

"Why on earth would he feel the need to deflect?"

"They were concerned how Remy would respond."

"Who was?"

Yes.

Good question.

And it was because Noel had been with me six years. Pre-divorce, and after. He knew Remy well, loved him and quietly grieved our end right alongside me.

And he never stopped sending Remy a custom-made dress shirt for every birthday (last year, Tom Ford, *from* Ford's modistes) and suits for Christmas (last year, Saint Laurent).

In return, Remy sent Noel things like monogrammed sheets and Montblanc pens.

Back in the day, I'd helped Remy pick. But even after we were over, Remy had not stopped. Though Remy had excellent taste, I suspected his assistant Lisa did the ordering.

So, Noel knew the man Remy was.

And the man he wasn't.

"All three of them," I told him.

He nodded, but I didn't feel he was committed to it. "It's an emotional time, and scary. But obviously, Remy set that to rest right away."

"No, he lost his mind and asked Yves what kind of father he thought Remy was that he'd be worried how he'd react."

Noel stretched out his lips and said, "Yikes."

"Then they hugged, and Manon and I started bawling."

He nodded. "I could have called that, at least the last part, not Yves. I never picked him as batting for our side, but what a lovely addition. And when he goes on the prowl, *rahrwwrr*."

I put my hands over my ears and chanted, "La la la."

"Stop it, Wyn," Noel chided. "You don't do that when Sah is dating someone."

"Only because that band-aid was ripped off when Remy caught...*gulk*."

I couldn't finish or think too long on the time Remy came over and shared he'd found our son and a girl doing things no mother needed to know her son did in his bedroom at Remy's house.

"And I do believe you two had your five thousand two hundred and seventh we're-fighting-because-we're-no-longer-screwing fight over how Remy made it easy for Sabre to rid himself of his pesky virginity by giving him a"—air quotation marks, which regrettably quoted an actual quote...of mine—"'bachelor pad within a bachelor pad.'"

"Sabre practically has his own wing of Remy's house," I defended.

"Boys gonna fuck, baby, girls too," Noel returned. "Be ready for when Manon decides you're well and truly the Mom Friend and no longer the Mom Unit, and she gives you the dirty."

I might vomit.

"Oh my God, how have I not fired you in six years?" I asked.

"You have. I just kept coming back. You barely know how to use our phones, no way you'd be able to call in a want ad."

Maybe now I was realizing why he never let me do anything practical. When someone made themselves your right arm *and* your left, you couldn't exactly cut them off.

"Noel, do we not have work to do?" I asked, reaching for my coffee.

"We do, indeed, but spill. How was Remy with you?"

Noel lived for the day we got back together, and that wasn't about my connections with various ateliers and how that might affect his future presents.

That was because he wanted me happy, and Remy too.

"The same," I lied.

Noel's shoulders slumped.

And I really wanted to tell him.

But I wasn't about to get his hopes up by sharing the knowledge that Myrna was out and Remy was sending strange signals.

I wasn't going there.

So Noel's mind shouldn't go there.

For his own good.

And mine.

"So what had you so far away?" he asked as I took a sip. "And don't say Yves. That's hardly a blip for you two, outside someone needing to provide the Famous Gastineau Drama before you all decided to be real."

Vanilla latte.

Perfect.

As usual.

Honestly, I'd be lost without this man.

As for his question...

"Bea and I had a thing yesterday before I went to Remy's."

His face shut down.

I went alert.

"What?" I asked.

"Nothing," he said.

"What?" I pushed.

He sighed.

Then he said, "Okay, so, when I was arranging Cock and Snacktails, Bernice lost her shit...on Bea. And I'm me, and as she ranted and raved, in her sweet Bernice still ranting and raving way, I did my best to hold the floodgates, I truly did." Two fingers went up. Then they came down. "But I failed. And Wyn, the three of you, I do *not* get why you put up with that venomous snake. She's *awful*. And she's never been anything but *awful*."

I said nothing.

"She nearly ended Bernice and Cornell after she stuck her fangs in when Cornell screwed the pooch."

"Cor kissed an ex-girlfriend, Noel."

Noel lifted a hand and waved it in surrender, shaking his head at the same time.

"Not defending him, he fucked up. But his life is Bernice. I don't know what was in his head then, but I know men, not only because I am one, but because I've dated *lots of them*, and shit goes through our heads. Again, no excuse, but what-might-have-beens are shiny and distracting, and it isn't okay that Cornell got distracted. But he fessed up immediately and he was a mess when things got rocky in a way he thought he might not ever smooth them out. Fortunately, Bernice didn't let Bea's drivel penetrate, or he wouldn't have, and we all wouldn't now have the beauty that is Anton."

I felt something unpleasant skate over my skin. "And is that what you think happened to me and Remy? I let Bea's drivel penetrate?"

"I think everyone who understands these things knows there are two preeminent architects of our age. Prentice Cameron in Scotland, and Remy Gastineau in Phoenix. And I think one of the people who knows that is Remy. I think his ego got the better of him, and when you started to compete in your own field with his success in his, he started acting like an ass. And I think that Bea was in fits of fucking glee that he did, and she pounced on that faster than you can say, 'we need a marriage counselor.'"

I stared in his eyes and whispered, "That's what I think too."

He whirled to the desk, fell to his forearms and whispered back, "Oh God, gurl, really?"

"I've let him go, Noel."

His face fell. "Oh God, gurl. *Really?*"

"It's time. High time. Past time. It's just..." I nodded once, decisively, "time."

"Because of that Myrna."

I shook my head. "It's just time."

"Manon hates her, baby," Noel said.

Important note: Noel was tight with all my kids too.

Oh hell.

I had to spill.

"They've broken up. She's moving out."

Noel brightened.

"We're over, honey. Don't get excited," I said swiftly. "It's done. He's moved on. Now, I need to too."

"Well, I suppose there are silver linings here, what with you realizing you weren't really over him and Bea got you in her evil clutches. But this still makes me sad."

"Bea isn't that bad."

He twitched his head so he was looking at me out the sides of his eyes.

"Is she?" I asked hesitantly.

"I wasn't around when she was brought into your crew, but since I met her, I've been fighting asking if I could hand her a piece of coal so she could shove it up her ass and make me a ten-second diamond. And trust me, I know you care about me. I know I'm family to you. I also know you're my employer. So understand, I know me talking trash about a friend is not cool in the best of circumstances, and you having future payments of my mortgage in your hands, you understand the risks I'm taking in sharing this opinion."

"And Bernice?"

"I'll let Bernice share Bernice's take during Cock and Snacktails."

I drummed my signature "wildfire red," long, rounded nails on my raven-black desk blotter and stared at my pearl-gray walls.

"How about we get back to work," Noel suggested.

I stopped drumming and took a sip of my latte before I answered, "Yes. Let's."

He started walking the long walk to his office that was outside my office.

But I stopped him when I called, "Did you really order lobster rolls?"

Noel didn't break stride or even look back when he answered, "Those are Remy's favorite, darling."

Well then.

Whatever.

He closed the door behind himself, and I glanced around.

When I'd decided to expand the brand into exclusive subscription boxes and online sales of curated pieces, I also decided that brand needed a head-quarters.

So I left my home office and took this space between Thomas and McDowell, close to the Botanical Gardens, that had been abandoned during the recession before it had ever gotten the chance to be anything.

And in it, among other things, was my office. Long, starting with an area that looked like a living room, complete with flat screen TV, and ending with my white desk in front of my built-in covered in a sheen reminiscent of mother-of-pearl.

The room had recessed ceilings, lit exquisitely. Two crystal chandeliers dripping from carved installations. A couch upholstered in gray silk with various toss pillows covered in white, black or gray. There were mirrors. There were black-shaded, crystal-bottomed lamps. There were fabulous leather armchairs. There were black-framed, black-and-white photos of me with clients or sitting beside runways.

Even if the building was surrounded by the city but felt like it was in the middle of nowhere, my office was elegant, glamorous, luxurious, and the like of which Fiona Remington (now a good friend), or Helena Abraham (another client), or Chloe Pierce (daughter of perhaps the most famous actor in the world, Imogen Swan), would not walk in, stutter step and think, "What on earth?"

The reception area was much the same, but dialed down several notches, and Noel's office was half the size of mine, in the same colors but had more blacks, whereas mine was more whites, and that dial for him had gone back up (*way* up).

Attached was an open office space for the rest of my staff.

Beyond that were two massive spaces: one, a warehouse where the subscription boxes were carefully hand compiled and sent out four times a year. The other where we kept our limited, exclusive stock of clothes, shoes, handbags, accessories and makeup items I deemed worthy of *Wyn's List* and sold on my website, this stock shifting out for a new list that shifted in every two months.

Outside Noel, who along with taking direct care of me, managed our two managers (subscription boxes and website sales), I also employed our receptionist, Jana, two computer engineers (one in charge of maintaining our website, the other in charge of all of our machines), one IT tech (who designed and sent newsletters and assisted the engineers), two creative directors (who reported directly to me, one who designed all editorials, the other who designed catalogue shoots for sales and marketing), three customer service reps, five stockists (who saw to inventory and filled orders), a marketing director and assistant, a rotating intern (who assisted Noel), and another who shadowed me. We contracted with various photographers, hair stylists and makeup artists when they were needed. And finally, I had a scout, Sabrina, who did what I used to spend a lot of time doing: traveling, shopping and monitoring trends.

I, however, with Noel and Sabrina, went to the runway shows.

In other words, Noel took care of me and the local operations.

And for the most part, Jana, my current intern, Maria, and I took care of personal clients, of which I had many, and many of those were famous.

I limited the number of our subscription boxes—we mailed twenty thousand of them four times a year—and our waiting list to get one was just under fifty times that.

And every curated collection I created sold out weeks before it was rotated, and I had current designers and up and comers, clamoring to be selected.

I was a small one, but there was no denying I was my own brand of a fashion mogul.

And I might not sit to the side of Anna Wintour next to the runway at Prada.

But I hadn't been in a nosebleed seat since I dressed Fiona for awards season.

And truthfully, my seats before that far from sucked.

Twenty-two years ago, I had interrupted the pursuit of my own dream while Remy continued on the path to his, for nine years.

I did not regret this or wish that time back. I made precious memories with my babies when they were babies and I gave time to my husband, who I adored, to do the thing his father demanded he not do: follow his own dream to building the structures into realities that had plagued his head since he was a little boy.

But once I began again, I hit the ground running, I'd busted my ass and—I took my office in again—I'd created *this*.

And for the last three years, I'd obsessed on failure.

The one I'd made of my marriage.

That wasn't all on me.

It wasn't all on Remy.

And it wasn't all on Bea.

Last, there was no point dissecting it now because there was one thing it was.

Over.

On that thought, I set Bea aside, Myrna, and most importantly, Remy.

And I got back to work.

CHAPTER 6

Rocky

Wyn

S aturday evening, I was running on time for a change as I got ready to go to Cock and Snacktails at Kara's house, when my phone rang with a call from my daughter.

Sitting at my vanity doing the final touches on my makeup, I put her on speaker.

"She lives!" was how I answered it.

"Boo, Mom. I'm a girl on the go."

"So on the go you can't return a text from your darling mother?"

"Okay, you have to promise not to get mad."

This was never a good opening.

Nevertheless, Manon used it a lot.

I braced.

She continued.

"I had a test and paper due this week, and I couldn't really afford the time to drive up to Phoenix for Yves's thing. But he was ready to do it, and I couldn't say no." Big breath and the real whammy. "And I have a new boyfriend. He's a graduate student. And I'm kind of...*obsessed* with him."

I immediately stated the obvious.

"I hope you were more obsessed with that test and paper."

"He finds girls who don't take their studies seriously unattractive."

"I like him already."

She started laughing.

I grinned at my vanity mirror while I swiped on mascara.

"So, Yves, Sah and me have talked...*a lot*, and we want to know if you and Dad are getting back together," she said.

I swiped a black streak across my upper eyelid.

"What?"

"He's dumping that cowface," she pointed out.

"Manon, don't call Myrna a cowface. She isn't a cowface."

"Okay, I'll call her what she is. He's dumping that bitchface."

She was funny.

She was also entirely inappropriate

"Is this the girl I raised?" I asked.

"Mom, she was *not cool* and I'm so glad *she's gonna be gone*. She was just like...*weird* with me all the time. Sometimes, when Dad was teasing me or giving me a hug or something, I'd catch her watching us like she was watching him flirt with another woman, and it made my skin crawl."

What?

Euw!

"You'd never told me that."

"Because you'd probably say something to Dad about it and then you guys would fight, and it didn't matter because Dad didn't miss it and he liked it a lot less than me. He wasn't ugly to her in front of me, but I knew when he'd address it because she'd be sugar sweet for a while after."

Well, at least there was that.

"And anyway, I got the hint that he was just not ever really into her," she went on.

I did not care about this (lie).

This had nothing to do with me (truth).

Bigger truth: I needed to let this slide and steer this conversation into different waters that included putting the kibosh on the kids thinking, now that Myrna was out of the picture, their dad and I were reuniting.

I didn't get the chance to do that.

"They didn't fight," Manon said.

"Sorry?"

"They didn't fight. It was creepy."

I'd grabbed a Q-Tip and some makeup remover to begin the preparations to repair the mascara swipe, but I stopped moving when she spoke.

"This is why I'm obsessed with Benji," she declared. "We fight all the time. I *totally* get it now."

Oh boy.

"Manon—"

"I'll spare you the specifics," she allowed (thank God). "But the first time I didn't take his shit, the look on his face, Mom. *Whoa*. It was like some veil had been ripped away. He's hot. He's tall. He's smart. He's going to get his Ph.D. I'm sure in the classes he teaches, the girls write things on their eyelids like that chick did in *Raiders of the Lost Ark*. So, he's twenty-four and acting like I'm five and he has to guide my way, when I'm twenty. I have a job I don't need because my parents can afford my college, but I know I need to learn how to go to work and earn money. My grades are great. I'm gorgeous. And he isn't the only bonbon in the box. Which was what I told him. And he realized he couldn't steamroll me and seriously, for him, *huge* turn on."

Oh Lord.

"Manon—"

"So yeah, I get it. A woman doesn't want to be a Myrna, where you're just kinda...*there*, for company or whatever she was to Dad. She wants to be a Wyn, where she's half of the dynamic of a relationship, with emphasis on the word *dynamic*."

This was supremely annoying.

Because it told me that Remy was right all those years ago, and at least one of our children learned that strength and passion and knowing your own mind and asserting it were essential to any relationship being healthy.

"So. You? Dad? What?" she prompted.

"Your father and I are divorced, Manon," I said gently.

"Yes, I know that. So why was he sitting on your chair and holding you at his side?"

"It was an emotional evening."

"Mom."

She wasn't buying my crap.

"Just because we're divorced doesn't mean he's quit caring about me, honey," I told her. "And something had upset me before I showed at his house, he knows me well, he noticed it, and he was concerned about me."

This was my guess, but I was sticking with it like it was etched in stone.

"What upset you?"

"I'd exchanged words with Bea."

"Good," she said sharply.

Wow.

Manon too?

"What do you mean, 'good?'" I queried.

"Mom, she's your friend and she can sometimes be sweet, but only if you have a vagina. Mostly, she's bitter. Jordy left her and she swallowed that pill whole. It was like she joined a cult. The bitter cult. And she's a zealot. Every man is Jordy for her, even though I'm now seeing why Jordy said, 'This is for the birds, life's too short. I'm outta here.' I mean, like I just said, a woman doesn't always have to make things roses in a relationship. But Bea's always been a pretty negative person, and that's a serious drag."

I had, for a long time (or until recently), wondered why Jordy had called it quits.

They had never been lovey-dovey, but as far as I knew, he hadn't cheated, she hadn't either, he didn't have some other issue like an addiction or something, neither did she. I didn't even know they were having problems.

He was a quiet guy, but when he talked, he had a wry sense of humor and an interesting, if twisted way of looking at life that I found fascinating, but he was also a nice guy.

Bea had never demonstrated devastation at this loss.

She'd been angry and self-righteous and stayed that way.

"So you and Dad are a no go," Manon noted, and she didn't quite hide the dejection in her voice.

"We are, Manon, I'm sorry."

"And this thing we're all meeting for tomorrow? And by the by, I'm staying at yours in case bitchface isn't out of Dad's place yet, and I'll be there around ten."

"This thing for tomorrow is your dad's way of making sure Yves knows we're his safe haven no matter what."

"But he's inviting us to yours, not his?"

She was as confused as me.

"Maybe he's concerned about the situation with Myrna," I suggested.

"Maybe." She wasn't buying it.

I wasn't either, but I didn't share that.

"Listen, honey, as much as I love talking to you, I've got a girls' night tonight."

"Is Bea going to be there?"

"No."

"Good."

Yes.

How I missed what everyone saw, I didn't know.

Maybe it was just that I loved Bea, and I didn't want to see it.

"You want anything special for tomorrow?" I asked.

"You feel like a trip to Bosa in the morning?"

"Cinnamon swirls or buttermilk?"

"Both."

Yves would love some donuts too.

"They'll be waiting for you."

"Love you, Mom."

"Love you too, my gorgeous girl."

We hung up, I fixed my eye, finished with my hair, got dressed and then wandered into my bedroom.

But I didn't do what I needed to do: wander out and into my car to go to Kara's.

For some reason, I went to the French doors that led to the private, master suite patio, and looked out to the backyard.

My lot was even bigger than Remy's, on a cul-de-sac and maybe a ten-minute drive, at most, north from his house, off Central to the east.

My house was also only ten years older than Remy's, and the lush, mature landscaping and trees reflected those sixty years between when they were planted and now.

The pool was large, kidney-shaped, and Remy'd had it resurfaced so that the water was a deep, Mediterranean blue, not chlorinated aqua.

The space back there was open, with lots of grass, lavish greenery around the edges to help buffer the sound from Central, which was a busy city street only a block away. It also made the backyard seem like an oasis.

The entire time we were together, regardless of his hectic schedule as budding then successful architect, husband and dad, he tended our outside space himself, including the pool. He didn't let anyone touch it, exempting Sabre and Yves when they got old enough to help, not exempting me and Manon.

Another thing he'd inherited from his father, who did not do a day of manual work in his life, but he did have firm ideas about gender roles.

This meant the yard and cars were Remy's (and his sons') domain, so was the garbage and recycling, neither mine nor Manon's hands touched any of it.

Ever.

This segued into him feeling the house and the work to be done in it (unless it was maintenance or repair) was mine.

And I was not in agreement with this idea.

I would far rather garden or skim the pool than do laundry or grocery shop. I loathed both.

We fought about this after I went back to work, and I didn't have time to keep house without help. And some of those fights got intense because I wanted to step over Remy's firmly established boundaries, and I wanted him to do the same.

In the end, we made enough to hire cleaning people, the kids got old enough to do their own laundry and have specific chores, and then Remy and I both had PAs who could do other tasks, like running errands and doing the shopping.

However, being honest with myself, I never quite let go of how irritating I thought it was he couldn't see I no longer had time to do tasks that were much more frequent, like cooking every night (and having the food in the house to do it), not to mention the never-ending laundry.

Now, I wished I'd let it go because really, it didn't mean anything.

And Remy always took excellent care of the yard and pool in a way it wasn't like he spent a half hour mowing the lawn and then done. He spent hours every week on both.

And when he left, I had to find someone to do it. I'd hired a pool service and they'd cleaned the pool, and I'd watched them then cried for an hour.

A solid *hour*.

Outside our boys, once it was resurfaced, no one's hand had touched that pool. Even to do repairs on the equipment.

Just Remy.

It was like someone touching it defiled our marriage.

It was lunacy.

But that was how I felt.

I totally ignored the gardeners when they showed, and I'd struggled with using and even lying beside that pool (both of which I enjoyed doing) ever since.

I sighed, letting this go, deciding to take a swim in the morning and wash those thoughts away, then realized it was September and the pool was probably freezing before I turned my mind to assessing which handbag I was currently using.

I noted I needed a change to match my outfit and headed out to the kitchen to get it so I could take it back to the closet to do that.

I was in the hall when I realized my son was home from rugby practice (the league didn't start until January, but they kept conditioned all year long, and by the by, his father was his coach).

That "by the by" was important, since I could hear Yves with company in the kitchen.

And hearing the voices, I knew that company was Remy.

Therefore, I walked into my glorious kitchen with its acres of marble countertops, cream cabinets and unambiguously French country flair, and saw father and son casually leaning against that luscious marble, enjoying a post workout beer.

Father.

And son.

With that father no longer being married to me nor an inhabitant of this house.

And that son being seventeen.

Both pairs of eyes came right to me, but only the older pair did a head-to-toe sweep and back again, this ending in a smirk.

Yes, you better believe I dressed for Cock and Snacktails that would take place around an island in my friend's kitchen.

Thus, I was now wearing dark-wash, high-waist jeans, a green blouse with big white flowers on it and interesting exaggerated cuffs that went over my red fingertips, with high-heeled, fawn suede booties on my feet.

"Did I miss something in my morning scan of the *Arizona Republic*? Has the state decreased the legal drinking age to seventeen?" I asked the room at large.

The smirk became a smile.

"Mom, I'm at home," Yves replied.

I raised my brows at my boy.

"He needs to learn to hold his liquor," Remy stated.

My attention returned to him because we'd already had this argument about Sabre.

I had, incidentally, lost.

But I was okay to try again.

"You know my feelings about this, Remy," I told him.

"I do. And you know I don't agree with you," he replied.

"And you know I don't care if you don't," I shot back.

"Wyn, do you want him to be a sloppy, teenage-boy drunk?" Remy inquired.

"No," I replied. "I *know* my son is intelligent, so he will understand when it's explained to him that alcohol affects your mood, thinking, coordination, inhibitions, and copious consumption over time can significantly affect your health. And as he'll understand this, when it's legal for him to drink, because he's remarkably intelligent, he'll do it in moderation."

"Baby, boys will be boys."

It was the "baby" that got me, in both very good and very bad ways, thus it ratcheted up my annoyance.

"Yes," I snapped. "And boys being boys means they might feel peer pressured into trashy, locker room talk about girls. And I *know* you've firmly *stressed* that even if said girls are absent, that is *still* a violation of them. And if they *ever* were to consider engaging in such vile byplay, they should remember their mother and sister and know such things had been said or were being said

61

somewhere about both of them and consider how that feels. But more, how it would make their mother and sister feel. And not only refrain from doing it but tell the buffoons who are doing it to shut their damned mouths because they're behaving like buffoons."

"Fucking love it when you slip words like 'buffoons' into one of your rants," Remy murmured.

"Remy!" I shouted.

"It's just a beer, Wyn. It's not talking smack about a woman because, yeah, Sabre and Yves know never to do that shit, but also, we've just found out, Yves wouldn't anyway." He looked to his son. "And no trash talking guys either, kid. What's good for the gander is the same for the goose."

Yves, my perfect final child, lifted...his...blasted...*beer*, smirked at his dad and said, "You're heard, Father."

Then he shot back a slug.

"Oh. My. God!" I yelled at my son.

"Don't you have somewhere to go?" Remy asked.

I opened my mouth, but no.

No.

This was not us anymore.

It wasn't.

He wanted to have a beer with his underage child?

Fine by me!

"Enjoy yourselves," I bid, nabbed my bag and stomped out of the room in the direction of my closet.

I heard Remy's chuckle.

And joining it was a replica of the same.

God!

Why could I not have three girl children?

Why?

Manon was *sheer perfection* when she wasn't hinting at the sexual relation-ship she was having with her boyfriend (and even, kind of, when she was).

Ugh!

I switched out purses, checked my lipstick and hair (no, I did not do this for Remy (yes, that was a lie, I did this because Remy was there)) and marched out, shooting a glare to Remy and blowing a kiss to my son.

God.

Yves

SABRE'S FACE was already on his laptop screen, and they were shooting the shit while they waited for Manon's face to hit it.

It did with her saying immediately, "I'm on a date, you dorks. What's the freaking emergency I have to race to my stupid computer?"

"Mom and Dad are totally getting back together," Yves declared.

"What?" Sah asked.

"They're getting back together," Yves repeated.

"They aren't, brother, I talked to Mom about it today," Manon said.

"When today?" Yves asked.

"Before her girls' night."

"When she was in the car or something?" Yves pushed.

"No. I don't think so. I didn't ask. Why?"

"Because me and Dad were in the kitchen having a beer—"

Manon rolled her eyes and interrupted him. "You will note Dad didn't initiate *me* to alcohol with Gastineau Family Hold Your Drink 101."

"Because Mom had been letting you have a half a glass of wine at dinner since you were fifteen, a full one starting at sixteen, and she mixed your freaking martinis herself the first time you came home for a visit from school," Sah pointed out.

Manon shut up.

"Why do you think they're getting back together?" Sah asked.

"Well, first, she didn't kick Dad out. She just started bickering with him immediately, like he never left," Yves explained.

None of them said anything.

But they all knew what that meant.

Manon spoke first.

"She seemed pretty...*firm* about that not happening, Y."

"She was looking MILF, as usual, and I can say that because I'm gay," Yves said.

Manon grinned.

Sah laughed.

"And she walked in, and for a second there, I thought I needed to figure out how to disappear in a puff of smoke because I thought he'd jump her," Yves finished.

"This is gross," Sah muttered.

"There are worse things than your parents having a very healthy sex life," Manon sniffed.

"Did you hear me a second ago saying this is gross?" Sah asked.

"You guys, shut up. They're getting back together," Yves pressed. "He called her 'baby.'"

Both his older siblings focused on him, he could tell, even if they were looking at his face on a screen.

"He did?" Manon asked quietly.

Yves nodded.

"What'd she do?" Sah asked.

"Nothing, it was like when they were together. They just kept squabbling. Mom was on a roll, it was her usual, totally hilarious. And Dad *totally* did not miss how hilarious it was."

"Yves, bud, I hear you, but I wouldn't get your hopes up," Sabre said.

"Yeah," Manon agreed, though she now seemed unsure.

"You weren't there," Yves told them.

"Just, you know, you're home and around them more, so be...you know, cautious, okay?" Sah advised.

They'd all been crushed when their dad left.

Sure, their parents fought, but most of the time, it was like today. They were just two strong personalities who had no problem laying it out. Their mom would be funny, their dad would be cool and egg her on, sometimes it'd escalate and then they'd disappear in their bedroom where the argument might get loud, but then it'd get very quiet for a long time.

So there was love, a lot of it in that house, and having half of the engine that drove that love walk out the door, the buzz of the house had changed drastically and it had been hard to take.

The three of them didn't lose him, just time with him.

But Mom lost him, and it was killer, watching that.

And maybe it was good advice to be cautious.

But since they broke up, his dad never followed him home from practice with the lame excuse that he was bringing the booze over for their get-together early, but also to grab a beer and shoot the shit, and that was not about him initiating Yves in Gastineau Family Hold Your Drink 101.

Dad could do that at his house.

It was about Dad being in a place where he could see Mom, and she could see him.

"I'll be cautious," Yves said.

And he would.

But still.

Their parents were getting back together.

"Can I go back to my date now?" Manon asked, and it wasn't snotty. She wanted to know if Yves was cool.

"Yeah, sister. Have fun," Yves said.

"Later, bros," she replied then her face blinked out.

"You good?" Sah asked.

"Yeah," Yves answered.

"See you tomorrow," Sabre said.

"Tomorrow, brother. Later," Yves replied.

Sah blinked out too.

Yves shut his laptop.

Then he picked up his phone and called Theo.

"Hey, babe," Theo answered.

"Hey," he greeted his boyfriend. "So, one, I'm a man now, my dad gave me a beer, and two, strap in, because I'm springing you on them tomorrow and then you'll be on the Gastineau train and we're all along for the ride, which is sure to be rocky, of Mom and Dad getting back together."

Theo's laugh was deep and rich, and Yves felt it in the two places he always felt it. In his chest, and points south.

"Looking forward to it," Theo said.

Even though his man couldn't see him, Yves smiled.

"Are you sure this springing me on them gig is the right way to play it?" Theo asked (again, he'd mentioned it before).

"One, Dad knows you," Yves pointed out, because that was true. Theo played rugby with him and had for the last five years, and his dad had always been their coach. "Two, yes. I'm sure."

"That's what I'm worried about," Theo muttered. "The him knowing me part."

"Thee, I told you how it went Wednesday."

"Him being cool, and him being cool with us doing each other are different things."

Yves didn't know what to say to that.

Then he figured it out. "He doesn't know specifics."

"He's still going to know we're doing each other."

"I haven't told them I've *gone there*. Just that I'm gay."

"Your mom will convince herself you're a virgin until the day she dies. You told me she's in denial about Sah."

"I didn't say *denial*, I said she refuses to talk about it, and it takes her at least ten minutes to look any of his girlfriends in the eye."

"Denial."

Yves smiled again.

"Your dad, though. You told me he told you when he gave you the sex talk that he'd lost his virginity at sixteen and he understood the sex-on-the-brain thing. Just be smart about the sex-on-the-brain thing. So he gets it, he's a guy, he's been our age, which means he'll totally know we're fucking."

"Shit," Yves muttered. Theo was totally right.

"Tell them about me and then text me if it's cool to come over, okay?" Theo said.

"I don't want it not to be cool," Yves admitted.

"You want to force their play so they've got no choice but to play it cool with me when you gauged shit wrong the last time and hurt your dad's feelings. Don't do that again, babe. I think you learned benefit of the doubt is the way to play this."

"But you don't think he'll be cool with you?" Yves asked.

"What I think is, it'll be a shock to him, and you need to give him a beat to come to terms with that before I'm in his space."

Yves saw the wisdom of this, so he said, "Okay, you're good with being standby until I text you?"

"Fuck yeah. I can't wait to try these crab cakes."

And again, Yves smiled.

CHAPTER 7
Yea

Wyn

"I'm a yea," Kara stated, leaning into her island with her martini glass coasting over a plate of brie and thinly sliced apples.

Not a surprise, as Kara was my take-no-prisoners, eat-no-shit girl.

She was also petite, red-haired, wore glasses, had two children in their late teens who were more intelligent than our collective group, and thus they scared me, even as I adored them. She was also so good at makeup, a couple of times when our artists let us down and didn't show up, in a pinch, she had shown up, and done a beautiful job.

Her full-time gig was as a pediatrician, though.

"I don't know. I say nay and a meeting," Bernice stated, sitting back, one arm wrapped around her middle, the other one holding up her martini glass.

Not a surprise, as Bernice was my heart-of-gold girl.

She was also delicately boned, dark-skinned, had a mass of fabulous braids knotted up in killer ways I took note of, because I wanted some of our models with that style for a future *List* and I was going to need to talk to her stylist. She had two boys who were the light of all of our lives, and she'd met her husband Cornell in a very traditional way: he was a pilot, she had been a flight attendant.

Since then, they'd made babies and she'd made a move that kept her close to home.

She was now air traffic control.

"I'm the newbie, I abstain," Noel put in.

That night, Noel had been there when I got there, and he explained his presence by saying, "I've waited six years for a seat at this table to open, I wasn't missing my chance."

He was, of course, the perfect addition.

But now the vote of whether to oust Bea by just ghosting her (Kara's "yea") or to see if we could work on current issues by sitting her down and talking about why she was so negative all the time (Bernice's "nay and a meeting") was down to me.

"You know, I have to say, as much as it makes me sound like a bitch, I've been going through the motions with her for a long time," Kara said. "Having her around, calling her for Cock and Snacktails, inviting her to things was just habit. But in thinking on it these past few days, when she is around, I try to avoid her."

"She's a good soul," Bernice said.

"She is?" Noel asked.

It was, as we were showing, arguable.

But in some senses, she was.

This was why I piped up.

"Once, when Remy was in Houston visiting a site, I got sick. Weather flared up there and he couldn't get back. The kids were little, I'd had all three by then, and I had a really bad flu. Like, nearly delirious, pass-out-and-lose-three-days flu where you just sweated out a fever and hoped. After waiting for a flight to be cleared for takeoff, giving up, renting a car and driving, it took Remy thirty-six hours to get home. In the meantime, Bea came over, took care of the kids and me, and she was there the whole time."

Kara and Noel didn't say anything.

But Bernice did.

"I will admit to what we were discussing earlier, and she absolutely tried to drive a wedge between Cor and me. But when my mom passed—"

Bernice stopped.

It had been years, she still wasn't over it.

It had been years for mine too, so I got her.

"Langston and Ruth were here, we were all a mess," she went on, referring to her big brother and younger sister. "Cor was trying to hold me together. And Bea came over and just did stuff. No questions, she just got to work. Like cleaning the dishes and bringing in food and making us eat and setting a meeting at the funeral parlor and with the pastor. She didn't say anything about it, didn't make a big deal, and when we pulled ourselves together, she just faded away. But the truth of it is, if she didn't hustle us to the car and drive us there herself, I don't even know if Mom would have had a service until maybe weeks later."

"I'm seeing now why you put up with her shit," Noel remarked.

"I told you she isn't all bad," I said.

"You're right, she's had her good times with me too. She's also, as we talked about, had her bad. But Wyn, seriously? She was the worst with you," Kara said, and it surprised me.

"Do you think?" I asked.

"Uh, yeah," not Kara, but Bernice answered.

"Really?" I asked Bernice.

She nodded.

"I talked to her, you know," Kara said. "After the Cor debacle, and when she seemed to be setting her sights on Remy, I sat her down and told her to lay off."

"*Really?*" Noel, Bernice and I said at the same time.

Kara sipped her dirty martini and nodded. "It was too much. It was constant. It actually kinda freaked me out."

"What did she say?" Bernice asked.

Kara shrugged. "At first, she stuck to her guns, was belligerent, said he was too alpha and maybe she shouldn't be asked to be different, he should, which was hogwash. I mean, Remy is alpha, but he's not a dick, and she was using those terms interchangeably. When I pushed it, she was vague. Looking back, it was kind of a confront the bully, the bully backs off situation. I didn't let her get away with her lame excuses, she said whatever she had to say to get me to shut up about it, except that she'd do better. Then, of course, it came as no surprise she didn't do better."

"I just passed it off," I mumbled.

"Because you love him, and nothing anyone said about him would change that," Kara replied.

It was Bernice mumbling when she said, "Until it did."

"Bea didn't break us up, Remy walked out," I reminded her.

"You know that wedge she had for me and Cor?" Bernice asked.

I nodded, because I so did.

"Well, she chucked that aside and grabbed a jackhammer to pick away at you and Remy," Bernice went on.

I sat still and said nothing.

"Honest to God, it says a lot about the man he is, and the respect he had for you and your decisions, also the faith in your marriage, that he didn't tell you he didn't want you around her anymore," Kara put in.

"Why would he do that?" I asked, ignoring the "faith in your marriage" part because a creeping feeling was sinking in.

"Oh, I don't know, because she dug into him right *to him*," Kara replied.

Oh my God.

He'd never said anything.

"She did?"

Kara nodded.

"I remember when he was talking about that project in Chicago, and you had that fundraiser you were doing with the queen bees of Scottsdale, which was a massive score for you, and he mentioned he was flying to Chicago, and she said, 'Of course you are,' all snotty," Kara told me. "He couldn't miss what she meant. He was leaving you with the kids when your plate was seriously full."

"Sabre was fifteen then, sixteen?" I noted. "So Manon was thirteen and Yves eleven. It wasn't like, for the most part, they couldn't look after themselves, or Sabre couldn't look after them. And I worked from home then. I was just across the garage. What was she on about?"

"That wasn't her worst offense."

We all turned at these words and saw Reed, Kara's husband, strolling in.

He went right to his wife, and the brie, put some on a slice of apple, popped it in his mouth and chewed.

"Did I say you were allowed beyond the estrogen barrier?" Kara asked.

Reed tipped his head to Noel. "He broke the seal. For years I've been dying to tomcat with you kittens. Here I am." He then faced Noel. "Thanks, man."

"One, I love you, your phraseology is *everything*, and two, you are more than welcome," Noel replied.

They smiled at each other.

I had no time for this, no matter how cute it was.

"What was her worst offense?" I asked.

Reed looked to me. "She's a man-hater, Wyn. This was why Jordy left. She never ceased trying to emasculate him. Honest to Christ, I have no idea how he put up with it for so long. I don't even know how they got together in the first place."

I hadn't thought about it until right then, but before she set her sights on Cor, and Remy, and yes, even saying things about Reed, she made comments about Jordy that weren't...right.

Not from a wife.

But it was her, it had always been her. And if I carried that further, when Jordy was gone and she moved it to the other men in her circle, we were used to it and used to not processing it in any real way, so we didn't.

"And even as a man who feels he's pretty damned manly," Reed carried on, "I'll allow that there's every possibility Remy's dick is way bigger than mine." He turned to his wife. "Figuratively speaking, sweetheart."

"Of course, I will state with witnesses how satisfied I am with my husband's package," Kara, hand on heart, announced.

"Oh my *God*, I am *so glad a seat opened at this table*," Noel breathed.

Bernice giggled.

I wanted to find this amusing.

I did not find this amusing.

"And?" I pushed, aiming this at Reed.

"And, if you women weren't around, she went for his jugular. She was a virtuoso with it. Always saying shit that was meant to make him bleed, but she had plausible deniability and it struck at his manhood. Like, 'Oh Remy, you're too sensitive, of course I didn't mean *that*.' I mean, no man wants to prove to some bitchy woman he's *sensitive* by being, well...sensitive to her bullshit. It was masterful."

"Like what would she say?" I asked. Even though I didn't want to know, for some reason, I really needed to know.

"That's part of the genius of it," Reed said. "I honestly cannot remember a bitchy thing she said, but I do remember a lot of times Remy looking like he wanted to strangle her and thinking after she said something, '*Fucking ouch.*'" He reached for an olive, popped it in his mouth, chewed, swallowed and finished, "But it wasn't just Remy. She did it to all us men. It was just she kept the real zingers for him."

I stared down at my martini not knowing what to make of this, but knowing it made me feel exceptionally uneasy.

"I still think we should find out what's behind this," Bernice said, but there wasn't a lot of *oomph* to it. "I'm not real hip on having someone in my life who I care about, who I just give up on."

"You're such a buzz kill, always having a conscience and shit like that," Kara complained.

Bernice smiled at her.

I took a sip of my martini.

"Have you gotten to the part where Remy isn't over her yet?" Reed asked.

Noel was also sipping at his martini, and he almost did a spit take.

Bernice made a "peep" sound.

Kara smacked Reed's arm and snapped, "Reed! What the hell!"

My chest caved in on itself.

"What?" Reed asked. "Should I take that as a no, you haven't?"

"Don't you men have some kind of code or something?" Kara asked.

"Not when one of my male friends, which Remy still is.... You got Wyn, I got Remy, but I'm taking Wyn back, as you can see." Reed threw his arm up his front to indicate his current location. "I'll finish what I started by saying, not when one of my male friends has his head up his ass, which Remy does."

"You girlies *so* should have introduced testosterone *years* ago," Noel noted. "I'd say, around three of them."

"Remy just broke up with his live-in girlfriend," I choked out.

"That woman was not a keeper," Reed declared.

"Oh my God," Kara said slowly to the ceiling. Then to her husband, "You are not getting sex until the end of time."

"What?" Reed asked.

"Did you just refer to a woman as a 'keeper?'" Kara asked back.

"Please do not sit there with your hens telling the rooster that you do not refer to men in the same way I just did to that woman Remy was seeing," Reed returned.

"Now did you just refer to us as hens and yourself as a rooster?" Kara demanded.

Reed grinned at her then reached for a bacon-wrapped date stuffed with bleu cheese.

He ate it.

"Chiming in here," Noel said. "Men, like I'm sure is the same with women," he spoke that last quickly and in Kara's direction, "do not find every reason under the sun to go invade an ex's space to fight with her," again to Kara and swiftly, "or him."

"You and Remy do spend a lot of time together," Bernice commented carefully.

"Flipside, if a woman, or man, isn't into it, they do not allow the other person to invade their space and engage in said fight," Noel concluded.

"We all know I wasn't over Remy," I pointed out.

"Did it occur to you, honey, that he had a woman at home, but he was at your doorstep a whole lot?" Reed asked gently. "And then maybe wonder why?"

I looked to my drink again.

Then, even if it was mostly full, I drank half of it.

"That hadn't occurred to her," Kara said, *sotto voce.*

"It destroyed me when he left," I said to my glass.

No one had a response.

I looked to the beloved faces around the island all gazing at me gently, but intently.

"We were perfect together. Then we were not. He walked out, and the only way I could deal was not to admit to myself that I wasn't dealing and that I was hanging on to him even when he moved into an apartment, then bought and furnished a home, then entered into a relationship with another woman where she was sleeping beside him every night."

Not one of them, even Reed, could hide their flinch at my last.

"You've had lovers," Bernice said softly.

I faced her. "Not in my bed, *his* bed, *our* bed. Neither of them met our kids. And I never spent the night with them night after night for *a year*."

Bernice pursed her lips and looked to Kara.

I kept going.

"We fought about me going to California. We made up having sex. I went to California. I came back. And he had an apartment to go to. Not a hotel. *An apartment*. He'd been planning," I reminded them. "Planning and following through with that plan before the California trip, which was *a day*. I was gone at seven o'clock in the morning and I was back in my bedroom, watching my husband pack, at ten o'clock the next day. When the kids went to him that next weekend, they had beds. You can buy beds in a week. He did not. He already had them, and told me so when he called, one day after he left, to share he wanted them for the weekend. He did not tell me any of this. He did not warn me about it. He did not warn me he was thinking about it. About leaving. About ending us. He did not agree to discuss it after. He filed when he could file. Our attorneys ironed out the arrangements. And he divorced me."

No one spoke.

I did.

"I asked him to talk to me. I asked him to come back. I asked him to go to counseling. He said what needed to be said had been said. He didn't come back. He built a new life without me, and he didn't let another woman in his bed, he *installed her in his home* and in *my children's lives*."

"Babe," Kara whispered.

"Now, she's out and what? He realized what he lost? Or he's looking for a rebound?" I asked. "Well, no. Because yes, indeed, I did just come to terms with the fact that I never stopped loving him. And maybe somewhere in his heart, he never stopped loving me. *But he gave up on us*. Not on *me*. On *us*. He just *gave up*. We were *perfect*, and many might argue my definition, but we *were*. And he walked away. And when he did, it hurt so bad, I couldn't face it until *three years later* with a martini in my hand and my best people around me and..."

My voice cracked, my glass was swept away, and Bernice's arms were around me with Noel patting me on my back because I'd lost it.

Three years of wracking grief and despair and heartbreak poured into

Bernice's (rather fabulous) yellow blouse, and I was ashamed to say, this went on for a while.

Eventually, through my sobs I heard Reed growl, "That stupid motherfucker."

"Reed, honey, chill," Kara whispered.

I sat back abruptly and swiped my face, announcing, "I'm okay."

"Gurl, you're a fucking *mess*. Shut up with that," Noel replied.

I shook my head, short quick shakes while sniffing.

"I'm fine. I will be fine. Eventually, I'll be fine." I cleared my throat and picked up my glass again, taking a sip, then repeating, "I'm fine."

"You have to know, if there's one place in the world it's okay you're not fine, it's here," Kara said.

I nodded to her and looked to Reed and stated, "She slept at his side."

He winced and whispered, "Sweetheart."

"He didn't cheat on me. We were over. But do you get me?" I asked Reed.

He didn't answer me.

He looked at his wife and his voice was rough when he declared, "If you ever think of leaving me, I'm chaining you to my side."

Her face got soft, and she touched his chest.

Bernice scooted her stool very close to mine on one side, and Noel did the same on his so I was sandwiched between them.

I reached for a date, but before putting it into my mouth, I said, "We're not the sort of people who give up on a friend. Maybe Bea's hurting and all of this has been a cry for help we've been avoiding because we didn't want to confront it. We'll talk to her. And then what will be, will be."

"I'm a yea with that," Kara said.

"Me too," Bernice said.

"The estrogen barrier is back up on that one," Reed said.

"Word, my brother," Noel said.

I popped the date in my mouth and chewed.

I was sure it was delicious.

I didn't taste a thing.

CHAPTER 8

Now?

Remy

The next night at 5:55, Remy pulled into the driveway of his own house (or he still thought of it that way) not feeling like he had the many other times he'd done it over the last three years.

That being lowkey rage that he'd have to walk up to and hit the doorbell on the door to a home he'd paid the mortgage on for fifteen years.

It was something else that was uglier and harder to take.

He felt miserable.

Not about what was to come.

With that, he had a game plan. Yesterday, he'd instigated it and today he would bring it forward.

No, that miserable feeling was about the fact it was all on him that he had to walk up to that damned door and ring the bell because what was beyond—especially one particular thing that was by far the most important—wasn't his anymore.

The catering van was at the curb, and he'd come hungry because Lucie had been Wyn's (more aptly, Noel's) favorite caterer for four years, so he knew what was in store.

And he ignored the wrench in his gut when he rang the doorbell, including the familiarity of the feel of it, something he'd been able to ignore by covering it with anger about whatever he'd concocted to come get up in Wyn's shit about.

He still had the key (she'd never asked for it back, he'd never offered). After he'd walked out three years ago, he'd also never used it, even if he'd invented ways to be extremely pissed off at her and had come over to share that.

He loved every being in that home (save Lucie, but he loved her food).

He was still glad it was Wyn who answered the door.

She did it differently, not the way she'd done it since he'd left.

This time, she appeared flustered.

He'd get why when she said to her feet, "For something like this, Remy, please, don't ring the bell. Just come in."

Which meant maybe she wasn't big on him ringing the bell on the door to his own home either.

"Hey, and thanks," he murmured, moving in.

Her eyes skittered through his and she said, "The kids are in the kitchen."

He didn't go into the kitchen. He waited while she closed the door.

Then he told her the truth, but he did it having a purpose.

"You look good."

Her gaze finally came to his face. "Well...uh," she tucked hair behind her ear, and Jesus.

Jesus.

He forgot how fucking cute she was when she was uncertain of her footing with a man she was attracted to.

She was the single worst flirt he'd ever encountered.

It was the most effective flirting he'd ever experienced.

"Thanks," she finished.

"I brought over Dom. Were you intending not to let your underage son drink it at his own truth and bravery celebration?" he teased.

She scrunched her face (*fuck*, he forgot how much he liked that too) and pushed out, "Don't be an ass."

He smiled at her.

She then swanned into the kitchen, and he watched her ass as she did it.

He really wanted to believe her outfit of white, wide-legged, ribbed knit pants with a matching top that had short sleeves and buttoned to a vee-neck (both the pants and the top hugging areas of her body he'd spent years worshiping) was for him. But he knew the last time she'd worn true knockabout clothes was the day they'd painted Sabre's nursery together in their first house.

Even when the kids were little, she turned herself out, and it was not lost on him the job he left her to at home when he went to work was tough, carried incredible responsibility, as well as a huge workload.

That, he'd figure out later, was never for him.

It was the way she was. It was *who* she was. And before the term "self-care" became the lingo, it was what she carved time out of her day, every day, to do for herself.

Except for a rough patch that lasted about eight months when Yves was newborn and the other two were under five, Remy was making his name, so he was also working longer hours and things got hectic for her, that had never changed.

What she was wearing right then was as casual as it came.

Unless she was nude.

"Your father has arrived," she announced grandly as she hit the kitchen.

"Daddy!" Manon cried and then she was on him.

And since his daughter heard the doorbell, knew it was him, and she had never in her life hesitated rushing him, shouting his name, and falling on him, he gave her a hug, murmured in her ear, but looked at his two boys who were also in the room.

Both darted their attention back and forth between him and their mom.

They'd left her to get the door for their own reasons, which Remy was seeing aligned with his.

Good to have additional evidence they hadn't raised idiots.

He felt his lips tip up and Manon jumped back from him.

He looked down at her, forgetting for a second he had a number of motives for why he'd arranged them all to be there, and since he'd arranged it, he'd added one more.

Her mother was the most gorgeous woman Remy had ever seen.

But damn, did they make a beautiful girl.

"Are you going to pop the cork?" she asked. "I'm *dying*."

"I don't know, precious, you're underage. We'll have to ask your mom."

She blinked in confusion.

Yves burst out laughing.

"Stop being difficult, Remy," Wyn demanded with unveiled exasperation, having put the whole length of the massive, very long, not as wide but still wide, island between them.

"Hey, Lucie," he greeted the woman who was shifting this way and that on the island, enough food there was no way in hell the five of them would get anywhere near going through it all.

God, he missed Noel.

And that amount of food was all Noel.

Remy's dad came from wealth.

His mom came from wealth, even if, by the time it got to her, it was mostly gone.

Remy's dad worked far more hours than he spent with his wife or son to make more wealth.

And considering the fact both of them had made a deal with the devil and drove a hard bargain seeing as the devil met them each in turn and realized he'd met his match, they were unlikely to die until Remy had long since kicked it.

But once they did, they were going to make his kids very rich.

Wyn, on the other hand, had grown up on a small farm.

Her dad worked the land but also worked as a janitor in an automotive parts factory. Her mom worked reception for the local dentist. And still, with four kids, they barely made ends meet.

They were also the kindest, gentlest, most loving human beings Remy had ever met (outside their daughter), and when they both passed, Remy grieved twice, losing them and having to experience the agony of watching Wyn do it.

But near on their whole lives, they were two steps up from dirt poor.

Wyn had never washed that taste from her mouth. Not sipping wine on the Seine. Not declaring ouzo disgusting on Crete (the moment he discovered she hated licorice and all things aniseed).

When he met her, he'd been fucking around going back to school to get his architect's degree, trying to prove a point to his father, at the same time knowing eventually he'd give up as his father suspected he would and goaded him about incessantly. Then he'd be swallowed by his family's company.

It was meeting Wyn that had lit the fire in his belly to make something of himself to show her, but also show his dad.

To follow through with something.

Something important.

But most of all, to build a life with his hands, his work, his ideas, all things *his*. A life he would give to her where she could stop carefully unfolding the paper around flour packets so she could be certain to save that half a teaspoon that got caught in the folds.

He'd never, not once, mistaken he was who he was because of Wyn, and no small part of that was when they made their family and she let him work. She'd given him time and space to test the lengths of his ambition, and best them, then reset them, while she took on the work of their home and their kids.

In return, they both had built a life where she didn't have to worry about the flour packets.

But he'd failed in his mission to eradicate her innate need to do so.

"Hey, Remy," Lucie replied.

"Looks fantastic," he told her.

She shot him a smile then turned to Wyn. "I'm taking off. We're recycling, yes?"

Wyn nodded. "But do you want to stay for a glass of champagne?"

"I'd love to, but it's a banner Sunday. I have another job on the go. I have to check on them."

"Oh!" Wyn chirped. "My God. Sorry. Okay. Thank you for taking us on."

"I will never say no to you," Lucie replied.

Remy knew why she wouldn't.

She'd been a woman with a dream and a food truck.

Noel had been to that food truck. And since that man could make friends with a gnat, he'd made friends with Lucie and found out catering was where she wanted to go. So, when they'd had the work, he'd suggested her for the job. Wyn had taken a chance. And most of Phoenix and Scottsdale's elite had eaten her food.

And now she had more food trucks and a successful catering business.

Lucie said goodbye to them all and they all returned it with Sabre saying, "I'll drop those trays by your kitchens before going down to Tucson in the morning, Lucie."

"You don't have to do that," Lucie replied.

"Won't be a problem."

"You're the best."

He smiled his cool-guy smile and Lucie took off.

Fortunately, she was halfway down the walk (he could see through the window over the sink, which had a view to the front yard), when Manon chanted, "You like her, you like her, you *so, so* like Lucie."

"Ef off, you dork," Sabre growled.

Remy was at the wine fridge, and he could growl too.

"Son."

"I didn't say the full word, Dad. And she's being a pill."

Remy got out the Dom Perignon and said, "Manon."

"All right, Dad," she muttered, then stuck her tongue out at her big brother.

He sighed.

Wyn came out from behind her fortress of the length of the island to move close enough to Remy to slide the coupé glasses toward him.

No flutes for Wyn.

Coupé glasses held far less liquid, but they were far more chic. He didn't think she even owned a flute.

And that wasn't about appearances.

That was about aesthetics.

That was something they had in common.

Not a detail of their home did they fight about.

79

She had perfect style.

And he had perfect design sense.

It was a perfect match.

He popped the cork.

"Yippee!" Manon yelled.

He grinned and grinned bigger when he saw Wyn smiling.

He poured glasses and the kids approached the island as Wyn passed them out.

Ballsier than any male he'd ever met, it was not a surprise when Sabre got there first with the toast.

Glass raised, he said, "Here's to courage and truth and all that jazz, and for essentially existing, Yves giving us an excuse to eat crab cakes!"

"I'll drink to that!" Manon cried.

Remy would too.

They all raised their glasses and drank.

He'd have to wait until he managed to maneuver the kids being gone and him still there before he got into one of the things he'd engineered this celebration for.

But now, since they'd just done the important part—making sure Yves knew he had their unconditional love and support—Remy could get to the add-on.

"Thought I'd see Theo here," he said, then smiled into his glass as Yves choked.

"Oh man," Manon mumbled.

Sabre grunted.

Yeah, the kids knew.

They were close. Now, and they always had been.

Thick as thieves.

All their lives.

He'd never had that, until Wyn gave it to him.

Then he had it every day.

Until he walked out.

He quit smiling.

"Theo?" Wyn queried.

"You know?" Yves asked, his eyes glued to his dad.

"I didn't until yesterday because I didn't know your orientation until this week. Now that I know, you men are very bad at hiding it. And how about until your old man gets used to things with you and Theo, we have a little less patting on the ass?"

Manon burst out laughing and Sabre's chest moved with the same, but silently.

Yves was bright red.

"What are you all talking about?" Wyn asked.

"I have a boyfriend, Mom," Yves said.

Her head jerked and her thick blonde hair swayed around her shoulders.

"Theo...from the squad?" she asked.

"Yeah," Yves answered, sounding strangled.

"Oh my," she whispered, then recovered. "Well, I suppose we don't have to worry about anyone confronting you with bigotry. He's, what? Six ten and five hundred pounds of solid muscle? And you're no slouch. You'd have to have a death wish to try anything with either one of you."

Yves relaxed and chuckled. "He's six five, Mom. And he's only about forty pounds bigger than me."

"He's also older than you," she noted. "He's in college."

"He's one year and two months older than me. He's a freshman in college, I'm a senior in high school. He's nineteen. I'll be eighteen in a few months. It isn't a big deal."

"One year and two whole months," she murmured, a light in her eye.

She was playing.

She was pleased.

She was maybe even relieved she knew the kid and knew he was a good kid.

Of course, she was also a woman, so she saw her good-looking son and knew he wasn't taking whatever he could get, but instead, he'd scored a good guy who was also good-looking.

Which meant she wasn't a man, so she wasn't thinking any further than that.

And Remy wasn't going there.

He'd already had to deal with it in his face when he'd come home from his office to grab something he'd forgotten, saw Sabre was up from school, and walked in on him giving a girl a ride in his bed.

Now, until he had grandchildren, and therefore the bonus of such activities to spoil, he wasn't thinking about it again with any of them.

"He's on standby to come over," Yves said.

"On standby?" Remy asked.

Yves nodded to him. "I was going to tell you about him and ask if he could come over so you could meet him. And he's waiting for my call, or, um, text if you're not ready."

"I coach him, son. I spent two hours with the guy yesterday."

"Well, you know, as my...uh..."

"Boyfriend?" Wyn provided.

Yves smiled at his mom. "Yeah, that."

She glanced at Sabre, who was shoving a crab cake in his mouth, then she said, "By all means, phone him with urgency before Sabre eats all the food and we look ungracious due to the fact we've asked him to a meet the parents and yet we can't offer refreshments when he arrives. But instead, he'll be mocked by a variety of catering trays with nothing but crab dust inside."

That was when Remy laughed.

"I knew you'd say yes, and me and Yves double date, so I also know how much that guy puts away. I'm getting my fill before he gets here," Sabre stated with his mouth full.

"You double date?" Wyn asked.

Sabre shrugged...and shoved another crab cake in his mouth.

"How long have you and Theo been together?" she asked Yves.

"We hoo...um, started dating in April," Yves answered.

Wyn nodded to her youngest, wisely not making an issue of the fact that he'd hidden a boyfriend for six months. Yves had his reasons, and they didn't need to put him on the spot to explain them.

He'd come out, and a few days later, shared about the boyfriend.

All good.

Also, a reminder to Remy of something else about his wife.

With the way he'd grown up, he'd had no clue how to be a parent.

She did because she'd had excellent teachers.

From the beginning, they hadn't fought about it, and he hadn't fumbled. He knew the foundation she was standing on with her parenting, so he'd watched and taken her cues.

He couldn't say they'd never disagreed on parental decisions, case in point, him feeling with his sons he should demystify booze (however, he had not missed she'd done the same with their daughter, but since he agreed, he didn't call her on it) so it wouldn't seem the illicit thrill other kids thought it was.

But on the important things, like this, they were always rock solid.

She looked to her oldest.

"Do you have a girlfriend?" she asked Sabre suspiciously.

Sabre shook his head and swallowed more food. "No, and I'm not hard to look at, but I'll sure be able to tell how into me she is when we sit down and eat with two Adidas models." He turned to Yves who was shoving his phone in his jeans, after no doubt texting Theo. "Which, by the way, I'm batting zero, man."

"Let me get this straight..." Wyn started.

Oh shit.

"...you *test* your dates by using your brother and his boyfriend?" she finished.

"Babe," Remy murmured.

"Yeah. And it's good I do because they all fail," Sabre said to his mother.

She looked up at Remy and her hazel eyes flashed more green than brown, and he absolutely knew what that meant.

When she wasn't angry, they were an equal mix of both.

When she was a little angry, they were an equal mix of both.

When she was pissed, out came the green.

"You get to handle this one," she ordered.

"Relax," he replied. "It's actually kind of ingenious."

Those eyes flashed again as they widened.

Jesus, he fucking *longed* to kiss her.

He'd longed for nothing in his life.

Not parents who loved him, not even after getting hers and knowing how much he'd been missing.

Not the end of their dry spell, as decreed by Wyn, that they couldn't have sex for one month prior to their wedding, "So on our wedding night, it'll be special."

Before that (and after, honest as shit, he didn't know how either of them were able to walk enough to get on a plane after their honeymoon), they'd fucked like rabbits, and she was phenomenal.

And she'd been so happy and excited in the run up to their wedding, she shone like a goddamn sunbeam.

It had been torture.

But he longed to kiss her right then.

In the kitchen they'd renovated, next to an island he'd eaten her out on countless times and fucked her on countless more.

Christ, what had he done?

"Remy?" she whispered.

"Right here, baby," he whispered back, tasting acid in his mouth and feeling it drip down his throat into his gut.

"You okay?" she asked.

"Mm-hmm, fine. Good," he muttered.

She studied him a second and he noticed the green was gone.

Now, her eyes were more brown than green.

He knew what that meant too.

She was worried.

But she muttered back an unconvincing, "Okay."

She turned to the island.

Remy drank half a coupé glass of champagne before he did the same, and it wasn't near enough to wash that acid away, and that had nothing to do with how much liquid a coupé glass held.

But when he took them in, he caught their kids in various versions of pretending they weren't watching every move and listening to every word their parents said with the intensity of the world's highest-powered microscope.

And that was when he thought...shit.

He better not fuck this up.

No.

He'd already fucked this up.

And Christ.

Now?

He simply *could not fuck this up*.

CHAPTER 9
Lost

Wyn

"See you at practice, Coach," Theo said, standing at the door, where we were *all* standing.

And I was trying not to panic.

Because *they* were all standing at the door, Remy was too, but they were preparing to leave.

And Remy was behind me, and apparently, he was *not*.

Suffice it to say, with all that was happening, I did not want to be alone in the home I'd lived in with this man, the home we'd raised our family in, the home we'd done countless things in, in a variety of places—laughing, talking, listening, comforting, fighting...and having sex.

Especially after the expression that took hold on his face earlier.

But that looked like what was about to happen.

"Yeah, son, see you Saturday," Remy replied.

"Mrs. Coach, thanks for the food and letting me drink champagne, even underage," Theo teased me.

I said nothing about the "Mrs. Coach," which was both a respect and a nickname that all of Remy's players had always called me.

When Remy had left, I had stopped doing some of the things I did as the coach's wife.

But since I was a mom of one of the players, I'd never stopped going to matches.

Even so, that was the first time in years anyone had called me Mrs. Coach.

And the hit of nostalgia with Remy at my back in the house we'd raised our family felt too good.

"You're welcome, Theo," I murmured.

"I'll be home before curfew, Mom," Yves said, coming in to kiss my cheek.

Then, with no further ado, in fact looking like they were hustling, Theo and Yves were out the door.

I didn't have time to blink, definitely not time to consider how much I liked Theo, before Sabre was in my space, kissing my cheek and saying, "I won't be home before curfew because I'm crashing at Dad's. But I'll be over in the morning to pick up the trays. Love you and thanks for the grub."

"Yeah," Manon pipped. "You're good to help Mom clean up?" she asked her father.

Oh no!

I opened my mouth.

Remy got there ahead of me. "Absolutely."

"Awesome!" Manon cried, sounding oddly desperate. "I'll be back in a few hours, Mom. Love you."

No kiss from her because Sabre had her by the hand and was practically dragging her out of the house.

The door closed.

I looked to Remy. "When did Sah and Manon have the same high school friends they *had* to catch up with *together* when they were in town, as a matter of what seems apparent urgency?" I asked skeptically.

"I've learned there's no way to keep up with them, so I don't. I just go with their flow," Remy answered, then started moving to the kitchen.

Okay.

No.

I rushed to follow him, stating, "You don't have to help. It won't take any time at all to sort this out."

"Then it'll be good it takes less when I help," he replied.

Shit!

"Remy—"

"Also, I have something to tell you, and the kids shouldn't be around when I do."

Shit.

I stopped at the island and watched Remy glancing about the room.

Sabre hadn't lied, Theo could pack it away, but there was still a ton of food left.

"You want me on dishes, or packing up the food?" Remy asked.

He was hopeless at food storage. Haphazard and prone to use Ziplocs, which I detested because I felt they should be used more than once, and as such, they needed to be cleaned in between, and that was annoying because it took forever for the insides to dry.

I gave in to him being there by saying, "Dishes."

He nodded and started to collect glasses.

I went to the cabinet where I kept my plethora of food containers and tried to ignore this new hit of nostalgia: Remy and me, after a party, in the kitchen, sorting things out.

Remy's gender divide didn't include dishes, especially after a party.

Why?

Because Remy liked to be around me.

If he wasn't home, until I made it perfectly clear things didn't get done by housekeeping fairies, he just expected things to be done.

But if he was home, he didn't like me away from him for very long. Which meant he didn't mind the time it took me to switch out a load of laundry. But he'd eventually become an excellent sous chef, cooking at my side if he was there, and until we transferred that chore to the kids, we always did the dishes together.

I got out some suitable containers and asked, "Do you want to take some of this with you?"

He had his back to me and was at the sink when he answered, "Yeah."

I started my process by loading him up with lobster rolls.

I also asked, hiding my trepidation because I'd then get an answer, "What did you want to talk about?"

"Myrna's gone."

My head shot up from packing the rolls.

"Remy," I warned.

He turned to face me. "Hear me out."

"This isn't my business."

"She pierced holes in my condoms."

A wild rushing filled my head, which was not unfamiliar but had not happened often in my life.

The first time it happened was when Remy came home from work and told me one of the senior architects at his firm had taken credit for some of Remy's designs.

The second time it had happened was when Manon's second grade teacher called us in for a meeting and told us Manon was "flighty" and "slow," she had trouble controlling her in class and may need to put her in special ed, and we had to work with her to get a lock on her "behavior problems" at home.

Remy had had to deal with that meeting, because I was so livid, I was incapable of speech (my girl was reading by four, and doing small sums by five, for God's sake).

Out of the meeting, he'd continued to deal.

This being having Manon tested. Finding her IQ was not genius level, but it was significantly elevated. And then taking her out of a school where a teacher deemed her "slow" when she was actually bored because she wasn't being challenged. We'd then put all three kids in private school.

And the last time that rushing occurred was now.

"She...pierced..." I was so overcome with anger, I couldn't get it out.

"Take a breath, baby," he said softly, and I noted he was now across from me at the island.

"She...tried to..."

"She had a pregnancy scare. She knew my feelings on that and about her," he shared. "Therefore, this scare forced me to investigate, and I can't even begin to tell you how fucked up it felt to be my age and digging through shit to examine condom packets and find birth control pills she hid from me so I wouldn't know she wasn't taking them."

"Oh my God," I bit out.

"Obviously, we were over after that, and I asked her to leave. As you know, she didn't. We had a conversation about why she didn't, and I was forced to kick her out. I told her I'd meet her the next day, Thursday, so she could get her things. She didn't text me, but I saw on my security footage she'd tried to get into the house when I wasn't there. She failed because I'd had the locks changed. Since she didn't text, or come over when I was there, I got boxes, packed her shit and put it on the back patio. I told her if it wasn't gone by the time I got home from practice on Saturday, it was going to Goodwill. When I got home, it was gone."

I stared at him across the island.

"I never loved her," he announced.

Out went the rushing in my head and something whooshed through my heart.

"Remy, I don't need—"

"She asked to move in. I've no idea why I said yes. For the company. Because I wasn't paying attention. Because I was lost, and I didn't know it."

Lost?

He was lost?

"No clue," he went on, shaking his head. "Especially now, I've got no clue why I said yes. But she knew it wasn't serious. She knew there were not good odds for it going anywhere. She knew I didn't have those kinds of feelings for her. I didn't make her any promises."

Okay.

Now that I was over the shock of the first...

This was agony.

"I don't need to know this, Remy."

"Yes, you do, Wyn."

"Why?" I asked.

"Because after I told her I'd packed up her shit, she phoned and texted...a lot. I've blocked her, and I have seven voicemails from a blocked number. I haven't listened to them, but I know they're from her. My concern is, she's a problem that isn't going to go away."

Okay, wait.

What?

"This pregnancy scare was just a scare?" I asked to confirm.

He nodded. "Yes, fortunately. And I talked with Bill."

I felt the hair on the back of my neck stand up. "Bill?"

Bill was a good friend of ours. Bill was another coach in the league.

Bill was also a cop.

"He confirmed I had reasons to be concerned," Remy told me.

Okay.

Wait.

What?

My voice was rising. "You think she's going to...*stalk you*?"

Remy again nodded.

My God.

"Bill says, lowkey, she already is," he told me. "There's a version of it that they take seriously that happens through phones, email, social media. I've blocked her on that too, as well as company systems."

Right, right.

This was not good.

However.

"I still don't understand why I need to know this."

"Yes you do, baby," he repeated, and the gentling in his tone could not be mistaken.

I shook my head fast because we were not going there.

"One reason," Remy stated, and I lifted up a hand to stop him, but he carried on, "is Sabre likes her."

I dropped my hand.

"And I think I need to tell him all of this," he finished.

Oh.

This was about Sabre and how to handle dealing with his crazy ex-girlfriend with his son.

This did not make me relax.

I got even more tense because that was all this was about.

And more tense because I couldn't deny I was disappointed about that.

So, not as over him as I'd thought.

"When was the last voicemail that came in?" I asked.

"Yesterday, during practice."

"None today?"

He shook his head.

"Maybe she'll peter out," I suggested.

"Manon nor Yves cared for her, which was another sign I should have read, but I know she and Sabre have each other's phone numbers. He's home now. I can sit him down when he gets back tonight. Have a chat. But, for obvious reasons, I don't want to."

"What are those obvious reasons?"

I watched his jaw get tight and I knew what that signaled in this situation.

That hint of Guillaume in Remy. The dashing, debonair, perfect-in-his-own-mind Frenchman's (emphasis on *man*) hackles were raising.

"I don't know, Wyn, maybe because I'm not feeling admitting to my son I walked out on the best woman I'd ever met, that woman being his mother, and then hooked up with a crazy-ass version of *my* mother who thinks everything is about her, and when it isn't, she's willing to go the extra mile to make it about her."

The best woman I'd ever met.

The blow was so unexpected, silken with a sting, I had no hope of deflecting it.

Or easily dealing with it.

"Like I'm not really feeling standing here admitting that same thing to you," he went on.

"Remy," I forced out.

"She tried to trap me with a kid," he stated.

I shook my head, those short shakes again, doing a repeat of the hand lift to stop this. "I'm sorry that happened, but—"

"And what was your response?"

Down went the hand and I stared at him, now confused.

"Sorry?"

"You were not upset that someone in the sisterhood pulled that shit. You weren't self-protective, not wanting to hear that shit. You were pissed. *For me.*"

Oh boy.

My breathing stopped coming easy.

"Why was that your reaction, Wyn?" he asked.

I reverted to our subject.

"How about you sit Sabre down and tell him to be careful about any communications with Myrna, that the breakup was difficult, and she wasn't handling it very well. And that she'd done some things that were shady, and he needed to be cautious. And then see if she fades away. If she doesn't, you can take a different course of action."

"Good advice, as ever, babe, but you didn't answer my question."

"Remy—"

"I fucked up."

Oh God, oh God, oh God.

I couldn't do this.

"Remy—"

"I fucked *us* up."

Right.

I was incorrect.

This wasn't just about Sabre.

It was about us.

And I was not ready.

"Stop talking, Remy," I snapped.

"I got involved with an awful woman who very nearly managed to shift the course of my life irrevocably because I was completely lost without you."

Hang on a second.

My voice was rising now in an angry way when I declared, "That is not my fault."

"I didn't say it was," he returned. "That's all on me. It *all* isn't on me. But that sure as fuck is."

"What do you mean it isn't *all* on you?"

"The end of us. I shouldn't have left. I should have stayed. We should have worked it out. But that isn't entirely on me, even if this is."

He'd just said it was him, *I* wasn't the one who fucking left.

I didn't remind him of that.

"Remy, we're done, divorced, over. This conversation should have happened three years ago. It's too late now."

"Really? Is that why you just nearly lost your mind when you heard someone was fucking with me?" he demanded. "Is that why you saw I was struggling earlier, and you shifted right out of being pissed at your son for pulling shit and you got worried about me?"

"Our divorce doesn't erase our years together," I retorted.

"Bullshit," he shot back. "It's not about history or you giving some minimal shit about me. The kind of love we have never dies."

I took a step back.

"Do not retreat from this, Wyn," he growled.

"You need to leave," I whispered.

He threw both of his long arms wide, and it seemed his presence filled the room.

Definitely having trouble breathing because he'd just taken all the air.

"We need to talk this shit out...*finally*," he decreed.

"The finality of this happened *three years ago, Remy*!" I shouted.

"Yeah? So you got the answers to all our questions?"

"I—"

"What was my goal, that I failed at, when I vowed to link my life to yours?" he demanded. "When I stood before a man of God and made you mine?"

I had no idea what he was talking about.

"Failed at? You mean by leaving?"

"No," he gritted. "I mean by not taking care of you."

"What?" I breathed, now totally perplexed.

He'd never—*never*—not taken care of me.

Not until he walked out.

"And what were you missing that I needed that you didn't give me?" he asked tersely.

That question felt like a spear punctured my chest.

"What did you need?" I asked softly.

He emphasized his point. "So you don't have all our answers?"

"Stop doing this," I begged.

"No, Wyn, it's too fucking important and too much goddamned time has been lost," he denied me. "If you did not give a shit about us, about *me*, you would not look like you look right now. You would not get up in my face defending Manon's overspending, forbidding Yves's underage drinking, and you'd find other ways to tell me what you do to *our house* is no longer any of my business. Not sharing that after spending half an hour shouting at me about it."

I said nothing and concentrated on breathing.

Remy didn't return that favor.

"You're in love with me, Wyn, and you never stopped being in love with me. And I'm so in love with you, I can't even fucking manage my own goddamned life without you in it."

I dropped my head.

"Look at me," he ordered.

I lifted my head. "You need to leave."

"We're working this out."

"*She slept by your side for a year!*" I shrieked.

The room fell dead silent.

I obliterated it.

"Is that how in love with me you are, Remy?" I hissed.

"I needed to hand you the world, but you took it for yourself," he replied.

What?

"What the fuck does that mean?" I spat.

"I miss you. God. Fuck. *Christ.*"

He looked to the ceiling and the emotion rolling off him threatened to drown me. God, take my breath, drag me under, carry me away.

His gaze came back to mine.

"I fucked us up, baby. And I know, because, shit..." He stopped, visibly struggled and kept on, "If you found a man, if you did what I did to you, I'd not survive it."

"Be quiet, Remy."

"It'd destroy me."

"Be *quiet*, Remy."

"I have no excuses because my mind switched off the minute I walked away from you, and it didn't switch on until you told me Bea hurt you and it brought it all back."

Bea?

Bea brought it all back?

What did it bring back?

Oh God.

"And now that I'm with it again, I know, no matter what's happened between then and now, we have never been done, and we never will be," he declared.

I didn't respond, not only because I didn't know what to say, but because I was physically incapable of speaking.

"I tested you, and I shouldn't have."

He did?

"You didn't test me, but I still failed," he continued.

I didn't?

"And now I see you need to do the mental work I've done, but I'm not waiting for that, honey. You're either going to have to snap to it or I'm gonna give it to you. One way or another, we're gonna get to the place where we work it out, and then we're going to get back to where we should be," he finished.

I remained silent.

Then Remy shared he wasn't quite finished.

"I also see now isn't that time. You need some space. You need time to think. But I'm cleaning the kitchen. So you can either stay here and help me, or find somewhere else to be. But be sure to lock the door when I leave."

I didn't need time to think about that.

I nodded and walked right out of the room.

I hid in my closet, and yes, it was not lost on me as I sat curled in my velvet chair, with two doors closed between me and Remy, in a space as far from him in the house as I could be, that I was hiding.

I also did not think about us and all he'd said.

No.

For better, or worse, I thought about one thing.

The fact that Remy was totally going to mess up packing the food away.

And tomorrow, I'd open the fridge, see that...

And it would mean everything to me.

CHAPTER 10
Top of the List

Wyn

Tuesday evening, I was, of course, running late as I walked through the back kitchen, the dining area, past the hostess station and into the bar at Durant's, to see Fiona Remington sitting in a half-circle booth at the back.

People were glancing her way, but they weren't being overt or doing anything as crass as taking pictures, because it was Durant's and no one there would be so gauche.

She was wearing a heavenly combination of Gucci and Givenchy.

I approved.

With a glance and a smile at her bodyguard, Davey (who was in the next booth), I hit the table and slid into the seat.

"You're ridiculous," she stated, reaching to what I knew was a mojito, since she'd mixed some for us at her house in Malibu and shared they were her signature.

I also knew she was referring to the fact that only I would be fifteen minutes late to sit down with possibly the most powerful creative force in Hollywood.

I grinned at her and replied, "Life has been crazy."

She lifted a brow on an expressive face with big eyes and perfect black skin, all of this surrounded by a halo of soft curls, before she took a sip of her drink.

"My son came out as gay," I declared. "He's dating an Adidas model rugby player, who in another life was a gladiator who had no troubles ripping apart a lion but has the manners of a young man who got perfect scores in etiquette school."

Fiona put her drink down.

I kept blabbing.

"Me and the rest of my friend posse are currently procrastinating in calling an intervention with a member of our crew who we've just realized has been verbally abusing our husbands for more than a decade. And in doing so, bringing a toxicity she's been slowly poisoning a lot of things with that whole time."

Fiona tipped her head to the side.

I continued yammering.

"And although he's been eerily quiet for two days, my ex-husband threw down with me on Sunday about the fact that we're still in love, and we need to work it out, even though he walked out on me, and we've been divorced for three years."

"Jesus, Wyn," she said.

"Oh!" I cried. "And he kicked out his live-in girlfriend after he found out she'd poked holes in his condoms and stopped taking birth control in order to trap him with a baby he did not want, and now there's a slim chance she's going to start stalking him."

Fiona was silent.

A waiter showed up, put a glass of water in front of me and asked, "Can I get you a drink, ma'am?"

I looked up at him. "Dirty martini."

"Keep them coming," Fiona ordered.

He nodded and took off.

I looked to her and shared, "I drove."

"Okay, I'll drive you home and Davey can follow, because, sis, you need to get *drunk*."

I smiled at her.

My smile faltered and I feared I was going to burst into tears (the state, incidentally, I'd been in since I'd slunk out of my own closet to see if Remy was gone then locked the doors behind him).

I got a handle on that, and Fiona reached out and wrapped her fingers around mine.

So obviously, I lost my handle on that.

To grab hold again, I squeezed her fingers and said, "Now you. Please tell me you're in Phoenix to scout locations for a movie and you want me to consult on costumes."

She took her hand away and asked, "Do you want to get into costume design?"

"I want so much work I can't think about anything else, so"—I shrugged —"sure."

"I know you're an intelligent, together woman or I wouldn't allow you to dress me, so I know that you avoiding your issues is a temporary thing and I know you're going to buck the hell up and get your shit sorted after you give yourself this temporary thing," she said quietly.

I reached to my water.

"I also better not hear you have issues with your boy and this Adidas model," she said.

I took a sip and shook my head. "No. Absolutely not. I mean, does it hurt that he was so worried what his dad would think about him being gay that he hid his boyfriend from us for six months? Yes. Do I get why he did that? Not really, since his father is one hundred percent not that man. But I'm not gay. He experiences things in our society about who he is that I do not. I might not get it, but then I never will. I just have to allow him to take his journey as he needs to do it and provide cushioning as best I can if times get tough, and encouragement for the same if that's what's needed."

She grabbed her drink again and nodded before saying into her glass, "I hear that," and then taking a sip.

Of course she did.

"This friend?" she asked when she put her drink down.

"Bea. And that's tougher. Because it's easier to think on, so I haven't been avoiding it. And in thinking on it, the bad outweighs the good, by a lot. We have, however, decided not to give up, because there is good. But we need her to understand we can't carry on the way we are and hopefully more, let her know we're there if this behavior means she needs our support for something deeper."

"You're good people, Wyn," Fiona said.

I smiled at her. "Thanks, but there's more bad to that."

"And that is?"

"I have a feeling that..." I couldn't finish because I'd been thinking about it, however I wasn't sure I'd wrapped my head around it.

"You have a feeling that...?" she prompted.

I cleared my throat and looked to the bar to see if I could assess how long it would take to get my martini.

"Girl," Fiona called.

I pushed out a sigh and looked back to her.

"I have a feeling that Remy was pissed at me that he took her abuse, and I didn't shield him from it."

"I have very little information on this, outside the fact you're you, and you wouldn't be sitting a friend down to have words about things if it wasn't extreme, so my guess is, whatever she was doing to him was also extreme. Taking that further, if you didn't put a stop to it, well..." She hesitated and then finished in the way I knew she had to, but I didn't want to hear, "Yeah. It isn't his place to throw down with one of your friends. But, girl, it sure is yours."

"Shit," I whispered.

"When you were together, did he complain about her?"

She's a piece of work.

She's harmless, Remy. She's just got an edge.

Yeah, like a razor has an edge.

That had been one of several conversations we'd had about Bea.

What he said was never overt, like, *she's a bitch, she treats me like shit, Wyn, ditch her.* But then again, unless one of his friends was inappropriate in ways that Remy absolutely needed to know, I would not hold my tongue that they annoyed me, but I wouldn't say, they've gotta go.

"Yes," I admitted to Fiona. "I just blew it off because it was Bea. She could just be...mean. And I thought mostly she was dealing not in good ways with the fact her husband had left her. But I'm seeing now that she should have done that without taking it out on other people. At least not for ten years and counting."

"Still, not a lot to hang walking out on your wife and family on," she pointed out.

I was her stylist. I was also her friend. If we were in the same space and it was possible, we got together.

I was in LA more than she was in Phoenix, so I'd been to her home a couple of times and we'd both shared. Fiona, not as much as me, and I got that. She was who she was, and to be sure she was protected, I'd have to be much deeper in her life, and she'd have to know me a lot better for her to share meaningfully.

But she knew about Remy.

"On Sunday he alluded to failing me about something..." I shook my head. "I don't know, he didn't fully explain it but..." God! "It obviously really bothered him."

"You don't know?"

"No. Because he didn't fail me."

"But he thinks he did."

The waiter thankfully arrived with my drink, and he barely put it down before I picked it up.

"We'll order in a second," Fiona said quietly.

"Of course, Ms. Remington," he murmured and moved away.

I sipped.

"So?" she asked me.

"Yes, oh yes." I put my drink down. "He thinks he did."

"Are you not curious?"

"If I'd allow myself to think about it, I wouldn't be able to function, because that would be all I could do. Think about it."

"You *could* ask him, Wyn," she pointed out.

"I let him go on Wednesday."

"Pardon?"

"I finally came to terms we were done. I did this last Wednesday."

She stared at me a second.

And then she started laughing.

I wasn't sure it was funny.

She was still chuckling when she again reached to her glass and murmured, "The shit we do to guard our hearts."

"He left me, Fiona, and eventually moved a woman in with him."

She sipped, but didn't put her drink down when she replied, "He did. You were divorced when he did. She's gone. That was then. This is now. You *just* let him go and you're hanging on to that like it means something and missing what it really means. You've been divorced for years, and you *just* let him go, and he wants to work things out and what are you doing, Wyn? Holding back a man you love because...why...exactly?"

"He walked out," I said shortly. "And divorced me. I wanted to talk about it then. I wanted to work it out then. He didn't allow either."

She swung her glass toward me. "So you didn't get what you wanted, girl. Who cares? Again, *that was then, and this is now.*"

"So I snap to when Remy decides we're worth fighting for?"

"Hell yes."

My head jerked back in shock.

She lifted one long, elegant finger from her glass.

"Now, I said that, but what I did *not* say was that you should let him off the hook for doing something so entirely fucked up without engaging his damned wife in the process. I'm telling you to sit down and listen to what the man has to say. And then *you* can decide if it's worth fighting for."

Ugh!

"God, you suck. You're just supposed to be beautiful and talented and demanding and vain. Not wise. It's upsetting and annoying," I groused, grabbing my drink and maybe spilling a little of it.

But that didn't stop me from drinking it and then more of it because she was laughing.

I put my glass down and pinned her with my gaze. "Okay, *what are you doing in Phoenix?*"

I emphasized my words to share that we were no longer talking about me.

"I'm moving here."

Another head jerk.

Then a big smile.

"Really?" I asked.

She nodded. "I'm just...done with LA. I need a break. Phoenix is close. No snow. No natural disasters. And maybe I can go to the grocery store without someone taking a photo of me."

"Fiona, we don't have famous people wandering about willy-nilly like LA, but as much as I'd love having you close, please don't hang your hopes on that happening. You know Imogen Swan lives in Phoenix. There are pictures of her published all the time, and in some of them, she's grocery shopping."

"Well then, I just need a break. And I need to know if my real estate agent is giving me the proper advice. She's recommending Paradise Valley or Cave Creek. And all I know is Scottsdale. And no shade on Scottsdale, but I'm not sure I'm a Scottsdale gal."

"Cave Creek would be far more private, you'd be able to have some land, but it isn't super close to the city. However, it isn't too far from Kierland and that has great shops and restaurants, not to mention Cave Creek itself is a little touristy, but the good kind. It's a fun place. Paradise Valley has some amazing homes, is in the city, perfectly positioned between Phoenix and Scottsdale, but it wouldn't be private. And, although you might be able to score a decent sized lot, you wouldn't have a ton of space."

"Okay, then part two, I want your ex-husband to design a home for me."

I sat still.

My smile was slow.

And my words were too.

"You little minx."

She rolled her eyes.

"Please, Wyn, do not think I got where I am without using every damned card I have up my sleeve."

"You do know that if Fiona Remington called his office and shared she wanted him to design a home for her, he would take you as a client."

"I don't know this because Dan Parkinson did and they told him they would love to work with him, but Mr. Gastineau has a two-year waiting list. And Wyn," she indicated herself with her glass, "this woman is not waiting two years."

"Remy's people said that to Parkinson?"

She nodded.

"Well, he is in demand. But he's trained some amazing juniors in his firm and—"

"I want Gastineau. So did Parky. They said they'd work with him, but they couldn't move him up. Gastineau did Dobbie Heald's place up in Wyoming. I've been there and it's *sublime*. No one else will do."

I remembered that design.

It *was* sublime.

"Well, obviously, I'll leave here and call Remy and tell him I'm willing to sit down and discuss our future, but only if he delays every project he's working on and puts you at the top of the list."

"Oh honey, no. He can have a month or two to get sorted. I have to find the perfect plot of land and decide what I want to put on it. *Then* I want to be top of the list."

I burst out laughing.

She pointed to my menu and said, "I'm starving, baby. Let's eat."

I picked up my menu, glanced at it, then back to her. "I'll love it that you're closer."

"And I'll be happy to have a friend in town."

"Thank you for listening and not letting me pull shit, even on myself."

"I will be honest and say I didn't do it to get on the top of your ex's list."

I nodded.

"But it better buy me the top of your ex's list," she finished.

And again, I burst out laughing.

CHAPTER 11
Monkey Bar

Wyn

You're right. We need to talk.

The instant that text whooshed away, doing whatever geniuses had allowed it to do to go from my phone to Remy's, I had second thoughts.

However, I'd also had a second martini as well as two glasses of wine with dinner.

So I was on the other side of tipsy.

The dangerous side.

Fiona Flipping Remington drove me home with her bodyguard trailing, and I'd promised to view lots and properties with her tomorrow even though I had a very full schedule.

She was gone and now I was tipsy-texting.

I didn't care.

She was right.

I should hear what Remy had to say.

And really, what the hell?

He couldn't come right out and give things to me?

What was with the mystery?

Bluh.

Text him.

Talk.

Mystery solved!

So there!

I wandered into my bedroom then my bathroom, and I did my evening routine by rote.

Down to bra and panties.

Brush teeth.

Makeup off.

Cleanse face.

Use rice polish to gently exfoliate.

Night serum and under eye moisturizer.

Put on jammies (indigo satin with huge, swirling gold flowers, cami edged in a delicate line of indigo lace, long bottoms, and I made this choice because the set had a matching short kimono, and I wasn't done with my tipsy evening, so I needed the robe).

I then went to the kitchen, poured myself *another* glass of wine, and went back to my bedroom.

Moisturizer over the serum and then I turned off the bathroom lights, climbed into my huge bed, situated me and my wine in the middle, and I phoned Bea.

"So you've finally called to apologize?" was her greeting.

I blinked at my elegant, white, Dian Austin damask duvet cover.

"Sorry?"

"It's been nearly a week," she stated.

I wasn't certain why she shared this information with me.

But I was on a mission, so I got on with that.

"Bea, we need to sit down and talk."

"Great. Happy to accept your apology face to face."

Uh...*sorry?*

"What, exactly, do I have to apologize for?" I asked.

"Hanging up on me?" she asked back sarcastically. "Your inability to listen to some cold, hard truths without being ugly to me?"

"Are you for real?" I whispered.

"So you aren't calling to apologize? Instead, you're calling to...what? Hand me more of your denials that your ex was a piece of shit who walked all over you and..."

She kept talking, but I stopped listening because I sensed movement in the room and my head shot up.

There stood Remy three feet from the foot of my bed.

My mouth dropped open.

He spoke.

"You said we need to talk?"

"Who's that?" Bea asked in my ear.

"Call you later," I said hurriedly, hung up and dropped the phone on the bed. "How'd you get in here?"

"You never asked for the key back, Wyn, and obviously you didn't change the locks." He lifted a hand and his key ring dangled from his fingers. "Have you considered why you didn't do that?"

Okay.

Oh God.

Oh shit.

Ummmmmmmmmmmmmmmmmmmm...

He took a step forward.

I noticed he was wearing black joggers and a heathered gray, long-sleeved T-shirt that clung to his shoulders and pecs, and even in his casual, hang-out-at-home clothes, he looked like he was waiting for Grace Coddington to call him in front of the camera.

"Wyn," he called, his tone meant to get my attention, but it wasn't sharp.

I focused on his face, he instantly smirked, and I realized I'd been focused on his joggers.

Specifically, the crotch of them.

How was this happening?

"You wanted to talk?" he prompted.

I pulled myself together.

"Yes, but I didn't mean *immediately*."

"Are you doing anything else right now?" he asked.

"I *was* talking on the phone."

"You aren't anymore," he pointed out.

"Because my ex-husband showed up in my bedroom."

He nodded then asked, "Who were you talking to?"

Damn it.

"Bea," I mumbled.

I heard the breath hiss up his nose, but he didn't get into that.

He walked to the bathroom door, which, hidden in the dark, was a long space that included every nuance of every girlie-girls' dream.

He flipped the switch, actually all of them, as the area all the way back to the enormous custom closet lit up.

Then he said slowly, "Jesus. It's like Zsa Zsa Gabor threw up in here."

That hurt.

We'd always been at one with interior design choices.

"You don't like it?" I asked.

He turned as slowly as he'd spoken. "It's stupidly perfect."

"What's 'stupidly perfect' mean?"

"Only you could make Swarovski chandeliers work in a fucking bathroom."

"Remy—"

"We're gonna fuck in that bathtub, baby."

My nipples got hard.

"Remy," I whispered.

He came forward and sat on the side of my bed so we could face each other, but just down, so we could do it without turning our necks.

And he wasn't too close, which, at that juncture, I thought was kind.

"What were you talking to Bea about?" he asked quietly.

"I didn't get a chance to say much, she answered by upsetting me."

"Mm," he hummed.

Okay, he was here.

Let's go.

"I didn't protect you from her," I whispered.

His caramel eyes melted. "No, you didn't."

"She was terrible to you."

Still doing the slow thing, he nodded.

"How bad?" I asked.

"I hate the bitch."

Oh hell.

I wasn't sure Remy hated anyone, even his parents, and they were hate-worthy (according to me).

"Remy, why didn't you say anything?"

"Wyn, I did."

I clenched my teeth.

"She was your friend, and I kept telling myself she showed up that time you were sick with that flu," he said.

Oh God.

"I was so fucking worried about you," he continued. "You were slurring your words, talking about asking your mom to fly out from Indiana, not making a lot of sense. Then you didn't answer the phone. I couldn't get Kara on the line. Bernice was on a flight, Cornell too. Bill was on shift. He'd just broken up with Janelle, and that was ugly, so she wasn't speaking to any of us. Bea wasn't picking up. Lisa was in Houston with me. No one was available. So I was a goddamn wreck. You were completely out of it. People die from flus, Wyn."

Oh, Remy.

He kept speaking.

"And our kids. Stupid, fucked up, but all that was in my head was that scene in *Steel Magnolias* where Julia Roberts is flat out and the baby is sitting there crying and the spaghetti sauce is burning on the stove." He drew a breath. "But we had *three* babies."

Oh, Remy.

"Got a car. Weather was so fucking bad, it was insane. I couldn't stop until I was nearly across Texas. Hit a station to get gas, called, hoping you'd answer, but Bea did. And I felt so much fucking relief, I can't tell you. I don't know how I didn't fall to my knees. So that was what I'd tell myself when she unsheathed her claws. She obviously hated me, but she loved you."

"I wished you'd made it more clear," I said softly.

"And I wished you didn't put me in that position, and you just knew to take my back, and dealt with it."

I looked away.

He kept going.

"But you didn't, and, baby, that hurt, you throwing me under that bus, making me eat the shit she said to me, the shit you told me she said to you about me, and how goddamn relentless it all was."

God, I'd messed up.

I would do that. Tell him.

I'd rant about it, telling him all the ugly things Bea said about him.

No one wanted to hear the nasty things someone said about them.

And no one wanted to hear that someone they loved had listened to them and didn't put a stop to it. Definitely not knowing that person was speaking those words *to the loved one*, and that wasn't handled either.

God, *I'd messed up.*

"Eyes, Wyn. Give me your eyes, honey."

I looked back at him.

"I didn't think it was that big of a deal," I admitted.

"Yeah, I know," he replied.

"I'm learning there are downfalls to thinking your husband is a titan who can conquer everything."

His head ticked.

And his lips whispered, "Sorry?"

"You were bigger than her, stronger than her," I tossed out my hand, realized it held a glass, and I reeled it in before disaster struck with red wine on white damask. "You're you, Remy. You're smart and talented and handsome and funny. You were a great husband, we made beautiful babies, and we were happy. You had all of that and she had her moans and gripes. I just thought, since I got that, you did too, because you were so above her, she couldn't reach you."

"So above her, she couldn't reach you," he repeated so softly, I almost didn't hear him.

And he was no longer looking at me.

His gaze was aimed at my pillows.

"Remy," I called.

His attention came back to me.

"Please tell me you didn't walk out on me because my girlfriend was mean to you."

"I didn't leave you because Bea was mean to me. But I will say that it bugged the fuck out of me, and it didn't help things."

Okay.

Here we were.

"What were those...*things*?"

"Do you remember the Monkey Bar?"

I was on edge, freaked out, very scared, but Remy asking that, there was no way I wouldn't smile.

So I did.

"Yes," I answered.

His gaze was on my smile. It was warm and something else I didn't have time to gauge, maybe relief, maybe triumph, maybe a touch of both, and it lifted to mine.

And the solemnity of his tone stunned me when he asked, "Do you, Wyn? Do you really remember?"

"Of course I do. You took me there on our first date."

"Do you remember what you told me when we sat down?"

I remembered I couldn't believe I was with such an amazing man on a date.

But I didn't remember what I said when we sat down.

So I shook my head.

"You said you'd never been anywhere like that before."

"Okay," I replied.

"Do you remember what I said?"

Oh God.

Tears hit my eyes.

Because it was coming back to me.

And the word was husky when I said, "Yes."

"What'd I say?" he asked gently.

"You said, 'Get used to it.'"

"Give me the glass, honey."

I handed him my wineglass.

He reached long to put it on my nightstand, and he'd barely sat back before I fell in his arms.

I would have crawled into his skin if I could have, such was the power of how good it felt to have Remy's arms around me again, the depth of the emotion I was weeping into his tee, the strength of my need to be swept back twenty-five years and be sitting in a booth in the coolest place I'd ever been with the most handsome man I'd ever seen, and have him say, straight out, the minute we sat down to truly start our first date, that I was his.

I was his.

Get used to it.

So sure.

Completely.

Which meant he was mine.

Forever.

After a while, I realized Remy was holding me close with one arm, I was draped across his lap, and he was playing with my hair with his other hand.

God, that felt so *nice*.

I shoved my face in his chest.

"All right?" he asked.

No.

I nodded my lie and started to push away, but the hair-playing stopped and both arms came around me.

I dropped my head back to catch his eyes.

"You're drunk," he stated.

"Tipsy," I corrected.

He smiled.

"You're tipsy," he amended.

"Indeed," I agreed.

"I miss your taste. I miss your smell. I miss the noises you make. The way your face looks when you're turned on. I miss being balls deep in you. And I figure, if I kissed you right now, I wouldn't be able to stop making you come until maybe this time tomorrow. But only to pass out so we could start again."

I just stared up at him because he had all my attention.

"But no way in fuck am I doing that when you're...tipsy," he continued. "When we go there again, you're going to be fully lucid, I'm going to be fully lucid, and we're going to have our shit fully sorted."

"I—"

"Say goodnight, Wynnie."

I pressed my lips together because he rarely called me Wynnie. He was the only human being on the planet I ever allowed to do it, but when he did, it was always a precious gift.

I did it also because I was cross that he'd talk dirty to me and then just...leave.

Though he was right, if this happened, neither of us should be under the influence of anything.

Not to mention, there was more to go over (so, *so* much more).

But still, I missed his taste, his smell, his noises, the way he looked when we made love and him being buried inside me, and it was a dirty trick to remind me I did before he was going to just...leave.

"I'll toss your wine and clean the glass before I go. And since I brought the key this time, I'll lock up," he finished.

"You aren't pouring out that wine. It's a full glass. I'm not certain I've even taken a sip. I'll pour it back into the bottle."

A shadow drifted over his face, and he said, "It's just a glass of wine, Wyn."

"And I'm not so tipsy I can't pour it back into the bottle."

"Is it a special bottle?"

"A special bottle?"

"Special. Or expensive?"

"Not particularly. I actually don't even remember where I got it. I think it's from one of my wine clubs."

"Wyn."

I started paying attention, *close* attention, because the way he said that, the pain in my name, it came unexpected but it packed one hell of a punch.

"What?" I whispered.

"You can throw away a glass of wine."

"But I can also keep it."

"When you cry like that, you get tired. Do you want to get up and pour a glass of wine in the bottle, or do you want me to take it away so you can just turn the lights out and get some sleep?"

Door number two.

However.

"Will you pour it back in the bottle?"

"Wyn." That was sharp.

So my repeat of "What?" was too.

"You have Swarovski crystal chandeliers...in your bathroom."

"Yes."

"Your duvet cover cost over a thousand dollars."

Of course, he recognized an Austin.

"And?"

109

"Are your pajamas polyester?"

Well!

"Of course not." That was a snap.

He shook me gently. "Jesus, Wyn."

"What?" That was a snap too.

"If you wanted Swarovski, I could have given it to you," he said.

I blinked, rapidly, three times.

"Sorry?"

"Though, no way in fuck would I take my kids' rooms to do it," he went on. "We could have built on."

"Remy, they'd moved out and Manon was—"

"You figured out Bea, what's the rest, Wyn?"

I pulled out of his arms because...

Was he serious?

"Are you...is this some kind of...*quiz*?" I asked.

"He gave her everything. To keep her quiet. To keep her docile. To keep her from asking too many questions. To keep her from aiming her vitriol at him. Did my mentioning the Monkey Bar penetrate with you?"

Well, I thought it did, but apparently it did not.

I shook my head, "Remy, I'm not following."

"Why did I want to give you everything?"

I stopped moving.

I stopped thinking.

I stopped everything and focused solely on him.

"She knew he fucked around on her. No way he could be gone as often as he was for so much time without getting himself some," Remy carried on. "She knew. *I* was her *little man*. I was her *perfect boy*. I was her son, but I had to take up the fuckin' slack when he was gone, for fuck's sake. *I* was the one who was her stand-in to take out her rage that her husband turned to other women and was never home. And he kept that aimed at me by coming home with diamonds and furs."

I reached out, put my hand on his chest, and although I knew now he was talking about his parents, I didn't know why.

But what he was saying was scaring the hell out of me.

"Remy, go back and explain why you're sharing this with me."

"Because you are not her, Wyn, but I *am* him. I need to be him. For you. I didn't take you to the Monkey Bar simply because it was a cool place to go. I took you to the Monkey Bar because I knew I was going to make you mine, and you needed to know how things were going to be. You needed to know who I was going to be for you. From our start until our end."

And with that, he got up, nabbed the glass of wine, which was full, so it sloshed, but I did not care, and then he walked out.

I didn't follow him.

But when time had passed, I did.

I checked the front door (locked).

I checked the kitchen.

And saw he'd thrown out the wine.

CHAPTER 12
Four Years Old

Remy

R emy was at his desk in his office the next morning when, with very bad timing, two things happened at once. Lisa, his assistant, walked in and his cell rang.

He glanced at her then he looked down at his phone.

It told him Wyn was calling.

Fuck.

Considering the fact she hadn't phoned since he'd walked out on them three years ago (all their communication had been done through texts), he absolutely wanted to pick up.

But after the shit he'd pulled on her last night, he wanted to avoid her.

Because, yeah, he was quizzing her, and the pass or fail was their relationship.

And he had no fucking clue why he was doing that.

Things got worse when Lisa announced, "Your dad is on the phone."

Fuck.

His father had been calling the office frequently the last few days, and he'd been doing that because he was blocked on Remy's phone, as was Remy's mother.

"Remy, this is, like, the tenth time he's called, and he says it's urgent," Lisa went on as his cell kept ringing. "And he started this by saying it was urgent three days ago. I'm thinking it's urgent."

He needed not to avoid Wyn. If he was going to fix them, he had to stop bowing out when shit got real, which meant after he'd fucked up.

He also had to get this, whatever it was with his father, out of Lisa's hands.

"Tell him I'll call him back," he said, reaching for his cell.

"Remy—"

"This is Wyn," he told her, and her eyes got big. "Tell Dad I'll call him back, and I *will* call him back, Lisa. Right after I talk with my wife."

Her head ticked when he referred to Wyn as his wife, but then she did not delay.

She nodded, turned, and practically jogged out of his office.

For obvious reasons, Lisa lost Wyn when he'd split them up. They hadn't been tight, but they'd liked each other a lot.

Though, Remy knew, he'd been a much more laidback boss before he'd blown up his marriage. This meant, even before he'd watched Lisa taking a quick hike so he could talk to Wyn, he knew she wanted them to get what they had back.

The door was not closed when he took the call, put the phone to his ear and greeted, "Hey, baby."

"Hi," Wyn said softly.

He shut his eyes, swiveled in his chair, felt her word dig down deep in his gut and take root there, and only then did he open his eyes.

And was confronted with the view to the courtyard of his office building, a building he'd designed and built, and it housed only the staff of his firm.

That courtyard had been redesigned this past summer.

This was done by Sabre who was soon to graduate with a degree in landscape architecture.

Sah had shared he wanted to work with his dad, nevertheless, he was already being scouted. The evidence as to why was right in front of Remy.

The desert xeriscape was fucking fantastic. Intentional but chaotic. Providing shade from a few paloverdes, but with streaks of sun that were there no matter what time of day it was. There were riots of color in the spring, and unexpected elevations from creeping ground-cover plants to pots on plinths to hanging ones with trailing greenery.

Sabre had told him he'd been inspired by DeGrazia's gardens, and Remy could see that, but Sabre still had made it his own.

Remy loved it. He had his boy at his back whenever he was in his office.

And now he had his son's mother in his ear.

"Hi," he replied.

"I wasn't thrilled with how we left things last night," she said.

Shit.

"And I thought maybe we should make plans to talk sometime soon," she suggested.

Fucking fabulous.

"You name when and where," he said immediately. "And I'll be there."

He heard how pleased she was in her tone when she told him, "Theo is coming over to hang tonight, and I feel the need to be the overbearing mother who makes her point by showing every fifteen minutes and offering lemonade."

Remy started chuckling.

What he didn't do was tell her that was probably a good call.

Then he said, "Right then, my place, six, tomorrow night. I'll pick up Frasher's. We'll eat and talk. Sound good?"

"Frasher's," she said quietly.

And yes, he was not fucking around.

She was a midwestern girl. She liked her barbeque.

She liked her cornbread better.

Frasher's arguably had the best of both in Phoenix.

And Wyn would argue it was the best.

"Work for you, Wyn?" he prompted when she didn't say anything further.

"Sounds good, Remy. I'll see you at six tomorrow night. Do you want me to bring anything?"

Just you and a nightgown if you don't want to sleep in one of my tees since you hate sleeping in the nude.

He didn't say that since that was where he'd like to take them, and then stay in that place until they both died.

But it was far too soon.

"I'll have us covered," he said instead.

"Okay, see you tomorrow evening."

"See you then, honey. Later."

"Bye."

He wanted to talk more, but he had shit to do, including calling his father and finding out what was going on with him, not to mention work.

And Wyn was always busy.

Wyn had always *been* busy. She was just a busy person.

This, too, was a remnant of how she grew up.

Because it was all she knew.

A dad with two jobs and four kids, a mom with a job and four kids, and a farm to work, there wasn't a lot of time for any of them to be idle.

When he'd met her, Wyn was about to be promoted to a personal stylist at Bergdorf's and was already making moves to take that to a different level.

Even so, it was New York, she lived in Manhattan, and she didn't have a trust fund like he did. So she lived in a two-bedroom apartment with a kitchen the size of a closet and five roommates, and until she was promoted, she had a side job as a part-time waitress.

She never complained, likely because she helped with the farm, the house, and got her first paying job at age thirteen, sweeping up hair and laundering towels at the local beauty salon.

So yeah, Wyn had hustle, and even when she was a stay-at-home mom, that had never died.

But when she was at home, she'd given him the freedom to let work time be work time, and she hardly ever interrupted him at work. When she went back to it, he'd done the same.

And he didn't change that now by engaging her in a conversation she probably didn't have time for.

Instead, he let her go, swiveled back to his desk, put his cell down, picked up his desk phone and called his father.

"*Enfin*," his father said as a greeting.

(Finally.)

"Dad, I'm at work. What's so urgent you're blowing up my assistant's phone?"

"What's so urgent?" his father asked.

"Yes," Remy said shortly.

"*Fiston*, I haven't spoken to you in three years."

Again, short when he said, "No, you haven't."

"Neither has your mother," Guillaume went on.

"She definitely hasn't."

"Remy—"

"You can't have forgotten, Dad, that the last time I spoke with Mom, I told her Wyn and I were divorcing, and she said, 'Excellent, it's about time. That girl has always been trash. Now you might be able to meet someone worthy of you. Sadly, it's later in life. But fortunately, women are smart enough not to have issue with gaining the attention of a successful mature man.'"

And that might not be verbatim, though it was the gist.

But the first two sentences were word for word.

"We both know *que ta mère* often does not weigh her words."

"She called the love of my life, my wife of two decades and the mother of my children, trash."

"Remy—"

"And when I blocked her, *you* phoned to tell me to sort myself out, call her and make amends, when it should have been the other way around."

"Son—"

"Dad, there's no use going over this. It's done. Even more done than you can imagine since Wyn and I are reuniting. Now, just tell me why you're phoning."

"You and Wyn are reuniting?"

He tried to ignore how happy Guillaume sounded.

He couldn't when his father kept talking and told him just that.

"I'm delighted, Remy. This is the best news I've heard in...well, three years."

His mother could barely stand Wyn and didn't hide it.

His father cherished her, and he didn't hide that either.

Which was unfortunate, because Guillaume thinking Wyn walked on water exacerbated how much Colette detested her.

He shouldn't have said anything.

"Again, why are you phoning?" he pushed.

"Remy, I..."

He didn't go on.

"Dad, I have things to do—"

"Your mother had a touch of breast cancer."

Remy sat still, staring at his desk with his phone to his ear.

"It was a few years ago. Nothing since. They took it out. She...refused further treatments because..."

Because her hair might fall out or her skin might wrinkle, or whatever it was that would affect her looks was out of the question even if it might save her life.

"We've been lucky. There was not a recurrence. That luck ran out," Guillaume concluded.

"She has it again?" Remy asked.

"Yes, and it's much worse and very aggressive. And although she will be doing a few treatments to see if things can be...*prolonged*...it will...it's impossible...at her age with the advancement of the disease." He took a second. "I'm sorry, *fiston*, they're not giving us very long."

Remy sat in silence.

"Remy?" Guillaume called.

"And again, why are you calling?" Remy asked.

He heard his father's sharp breath before, "*Qu'est ce que tu viens de dire?*"

(What did you just say?)

"I said, why are you calling?"

Guillaume's words were sharp when he replied, "I just told you that your mother is dying."

Remy sat back in his chair.

He considered what to say next.

He made a decision.

And then he shared, "When he's up from school, Sabre stays with me most of the time. As much as it pains me, it wasn't a surprise when all three of my kids were devastated I walked out on their mother. But I'm fortunate. They love me more than I deserve. And I think Sabre understands in a way I don't think he even gets *how* he understands that maybe most of the pain in all of that was felt by me. Even after what I did to his mother, our family. And that's why he sticks close to his dad."

He took a breath.

Guillaume didn't say anything.

Which was good because Remy wasn't done with his story.

Not even close.

"He was up from school, we were sitting by the pool, and we got to talking. I don't remember how it came up, but he told me his first memory was sitting in the sand with me, and the only other thing he remembered was his mother's red swimsuit. But I remembered all of that. I was showing him how to make sandcastles on Paloma Beach. He was four."

"I remember this too, when you were with us in France. He was so little," his father said softly. "You and both of your boys, once so little to get so big."

Remy didn't get stuck in his father's gentle reminiscing.

That wasn't even close to what this was about.

"This made me think," Remy continued like Guillaume didn't speak. "So when I went down to Tucson for a dad and daughter date with Manon, I asked about her first memory. She said Christmas. Me taking a picture of her and her mom was helping her open a big present. She, too, was four."

Now having a hint where this was going, it was hesitant when his father tried, "Son—"

"I haven't asked Yves. I should. I've no idea, but I hope I could imagine. Sandcastles and family vacations, and Christmases and Mom and Dad together. I'd hope it was something like that. And I have a first memory too, Dad, as we all do. Mine is Mom throwing a shoe at me and hitting me in the face."

"Remy," Guillaume said quickly, to cut him off, divert him, move this somewhere where he didn't have to deal.

"It was a pump. The spiked heel cut my cheek. I don't remember why she was furious that time. In my memory, I was scared, but I wasn't shocked. I'd seen it before. Her tantrums. I'd see it after. Her tantrums. But that was my first memory. And I was four years old."

Guillaume said nothing.

Remy did.

"That cut didn't scar. But she'd leave scars, not many you could see, but that doesn't mean there aren't many."

"Your mother is highly strung," Guillaume, as usual, defended.

"She beat me with a brush when I was six."

"*Mon Dieu*—"

"She broke my arm, twisting it, when I was eight."

"This really is not the time to—"

"Also when I was eight, I was her date to some event, a fundraiser, black tie. I wore a tux because I'd had a custom-made tux since I was six. And she'd drilled me on how to behave at dinner since I could sit up straight. But still, I did something wrong, that something being I was not you, and she had to take her eight-year-old to an event as her date. When we were in the car coming home, she shouted at me about all the things I'd done wrong, embarrassing her, and she slapped me so hard, *repeatedly*, I had a black eye the next day. But I didn't embarrass her, *you did* by not being there."

"I should have been home much more, for her, for you, for both of you. This was *my* failing, son."

"Yes, you should have. Absolutely. Though you didn't break my arm or shove me into an armoire so hard, I cracked my head against it and got a mild concussion. *She did.*"

"This was all a long time ago, and look what you built, who you've become, the woman you made your wife, the family you created—"

"Yes, let's talk about that. We already got into her calling Wyn trash. But do you know that the last time Mom phoned Manon, before I took my daughter's phone, blocked her grandmother's number and deleted her contact, was maybe two days after I left Wyn. And Mom told Manon it was now time she stepped in and 'took her in hand.' And therefore, if she had any hope of landing an appropriate husband, she immediately had to start dieting and take off twenty pounds."

"Women of your mother's generation have an unhealthy idea of—"

"My daughter is not overweight, Dad. But if she dropped twenty pounds, she sure as fuck would be underweight. But even in that dysfunction, Mom called her and said this shit to my fucking daughter *two days after I walked out on my family.*"

"Remy, we should discuss all of this, I agree. It's long since time. But I will say that none of it trumps the fact your mother is *dying*," Guillaume snapped. "And she misses you. She misses her grandchildren. But mostly, she misses *her son. Non, je déteste sérieusement* the manner in which I forced her to behave those years she had sole charge of you due to my shortcomings. But this is all water under the bridge now."

Water under the bridge?

"Dad, I lived my whole...*fucking...life* scared out of my goddamned mind I'd put a foot out of place, and she'd lose it with me. And at the same time I was doing everything I could to be her perfect boy, I was doing it to be *yours* so you wouldn't leave us. Leave her. Leave me *with her.*"

"*Mon beau Remy*—"

"And being groomed to be all things to both of you all my life, when I found a woman who loved me for me, I didn't see that. I needed to be that for her too. And when I couldn't be, I couldn't deal."

His father sounded like he was getting pissed when he asked, "I'm sorry, are you blaming your mother and me for you failing your wife?"

"Yes," Remy replied firmly. "I am."

"*Merde,*" he bit and then, "That is *not* the son I raised."

"It fucking is," Remy gritted out. "One thing I learned very well, Dad, is that I had to be all things to all people. I had to be perfect. But most of all, to keep the woman I loved happy, that woman being your wife, my mother, I had to be all things to her."

"Wyn is not your mother," Guillaume scoffed.

"No, she isn't. But I'm my father and I'm *her* son."

"And because of all of this, you will keep yourself and your children from your mother when she's dying," his father stated flatly.

"No. I'll tell the kids. And I'll tell Wyn. And I'll let my children individually decide how they want to handle it. Wyn can also decide what she wants to do. But I'll come home to say goodbye."

"I am now uncertain that's my wish, if you're coming home simply to upset her."

"Even if she's dying, if they decide to come with me, I won't allow her to abuse my family," Remy warned. "But I'm not coming home to force her to fix things that can't be fixed. Like I said, I'm coming to say goodbye. And if she lets it be that, that's what will happen."

"Then perhaps when you're here, you and I can have a conversation."

"About what? Your 'shortcomings'?"

"No one is perfect, Remy," he bit out. "Including you."

"I think you missed the point earlier, considering I just told you I learned that when I was four."

Guillaume said nothing.

119

"I need some time with the kids, with Wyn, to decide what we're going to do, and then I'll call to let you know when to expect whoever is coming."

It was very soft when his father asked, "Do you doubt I love you?"

"No, I doubt you know what love is."

Remy heard his father's hiss of breath and he wanted to feel nothing, but he didn't because this was his dad. And unless you were a psychopath, no matter the time or maturity or wisdom you amassed in your life, you gave a shit about your parents. What they thought of you. What they felt for you. And what they felt about how you thought of them.

"*Ça me blesse,*" Guillaume whispered.

(This wounds me.)

"That was harsh, but I'm sorry, Dad, it was also true."

"I will be gone one day too, son, and when I am, when my presence on this earth and your feelings about our family history don't blind you to it, you will understand."

"I walked out on my family once in my life and it destroyed me to the point I've been functioning on autopilot for three years, and now I will do whatever is necessary to rectify that mistake. You walked out on us all the time and never understood the devastation you created when you did, or you ignored it because dealing with it didn't fit into your life. So, in a way, I already understand. But don't fool yourself to make yourself feel better. I also never will."

"You are forgetting in all of these daggers you're aiming my way, that not only is your mother dying, *I'm* losing the love of my life."

"The love of your life?"

"Surely, you cannot doubt that," Guillaume huffed.

"Wyn is the love of my life too."

"As she should be, she's an incredible woman."

Remy kept talking, again like his father didn't speak.

"And because I was lonely and stupid and couldn't face the fact that I'd failed my wife and family, I let another woman into my bed, and I will regret that until my dying day. What were your excuses?"

Another sharp breath and then, "Please call me when you know your plans."

Which meant they were done, and Remy was good with that because he had work to do.

"You'll either hear from me or Lisa."

"Fine."

"Take care."

"I will give your mother your love."

Remy blew out a breath.

And then he said, "Goodbye, Dad."

And with a good deal of relief, he put the phone in its cradle, that conversation out of his mind, and got to work.

CHAPTER 13
Do It

Wyn

As I walked up to Remy's house the next evening, I focused on each step I took.

This was because he had the door open, was lounging in it wearing another pair of faded jeans, a pale green, slightly oversized button-up, which fell open at the throat and rested beautifully on his broad shoulders, and he was watching each one of those steps.

I didn't stop to greet him at the door.

Before I'd fully arrived, he turned to the side, an indication to come in.

I only spoke when I'd squeezed by him, he'd closed the door and turned to face me.

"Hi."

He smirked, I felt my vaginal walls contract, and he replied, "Hi. Hungry?'"

I nodded.

He took my hand (yes, *took my hand*) and led me to his kitchen.

And right into it.

Okay.

After he'd walked out on me, he'd spent precisely (I counted), five and a half months in his apartment before he moved into this house.

As such, I'd been to that house for another family meeting, before the one Yves had called last week, to discuss Manon's high school graduation party.

Also, as we decided was fair to each other and the children so they didn't have to split their celebrations, Remy had hosted each of our children's birthday parties once in the time since we'd been apart (I had the other times, it was coming up to his turn again), and I'd attended.

And in the beginning, pre-Myrna, when we were attempting to be good, divorced parents, I had spent Christmas Eve there and Remy had made his mother's (read: one of his mother's housekeeper's) famed etouffee. It was our family's Christmas Eve tradition and one of the few things he allowed into our lives that had anything to do with Colette.

In other words, since it was open to the family room, I'd seen it. I'd walked by it.

But I'd never walked *into* his kitchen.

And I didn't understand why being in his kitchen felt so profound.

But it did.

He let my hand go, went to the oven and opened it, asking, "Do you want wine or a martini?"

"Wine," I answered as he pulled out the takeaway from keeping warm.

"Right," he murmured, setting the food containers on the counter and reaching to get down plates.

"You do drinks, I'll serve up," I offered when he had the plates on the counter.

He looked at me, nodded, then moved out of the kitchen to his wet bar where he stored his wine.

Though, Manon told me, in the other wing of the house there was a walk-in wine room that was, "*So rad*, Mom, *you wouldn't believe.*" Apparently, you could see it from the pool. However, I had not seen it as I had not been in that wing or near his pool.

Remy had lived there two and a half years, and I'd been in the living room and family room.

And that was it.

I shook off these thoughts, and how they were distressing me, and got down to sorting the food.

When I opened the lids, it was no surprise to see he got me my favorite. Combo platter with pulled pork and brisket.

It was also no surprise Remy got a combo too: pulled chicken and turkey.

He had always, from the time I'd met him, had a mind to healthy living.

This didn't mean he didn't drink or eat sweets or snack. He did.

Just that, for the most part, he selected healthy choices and never really went overboard on anything.

It also meant, even after he quit training for triathlons, he ran, went to the gym and lifted weights, and always played rugby.

Rugby was his thing. He went out of his way to follow the MLR in the U.S., the same with the European, Australian and New Zealand leagues.

He was so into it, he'd played in a league in New York, and one of the first things he'd done when we moved to Phoenix was find one here.

Then, in usual Remy fashion, five steps ahead of any game, he got deeply involved in the junior league, building that up, as well as the senior league.

He did this because he loved the game. He did this because he wanted others to love it.

And he did it because he knew he couldn't play in the adult league after a certain age because he might get hurt, being mid- or late-forties and playing with guys in their twenties and thirties. But he wouldn't want to quit.

He'd also given this to our boys.

Sabre and Yves both played junior, Yves still active, and Sabre had found a team in Tucson.

They loved playing and I loved watching, regardless of the fact that, more often than not, they'd end up bloody.

Still, they were all very good at it, the best on their teams (I will admit to some prejudice about that). And it was an interesting sport, far more than any other (I will admit to some prejudice about that too).

I, on the other hand (and I'd given this to my daughter), loved food, but hated physical activity.

I'd struggled with this in my twenties and thirties.

But in my forties, I realized it was who I was.

I was not sedentary by a long shot. And although I could go overboard, sitting around eating wasn't my way of life.

My epiphany to being at one with this came when, one day, I heard that Tina Turner said she stayed in shape, and had those amazing legs, simply by walking every night after dinner.

That might be a fib, and it should be said she made this comment while she was touring, and I'd seen her on stage, so walking wasn't all the exercise those great gams got.

But it made me think.

And after some reflection, I realized I liked to walk too. I also liked to stretch.

So I didn't knock myself out, but I did both.

Not every day, but regularly, I'd walk. Sometimes I'd do it twenty minutes, sometimes I'd get into the music or podcast I was listening to, and I'd walk for over an hour.

But even if that was as and when, nearly every morning before I took a shower, I did some stretches and some crunches to keep my limbs supple and my core strong.

But that was it.

And unless I found something else I liked, it always would be and I was okay with that.

This was even if (the same as when I first met Remy) I'd carried extra weight. I'd then put on some when I was pregnant with the kids, and I didn't take it off. And sadly, my coping mechanism after Remy left meant I'd added a size.

But two nights ago, my ex-husband said he wanted to fuck me in my tub.

And since then, I'd reflected on those words.

After he left, I'd convinced myself there was a time when Remy wasn't attracted to me.

But taking some time (a lot of it), I realized he had never, not once, given me indication he was not attracted to me sexually or aesthetically, this being during pregnancy, post-pregnancy, in the years in between as life happened, which meant age happened, and both happened to me.

In fact, I'd always been curvy, from the minute I met him. Sure, I was curvier now, but he got three kids out of that.

I also remembered that I was not one of those women who had to put up with her man admiring other women, because he never looked. Never. Not once that'd I'd noticed in decades.

It was me for him.

He was just into me.

Then.

And, apparently, now.

Which might be why Myrna hurt as bad as she did and why I'd talked myself into thinking he'd lost interest in me.

For Remy, it had always just been me...until her.

Though, it was perhaps more important, after struggling with my body image and confidence as many girls and young women my age did, I got over it, and not just because my husband made no bones about the fact he was very attracted to me (even if that helped a ton).

I was around beauty for a living.

I saw it in its classic sense. I saw it in its atypical sense. I saw it in its edgy sense. I saw it in its unexpected sense.

And thus, I saw it was everywhere, in everyone, with one key component that was the same for all.

The people who had it knew they did.

If you thought you were beautiful, you just were.

When I realized the key to being beautiful was knowing you were, I realized I was beautiful.

And that was the end of it.

So there I was in Remy's kitchen facing a version of us in food form.

Remy had his turkey and chicken, I had my beef and pork, and that was who we were. It always had been.

And it worked.

Not because he didn't mind if I stole some of his, or I wouldn't complain if he took a forkful of mine.

And not because I was a together twenty-something when he met me, and I got I was all that.

But because that was the place Remy put us from the minute he met me.

And he'd never moved us from that place.

Not even when he left me (no, I had not missed the admiring glances or even the smirks during birthday parties or Christmas Eve, not to mention some of the times he came over to pick a fight, I was just determined to think they were about something else).

If he'd been a different man, I might not ever have come to terms with my body, face and style. Say he'd been Bill, who was a nice guy, but I'd always cringed before he'd broken it off with Janelle and we were around them, and he'd say things to her like, "Babe, maybe you should lay off the fries."

Remy would never do that, and not because it wasn't nice or appropriate.

But because it wouldn't occur to him. If I wanted fries, he'd want me to have them, and if they landed on my ass, he didn't care because he loved my ass however it came.

Because how it came was with me.

"I've got a Zinfandel or a Bordeaux here," he called, breaking into my thoughts. "But I can go to the wine room and grab something else."

"Zinfandel," I told him, getting out of my head and into piling the food on the plates.

He arrived with the uncorked wine and the glasses.

He poured through an aerator as I finished with the food.

That was more Guillaume in Remy.

He knew good wine. He understood why it was good. And he knew it was important to aerate a young wine to relieve the tannins.

I had an aerator. But I rarely used it. I just opened the wine, poured and drank it.

Though, I did taste how much better it was when it was aerated.

Remy set the glasses at the end of the countertop where there was a large seating area with four stools, instead of taking them to the round dining table in the corner of the family room with its smoked glass top sitting on a thick, geometric walnut base.

I was relieved he didn't treat this as formal.

We were far from casual, hanging out, talking.

But it still felt nice—comforting—that he went that route.

And I wasn't surprised when he got out cloth napkins with lime green and robin's egg blue boomerangs and chocolate brown lines with coral and aqua balls on the ends.

Remy had outlawed paper napkins, plastic cutlery, straws and any but necessary use of paper towel in our house around the time he switched to committing to using at least sixty percent of reclaimed materials for all his builds.

He never, however, gave up on the Ziplocs.

This thought meant I was smiling to myself when Remy hustled me out of the way to commandeer the plates and grunted, "Sit."

I sat, he set my plate in front of me, grabbed cutlery while I put my napkin on my lap and he asked, "What's with the smile?" as he sat beside me and nabbed his napkin.

I pulled mine from my lap and held it up to him.

That was when he smiled and said, "Manon. Last year. Christmas. As a joke. I told her I was not George Jetson. She told me they worked with my house vision. I think she thought I'd bury them in a drawer. But I use them because they make her smile. I have a service that does my laundry, and when they go in, I request they come back ironed."

That made me laugh.

It also made my heart swell.

He really did love his daughter.

All his kids.

But there was something sweet about the fact Manon was Daddy's Girl.

It was sweet because I had a sister.

And we both knew how beautiful it felt to be Daddy's Girl. I loved that my daughter had the same thing.

While I was laughing, Remy invited, "Dig in."

I did that next.

Remy did too, but he also started the conversation.

"Before we get into the nitty-gritty, I have—"

"Can we not?" I blurted, the words coming out even before the thought behind them hit my brain.

"Sorry?"

127

I put my fork down, grabbed my wine, took a sip (excellent) and set it down before I looked to him.

We were at corners from each other, and I knew, if I shifted the right way, my knee would touch his.

I didn't know for certain what I wanted. In between bouts of Remy, I was staying busy with life and keeping whatever was happening with Remy to happening *with* Remy.

It was hard, but it was also the best way forward.

Reflecting about where my mind had gone and finally being honest about my behaviors (and his) was one thing.

But there was no use obsessing about Remy when he had the answers, or we could work on the answers together, or we could see there were no answers, but that had to happen together too.

But now...

Now, for some reason, I just wanted barbeque, our daughter's napkins and Remy.

"The nitty-gritty," I said softly. "Can we just...?"

I trailed off because I didn't know how to say what I wanted without taking us, and especially him, places we weren't ready to go yet.

"Get to know each other again?" Remy suggested. My tone had been soft, his was gentle. But when I didn't immediately answer, he went on, "Pretend?"

Pretend.

Pretend this wasn't just his house and our house was now just mine?

Pretend the last three years didn't happen?

Just...*pretend*?

"Fiona was in town this week. Noel was full throated in his complaints about the fact he had to rearrange my entire schedule yesterday afternoon so I could view properties with her. But it was all worth it because I really like to spend time with her. She came over for a glass of wine before she had to leave last night, and I will never forget the look on Theo's face when Fiona Remington walked into the living room."

Speaking of looks I wouldn't forget, Remy Gastineau had given me many in our lives together.

The one he had when I walked down the aisle to him.

The expression on his face when I told him I was pregnant with Sabre (and then Manon, and then Yves).

The way he looked the first time Sabre was placed in his arms (and then Manon, and then Yves).

The one he wore when I walked into Spring House, up in Montana. A house he'd designed and built. And I'd wandered around it, knowing it was different. Knowing he was shirking off the tethers of his firm. What he was told to do, what he was supposed to do, clearly making his own mark. And I told him it was by far the best work he'd done to date. Then he'd told me he wanted to quit the firm and start his own. And I'd instantly said, "Do it."

And that one right there.

The one that was him and me eating barbeque at his counter in his house and pretending we hadn't imploded.

That we were still us.

At the same time giving him another massive hint that was where I wanted us to get back to being.

"If Theo sticks around, he might want to get used to that," Remy noted.

"My clients don't tend to walk into my living room, Remy."

"Manon has worked the last three summers in your warehouse, Wyn, and she's getting a degree in fine arts. That degree has a zero-point-one job placement rate, unless she gets a couple of graduate degrees. She's unofficially mentoring herself at your shop, likely because she wishes Noel was her brother by blood and she doesn't want him to feel his position is challenged. Regardless, it doesn't take a psychologist to see, if you allow it, this is going to be a family business. And although Theo is a solid guy, I don't like the idea of Yves sticking with the first person he's with rather than having some experience and knowing what he really wants. But if they work, Theo will be in our family."

"I need to start taking Manon to shows," I murmured.

"You do," he agreed.

We shared a familiar weighted glance while sharing familiar agreement about one of our kids.

Then I turned back to my barbeque, and in between bites, I told him, "I mentioned Fiona for a reason."

"Let me guess. She's not finding a house. She's finding a lot and wants me to scrape the house on it, if it has one, and build one for her."

I faced him again. "How'd you guess?"

He smiled, shook his head and went for his wine. "Because I never should have done the Heald home. I've had calls from A-listers, B-listers, aging Hollywood royalty and a straggle of wannabes."

"This is good," I said.

"This is a disaster," he replied. "Because, honey, those people are pains in the ass."

"Fiona isn't," I disagreed, and I would know, because I had a lot of clients and a goodly number of them were a pain in the ass.

"They all are," he refuted. "I swore to myself after Heald, not again. Christ, it's a wonder I didn't do time for murdering him when I worked with him. I changed my design fifteen times at his demand."

I couldn't believe I forgot this. It had done Remy's head in. The guy was ridiculous, not only with his indecisiveness, but his demands on Remy's time.

"Since then, I've had preliminary consultations with three actors, a director and a producer. All big names. All came to their meetings with definitive ideas, but before a week was up, they were already phoning repeatedly to suggest changes and additions. Now, I put them off before it gets to the consultation stage."

"I don't think Fiona would be like that. She's decisive. Case in point, she found a piece of property north of Carefree yesterday and she's buying it."

He shook his head and went back to his food.

"Remy," I called.

He shoved some turkey in his mouth and looked at me.

"Do you really have a two-year waiting list?" I asked.

"Literally, for someone to get direct to me, yes. For one of the talented people I employ, no. But it's anywhere from eight months to a year. But they all want me. And I don't bump people up the list. So if they want me, they wait for me."

Well, damn.

Now I was in the position of asking my ex-husband, who I'd fallen into working on our relationship with, for what amounted to a very big favor.

Remy knew me, which was why he asked, "You told her I'd do it?"

"I told her I'd ask, and this is going to sound like pressure, still, you should know. I might not have texted you the other night if Fiona hadn't told me I should."

"Typical, she gives something, she gets something," he muttered, and in his mouth went some beans.

"That's life, for the most part," I pointed out.

"Not for everyone. That's just how those people work," he replied, and I felt my eyes narrow.

"You hardly hobnob in Hollywood to *know how they work*," I noted.

He took another sip of his wine before he looked me direct in the eye. "You think I haven't lived my life around entitled people and don't know how they work? My life has been the figurative carrot and stick. Emphasis on stick, Wyn. And I didn't work my ass off to manage my own goddamned firm, to have a new line of privileged assholes taking their whips to me. If they want me, they can wait for me."

Emphasis on stick...

Taking their whips to me...

Entitled people...
Privileged assholes...
We were both creative.
We could both be prone to drama.

But this was intense language, and because it was, an unexpected cold started creeping over me.

"Are there deeper issues we should be talking about?" I asked hesitantly.

"Not if we're not getting into the nitty-gritty," he answered.

"I think maybe we need to."

He sat straight.

And then he announced, "Great then. Mom's dying of cancer."

I gasped.

"Yep," he said. "She wants me to come and see her. She wants the kids to come and see her. Or, at least, Dad does since he called to share this. Therefore, I'm sure you won't be surprised, he was thrilled we're working on things and I'm sure he wants you to come and see her, but mostly that means he wants you to come and see him."

"Remy," I whispered, watching him closely because this had to be confusing news to him.

But the bottom line was, your mom was your mom.

"And by the way, he's been calling these last few days, but I didn't talk to him until after I got off the phone with you yesterday. And that was the first time I'd talked to him in three years."

Another gasp and then I asked, "Three years?"

A short nod and then, "Not a surprise, Mom was far from upset we broke up and she was happy to explain that to me as only Mom can do. Dad was devastated, but he didn't call to share that. When I hung up on Mom and blocked her, Dad called not to say how upset he was that I'd done something as fucking stupid as leaving my beautiful wife. Nor did he call to try to explain why Mom behaved the way she did and apologize in her stead. He demanded I make amends. *To her.*"

"Some things don't change," I said hesitantly, saying this, but thinking how much I wished they did, especially around this very thing for Remy. And more hesitantly, I asked, "Are you going?"

"Did you fuck someone after I left?"

Hang on.

Wait.

Okay.

Um.

Hell no.

131

Remy did this, and it *always* happened around a discussion about his parents.

Precisely, anytime I got near to understanding how he truly felt about them.

Obviously, it wasn't hard to discern they weren't close. Equally, it wasn't hard to discern they were difficult people, so it would be no fun having them as parents and that easily segued into them not being close.

But any deep discussion about this was a no go.

He'd try deflection. Or he'd attempt distraction.

Or he'd pick a fight.

All of which he was doing right now with that one question.

"Let's stay on target," I suggested.

"No, Wyn. I'd like to know how guilty I really should feel about how I fucked up with Myrna."

Do not bite, Wyn!

"You don't need to feel guilty, Remy. We were divorced. You were free to do what you wished." It took a lot, but I said it, and I wasn't sure I meant it, but that didn't stop it from being the truth. "Now, let's get back to the equally uncomfortable subject of your mother dying."

"I was free to do what I wished, so you were too, is that what you're saying?"

"Okay, let's just get out of the nitty-gritty," I requested, maybe somewhat desperately. "How was your day?"

"My day was shit because my mom's dying, my kids have to go back and forth between two houses because I failed my marriage, and my wife is dodging a direct question because she doesn't want to say to my face she took a cock that is not mine."

Ding!

Done.

"Remy!" I snapped. "Stop being an ass."

"Just tell me, did you fuck someone else, Wyn?"

"We never have to talk about this."

"Okay then, I'll let that slide for now. Do you forgive me for Myrna?"

"I don't even know all the reasons why you walked out on me," I reminded him. "Let's not put the cart before the horse and get into all of this."

"So that means...no. You don't forgive me."

"I know you don't have a close relationship with your mom. I know why. Now she's ill and she wants her family around her, and her family is my family, so we need to talk about that."

He shook his head. "You don't know why, Wyn."

"Sorry?"

"You don't know why I'm not close with my mother."

Oh God.

Now that we were here, with that new look on his face, did I want to know?

I wasn't sure.

My mouth was because it ordered, "Then tell me, Remy."

After decades of evading this, he immediately turned his head and pointed to a white scar that was around three inches long. It marred his tanned skin about an inch down from his hairline, just behind his ear.

I'd asked him about it years ago.

He'd told me it was a rugby injury. He was down on the pitch and got stepped on by some cleats.

Now, I sat frozen to the spot, knowing that was a lie.

He turned back and shared, voice detached, "Dad was away on business, but he was supposed to come home. He didn't come back when he was supposed to, even when he did."

I sensed where this was going, but I didn't say anything.

Remy kept sharing.

"He had a local fuck."

Yes.

That was what I sensed because Guillaume cheating on Colette, and Remy knowing it, was one of the things I did know about his folks.

"I'd met her," he carried on. "He took me to her place once and I hung in her family room while they fucked in her bedroom. We were supposed to be having father and son time. Her name was Estelle. She was gorgeous. Brashly gorgeous. What my mother would refer to as low rent or trashy. She was a lot younger than my mom too. She made me an ice cream sundae and told me I was a heartbreaker. Then she took Dad down the hall, and as he was walking away, he told me to be quiet and behave."

I could not believe my ears.

"My Lord, Remy."

"But that day, the one he was supposed to come home, he called Mom and told her he was going to be away another couple of days. She was furious. But this time, she held it in check. At least she did until she got another call. I don't know who it was from, probably a friend of hers. One who saw Dad with Estelle. He was in New Orleans. He was home. But he didn't come directly back to his wife and son. He went to his local fuck."

I reached out and touched his arm, murmuring, "Oh, honey."

"Though, he sent flowers," he continued. "Or his secretary did. When

Mom got them, that was when she lost it. Took the vase, struck me with it. It broke on my skull, and the edge cut me. It cut deep. Water all over the place. Red roses everywhere, all mixed with my blood. Mom was hysterical. Our live-in, Marjorie, took me to the hospital and called Dad's secretary. He came home then. Home. Not to me in the hospital. To our house. To her. Soothing her, telling me when Marjorie brought me back that we had to understand how delicate she was. How women reacted to things differently. How very, *very* good we had to be not to upset Mom."

There was no buzzing in my head this time.

It felt like my veins had turned to acid and I was deep breathing while trying not to come out of my skin.

Remy, however, grew silent and I knew story time was over.

"How old were you?" I asked.

"Seven."

Seven.

He'd been *seven*.

Good God.

I continued deep breathing, but now while trying not to will my body to dematerialize in Phoenix, rematerialize in NOLA, so I could slap a dying woman silly.

I then tried to leech all accusation out of my voice when I asked, "Why have you never told me this story?"

"Because I learned to be very, *very* good not to upset the women in my life."

I sat back like I'd been struck, but he leaned forward.

"You don't get it," he said harshly.

And his face was suddenly ravaged, a hundred times worse than the harshness of his words.

"Then explain it to me," I replied gently.

"It's all I knew. Don't make waves. Smooth things over. Be good."

"Okay," I prompted. "For her, but for me?"

"Of course for you. More for you than I'd ever do it for her."

This made sense.

And yet it really, *really* did not.

"I want to understand, Remy, I truly do, but I can't say I'm getting it."

"I love you."

I sat still on my stool, staring at him.

"Nothing should touch you," he went on.

Oh God.

He kept going.

"You don't feel pain. You don't get upset. Nothing touches you, Wyn. I have to make that so. Do you get it?"

God.

"Life isn't like that, Remy. It's impossible to make that so."

"I know that. I'm fucked up, but I'm not stupid."

"I wasn't saying you were."

"I'm saying *I* don't make you feel pain. *I* don't upset you. *I* don't cause you harm in any way."

"You never would," I assured, then added, "I knew that. I never doubted it."

"She broke my arm. She gave me a concussion. And once she shook me when we were on the stairs, lost control, and I fell down. Half a flight. I dislocated my shoulder."

Some force surged through me so strong, it drove me to push my stool back and stand up.

Remy stood up with me.

Broke...

Concussion...

Lost control...

Half a flight...

Dislocated.

"Why didn't you tell me?" I whispered, my words strangled.

He pointed at my face, and if I thought his expression was ravaged before, I didn't understand the meaning of the word.

It was that now.

And I felt it.

I felt it in every cell that made me.

"That," he growled, jerking his finger in my face gain. "That right there is why I didn't tell you."

"Do you not think I should know my husband's mother beat him?"

"I absolutely do not think you should *ever* know that, and it is fucking *killing* me telling you now."

"Remy," I breathed, wanting too much all at once.

To shout at him, scream, rant, rave, dissolve into anger to balm the hurt that he never trusted me with this.

But the bigger needs were to touch him, smooth my hands over him, make him absorb how loved he was, find a way to go back in time and save him from his mother, from that fucking father of his, from his unhealthy need to shield me from, from...

Shield me from him.

Shield me from *the man I loved*.

"I needed to know all of that," I said.

"You don't need to know it, Wyn. I'm looking at you right now, and it's written all over your face how much you don't fucking need it."

"I need every part of you."

"Not that."

"Every part, Remy."

He reared forward so fast I didn't have a chance to lean away.

"*Not that!*" he roared in my face.

I went silent.

Then I demanded, "Give me your phone."

"What?"

"*Give me your phone!*" I screamed.

His movements wooden, he reached to his back pocket, pulled out his phone and handed it to me.

I looked down at it and asked him, "Same passcode?"

"What are you doing?"

It was the same passcode because I entered it, my birthdate (for God's sake!), and I was in.

I went to his contacts.

"Wyn, what are you doing?"

"I'm calling your fucking father."

He slipped his phone out of my hand.

My head shot up. "Give that back."

"I'm seeing we both need to take a breath, drink some wine and—"

"Give it back."

"Wyn, there's no point phoning him. Trust me, he doesn't give a shit."

I put my hands in his chest and pressed hard into the firm bulges of his pectorals.

Then I fisted my fingers in his shirt, pulled out then pushed in.

After that, I let him go, walked around him, through his kitchen to the back wall and stood at the wall of windows, staring at the lit, deep-clean aqua of his pool.

He had a dinette set out there: white table, white bucket chairs. A seating area with four white armless chairs facing each other, two-by-two. Not to mention, two other seating areas that had loungers.

Every inch was perfection, not even a hint on that white of the famous Phoenix dust that coated everything, and my guess was, he maintained it himself.

She shook me when we were on the stairs, lost control, and I fell down. Half a flight.

I closed my eyes.

Half a flight.

Twenty-four years, I didn't know.

Twenty-four years.

And I didn't know.

Remy was behind me when he said, "She's dying, and I need to go see her. I also need to talk to our kids, give them the information to help them make the decision on their own of whether they want to go or not."

I opened my eyes. "Does that information include them learning their grandmother physically abused their father and their grandfather doubled down on that abuse by making his son responsible for it?"

Remy didn't answer.

I turned and looked up at him. "You are not going to that den of jackals without me."

His torso swayed back, and his brows shot up.

"She might be dying, but a cat's at her most dangerous when she's vulnerable. No way...*in fuck*...are you facing that bitch without me."

There wasn't a lot of space between us, but after I said that, Remy negated it by moving into me. He then smoothed my hair from my face and held my head in both hands before he dipped down so we were nose to nose.

"I hate that you know," he whispered, and that was no lie, I could see it in his eyes.

This *was* killing him.

"I hate you didn't tell me," I retorted.

"Do you understand why I didn't?"

"No, I don't, Remy. I really fucking don't."

He closed down, started to move away, but I shot my hands up, caught his wrists and stopped him.

"Don't you *dare* move away from me," I snapped. "You did that once and it's not happening again."

He stood stock still.

"We're telling our children and they're all coming. Your entire family will be with you when you go back there, Remy."

"It should be their choice."

"They're coming."

He took a second with that before he agreed, "Okay. We can tell the boys, but Manon never knows."

I felt my brows shoot together. "She will know."

"No way, baby."

"We are not her, Remy. Manon and I are not porcelain dolls who shatter at a blunt touch and cut you with our edges. We're not that. Stop treating us like that."

He looked in agony when he said, "I don't know any other way, Wyn."

"Then it's time to learn."

He took another second with that and then he said, "I'll bump Fiona to the top of the list."

God.

This man.

I pushed through his hands on my head to plant my face in his chest.

He wrapped his arms around me, and I felt his breath in the side of my hair.

I stood in his arms, taking on the crushing weight of understanding I didn't have the information, but that didn't mean I failed to understand, *for decades*, my husband was battling some pretty fucking significant demons.

His mother had essentially shoved him down the stairs, he'd twisted this in his head that he had to be all things to me (as well as, obviously, Manon), and I had bitched to him about Bea's ugliness, telling him the nasty things she'd said about him.

He should have told me.

But I knew one thing.

The Gastineau family were skilled with façade.

And I'd just learned Remy was the master.

This did not enrage me.

No.

No matter what I'd lost to it.

Nope.

You see, I did not go from a loving family in a small house on a small farm in a small town in Indiana to styling award-winning movie stars by backing down from a challenge.

Oh no, I did not.

If I wanted something, I got it.

I wanted my husband back.

All of him.

And by God, I was going to have what I wanted.

"Do you want Lisa to make the arrangements, or Noel?" I asked his chest.

His arms tightened. "Lisa can do it."

"Do you want me to call the family meeting, or do you want to do it?"

"I'd like to further discuss Manon being there."

138

I tipped my head back. "No, Remy. From here on out, from Yves being gay to you surviving your upbringing, there is no more hiding in this family."

"She has to know she can count on her father for anything."

"And you have to get, *she already does*." I shook my head. "How perfect do you need to be, Remy?"

"I walked out on you when your business exploded, and I understood that you never again had to count on me for anything. How perfect do you think I need to be, Wyn?"

My *God*.

This man.

I forced my hands between us only to lift them and cradle his jaw. "I counted on you for everything."

"If you did, you'd know you could throw away a glass of wine, because there's more where that came from, and if that's what you wanted, I'd break my back to make sure there always would be."

Oh.

My.

God.

I closed my eyes, shoved my fingers up into his hair and pulled his forehead to mine.

"I need to know," he said, his voice thick, and I opened my eyes.

"Know what?"

"Is this what it seems? Are we working on us?" he asked.

"Yes," I said instantly.

That was when my arms got caught between us when he crushed me to him.

His face was in my neck, which meant I told his ear, "Let's eat. Talk about our days. Get you through this with the kids, your parents, and then we can... figure out all the rest."

"All right," he said into my neck.

"Somewhere in all that, I'll call Fiona and tell her it's good to know the right people."

He gave me a powerful squeeze that nearly made me peep.

Then he lifted his head and I saw conflict mixed with warmth and humor in his eyes.

This was the gift my husband gave me before he gave me another and smiled.

CHAPTER 14
Really

Wyn

"I'm going too," Noel declared, pacing my office while I leaned against the front of my desk watching him.

"Noel, I told you this in the strictest of confidence," I reminded him severely. "And anyway, you have to remain here to hold down the fort."

He stopped pacing and glared at me.

"I met her. I liked her. I thought she was fabulous. A killer queen. The bitch even smoked cigarettes in vintage holders, and cigarettes are revolting, but she rocked that."

I'd shared with Noel...well, pretty much everything about the night before at Remy's. And clearly, Noel was feeling personally deceived that she'd turned out to be a monster.

Also clearly, Colette should have quit smoking a long time ago.

Last, even I had to admit she was fabulous.

Definitely a killer queen.

"I regret to inform you of this, but I thought you two were just in competition for Remy's attention," he went on. "That happens."

"I love that you feel a part of my family," I said.

He waved a hand to wave this comment away because Noel didn't do sentimentality.

"I love how much you care about him," I kept going.

"I love that you two are working things out," he replied. "Though, I don't know why you didn't spend the night with him. He needs comforting."

Dear Lord.

"Working things out is not the same as things being worked out," I returned. "A lot is going on and we don't need to confuse the situation by getting physical."

"Have you considered the fact things getting physical might go a long way to working things out?" he asked.

"I can hardly pounce on him the night he shares his mother is dying, and oh yeah, she also physically, and along with her husband, mentally and emotionally abused him his whole life."

Though, I had to admit, once I got over the shock of it all, being alone with Remy, spending time with him in his amazing home, that option had been preeminent on my mind.

And, I had to admit, I didn't want to be talking about this with Noel, because that thought was *still* preeminent on my mind.

I had decided to work things out with Remy.

And one could say I was keen to *work things out* with my husband.

We hadn't touched in that way since...

Well, since he came over about a year and a half ago to pick a fight, we'd both lost control and ended up having sex against the wall in my foyer.

That was the last time I'd had sex.

After he'd filed for divorce, I'd dated, and since Remy, taken two lovers.

But after that time in the entryway, that was over.

Not because I thought we'd get back together.

Just because, unconsciously I was holding on, and the reminder of how we were in that way, it was ridiculous, but seriously...

Remy ruined me for all other men.

Now, we were working things out.

And I was intent to get my husband back...and give both of us *that* back.

However, he was dealing with a lot, and although we had a history of working things out sexually after arguments, when things were emotional for Remy, he craved affection.

Heck, when my mom and dad died, Remy and I spent hours cuddling (literally *hours*). Or he'd play the piano, and no matter how much I had to do, I'd set it aside and sit close to him, reading, just so he could see me.

It had not been lost on me why this was, his mother and father being as they were.

Now, truly knowing the way his mother and father were, I felt it imperative to give him my time, attention and affection but not push him to…well, *perform*.

"Uh, yes you can," Noel shot back. "Men feel comforted by precisely two things. You cooking them their favorite foods and you giving them an orgasm."

I looked to the ceiling.

My cell rang.

So I aimed my eyes down to my desk and saw my daughter was calling.

I picked up the phone and answered, "Hey, honey."

"Mom, love you, and I love that you and Dad are *so totally* getting back together even if you're trying to be careful with our feelings in case it doesn't work out, when it absolutely will, but all this family drama is *killing* my social life."

Needless to say, I'd called the family meeting via text, telling the kids I wanted them all at their father's house by seven that night for his steak tacos and discussion.

I knew this was doable because I knew their schedules. We had a family calendar on our phones, and yes, more evidence that I'd been ludicrously blind, and completely missed how my husband was reaching out to me even as he pushed me away, because Noel and Lisa had not once ceased in adding Remy and my details into it.

Therefore, I knew both Sabre and Manon were finished with classes that day by early afternoon, (Sabre's last class finished at three). This meant they had time to get packed and drive up.

"Save the environment, drive together for once," I ordered my daughter.

"Benji's driving me up. We're going to multi-task and add a meet the parents," she declared.

Oh no they weren't.

I pushed up from the desk. "Manon, if Benji is important to you, I'd love to meet him. But this isn't the time."

"If he's gonna be a keeper, then he has to be introduced to Gastineau Family Theatrics. I'll need to assess his reaction to that, and I figure that should be sooner rather than later."

And there it was.

Reed had not been wrong.

Women also referred to men as "keepers."

"Really, honey, this isn't the time."

"I talked to Yves and he's bringing Theo. Though, that's probably more about Dad's tacos."

Damn it.

Though, it probably was. Remy's steak tacos were simple, but they were amazing.

"I'll talk to your brother because he's not bringing Theo."

"It's not a big deal, Mom, we all knew you'd get back together eventually."

I drew in a breath.

And then I said, "Okay, yes, your dad and I are talking. However, this meeting is not about that, and it isn't appropriate for Benji to be there."

She started to say something.

But I didn't hear it because Noel was there, taking my phone right from my ear and putting it to his.

"Doll, you've got Noel. Don't fight your mom on this one. You with me?" Pause then. "Mm-hmm." Pause and, "Mm-hmm." One last pause then, "All right. We'll do brunch. Byeee."

He took the phone from his ear, disconnected from my daughter and handed it back to me.

"She's going to contact Sah. They'll come together. Benji is out...for now."

"It's unpleasant, being grateful to you and annoyed at you at the same time."

He just grinned then asked, "Shall I call Theo?"

Before I could answer, my phone rang again.

Noel and I both looked at it.

But it was Noel who again slipped it from my hand, took the call and hit speaker.

"You got both of us, beautiful," he announced to Kara.

"Excellent," Kara's voice came from the speaker. "I've got a few minutes between patients, and this is a time saver. I'm officially changing my vote. I'm ghosting Bea. She called last night and unleashed the verbal hounds. Don't worry. She won't care about the ghosting since I ended the call by telling her to go fuck herself."

Noel and I stared at each other.

He looked like he was trying not to laugh.

I felt sick.

"And, not quite an aside, but it has to be an aside for now since I have to call Bernice too and I have five minutes before I have to hit an exam room, but you're up for Cock and Snacktails next, Wyn. And during them, you'll be telling us all about Remy being at your house late on a Tuesday night," she continued.

Translation: Bea had heard Remy's voice over my phone and had called Kara to bitch about me...and Remy.

That whooshing started to happen in my head again.

"No can do, sister," Noel spoke for me. "Seeing as she, Remy and the kids are heading to NOLA to bid adieu to a dying Colette."

"The witch is almost dead?" Kara breathed in what sounded like excitement.

"Thank God I'm not a child and you're not my doctor because I fear you lack empathy," Noel drawled.

Kara ignored him and asked, "Wyn, you're going with them?"

"Yes, because his mother is dying, and Remy and I are talking things through."

"*Ah-ha!*" she crowed like a mad scientist who just made a breakthrough. "I totally knew you'd get back together. Now I'm going to be late for my patient because I also I have to call Reed. He's going to be so excited. He'll probably break out the purple box."

Oh, for heaven's sake.

"What's the purple box?" Noel asked.

"Our sex box," Kara answered.

"New rule!" Noel cried. "No phoning between patients when you don't have time to get detailed *in all the things*."

I broke into their repartee.

"You need to make your calls, and I need to contact my youngest son to share he can't bring his boyfriend to a family meeting that will include him learning his grandmother is dying and we need to go to New Orleans to say goodbye. I also might need to get some work done. And Noel does too. So we're saying goodbye now."

"Wyn?" Kara called.

"Yes, honey?"

"I'm really happy you and Remy are talking."

"I think she got that with the sex box," Noel remarked.

I shot him a look and then said into the phone, "I am too."

"Really?" she asked.

There was a wealth of feeling in my one-word response.

"Really."

"Awesome," she whispered. "Later, my lovelies."

Then she was gone.

The instant she was, Noel asked, "Do you know what's in this purple box?"

I looked at him, and it wasn't only to avoid his question (because, yes, I did know), that I said, "I love you."

He shrugged. "I'm lovable. And I love you too because you're fabulous. And as you know, I don't do mushy. So I'm going back to work now."

With that, he strolled out of my office.

I watched him go.

And then I called Yves.

After I sorted things with my youngest, I was able to get fifteen minutes of work done before my phone buzzed.

It was a text from Remy.

I'll hit AJ's on the way home. Come over when you want. Lisa's couriering over a key. The security code is 21209. See you tonight. Love you.

Twenty-one was Manon's birthday (October).

Twenty was Yves's (January)

Nine was Sabre's (August).

That got me.

Remy was couriering over a key.

That got me more.

And even more was Remy hitting AJ's, which he used to do a lot.

What got me most was the last.

I touched the phone to my forehead and took a second, pushing into the back of my mind the vision of Remy shouldering his life with me in the form of literal baggage and walking out of our home. Then remembering the Remy of last night who bought me Frasher's, and we ate it using our daughter's napkins.

Then I texted back, *Should be done around five. So I'll be at yours at 5:30. Too early?*

I got back, *I'll aim to be there then too.*

It was hanging.

Just hanging.

And I couldn't leave it hanging.

Because this was Remy.

And my hold might have slipped along the way.

But from our first date, he'd been mine.

So I didn't leave it hanging.

And that meant I texted back, *See you then. Love you too.*

He didn't reply.

But that felt so right, even though I gave myself five minutes, I fretted about it for maybe one.

And then I got back to work.

CHAPTER 15
Scottish Royalty

Sabre

Sabre did not get a good feeling when he walked out of his last class and standing across the way was Myrna.

Especially after his dad sat him down and shared that Myrna wasn't taking the breakup real great, she was doing some weird shit, and Sabre had to be on the lookout because of it.

Dad didn't dog her, but Sabre could tell he was tweaked about it.

And now, seeing her standing there, Sabre was too.

Then again, after she was gone from his dad's, but before his dad chatted with him, he'd texted her to say he was sorry it didn't work out and maybe they could grab coffee sometime.

He did this because he dug her. She was a cool chick. When Dad wasn't around, she smoked pot by the pool, and she mountain biked, and she had that old truck because, "we discard things we shouldn't and we'll pay for it soon, Sabre, seriously." This meant she gave a shit about important stuff, like the environment.

So yeah.

She was cool.

A decent person.

Sabre would never say his dad played her dirty.

But to Sabre's way of thinking, as hard as it was to admit this to himself, Dad hadn't done Myrna right because he never should have let her move in.

This was because it wasn't lost on anyone Remy didn't really even let her move in. None of her stuff was anywhere, except her truck in the garage and her coconut milk in the fridge. But nothing personal. Nothing that meant anything.

Seriously, it felt like she was just staying over but for a really long time.

More importantly because his dad and mom were always going to get back together.

Sabre didn't know what blip they were having, but from the very beginning, even though it lasted too long, he didn't freak about it like Manon and Yves did, because he knew it was a blip.

So, from the beginning, he knew Myrna was temporary.

And his dad treated her like that.

He wasn't mean or anything.

But he was never (not even close) with Myrna like he was with their mom.

Jesus, he was more into their mom when they were broken up than he ever was with Myrna.

Myrna wasn't sixteen. She was an older woman. Maybe she knew the score.

But Sah figured women might not ever get over that kind of shit, seeing things as they wanted to see them, instead of how they really were.

Sabre was only twenty-two and he'd already had that kind of crap up in his face more than once.

So yeah.

He wasn't feeling her being in Tucson, on campus, waiting for him outside his class because she had never come down to visit him at school, not alone, also not with Remy when he came down.

He went to U of A so that didn't take any super sleuthing.

But to be outside his class?

What? Did she somehow scam on where he lived and follow him or something?

So, was she standing out there for an hour waiting to ambush him?

Okay, yeah.

Dad was right.

Sah hadn't even said hey to her, and he knew his dad had downplayed it.

She wasn't doing weird shit.

She was doing *super* weird shit.

She bopped forward in a way that he'd never seen her move, all fake casual and girlie.

"Hey, Sah!" she cried.

He moved toward her, and when he got close, he said, "Hey. What are you doing here?"

"Wondered if we could go grab a beer or something?" she asked.

He shook his head. "Sorry. No. Yeah, I mean, when I'm back home, maybe we could do something to keep in touch." *Never gonna happen, not now.* "But I've got something I gotta do."

She looked weird, panicked or some shit, when she pushed, "Okay. But do you have, like, ten minutes, like, right now? It's important we talk."

"About what?" he asked uncertainly.

She got another weird look, it seemed fake serious when she said, "Your dad."

Here we go.

Fuck.

"What about Dad?"

She glanced side to side, reached in, grabbed his hand and started walking him toward a door.

Because he didn't want to seem like a dick by pulling away, especially from some chick who'd just been dumped, he let her hold his hand for a few strides. Then he broke free to open the door and they walked outside.

He led her to an area in the quad where there weren't a lot of people and turned to her.

"Okay, what's happening?" he prompted.

She glanced around and requested, "Can we go somewhere and sit down?"

Occasionally, when his dad was working late or out of town on a job, Sabre had been alone with her, but only because they lived in the same house. They'd never intentionally spent time together and had not once been out somewhere together.

This was hella bizarre and it was giving him the creeps.

"Right, Myrna, I don't want to seem like an asshole, and I know you and my dad's breakup is new, but this is freaking me out."

She jumped toward him again and he braced. He also didn't feel a lot better when she grabbed onto his biceps and squeezed.

He didn't think she'd ever touched him.

Now, with the hand holding, she'd done it twice.

"I know this is weird. And I'm sorry it's weird," she said earnestly. But he sensed that was fake too. All of it. Including her being sorry. "And I'm sorry it's going to get worse, but I don't know where to take this."

"Take what?"

"I'm pregnant and your dad kicked me out because I want the baby, and he wants me to get an abortion."

Sabre didn't move.

"I mean, that's not okay," she said. "We made this baby together. And it wasn't like he didn't *know* I wanted to start a family. I told him. Then I fall pregnant and he's acting like he didn't know that, and he's pissed and shouting at me, and Sah, I wanted to work on us. But even if he was intent on being an asshole, he could give me a chance to get my shit together. I mean, I don't just have myself to consider. I have our baby now too. In the end, he threw my stuff in the backyard and told me to come get it or he was going to have Goodwill come and take it away."

His voice was strange when he asked, "Dad threw your stuff in the backyard?"

"Yeah, it was all over. It took me hours to collect it. And some of it was drenched because he threw it in the pool."

"And you're pregnant."

She ran her hands down his arms to catch both of his and smiled huge at him.

"Yes. I'm carrying your little baby brother or sister."

"And Dad wants you to get rid of it?"

She frowned and nodded.

"And you drove all the way down to Tucson to ambush me after my last class and tell me my father is a colossal dick because...why?" he asked.

Her head jerked.

Sabre pulled his hands from hers and took a step away. "My dad might not want another baby, but he wouldn't get pissed you wouldn't get rid of it and kick you out. And he would never throw your shit in the backyard."

She took a step toward him, but he just backed up again, so she stopped.

"Sah, I know you love your dad, but he did do that."

"And you're here telling me this because you think I can do something about it?"

"Whether your father likes it or not, I'm part of your family now."

"That's why you're right here, right now, to tell me that and not because you're pissed Dad broke up with you and you're doing crazy shit to get back at him."

Her mouth shut and her face got hard.

Christ.

She was doing seriously crazy-ass shit to get back at his dad.

"Are you even pregnant?" he asked.

"Yes," she snapped, too fast.

"You're not, are you?"

She jerked up her chin. "Yes, I am."

"Is it Dad's?"

149

Something eerie as fuck moved over her face, and she hissed, "I cannot even *believe* you asked me that."

"Myrna, are you pregnant?"

"Yes."

"Don't fucking lie to me," he bit. "You've cornered me, talking trash about my dad, and it isn't like this shit doesn't pan out one way or the other. You're either pregnant, or not. And if you are, it's either Dad's, or it isn't, and it's easy to find out of it isn't. In a few months, your jig will be up. So just tell me, are you dicking with me?"

"He threw my stuff in the backyard, Sabre."

"I don't believe that."

"It was boxed, but he put it out there and—"

There it was.

It was boxed.

She didn't get out when Dad told her, so he put her out.

That's a really different thing.

He shook his head, took another step away and said, "Listen, I am not in your shit with my father. This not only has fuck all to do with me, it's seriously gross. You got an issue with him, take it to him. But if you guys are done, you're just done. Get over it. Move on. Don't go all stalker, for fuck's sake."

"Your father doesn't like you to speak that way in front of women," she sniffed.

"Bet he'd like it less some crazy chick shows at his son's school and lays a bunch of sick lies on him," he returned.

She changed again, her face twisting, and she shared, "He *used* me."

"I'm done with this conversation. Goodbye, Myrna. Hope you get your shit together."

He moved away, but she dogged him, walking at his side. "I barely left, and he's getting back together with your mother. She was over at his house last night."

Sabre stopped dead and turned to her. "How do you know that?"

"That was *my* house, like, *a week* ago," she said, rather than tell him her crazy ass was staking out his father's place.

"It was never your house, Myrna. You always just lived there," he pointed out.

She looked like she'd been slapped.

But for fuck's sake, get with the program.

"Dad has a friend who's a cop," he warned her. "And I'm sure as shit telling Dad you're pulling this crap. I'm also telling his friend."

"He shouldn't have used me as his fucktoy."

"I don't remember him drugging you or locking you in the house," Sabre shot back. "Christ, get away from me and stay away from my dad."

Thankfully, she took a step from him, returning, "You're just like him."

"Yeah, I am. And thanks for the lesson. Because now, if I ever walk away from a woman I care about, and I hook up with some rebound piece who seems immune to understanding the situation even though it's all fucking around her, I need to cut her loose before she whacks out."

Something edged into her eyes that looked like sanity returning, but even so, she mumbled weakly, "He knew I loved him, and he used me anyway."

"You know what? If this is the shit you've been laying on him, if it was me, your stuff would be in the fucking pool."

She flinched—he was too pissed to care, which pissed him off even more, because he'd just learned he didn't like being a dick to girls since, until that moment, he'd avoided it—before she said in a super-hurt voice, "Fuck you, Sabre."

"Thanks, no," he replied.

She shot him a new look. One he didn't get, and he didn't try.

She then turned and walked away.

Sabre took a second to get his shit together before he jogged the eight blocks to his apartment.

He packed some stuff and had just enough time to hork back some trail mix and refill his water bottle before he had to throw his bag in his truck and drive to Manon's house to get her when she told him she'd be ready.

But when he went up and knocked on the door, he waited outside too long.

And when she answered, because Manon was his mom in all but looks and age, she said, "I'm running late. Hang tight. I'll be ready in a jiffy."

He walked in and was glad her roommates weren't there because he'd fucked one of them, and he wanted to fuck the other, and that was a hassle he didn't need right now.

It was also another lesson.

It seemed the signs were telling him he needed to quit playing and get his head out of his ass because he could end up with some *Fatal Attraction* bitch like Myrna if he didn't.

Shit.

He hoped this whole drama his mom and dad had going on that was just them telling their kids what their kids already knew—they were finally going to sort themselves out—didn't mean his mom was going to spend the night at his dad's house.

Yeah, sure, he wanted Mom back with Dad in all ways that could be for them both.

But Sah needed time alone with Remy so he could break it to him that Myrna had about fifteen screws loose.

He wasn't in the frame of mind for Manon's being-late bullshit, and he got pissed at Myrna again because she'd put him off his game.

Normally, if she chose the time, he'd show at least ten minutes late to pick her up, or if he was choosing it, he'd tell her fifteen minutes earlier.

This was something in high school Sah caught his dad doing when he was on the phone with Noel sorting something out with his mom.

"What's with the game playing? Why isn't she just ready on time?" Sah asked Remy when he got off the phone with Noel. "It's rude to be late. Mom's not rude in, like...*anything*. It's weird she's always late."

"Mark this, son," his dad had started his reply in a voice that Sabre always took notice of and paid extra attention to. "You'll find a woman and there will be things about her that don't mean anything. You'll think they do, but they don't. Don't blow them up and make them mean anything. Do not...*ever*...let her walk all over you. Much more importantly, do not...*ever*...walk all over her. But when something doesn't really mean anything, find a way to deal with it, and then let it go."

Having that memory, he should have realized shit was weird with his parents, because it seemed all of a sudden his dad started to get ticked about his mom being late.

Also having that memory, like he'd ever in a million years believe Remy would tell Myrna to have an abortion, and when she didn't, he threw her crap in the pool.

Jesus.

It might have been clear to just about anybody (except, obviously, Myrna) his dad and Myrna were not a love match and there wasn't a future for them. But his father had always been nice to her. Affectionate. Attentive. Only when she'd get weird about Manon would Remy cool off.

He just wasn't that guy.

Manon came out and the first thing he did was ask, "Got your phone charger?"

"Crap!" she cried then ran back to her room.

Not like there weren't a million of them at his mom's and dad's houses, but the way Manon used her phone, she'd probably run out of juice in his truck. And since Manon kept stealing his chargers, he didn't keep one in his truck anymore, so she'd be S.O.L.

He took her water bottle himself and filled it because she'd forget that too, and then they'd be stopping to grab her some water, which would be annoying.

When they left, he took her bag and threw it in his truck himself.

And when they were both in, she teased, "You are so Dad."

He knew she meant that he carried her bag.

"And?" he asked.

"Chivalry isn't dead," was all she said.

He didn't reply.

They were on the road awhile before he realized he wasn't hiding how creeped out he was because she asked, "You okay?"

"Fine."

"You have a weird vibe."

"I'm fine."

"Is it about Mom and Dad getting back together?"

"I'm beside myself with glee they're getting back together," he tried to joke. "So, again, *I'm fine.*"

"Whatever, weirdo."

Her saying that meant she wasn't buying his shit, but she was giving him space, which was good because he wasn't dragging her into this mess, and he needed his space right about now.

When they got to their dad's, Manon was all over Remy, and Sah went to give his mom a hug.

But after the greetings, there was more weirdness, because Mom and Dad were cooking together in Dad's kitchen like they'd done it a million times before.

They had.

Just not in Dad's kitchen.

Mom was pickling the onions and making the lime crema. Dad was flavoring the filets with taco seasoning.

Dad seemed tight.

Mom was being too loose.

All right.

This was not about them getting together, because first, it looked like they just were, and second, they would not be acting funny if that was it.

This was about something else.

Had Myrna pulled some shit with them too?

He'd barely gotten himself a beer before he figured all this out and he didn't delay any further in finding out what was up.

"What's going on?" he asked.

"Yves will be here soon. We'll talk then," Wyn said.

"You guys are being weird," he accused.

"They're not being weird," Manon put in. "They're being like they always used to be, just doing it at Dad's. You're the one who's being weird."

"For the last time, I'm not being weird," Sabre clipped.

Which, of course, bought him his dad's attention.

Remy didn't tell him off for talking in a mean tone to his sister, something his father did not tolerate (truth, though, was their dad didn't like that anytime, even when Yves and Sah were having words, but definitely Manon was a no go).

Remy just studied him.

Too closely.

"Just tell me," he said right to his dad. "Are you both okay?"

"We are both great," his father stated firmly.

Yup.

They were back together.

He grinned at his dad.

Remy grinned back.

For the first time since he walked out of class, Sabre chilled out.

Yves showed and it nearly made Sabre laugh.

Mom and Dad had said to be there by seven and they were all there before six.

That meant they all knew what this was about, and they were all ready for Dad's tacos, which was apparently shorthand for another family celebration.

It happened after Dad asked them to grab drinks then go into the living room, not the family room, to have a "chat."

And after they went there.

When his father started talking.

It was then, for the first time in his life, Sabre realized just how freaking lucky he was up until then with the hand life dealt him.

No, with the parents God gave him.

Because it didn't affect him too much his grandma was dying of cancer.

It might seem mean, but the woman wasn't very nice. She treated his mom like shit. She was bizarre with his father, all fawny and gross. And she said things to Manon that weren't okay.

It wasn't about being an old lady either. Their gramme, Mom's mom, had been the exact opposite in every way.

Colette Gastineau was just...like...a little psycho.

It was what came after.

The words coming from his dad's mouth.

The dislocated shoulder.

The broken arm.

The concussion.

The news his father had had a tux since he was six (like, what the fuck? How creepy was that?).

And more.

The way his parents were both standing, like the edge couldn't come off enough even for them to take a seat.

The way Mom was holding Dad's hand and you could see she was pumping it, like she was pumping love into him through their fingers.

The way Manon started weeping quietly and Yves had to grab hold of her and didn't let go.

"So," his mother finally took over, which was good, because Sabre was pretty sure his ears were bleeding, "I'll be calling school, Yves, to sort things for you. Sah, Manon, you need to talk to your professors. We're all flying out Thursday, mid-morning, and returning Monday afternoon. You can be back in classes on Tuesday."

"'Kay, Mom," Yves said.

But Sabre was looking at his father.

"All this shit went down, what did your dad do?" he asked.

"Dad worked and was away from home a lot," Remy answered.

"So, like, he didn't know his wife was beating the crap out of his son?" Sabre demanded.

Remy tilted his head to the side and said quietly, "He knew, Sah."

Sabre looked at his mother.

Oh yeah.

What was on her face was in his heart.

That's how he felt.

Black as pitch.

That bitch was a bitch.

But that guy? His grandfather? Knowing this shit was going down and doing fuck all?

What in the absolute fuck?

"Manon, honey, are you okay?" Remy asked his girl.

"Yeah, she's okay, because her father treats her like gold," Sabre answered for his sister.

Remy's gaze shot to Sah, so did Wyn's, but he pushed out of Dad's kickass sofa that Manon said the leather felt like "butter."

"And I'm okay because, even when I fucked up and had that party when you guys were in New York, you were pissed at me, but you were cool to me," he went on. "I mean, you didn't break my arm or shove me down a flight of stairs or anything."

"Sah—" Remy started.

"And Yves is okay because he had the weirdest coming out ever, seeing as his dad got up in his shit not because he was gay, but because Yves thought he might get up in his shit because he was gay," Sabre kept going.

"Son—" Remy tried again.

"But *you've never* been okay because your dad was a motherfucker and your mom is a bitch," Sabre finished.

"Don't call your grandmother a bitch," Remy rumbled.

"*She beat you!*" Sabre thundered, and he didn't like how the room got all still after he shouted, but he wasn't done. "She treats Mom like shit. She says crap to Manon that is not all right. And the woman beat you. No. Hunh-unh." He shook his head. "I'm not going there to say goodbye. I'll go and tell her I'm glad she's dying, but I'm not going there to tell that woman goodbye like I give a shit she lives or dies."

"You will not tell her you're glad she's dying, but you will go there, Sabre," Wyn declared. "Because every single one of us is going to be at your father's side when *he* goes there."

That shut Sabre up.

"Sah, come over here, bro," Manon called, and when Sabre looked at her, she had a hand reached his way.

"Yeah, bud, come over here," Yves urged.

He didn't go over there.

He looked at his father.

"How did you do it?" he asked.

"I think Dad's had enough," Manon said. "Please, Sah?"

But Remy asked, "Do what?"

"That shit, it's supposed to be, like, inherited. How'd you do it? You weren't like that with us."

"I found your mother," Remy answered.

"Then why'd you walk out on her?" Sabre demanded.

"Sabre!" Manon snapped.

"Honey, I think—" his mom started.

But Sah wasn't surprised even a little bit when his dad answered.

"Because I had been conditioned from a very young age to take special care of the women in my life. And that was ingrained so deep, I didn't realize your mother could take care of herself. That doesn't mean she didn't need me, or I don't need her. But I was completely unprepared for an evolved, functioning, mentally and emotionally healthy woman to be in my life. It was fine when she was at home taking care of you kids, because that meant I was taking care of all of you, including your mom. And it was fine when she was starting out, because I made more money and I still felt like it was me giving her the life she deserved. And it isn't okay, but I couldn't handle it when she started to become successful, not because she might overshadow me or make more money. But because it meant I wasn't taking care of her. It was messed up and wrong, but that was where my mind went. And that was why I left."

"We're talking, though," Wyn said quickly. "And we have more to discuss, but right now, with what's happening with your grandmother, we need to rally around your dad."

Like his mom didn't say anything, his eyes still locked on Sabre, his dad said, "It was wrong, Sah. I shouldn't have left. I regret it more than I can explain."

Oh yeah.

He already knew that.

And what his dad said made sense, but he wasn't on that.

He was stuck on something else.

"She was messed up and he just left you to that."

He was talking about his grandparents.

Remy knew that.

"Yes, Sabre, he did," his dad confirmed.

"I'm gonna go because Mom's right. You aren't gonna be around them without us around you," Sabre decided. "And I'll do my best to be cool with her because she's soon gonna be dead. But Pépé better stay the fuck away from me."

"That's fair," Remy murmured.

"I love you, you know that, Dad? You're a great fucking dad."

He heard Manon make one of her crying noises and felt his mom get close, but he didn't tear his gaze off his father.

"I know that, Sah."

"And a long time from now, when you die, it's gonna fucking *wreck me.*"

He wasn't standing a few feet away from his father anymore.

Suddenly, he was pressed up to his dad with his face in his dad's neck, his father's hand wrapped around the back of his neck and an arm curled around his back.

Remy's voice was gruff when he said, "I know."

Sabre's voice was totally fucked up when he said, "Fuck those fuckers."

"Son," Remy murmured.

The dislocated shoulder.

The broken arm.

The concussion.

Shit.

Fuck.

He was gonna cry.

His dad helped him do it, holding him with his face shoved in his dad's neck so no one would see.

The rest gave them time, but then they all piled on, because that was the Gastineau family, and they were in a group hug.

But Dad was the kind of dad he was.

So he kept Sabre's face shoved in his neck.

Then his mom said something bossy, and his sister said something goofy, and Yves said he was going out to start up the grill (which meant he was hungry), and they all drifted away, leaving Sabre with Remy.

One thing he knew, right then, he couldn't tell Dad about Myrna.

So he'd have to deal with that himself.

Somehow.

He pulled away, but Remy didn't let him go too far, keeping his hand at Sah's neck.

"Best son a man could ask for," Remy whispered.

"I bet you were better."

Remy's lips thinned, and Sabre decided right then he needed to rein in the Gastineau/Byrne hothead they both gave him and learn when to keep his mouth shut.

"I just hate that was your life, Dad."

"I got that, Sah. But none of what happened to me was near as bad as telling you all about it. Now it's over. We're gonna have tacos. We're going to deal with what happens in New Orleans as a family. And when we come back, I'll need to figure out a way to talk your mother into maintaining two houses. Because she's never giving up that bathroom, closet or kitchen, and no way I'm giving up my wine and poker rooms. So we're gonna have to be like Scottish royalty and spend summers in one house then go down the street a mile and spend winters in another."

That was the first time in hours Sabre laughed.

Better, his dad laughed with him.

"ARE YOU FUCKING KIDDING ME?" Yves nearly shouted.

"Baby, calm down," Theo muttered.

Tacos were consumed. Mom and Manon had gone home. His dad had gone to bed. Yves had stayed and asked Theo over.

Now they were in Sabre's room, which had its own full bath and a little space off it that had a wild, curved couch, a space-age curved chair and a seventy-inch flat screen.

Theo and Yves were sprawled on the couch, proving it was quality, since their combined bulk meant no couch could be seen and the thing hadn't collapsed.

Sah was in the space-age chair.

They all had beers, and since Remy knew they were drinking, he'd given Theo a look and said, "You stay if you've had too much, but you sleep on the couch."

Like either of those two would go there with Dad close by. They'd gone at each other when they got drunk when they were down in Tucson with Sah, and they were loud. And since they were the ones being loud, they had to know they were.

Now, he had to deal with Yves, who was usually so laidback, if he didn't look like Dad and had come straight out of Mom, Sah would wonder if he was switched at birth.

But he'd forgotten that, if Yves got pissed, hell was paid.

"No, I'm not, and keep quiet, dude. Serious," Sabre hissed. "We're far from Dad, but he's got dad hearing and you know it."

Yves's voice was lower when he asked, "She said Dad told her to abort a kid?"

"That and all the rest I told you, yeah," Sabre confirmed. "Obviously, with Grandma dying, I gotta talk to Bill because I can't tell Dad."

"You can't talk to Bill because he'd totally tell Dad," Yves refuted.

"Not if I tell him Dad's dealing with his mom dying," Sabre returned.

"He will, Sah. Because she's watching this house and that shit is creepy AF," Yves shot back. "But her somehow figuring out your schedule and driving all the way down to Tucson to be outside your class?"

"Whole new level," Theo chimed in.

"Bill will freak, and then Bill will tell Dad, and then Bill will be all over it," Yves said.

"Okay then, until we get back from New Orleans, we have to keep Mom on radar," Sabre declared.

"Word," Theo agreed.

"I'll keep track of Manon just in case Myrna loses another screw, but Dad can take care of himself. That woman can't get near Mom. First, because she's loopy as all fuck. But second, Dad would lose his mind if Myrna started fucking with Mom," Sabre finished laying it out.

"I'll find time to swing by here when you're with your mom," Theo offered, looking at Yves. "See if she's in her car watching. Take pictures of her. Note the time. Shit like that, which the cops will need if Coach eventually has to take it to them."

"Thanks, babe, you're awesome," Yves said to Theo.

"If my dad had a creeper, you'd do the same for me," Theo replied.

"Count on it," Yves confirmed.

They gave each other looks that made Sah want to gag, and since they had the important shit sorted, he got up and said, "You two have fifteen minutes to feel each other up while I drag my feet and get us more beer. But I'm timing it, so you better do that too. Because I won't make this offer again if I come back and see something I cannot unsee."

Theo looked to Yves. "You have the best brother ever."

Yves did not look to Theo.

He kept his eyes on Sabre and ordered, "Go get the beer."

Sah shot his baby bro a grin.

Then he seriously dragged his feet getting them beer because he even more seriously did not want to see something he could not unsee.

Hell, he'd been to a party once where he'd caught Manon making out with some dude and it put him off chicks for at least a week.

Also because he was the best brother ever, he got into his phone game.

And gave them twenty minutes.

CHAPTER 16

Play

Remy

S unday evening, Remy sat at his piano playing "Clair de lune" while Wyn sat curled into the corner of his couch, reading a book.

On the one hand, he loved this. It was peaceful, and he knew how much Wyn enjoyed his playing, specifically this piece. It was her favorite.

On the other hand, with all their kids gone, the third family supper in a row consumed, and Wyn firmly establishing herself in his life and his home, he'd prefer to be doing other things with his wife.

He watched her lips tip up softly and called, "Good book?"

She looked up at him.

"It is, but I was remembering *The Right Stuff*."

Remy didn't miss a note, even if he remembered that too.

She had to know he did, but she laid it out anyway.

"We watched that movie at your place in New York, and during the fan dance scene, I started crying. You teased me. I said I'd never heard that song and it was the most beautiful song to ever touch my ears. You paused the movie and got right up, went to your piano and played it by memory. I was so impressed I could barely stand myself."

He kept playing, now smiling, as he reminded her, "I got that, since, when I was done, you tackled me, and we had sex under the piano."

Her face grew soft. "You had that tiny loft. A bed, a couch, a TV. All of that barely fit because you had a grand piano."

161

He did.

Because his mother bought it for him, saying, "Uprights are common, Remy."

He looked down at his hands moving on the keys.

Wyn kept reminiscing. "So when I moved in, we were totally scrunched."

That memory was a load better.

Only when he finished the piece did he turn back to her, and this time he did it fully shifting his body on the bench to face her.

"What's going on with Manon and her guy?" he asked and watched her head tick at the change of topic.

But she went with his flow because she was determined to go with his flow because she was determined to treat him like he was china now that she knew what his childhood had been like.

He loved her sitting right there.

He'd bleed before she was again anywhere but with him.

But that shit was beginning to piss him off.

"She tried to reschedule their date for last night, but he said he had something on. According to Manon, he's playing games. Apparently, he was upset she cancelled the plans they had Friday night. She said two can dance that tango. So instead of going home yesterday, they stayed until today, because they also had brunch plans for this morning."

They did stay, with Sabre, oddly, having no qualms falling in with her plans to the point he horned in on Wyn and Manon going shopping yesterday, declaring, "I need new jeans," when Remy couldn't remember the last time his oldest son had gone to a mall. This to the point he gave his sister money and a shopping list to do for him for Christmas, and since Manon could happily live in a mall, she had no problem fulfilling his orders.

And because Sah went, Yves went too.

Remy did not. He wanted to give them time with their mom, he had a delivery he needed to be home for, and like his eldest, he hated the mall.

It wasn't shopping, he just wasn't a crowd person.

"Did Sah get new jeans?" Remy asked.

Wyn nodded.

"Did you tell Manon she needs to dump this guy?" he asked.

Wyn's lips tipped up again. "You think your daughter needs to dump every guy."

"Only when she dates putzes. And this guy is a putz, if he gets in a snit when it's more important she be with her family."

"According to you, they're all putzes."

"Because they've all been putzes."

Her smile came back.

"Do you think Sabre is acting strange?" Remy asked.

The smile went away, and she nodded.

"Yes. For Sah, he's being..." she looked like she was searching for a word before she found it, "overprotective of Manon, when Manon is handling learning what happened to you a lot better than I expected."

"He's giving me a break, or he thinks he is."

"Sorry?"

"He thinks I need to deal with Mom dying and he knows, usually, I'm overprotective of Manon. So he's taking that on because he feels I need to have time to deal and not worry about my daughter. And he made a show of making sure I knew he was on the job."

"We've got good kids, Remy," she said softly.

"The minute she was out, I bought new mattresses," he announced. "They were delivered yesterday while you and the kids were shopping."

That made his wife look like she was going to bolt.

Since she didn't, he went on, "Even so, I hadn't slept with her in that bed in weeks."

"Remy—"

"Because I fucked her, are you never going to touch me that way again, Wyn?"

"I think maybe we should get into this when—"

"She was my first, and only, after you."

Color came into her face, and yeah.

He was getting pissed off.

The worst part about it?

He had no right to.

Not about that.

He'd done that to himself.

Regrettably, it didn't make him any less pissed off.

"So you had a first but not an only," he guessed, feeling that knife sink into his gut.

"I think maybe this is something we should both let fade away," she suggested.

He didn't take her suggestion.

"How many were there? One? Two? Five?" he pushed.

"Remy." That time his name was a warning.

He wasn't sure ever in their lives together he'd heeded one of her warnings.

She also never heeded his.

And this time, it was no different.

"I know it's on me. I'll have to live until my dying day knowing I made it so you took another man...or men. But since you did, I don't think it's fair you make me pay for having another woman."

"This isn't about being fair, Remy, or making you pay. It isn't about her either. It isn't about...the others."

Fuck.

Others.

Plural.

Fuck.

"It's about me seeing to you," she finished.

"Seeing to me?" he asked.

"When you hurt...like that...you want affection, not sex."

What was she talking about?

"Sorry?"

"When you get hurt, when your feelings hurt, or you get sensitive or emotional..."

Jesus Christ.

"...you like to cuddle and get in your head playing piano with me close," she concluded.

"This is one of the major reasons I did not want to tell you about my parents," he growled.

"What?" she asked.

"I don't want to *cuddle*, Wyn. I'd much rather be buried in you than buried in Debussy. *You* like me to play. *You* like to cuddle. I do it for *you*."

"Do you...not like to play? Does it...remind you of your mom?"

"For fuck's sake, Wyn!" he exploded, standing. "I'm not some wuss-ass bundle of fragility you have to coddle just because my mother was fucked up. Every piece of my life is not about her, every part of me is not about her."

She uncurled her legs on the couch to sit straight, but she didn't stand up.

And she said pacifyingly, "All right, honey."

This, of course, made him angrier. "And don't do it now, for fuck's sake."

"You use the F-word a lot when you won't let your sons do it," she remarked.

A diversion tactic.

He wasn't diverted.

"That's because you let me be just who I am and I have a foul mouth, and yeah, maybe that's because my mother used to smack it when I got older and started to defy her. But that still doesn't mean everything about me is about her."

She looked stricken.

And it gutted him.

"She used to smack your—"

"*Jesus Christ, let it go, Wyn!*" he roared.

She closed her mouth.

"You do see me standing right here?" He slapped his hand on his chest to emphasize his question.

"Yes, Remy, I see you," she said gently.

He had a bad taste in his mouth as he spat, "Don't be docile and meek because you don't think I can handle shit."

She shut up again.

"I'm not exactly a hundred-pound weakling," he pointed out.

"No, you're not," she agreed.

"I had a growth spurt at thirteen, started filling out at fifteen, but before then, all that shit stopped mainly because she pushed me into a wall when I was eleven, and I got ticked. So I pushed her back."

Her eyes got round.

"She lost her shit, dissolved onto a chair, howling with crocodile tears, asking me what kind of son she raised and threatening to tell Dad I put my hands on her. My response was, 'Please, Mom, tell him.' She read that threat for what it was, shut shit down immediately, gave me a good look and realized that particular reign of terror was over."

"That particular one?"

"You don't go from taking all your perceived woes out on your child to being a functional parent. She found a different way to take her shit out on me, and I became her recalcitrant son. I didn't listen. I had no respect for my mother. I wasn't polite. I didn't love her, or I didn't love her enough. It was relentless. And that was almost worse. Sometimes, I wished she'd go back to hitting me, because it seemed I could never do anything right. No matter how hard I tried, I couldn't make her happy. I couldn't settle her down. I couldn't be what she needed me to be to make her normal, to make her love me."

Wyn was now pale, her gaze wounded.

But she wanted this, said she needed it, and Remy was done with it. He wanted it over, he wanted them to move on from it, so he had to give it to her.

All of it.

Thus, Remy didn't stop.

"After I got older, after it sunk in he wasn't going to come to my rescue, and the end was in sight because I was in high school, I could drive and I had things out of the house I could do to escape her, friends I could be with who made me feel normal and made me realize I was, but she wasn't, it became a self-fulfilling prophecy for her. I didn't listen. I had no respect for her. And to her, I was not polite. I put up with her because she was my mother, but I didn't like her all that much and I wasn't shy about behaving like I didn't."

"But, do you like to play piano?"

For fuck's sake.

"I love to play," he replied. "I love that my kids play. I love that my sons are better than me. I love music. And I love that my wife thinks it hot that, even if I like all kinds of music, if given a choice, I don't turn on rock, I listen to classical."

"Okay," she said quietly.

"I'm not an idiot, Wyn."

Her back went up on that one.

Visibly.

"I never said you were," she retorted, and there was a snap to it.

Finally.

"I had friends," he carried on. "They had parents. And absolutely, I worked my ass off to try to earn her love, then try to make her version of love stop and shift to one that didn't hurt. I did the same to try to figure out the son my father needed so I could be that so he wouldn't go away. But I saw how my friends were. How their parents were. I realized eventually that what I had was not that. Even if I didn't understand it wasn't healthy, I did understand it wasn't normal and I came to understand it wasn't about me. Obviously, with what happened with us, it dug deeper than I thought. But theoretically, I got it."

"Right."

"So I'm not fucking fragile. I get it. I got it a long time ago."

"Right."

That was not convincing.

He understood why.

"The way I blew us up was not conscious, Wyn," he bit out. "If I knew what I was doing, I never would have fucking done it."

"So you're over it...but you're not over it?"

"You never get over it."

"Remy, you've got to understand I'm not in a place where I'll ever understand," she said carefully.

He loved that for her.

But they had to get past this.

"Do you know the man you married?" he asked.

"No."

Okay.

Yeah.

Nope.

Not pissed anymore.

Furious.

"Are you shitting me?" he asked.

That was when she stood because that was when she lost it.

"Remy! I just found out you were significantly abused in every manner that could be *three days ago*. And I've been with you a *quarter of a century*."

"Yes, and it was my choice not to tell you," he replied.

"It was mine to have."

Was she serious?

He shook his head. "Oh no it was not, baby."

She asked his question. "Are you serious?"

"It's mine to give, and only mine to give. And I have to say, I'm not feeling it I was forced to give it. Especially right now."

"Forced?" she whispered.

"That's not on you," he assured. "That's on Mom."

"You cannot know that you're not making a lick of sense, but trust me, *you are not making a lick of sense*."

With strained patience, he explained, "If her shit didn't cause me to do something I shouldn't have, and I didn't find out the woman was dying in the middle of reuniting with you, you never would have known."

"I never would have known," she breathed.

Again, wounded.

"Wyn, I told you I hated that I had to tell you *when I was telling you*."

"Two," she bit off.

"What?" he asked.

"Two. I slept with two men after you."

Remy stood completely still.

"Is that not yours to know, Remy?" she asked. "It's mine, I didn't really want it, but it's mine. I also didn't want to tell you. However, you wanted to know, so I told you. Is that the same thing?"

"Right now, you're throwing your fucks in my face?" he asked with deceptive quiet.

"The fact I had those fucks is not on you, honey, they're on your mom," she returned.

Christ, he hated it when they were arguing, and she was right.

"*She* ended my marriage," Wyn continued. "*She* took you away from me. And you don't think I have the right to know why?"

"I told you," he reminded her.

"But you didn't want to."

"*It hurts you!*" he thundered. "Jesus, Wyn, *how are you not getting this?*"

"You're not fragile, Remy. *I'm not either!*" she shouted that last.

"*I know!*" he bellowed.

"*Then stop behaving like I am!*" she shrieked. "I am not her!"

"*I know that too!*" he shouted.

"Then don't act insulted when I say I don't know you, Remy. For God's sake, I just found out you don't like to cuddle."

Jesus fucking Christ.

He looked to the ceiling.

"What now?" she snapped.

He looked to her. "I like to cuddle, Wyn. I love being close to you. But think about it."

"Is this another quiz?" she hissed.

Right, it sucked, but that was valid.

"When did we do that and it didn't end up with us going at each other?" he asked, but not to make her answer, because he immediately told her. "When your dad died, and two years later, when your mom followed him."

"You adored them."

"Yes, I did. But not near as much as you."

Light dawned, he watched it.

"You were comforting me?" she asked, like she couldn't believe it.

"Baby, *your parents died*. Outside bed and outside anything to do with our kids, what's your favorite thing that I do?"

Her gaze went to the piano and then back to him.

"Play," she whispered.

"Play," he agreed.

"Oh my God, Noel was right."

"Sorry?"

"He told me I needed to pounce on you."

This meant she told Noel about him.

Remy was not ticked about that. She told Noel everything.

Therefore, he didn't get into that.

He confirmed, "Yeah, he was right."

She tilted her head to the side. "Do you want me to pounce on you, um...*now?*"

"No."

"No?"

He took the five strides separating them and held her face by her jaw.

"No," he repeated.

Then he dipped his head and kissed her.

God.

Yes.

Wyn.

It had been too long, and they were them, so it went from a touch on the lips to serious tongue, to her tearing at his shirt in maybe twenty seconds.

He pulled away to yank it off, but he didn't when she asked, "Is your bedroom really sunken?"

Remy didn't answer.

He didn't make a mental note to finally give her a full tour of his house either.

He grabbed her hand and dragged her to his bedroom.

Down two steps, whirling her in front of him, backing her to the bed, then taking her to it by falling into and *onto* her.

That was far as he got with "pouncing."

Wyn took over with mouth and hands and nails, eventually rolling him to his back.

This could be about her giving him what he needed in a sensitive, emotional time.

If it was, he could not give fewer fucks.

His wife was right there with her lush body, mass of hair, gorgeous face, talented mouth and hands, and the sting of her nails.

So he took it.

But when she was getting them both naked and was down to her bra and pulling off her jeans, he lent a hand and yanked off his own.

She then moved to climb on his hard cock.

That was when Remy took over, grabbed her hips and pulled her to a different location.

His wife on his tongue for the first time in years, he ground her down on his face.

She helped, rocking against him, her low noises pulsing through his dick.

No matter what, no matter when, from the first time to the last before this when they went at each other in the foyer of their house, she was like this.

She never covered herself to hide her nudity.

She never stole glances to make sure he liked what she was doing.

She was completely into it.

Him.

His.

Everything she did, he got off on.

Everything he did, made her soar.

Not once had it been awkward and hesitant, done by habit, going through the motions.

They'd always been as they were right now.

He could live on the taste of her, the feel of her pussy.

And she could ride his face or take his cock until she stopped breathing.

"Baby, baby," she whispered urgently. "You."

She was almost there.

He pulled her off, tossing her to her back, and rolled onto her.

Her hair all over his bed...

Fuck.

Fuck.

He was feeling less emotionally bruised and sensitive by the second.

Holding his eyes, even if hers were dazed, she opened her legs and hooked them around his thighs.

Not breaking their gaze, he took his cock in hand and guided it to her.

"Hurry," she breathed.

He slid home.

When she closed around him, that was when he closed his eyes.

Wyn glided both her hands up his back and into his hair, and Remy tracked every centimeter and committed it to memory.

He opened his eyes.

"Missed you, Remy," she whispered.

He felt the sting, the wet hit his eyes, but he didn't kiss her to hide it.

He moved inside her, she moved with him. Their breath started coming faster, together. Their movements started to get more urgent, together. They held each other's gazes throughout, and he would have liked for them to come together, but he'd eaten her, so she was closer and got there before him.

It was not a sacrifice, he got to watch.

Then he was able to give her the same.

When he came down, that was when he kissed her again.

And he did not pull out when he shifted to nuzzling her neck. He was going to stay inside as long as his cock remained hard enough to keep him there.

He smelled her perfume.

Van Cleef & Arpels *Bois D'Iris.*

It was in his nose and would be all over his sheets.

He had his Wyn back.

"It's a lot to ask, but I don't want you sleeping anywhere else but beside me until we figure this all out and get married again."

"Are we getting married again?" she asked while drawing patterns on the skin of his back.

He heard the lilt of her teasing, but he still lifted his head and made plain how unfunny he thought that was.

She didn't care.

"I like the idea of living in sin."

"We're getting remarried. It's going to be ridiculously lavish, everything you ever wanted, completely obnoxious, and you're putting your old rings back on your finger, but I'm getting you an eternity band to add to it. That Harry Winston one you saw in New York that last time we were there and tried not to let me see you liked it. The emerald cut one."

"Wow."

He'd had Lisa check the price when they got back home.

So...

"Yeah, wow."

"No, I mean, yes, wow, to the Winston but also wow, you have this all planned out."

"Have I ever fucked around?" he asked.

"No," she answered. "Though, honey, I'm all for lavish, but you know me well enough to know I would never be involved in anything obnoxious."

"I'm just saying, you'll get what you want."

And it wasn't like she didn't before.

But her parents insisted on paying for everything, and because they did, Wyn adjusted what she wanted to what they could afford.

It was a beautiful, amazing day, even if Colette minced through the affair like she had to be wary just in case they didn't clean up all the hog droppings.

But he knew his wife then and now.

If she'd had the money, it would have been vastly different.

"I know what you're saying," she said softly.

He moved them beyond that. "So start thinking about it because we'll need to do it before we get close to Sabre's graduation. I don't want to steal his thunder."

"You're certainly taking a lot for granted after one very nice orgasm."

"Just very nice?"

"Yes, though it was more like *very* nice. However, I have a feeling the next one is going to be better."

He made a noise that was a lot like a growl, which meant his wife reciprocated with a purr.

Yeah, the next one was going to be fucking *awesome*.

"Christmas," he said.

171

Her eyes got big. "Like, you mean, for a wedding?"

"Yes."

"I am obviously going to need to be married in Oscar de La Renta."

He grinned. "Obviously."

"It would take a small miracle to have a gown ready for December."

"Then New Year's."

Her eyes narrowed. "Remy, that's only an extra week."

"Good thing Monday is a workday, and you can get on it."

Her mind wandered, he saw it in her face. "This would be a perfect challenge for Noel."

"Baby, right here."

She focused on him again.

"Sleeping by my side?" he prompted.

And that was when he saw her face get soft, she cupped his cheek, and she whispered, "Just try to stop me."

Fuck.

Fuck.

He felt his stomach twist, his throat get tight, and his voice was hoarse when he said, "If I could go back—"

"Stop it, Remy."

"I hate I hurt you."

"I know. I hate it too, and part of that is knowing how much you hate it. But it's over."

"I'll never—"

She shifted her hand, so her fingers were over his lips.

"The hurt will never die if I have to live the rest of my life watching you suffer for it. *It's over*, Remy. There's more to figure out, but we'll figure it out. Now," she moved her hand, "kiss me before I go clean up."

"I love you, Wyn."

"I love you too, Remy."

"I know," he whispered. "Fuck, do I know."

After he said that, he kissed her.

But she didn't go clean up.

He went to the bathroom to get a washcloth to do it for her.

And after that, they discovered they both were right.

The next go was even better.

CHAPTER 17

French

Wyn

"When Pépé kicks it and we inherit his fortune, we're buying a plane so we can take family vacations like the Kardashians," Manon decreed.

"If I ever do anything like a Kardashian, shoot me, bro," Sabre declared.

"Only if you make me the same promise," Yves replied.

"Double suicide it is," Sabre agreed.

I looked between the front seats of our rented Denali to the back where my two big boys were crunching my girl in between, and I watched them solidify their agreement with a fist bump.

They were being funny, even if it disturbed me greatly that Manon was cold-bloodedly spending her inheritance before she got it.

But I wasn't surprised since she'd been confronted by the enormity of it considering Remy had just driven into the back drive of his parent's home in New Orleans. A drive that had been paved in bricks in the 1910s. A drive, Remy had told me, that replaced the dual line carriageway that used to be there when it became clear automobiles weren't going away.

The residents and guests staying at the house used that ingress, also using the stately porticoed door to the side for entry into the home. Other guests

173

used the front door that faced the veranda at an angle to the side. An odd arrangement, that Remy explained when I'd asked after it.

"It's about the windows, baby," he'd said.

And when he'd shifted my perspective, I saw he was right.

Because beyond the regal white columns, past the graceful hanging lantern, if you didn't get stuck on the manicured, potted, conical miniature evergreens dotting the porch among the curlicued wrought iron furniture, the fifteen-foot-high windows flanked by their narrow black shutters gave more than a glimpse of the opulence within.

Therefore, if that large, two-story home with its front veranda, top balcony and wide yard of velvet green skirted by a black-painted iron fence and trimmed by bird baths and meticulously tended greenery wasn't in-your-face shouting, *The people inside are loaded!*, a view through the windows did.

Colette was an only child of two only children. Thus, Colette had inherited her family's estate. Something they'd managed to build even if it had been 1883 when her great-grandfather left the plantation he could no longer maintain as he'd lost his free labor of enslaved human beings. So, he'd sold it, moved to the city, and made a second fortune in printing.

However, that fortune took a turn for the worse when Colette's father died of polio when she was little.

Since she was too young, and her mother didn't feel any need to keep her eye on things, the printing business suffered. This was due to the fact Mrs. Cormier left it in the hands of men who preferred to siphon money from her and her cossetted daughter, rather than keeping them in the style to which they were accustomed.

It took years, but that business eventually went bankrupt.

Even though Colette was of age when that happened and had a degree in English from Tulane, neither of them considered procuring paid employment.

Therefore, Colette and her mother were barely hanging on when Guillaume entered the picture.

I had no idea why they chose to make their official home in New Orleans rather than in Toulouse, where Guillaume's family was from, and where his family's business, which centered around shipping, was still maintained.

I just knew that Guillaume swept into Colette Cormier's life like a tornado, dashing her into a whirlwind of international travel, parties on yachts, gambling in Monaco, frolicking on the Riviera, and turning around the Southern belle's drooping fortunes, including spending tens of thousands on a complete restoration of her family home.

The inside, even I had to admit, was a dream of peaches, creams and pale yellows, greens, pinks and blues with ornate furniture, heavy, perfectly swagged draperies and Aubusson rugs.

The sitting room (my favorite, outside—something else I didn't like to admit—Colette and Guillaume's bedroom, which was impeccable) had a ballerina-pink wall that depicted a hand-painted mural of a grove of trees.

What I had never understood, even before I knew how his parents treated him, was how Remy grew up in that place.

It was gorgeous.

But it was like a museum.

I also knew, before what I'd recently learned, that Remy didn't have an emotional attachment to the home he grew up in, and he had plans for it when it was his.

He'd told me years ago he intended to sell the house and donate the proceeds to the EJI.

"Far too little, far too late," he'd muttered. "But that money should take care of the people who earned the man the means to build that house in the first place."

Needless to say, with three astute children who knew they had deep roots in Southern upper-class society, they'd asked the question, and Remy and I'd had an uncomfortable conversation with them to explain that they were the descendants of slave owners.

Their reactions told me not one of them would make a peep when Remy sold his childhood home, part of their legacy, and invest it in a better legacy, justice.

But now, I had less unpleasant things to turn my mind to.

They still weren't pleasant.

This was because Guillaume had come to stand outside the side door.

He was tall and straight and remarkably handsome, even in his eighties.

And it was an odd sensation to intensely dislike a man who looked so like three I adored.

But there it was.

"You good, Sah?" Remy murmured before he opened his door.

"I won't tackle him and punch him in the face, if that's what you're asking," Sabre answered.

My eyes again darted to the back.

"He's good, Dad," Manon threw in, her gaze on me.

She nodded to me.

She'd keep her brother in line.

But I knew the children I'd raised, and I knew she wouldn't have to.

He might not ask the man for a game of catch, but Sabre would be civil.

I still nodded back to my girl because she was being sweet, looking after her dad.

We got out, and although Guillaume came down the steps and allowed his fond gaze to linger on all of us, his arms didn't open to anyone but Remy.

I felt my hands clench into fists.

Remy walked into those arms, and that was when I felt my daughter's fingers close around my tightly balled ones.

I shifted so I was holding her hand.

Perhaps noting that Remy did little more than pat his father on the back before he started to pull away, he wasn't going to push it with an audience, so Guillaume let him go and turned to me.

"*Ma belle* Wyn," he murmured, his voice throaty, his eyes soft with shimmers of wet, openly and unabashedly overcome that Remy and I were back together.

"Guillaume," I replied, letting my daughter go and walking to him.

I kissed his cheek and suffered my own hug.

He then turned right to Manon like Sabre nor Yves were standing there and gave her the biggest smile imaginable.

"And how is the most beautiful girl in the world?" he asked.

"I'm good, Pépé," she muttered, jumping forward to give him a quick hug and a peck on the cheek.

I stiffened when he corrected her, because when he did that, it always rankled me.

"*Je vais bien,*" he said. "*Où ça va, merci,* Pépé, *et toi?*"

He was constantly on all the kids to speak French (especially Manon), something they were all haltingly fluent in because their father spoke it and we'd been to France often.

"*Ça va,*" she forced out trying not to show she was forcing it out. "*Et toi?*"

"*Bien, ma chérie. Surtout maintenant que tu es là,*" he replied. (Good, my darling. Especially now that you're here.) Then he turned to the boys. "*Mes beaux petit-fils!*" he cried.

"Pépé," Yves greeted, coming forward to get his brief hug before popping back.

"Granddad," Sabre said, and Guillaume's head ticked because he was stringent about being Pépé, or if necessary, but it was not preferred, Grand-père.

Their hug was swift and awkward, and Guillaume's gaze was on Remy when it was over.

"We've had a long flight. We need to get in and settled, Dad," Remy made a pass at explaining his son's behavior.

But now I had an understanding why Guillaume demanded his grandchildren use his native language, one that was not native to them, when they referred to him, and Remy steadfastly called him "Dad."

It was the same insolence that Sabre just demonstrated.

I wondered if Remy ever called him Père or Papa.

"*Bien sûr*," Guillaume murmured. "There are no surprises. The boys are in Velvet. You and Wyn are in Silk. And you, my darling," he turned to Manon, "are in Matelassé."

I clenched my teeth because the Velvet Room was a large room with a king-sized bed, and it was the only dark, clearly masculine room in the house.

It had been Remy's, and the painstakingly treated walls that were awash in violet and shimmering champagne were gorgeous, as were the drapes, which were acres of iridescent purple satin with a green sheen. The armchairs were covered in a bright blue-purple velvet, with the bed covered in black of the same fabric.

But there was one bed.

And my sons were no longer boys. They were grown men who hadn't slept in the same bed since they were, if memory served, in single digits.

They probably wouldn't mind.

But they weren't children anymore and shouldn't be treated like they were.

"Thanks, Pépé," Manon replied.

"Boys, get the bags, yeah?" Remy ordered, hitting the button on the fob to open the back of the truck.

The boys moved to the car and Guillaume looked to Remy.

"It's getting late, and your mother isn't feeling sprightly. But she wishes to see you, and once you refresh, she's waiting for you in the mural room."

Remy nodded, and as Sabre and Yves got close, he said, "One of you take the Gold Room."

"Remy, this room hasn't been prepared," Guillaume stated.

"If it isn't, I can put sheets on a bed, Dad. So can my boys. But my sons are grown and they're not sharing a bed."

"They're brothers," Guillaume pointed out.

"They're *grown men* and they love each other, but it's not cool to make them share a goddamn bed," Remy bit back. "If I had two grown daughters, I wouldn't ask them to share a bed either. If there's space to have, I'd want them to have their own space. And there's space to have. Right now, would you share a bed with Uncle Luc?"

"Of course not," Guillaume hissed.

"Well?" Remy asked.

A muscle rippled up Guillaume's cheek as father and son went into stare-down, and I looked on, realizing something else I never quite understood.

Remy and Guillaume had these clashes often.

I had read it as an alpha father who had born an alpha son battling, the elder refusing to graciously relinquish control.

The reason it always irritated me was that I'd met Remy when he was an adult, and in some way or other this always happened, so I didn't understand why Guillaume continued to test my man in irrelevant ways. I thought Guillaume should just be happy he'd raised such a strong, accomplished son, rather than constantly doing insignificant things that would remind him of his place.

Now I understood why Guillaume needed to establish his role with Remy.

My home, my marriage, my wife, my son—keep yourself in line.

I knew now the most important parts of that were *his wife* and *his son*, and regardless of what his wife had done to his son, it was Remy's place to keep things as they needed to be for Colette.

From the stories Remy told me, even before he walked away from the family business to go to school to be an architect, he rarely stayed in his father's line.

Now I knew he'd been so beaten down as a child, his inherent need was not to be held down by either of them ever again.

And even if Guillaume made the attempt, he knew that.

Therefore, as usual, it was not surprising when Guillaume gave in.

But I had to get a handle on how much it infuriated me, having learned what I'd learned, that the man still tried.

"I'll ask Melisande to prepare the Gold Room for Yves."

"Fantastic," Remy clipped.

I opened my arms to encompass us all. "Let's go in. I need to change out of these airplane clothes, and I'd love a glass of wine."

"When you come down, I shall have one waiting for you, *chérie*," Guillaume said immediately.

"I'd love that, Guillaume, thank you," I replied, smiling maybe a hint too beatifically at him, as Remy clamped an arm around my waist and hustled me to the steps.

The arm fell from around me, but his grip on my hand was tight as he pulled me inside, up the stairs and into a room that had matching silk jacquard in pale sage on the duvet covers as well as panels in the white walls.

This was not the pièce de résistance.

The gold and crystal chandelier hanging in the middle of the room was.

This was their guest suite, and it included a heavenly bathroom and a charming breakfast table in the corner by one of the windows that faced the street. And since those windows faced the street, this was the room with the balcony.

"You okay?" I asked just as my phone rang.

"I'm going into town tomorrow to buy a hip flask," he muttered.

He was joking, which meant he might not be having the time of his life, but he was fine.

I tried not to smile.

Sabre came in shouldering Remy's bag and rolling mine on its wheels across a possibly priceless rug. He did this bumping it into one of the two cream, button-backed, gold-framed regency chairs that flanked the fireplace. Likely equally priceless.

"Me and Yves are raiding the bar, what do you want?" he asked his father.

I burst out laughing.

My phone had stopped ringing, but it started again.

I pulled my purse off my shoulder to dig it out.

"Whatever looks the most expensive, pour me a huge glass of it," Remy ordered.

"Gotcha," Sabre said, dumping Remy's beat-up leather bag on silk jacquard.

I winced at the sight before I looked to my phone.

"Noel," I said to Remy.

"Take it," he replied.

I took it.

"Hey there."

"You are *Satan*," Noel stated. "First, the feathered de la Renta, that can happen in exchange for Fiona during awards season."

"Fiona makes her own choices. Though I will present her with Oscar."

"*Do you want to be remarried in de la Renta?*" he screeched so loud, I had to take the phone from my ear.

Remy's brows went up.

I put it back and said soothingly, "I'll talk to Fi."

"Fine. But there is not a fucking venue in this fucking city that is not fucking taken on Christmas Fucking Eve."

"Maybe we can do it in the backyard," I suggested.

"Are you *high*?" Noel demanded. "Give me January first. I have an *insane* spot open on the first. It's like, *a miracle*."

"Um..."

I couldn't say more because now that we'd discussed it, Remy was dead set on Christmas Eve for our remarriage ceremony.

"Oh my God, I'm going to fucking kill your fucking *husband*," Noel threatened, because he knew he was acting under Remy's orders for that.

"Think of this as a creative challenge," I tried.

179

"Goodbye," he replied and hung up.

"Let me guess, no luck on venues," Remy deduced as I tossed my phone and purse on the bed.

"He'll crack it," I assured, and Noel might be going crazy, but not only did he secretly love it, he'd crack it. "Though, he said he has something promising for January first. What do you think? New year? New start? New marriage?"

"Same marriage, and we're watching the fireworks over the Eiffel Tower on New Year's because we'll still be there on our honeymoon. That's booked. And I got that room because of my name and a cancellation. I'm not changing it."

I'd always wanted to see the fireworks over the Eiffel Tower on New Year's, so I said nothing.

I moved to my suitcase.

"Don't," Remy grunted.

I stopped.

He then moved to my case, took it the three feet I could have rolled it to the sofa, hefted it up, and opened it.

I'd forgotten without really forgetting that he was like that.

Bea would be in fits, my husband not allowing me to lift my bag two feet to a couch.

But Bea could go spit.

I started unpacking while I asked, "Do you want me to go with you when you go to her?"

"Do you want to go with me?" he asked back.

I stopped with my hands pancaking my pajamas and looked at him.

"I want you with me," he said softly.

I nodded.

Manon wandered in and promptly fell to her side on the bed like a wilting violet who had her corset on too tight.

"I always forget this place is so *bluh*," she complained. "It's gorgeous, but I can't relax for fear of a docent coming in with a tour group."

I swallowed a giggle and put my pajamas in a drawer.

"Your brothers have decided to get slaughtered, how about you join them?" Remy suggested.

"He wasn't good for much as a father, but Pépé does make amazing cocktails," she replied.

"It's good he's good for something," I said under my breath.

"Oh my God, Mom, do I need to keep my eye on Sah *and* you?"

"I'll be fine," I assured, grabbing my toiletry bags and moving toward the bathroom.

180

I was in the bathroom when I heard Manon ask, "I don't get it, Dad. With things the way they were, why'd you name us French names?"

I didn't hear his response.

Though I did hear the tone of Manon's, "Dad?"

So I dropped my bags and rushed out of the bathroom.

Remy had zipped open his case while I'd been out.

But he was standing above it, immobile, staring at his girl.

"Remy?" I called.

He jerked and only semi-focused on me.

"All right?" I asked gently.

"Why'd I do that?" he asked in return.

Oh no.

I stared at him because I didn't have an answer to this question.

He'd named all three of our kids. He was adamant about the names. He was adamant they be French.

I liked them, they were unusual (to me) and cool (to anybody, says me) so I didn't object. And now I was glad (I would have selected Joshua, Emily and Matthew, and they were so *not* Josh, Em and Matt it wasn't funny).

"I did it for him," he said. And the next was a muted explosion, the force of which had Manon jumping to her knees on the mattress. "*Fuck!*"

"Manon," I murmured.

She popped off the bed and left the room, closing the door behind her.

I then moved to my husband.

I put my hand on his chest and ordered, "Remy, look at me."

He'd still seemed unfocused, but he immediately focused on me.

"It doesn't matter why," I stated. "They're Sabre, Manon and Yves, and they were meant to be those people with those names."

"Yeah, but I did it for him, Wyn. *Shit*."

"But it doesn't matter."

"He doesn't even like Americans, did you know that?"

I closed my mouth because I was many, many things.

A proud American among them.

"He thinks Americans are harried and uncultured and worship at the altar of the dollar. And he finds the enduring American dream of possibly wedging yourself into upper middle class and a country club membership, pitiful."

I kept my mouth shut.

Then I opened it to note, "Of course he'd look down on the proletariat, Remy. His family has been bourgeoisie for the last three centuries. And let's not forget he left his son to an abusive mother in order to worship at that altar of money."

"Some of the time. The rest of it was to live his life however he wanted, including keeping his fucks. He had one here, probably always. He had women he visited in Paris and more in the country. Remember when I told you about that summer when I was twenty? Him and me in the garden at the house in Toulouse. He was smoking a cigarette and having a brandy and sharing with his son the finer points of being a man. Including how crucial it was to keep your mistresses happy, but your wife happier, just so she won't ask questions about your mistresses."

I made a face, even though I did remember that story.

"Yeah," he responded to the expression I made. "And I named our kids what I named them because I knew it would make him happy. I didn't even think about why I was doing it. Like I didn't think about why I left you."

"Remy, just because your father is who he is, you're a French-American man. You have dual citizenship. You made certain the kids did too."

His face twisted because he thought he'd done that for his father too.

This had to be stopped.

So I got closer, lifting my hand to his neck, curling it around and squeezing.

"Remy, France is wonderful. You love it there. Your dad is who he is, but you love your Uncle Luc, your Aunt Francesca. You adored your grandparents and they adored you. You picked Paris for our honeymoon, for goodness' sake, because you think it's the most beautiful city in the world, and you know I do too. You might not be proud of your father, but you're proud of being French. So stop it. It wasn't like that. You're you. You're American. But you're also *French*, and you gave that to our kids, and I for one think that's a beautiful thing."

"I hate it that he pushes them to speak French. I want them to speak French, but I know how it feels when someone pushes you to do something."

He did know that.

Oh, how he did.

I didn't focus on that.

"See?" I whispered. "You're proud of who you are and that has everything to do with your heritage and you gave it to them. And I love that. For me. For our kids. And for you. And that's why you gave it to them, honey. You didn't do that for your dad. You gave them *you*."

He spent a moment with that before he groused, "Shit, now it's not you, it's me who's worrying that every reaction I have, every meaningful thing I've done had something to do with them."

I wrapped my arm around his neck, set the other one to doing the same, and fitted myself to him, saying, "That's what I'm here for, to help you see sense."

He slid his hands over my hips to rest them just above my behind, with fingers encroaching, murmuring, "Yeah?"

I wanted to think how much I loved having his hands right where they were, having that back, having this kind of closeness with Remy again in my life.

What I didn't want was to say what I had to say next.

But we were in this moment, it was truth and logic, and I needed to call it to his mind.

"And to remind you that they're your parents. There's no escaping that. They made you what you are, either because of them or in spite of them. And although it's difficult for me to find any good in either of them, I know, even if it's slight, it was there because they made you."

Remy had one reply to that.

He dipped his head, and he kissed me, deep and wet and lovely.

When he broke it, his lips whispering against mine, "Let's unpack."

"Okay, honey."

I touched my mouth to his, pressed close and then moved out of my husband's arms in order to unpack.

Because once that was done, we could get on to the next thing.

And once that was done, to the next.

And eventually, I'd have him away from here.

And we'd be safe.

We'd be home.

CHAPTER 18
Three and a Half

Wyn

After Remy and I unpacked, washed up and changed into clothes that didn't smell like an airplane, we headed downstairs.

And hearing our descent, with military precision, our children filed out of the front parlor, and with Sabre handing Remy a very full glass of what looked like scotch on the rocks, they fell into formation around us before we headed toward the mural room.

Considering how they did this, I decided it best not to ask them to stand down.

Remy didn't say a word.

Guillaume had heard our approach too, came out of the room we were walking to, and watched quizzically as the Gastineau family approached as if on attack.

Another giggle fizzed up that I had to swallow down, this one hysterical, as I braced to face the woman who had harmed my husband.

I was his wife.

I was a mother, and thus knew the nurturing he should have had, but didn't.

And her abuse nearly cost me my marriage.

So I was obviously on edge.

But it wouldn't do for me to tackle a dying woman and punch her in the face, so I had to get it together.

We all stopped outside the room where Guillaume was out in the hallway barring even a view through the door.

"It makes me very happy you're all keen to see Colette," he murmured kindly. "But I'm not certain she's up for a visit from everyone. She, too, cannot wait to see you. But she'd prefer to do it in the morning when she always feels much better. So, if you will, only Remy and Wyn for now, *mes petits-enfants*."

I opened my mouth to tell the kids we were okay.

But Sabre spoke before me.

"We're going in with Dad."

"*Mon chéri*, this—"

"We're going...in...with Dad," Sabre repeated.

At a confrontation with another alpha, an invisible rod slammed down Guillaume's back, his gaze narrowed, and then I watched with grim fascination as he came to realize that his grandchildren had grown old enough to be told what had happened to their father in this house.

And I really did not want to feel it, but I was human, and the severity of the pain that washed over his features and swept through the hall couldn't be avoided.

I felt it sluice over Remy and I moved closer to him.

His fingers sought mine, and when they found them, they gripped painfully.

I didn't make a peep.

"Then you will be with your father," Guillaume whispered.

I looked up at Remy to see his face was carved from stone.

He was hiding his reaction to his father's pain, his guilt.

And...

Fabulous.

This was already going to be hard enough. We didn't need a repentant Guillaume on our hands.

"Allow me to let her know you're all coming. One moment," Guillaume went on, and then he moved into the room.

Remy turned to the kids. "I think—"

"No," Sabre cut him off.

And yes, my husband's face had been carved from stone.

But my son's was hewn in granite.

Manon leaned into her big brother and took his hand.

"I love you very much, Sabre," I said softly, then took my other two in. "All of you."

Yves's Adam's apple bobbed.

Without using a hand, Manon blew a kiss at me.

Okay.

Safe to say we were *all* on edge.

I turned back when I felt Guillaume rejoin us.

"She's ready."

We started to troop in, but we were stopped when Guillaume handed me a chilled glass of rosé wine.

"Something light and refreshing for now," he said. "I've opened a bottle of red to breathe that you can enjoy during dinner."

My sentiments were, Guillaume was more at fault for what happened to Remy than Colette because he was more than negligent by not putting a stop to it—he'd been complicit.

I had not prepared to be around the Guillaume that had played a large part in making the man I loved into a man I would love.

"Thank you," I replied.

He inclined his head and we all resumed trooping in.

And I wished I had my phone so I could take a picture for Noel, because she might be a monster, but it could not be denied, even at her age and in her condition, she was still fabulous.

This was demonstrated by the vision before us.

Colette spread across a settee in a pair of satin lounge pants the color of burnt sienna.

Up top was covered in a cream cashmere duster with a thin cable knit, and I didn't know what was under it, because she had a Dior gold silk scarf frothing at her neck.

Her feet were ensconced in slippers made of green suede with pointed toes, a matching pom on the top, but the sole was covered in soft beige fur that tufted out the sides.

Her hair was a sleek bob that curled under her jaw and was the same dark color with caramel hues that she'd had when I'd first met her.

Her face was minimally lined, these only around the sides of her mouth, and it was lightly made up. Foundation to even the tone, powder to take away shine, neutral base from lid to brow to give the eyes a lift, and a thin stream of liquid black liner with a just a hint of a cat's eye. Mascara. A touch of peachy-neutral rouge.

And on her lips, perfectly lined and filled, was her signature flamenco red.

She was thin to the point of emaciated, but this wasn't a concern. It was my understanding that she'd worked meticulously to remain underweight all her life, and I'd never known her to be anything but what she was right then. Though, truth be told, she did look like she'd lost weight she couldn't afford to lose.

The room wasn't cool, but a throw of an intricate design in shades of pink, red, ivory and burnt umber that had an impossibly long fringe at the edges, had been thrown back on the moss- green velvet settee like a production assistant had set the scene.

But it was clear it had been over her before we arrived, however, if it remained covering her, we couldn't see her outfit.

A dainty teacup and saucer in a bold millefleur design sat on a slender wine table in front of her.

And although I could understand a visit from your family after years of not seeing them would make you go that extra mile even if you were significantly unwell, she didn't appear fatigued or off in any way.

She looked like Colette.

Perhaps she wasn't going to go out and drum up a game of horse, but she'd never do that anyway.

But I could easily see her ordering Melisande to bring a bottle of champagne and some cheese and crackers, and entertaining for an hour or two.

Her eyes were locked on her son.

And she failed with her opener.

Dipping her head to the glass in his hand, she drawled, "Please tell me your marital affairs haven't led you to a drinking problem."

Not, "I cannot begin to explain how much I missed you."

Not, "It does my heart good to see you."

Not, "My handsome son."

Not even, "Hello."

I moved closer to his side.

"Heya, Granny," Sabre greeted with mock exuberance, and I was so jolted by his tone, I almost missed Colette's reaction to being called Granny.

She was Grandma or, as preferred (but none of my children really used it), Grandmama.

Never *Granny*.

She looked mad enough to bite.

No.

This woman was going for the drama and the sympathy.

She might be dying, but she wasn't dead yet.

I dipped my chin to hide my smile at her reaction to my son's words as Sabre kept talking.

"You're, you know, not well, and I looked up stuff about your condition and learned your immune system is probably messed up. Since we just got off an airplane, which are full of germs, we shouldn't get too close." He let that sink in before he finished, "Don't take it wrong that none of us are gonna give you hugs, you know, like the entire time we're here."

I heard my daughter make the noise I swallowed down earlier as I looked up at Remy.

His lips were twitching.

Seeing that I could think only one thing.

God, I loved my son.

"We'll take showers and everything," Sabre started talking again. "But unless we were here for a week or whatever, so we could make sure we didn't catch anything, and we're not gonna be here that long, we should probably keep our distance." He paused then said, "But you look real good."

Colette recovered quickly and replied, "Sabre, my love, you cannot know how much it means to me you cared enough to research my...condition and move to look after me."

"Well, you know, we heard word and we're all super worried about you," he replied.

"Yeah, Grandma, we're all worried," Manon chimed in.

Her gaze skimmed through Manon to light on Yves.

"Let me look at you, Yves," she called.

Yves moved up to my side.

She gazed at him lovingly, which wasn't surprising. He'd always been her favorite.

I took a sip of my wine in order not to gag.

"The vision of your father at your age," she remarked.

"Yeah," he grunted, and I turned my attention to him.

It was easy to forget, with how mellow my youngest was, that he could get upset or angry.

He was the latter now.

Even with Sabre's antics, he was not over the "marital affairs" comment.

Or his grandmother breaking his father's arm when he was a child.

"This means you're sure to find a lovely woman..." the pause was significant before she said, "like your mother."

"That'll be hard, seeing as I'm gay," Yves replied.

I went still.

I heard my daughter moan, such was the effort it took this time for her not to burst out laughing.

Sabre muttered an amused, "Jesus, bro."

Guillaume rounded to the back of the couch close to Colette's head, his eyes glued to his grandson.

Colette had gone white as a ghost.

"But don't worry, Grandmama, I've already found a super fit, awesome guy," Yves went on.

"Yves," I whispered.

"What?" he asked me.

I didn't have a response.

"I...well...you know..." Colette flitted a hand in front of her. "Boys do tend to experiment."

"I'm not experimenting," Yves said. "I'm like...*really* gay."

"Yves, I think you better let your grandparents have a minute with that," I suggested.

"Sure," he agreed amiably.

"Do you know about this, Remy?" Colette asked her son.

"Hello, Mom. Sabre's right, you do look well. I'm glad of it," Remy replied. "And yes, I know about Yves."

"And you're fine with it?" she demanded.

"About as fine as I am with him continuing to breathe, which I'm sure you can guess is a lot, though I'm sensing you don't realize it's one and the same thing," Remy said blandly.

Colette opened her mouth, but Guillaume rounded the couch, saying, "Melisande has prepared a lovely supper for you. I know your grandmother is tired and I'll need to see her upstairs and make certain she's comfortable, so sadly, I won't be joining you. But I'll let her know you're ready to be served. If you'd like to say goodnight to your grandmother and move into the dining room?"

"Cool, thanks, Pépé, we'll go there. See you tomorrow, Grandma," Sabre said, took his sister's hand, gave his brother a look, and with my other two mumbling their goodnights, they took off.

"Colette," Guillaume prompted in a tone that didn't say, *take my hand so I can escort you upstairs.*

It said, *we talked about this.*

She looked stubborn then lifted her chin, which only made her look more stubborn.

Then she said, "I'm so very happy to see you all—"

Guillaume shifted.

"Especially the two of you," she continued, but the last was nearly spat. "Together."

"Thanks, Mom," Remy replied in a bored tone.

She did an up and down to me and waited for me to say something to her to congratulate her on her effort of kinda, but not quite hiding she was insulting me, but I didn't say a word because I didn't have any in that moment that were polite.

She then looked to her husband and lifted her hand to him.

With supreme gentleness, Guillaume took it in his.

"See you both in the morning," Remy said, turning us and heading us to the door.

We were in the hall when Remy snorted like a bull.

Obviously, I'd heard him make the noise before, and it had two meanings, so I looked up at him to see which one this was.

It was the one which meant he was having trouble not laughing.

I smiled at him.

"I will never in my life forget Yves telling his grandma he's, like...*really* gay," he said.

I started laughing.

He looked down at me.

And proved how well he knew me.

"Three and a half more days, baby."

We turned into the dining room, and I replied, "Three and a half more days."

CHAPTER 19
Tradition

Remy

T he next morning, Remy had his back to the headboard and his wife riding his cock.

And ever since Sabre could think coherent thoughts, they'd practiced the art of fucking without making a noise.

Therefore, they were doing this now, even if Wyn was taking his cock like she was willing her body to absorb it.

"Baby," he murmured, tweaking her nipple.

She slid a hand back and claimed a fistful of his hair.

He heard the soft sound of warning, took her mouth to swallow the moan of her orgasm, and once she recovered from it, as if she wasn't serious before, she set her sights on pounding one out of him.

He didn't make her wait too long.

After it was over, she sat on his dick with her face in his neck.

"I need another hour of sleep," she whispered.

In their time zone, she did.

He'd woken her to fuck.

But although Wyn needed a solid seven to eight hours every night, Remy was one of those people who was good with five to six.

So he was awake.

"I'll clean you up and then go find coffee," he replied.

She nodded, her hair moving along his shoulder.

As he'd been doing since they added physically reuniting to the rest of it, random things that felt important, because they were, he memorized.

And so he memorized the feel of her hair on his skin too.

She climbed off him and curled under the covers.

He kissed her shoulder and got out of bed making certain those covers were barely disturbed.

He came back with a washcloth, and she adjusted enough to let him take care of their business before she let him kiss her lazily and she snuggled down in the bed.

She mumbled, "Love you," as he straightened.

But he took her in under silk and down and entrenched in one-thousand-plus thread count sheets, moved his eyes around the room, and then back to her when he said, "You were made to be right there."

She blinked up at him, turning her head a little on the pillow.

"Sorry?"

"This house suits you. You were made to lie under silk in Egyptian cotton with opulence everywhere you turn."

"That's only because you love me."

"It's because of who you are, which is who you made yourself. But honest to God, you were that woman when I met you, Wyn, you just didn't yet have the means to be who you were going to be."

She scrunched her nose and replied, "Once a farm girl, always a farm girl."

"You're that too," he replied. "But one who sleeps in expensive sheets."

She nestled her head in the pillow, ordering, "Go away. You being amazing is making me want to do things other than sleep, and I have to have my wits about me to wrangle three rabidly protective children. Not to mention, I'm not facing any day with dark circles under my eyes."

Although he wasn't a big fan of her blowing off what he was saying, to let her have her sleep, and since she was looking at him out of the corners of her eyes, he grinned before he leaned in and kissed her temple.

Then he left her to it, took a shower and shaved.

She was sleeping when Remy exited the bathroom, so he quietly got dressed and moved into the hall.

All the doors to the rooms were closed, except the door to his old room, and Remy didn't investigate.

His kids were in the same time zone as their mother and Manon and Yves had inherited her sleep needs.

Sabre, on the other hand, had inherited Remy's.

It was unlikely he was hanging in the parlor, more likely he was out for a run.

Remy wasn't about to run in that humidity.

Once, he wouldn't have felt it.

Now?

No fucking way.

Instead, he went to the kitchen in search of coffee and found Melisande, his parent's housekeeper.

She'd been with them for nearly seven years, lived in the carriage house across the drive and did everything for them from cleaning and laundry to cooking and running errands.

They'd always had a live-in, and as far as he knew, Guillaume had only fucked one of them. Her name had been Angela. She'd been there a very short time, and before her, and after, the rest were much older, and never conventionally pretty.

Melisande was different, however.

She was probably in her early thirties. She had a nice figure. And she was attractive.

She was also evidence his mother was slipping, as was his father, because, due to her no-nonsense personality, Remy was in no doubt Melisande wouldn't allow Guillaume to touch her.

Which was why she'd lasted that long.

"Good morning, Remy," she greeted.

"Morning, Melly."

"Sleep well?" she asked.

He nodded.

"Coffee and breakfast?" she offered.

He nodded again.

"Your father's at the table. So is coffee. Traditional southern? French toast? The House?" she asked after what he wanted for breakfast.

He smiled at her. "The House."

She smiled back because she knew that would be his answer, and Remy moved into the dining room.

His father's reaction to the news his grandchildren knew what happened in this house being too fresh, Remy was unprepared to see Guillaume at the dining table as he now was.

The last of a breed, sitting at a table with a live-in in the kitchen who made breakfast to order, coffee at hand in a silver pot that was used regardless that it had been crafted in Paris in the nineteenth century, reading an actual newspaper.

It was the newspaper that dug under Remy's skin.

Colette had always slept late.

But Guillaume had sleep needs like Remy.

So whenever his father was home, even if their housekeeper would be the one to wake Remy so he'd get ready for school, Guillaume was at the table before Remy in the morning.

And every time, the moment he saw his son, he'd cease reading and go direct to the funny pages, which he'd hand Remy to read when he was little, or the sports section when he got older.

And even as a little boy, so he could be like his dad, Guillaume made sure Remy had a cup of coffee.

It was a *café au lait*, and it was always more steamed milk than coffee. Caffeinated or decaffeinated, he never knew. He just knew drinking it, he felt grown up, like his dad.

And Remy never forgot how important he felt, lounging at the breakfast table with his coffee, his paper and his father.

Even as a little kid, if his dad was home, he'd get up early so he'd have time to do that.

And when he was in his teens, drinking real coffee and reading the paper, he'd never lost that feeling of silent, morning, man-to-man camaraderie he shared with his dad.

So now, when Guillaume's eyes landed on Remy, Remy was feeling a lot when his dad shook the paper closed, sat straighter in his chair, and said, "I suggest you consider your time at home with us a vacation from the news. It's far from pleasant."

"*Comme c'est le cas ces jours-ci,*" Remy replied, (as is the case these days), heading to the table, and reaching for the coffee.

This so he could ignore the warmth hitting his father's expression that he'd spoken French.

Remy poured his coffee and sat down opposite his dad, who was seated not at the head, but at the side of the table.

And it only occurred to Remy right then that this was another man-to-man thing with his son.

When Colette was around, he took the head, Colette sat to his right side, and Remy sat where he was, middle to the left.

Separate from his parents.

More aptly, at distance from Colette.

But when Guillaume knew it would be only him and Remy, he sat opposite.

Not the man of the house.

In a position where they could look right at each other when they spoke, and no one was lording over the other.

"Sleep well?" Guillaume asked, setting the paper aside.

Remy answered, thinking instead of what he did after he woke, "Very."

"Good," his father said quietly. Then he cleared his throat and began, "About Yves—"

Remy swallowed the sip of coffee he'd taken and cut him off. "This is not an issue and I'll not have it made an issue."

He had more to say, but Guillaume spoke, surprising him with his words.

"Of course it's not an issue."

"You don't—"

"Remy, stop being so American," Guillaume drawled, and Remy felt his neck tighten. "When I was at school, half the boys did things with other boys. Most of that was what your mother said, experimentation. But some of it was because they simply liked boys. It's exceedingly puritanical to think some mortal man interpreted the words of God to state this is wrong, when some men have loved being with men, and some women have loved being with women, and some love to be with whomever they please, since time began. I would think, considering this has always been the case, more than likely since history was even recorded, it's quite naturally *the case*. And since God made us this way, that's really all to be said, don't you think?"

He did think.

However...

"Mom was—"

He was interrupted again, and although he had no qualms with what Guillaume was saying, it was annoying not being able to finish what *he* was saying.

"I had words with your mother. She was taken off guard, though you know how she is with these things. Very traditional. It was just that we both were annoyed at being blindsided, as I can assume you'd well imagine. Which was why I brought it up. Yves is who he is, and he'll be our grandson and we'll be proud of him regardless. But perhaps a little consideration can be borne in mind in the future?"

"Mom will be proud of him?" Remy asked dubiously.

"She's exceedingly proud of all of you, *fiston*. Yes, including Wyn."

Remy sat back in his chair and took a sip of his coffee, allowing that to share he didn't believe what his father just said about Wyn.

Guillaume's tone was sharper when he asked, "Considering the fact we both lost you for three years after she said what she said, and I'd done what I'd done, do you not think your mother and I had long conversations?"

Remy made no reply.

"I've been besotted with Wyn since I met her," Guillaume continued. "If she didn't speak, and I just watched her and her mannerisms, I'd think she was French."

Remy sighed.

"And you know your mother. She gets competitive even if it isn't rational."

Remy made a noise in his throat that stated plainly, *I wonder why that is?*

Guillaume looked beyond Remy, to the palest, pale blue-green of the wall where a portrait hung of his great-grandmother lounging on a hip on a chaise longue, resting on her arms at the arm of the chair. She'd had her portrait done wearing long ivory gloves and a butter-yellow evening gown adorned with stitched-in ivory lace.

Her hair was parted in the middle and pinned at her nape, and his mother still owned the strand of a multitude of pearls draped at her neck.

His wife would one day have those pearls.

And she'd give them to their daughter.

Guillaume looked back to him and started, "I've made mistakes—"

Remy sat up in his chair. "Let's not do this."

"You are the best thing I've ever done in my life."

Those words coming unexpected, Remy froze.

"I look at you, your children, your wife, the family you created. Do you not think it pains me to see my son has all that I did not?" his father demanded. "The pain coming from the fact that I was...it was me who—"

"Dad, like I said, *let's not do this*," Remy bit off.

"Why did you leave Wyn?"

"Okay, *I'm* not doing this."

"She's an extraordinary woman."

"I know that."

"She loves you more than she loves even herself."

"I know that too."

His father's face got hard. "I'm trying to be a father to you, Remy."

"Too late," Remy replied mildly and took another sip of his coffee, ignoring the fact that his father looked like he'd been struck.

Then Guillaume asked, "What would you do if Wyn was like your mother?"

"No way in hell I would marry a woman like Mom."

"I'm speaking in hypotheticals."

"Even so, it's impossible to answer because even hypothetically that would never happen."

"What would you do if you loved a woman more than anything," his dad pushed, "and she was...not right?"

"I wouldn't fuck around on her making her even more...not right," Remy retorted.

His father's shoulders visibly tightened. "It's the French way."

"It's fucked up."

"Remy—"

"Let's not do this, Dad."

"Do you think, what she did to you, she did not do to me a thousand-fold?"

And again, Remy froze.

Guillaume kept speaking.

"Your grandmother was a vapid woman. I would have been uncertain she had much but air between her ears, except she was uncommonly cruel to her daughter. She wished her daughter's death, not her husband's. And she did not wish that because of love for her husband, but because she wanted no responsibility except selecting which gown to wear to which event she'd attend each evening. She was infuriated she was saddled with a child, a home and a business she had to see to herself. And as such, it isn't lost on you, she saw to all of them *very poorly*."

Remy didn't have anything to say, but even if he did, Guillaume wasn't finished.

"I took one look at your mother, I saw this extraordinarily beautiful woman who needed to be saved, and I was lost. I was young and that romantic notion was too much for me to ignore. I fell in love with her and set about saving her. It wasn't until much later that I realized the damage was done. But I was still in love with her, much more so by then. What did I do? I am a man and not a small man. When she slapped me, did I slap back? When she used her nails on me, did I bind her then cut them to the quick? When her tantrums woke the neighbors, did I gag her?"

"Well done for deciding to just absent yourself and letting your child deal with it," Remy replied.

"We left her four times, do you not remember?"

Remy felt his blood turn sluggish in his veins.

And it seemed his lips didn't move when he answered, "No, I don't remember."

"We were in France, without her."

Fuck.

He remembered that.

Maybe around when he was four. Definitely when he was six. His dad had even enrolled him in school that time. And again at seven. Last, not long after, when he was eight.

Respectively, the pump, the brush, the cut from the vase, and the broken arm.

His mom was not with them, but he didn't know they'd left her.

He just knew they'd left.

"To get me back, *us* back, she promised," Guillaume continued.

Remy said nothing.

"She lied," Guillaume finished.

"So why—?"

"Why did Wyn take you back when you left her? I love her. And after the last, when I told her she wouldn't get another chance, it stopped."

"It didn't stop, Dad."

"I had our housekeepers reporting."

He did?

"It didn't stop, Dad."

That was when Guillaume froze.

"It didn't stop until I was eleven. She shoved me, and I pushed her back. I told her—"

Oh Christ.

He told her to tell his father.

And telling his father, they both knew, meant his father would know he didn't push her for the fuck of it.

He pushed her because he was fed up and was pushing back.

Now he knew, that if he'd told his dad...

"You told her what?" Guillaume prompted.

"She threatened to tell you what I'd done. I told her I wanted her to. After that, the physical stuff stopped."

Abruptly, with an awful look on his face Remy could barely witness, Guillaume started to rise from his chair but stopped and settled back when Melisande arrived and set in front of Remy a plate filled with oysters fried in cornmeal and poached eggs covered in hollandaise sauce with creole seasoning, on top of ham and biscuits.

"The House," or the breakfast Cormier men had been eating in that house for over a hundred years.

Not the women.

They got one egg, half a biscuit, the ham and sauce, but nothing fried, and it was assumed they wouldn't finish it.

Wyn ordered it without the oysters, which was to say, two eggs, not one, and a full biscuit.

Manon had it as it was and ate every bite.

"Thanks," he pushed out.

"Anything else, Remy?" Melisande queried.

"I'm good."

"For you, Mr. Gastineau?" she asked his dad.

Remy looked and saw his father had smoothed his expression.

"The others will be waking soon, my dear, perhaps fresh coffee?" Guillaume ordered.

She nodded and reached for the pot. She then left.

That was when Guillaume got up and stood at the window to look out.

Remy stared at his back and wondered, holding himself so tight, if the compression would get too much and he'd fly apart.

"Dad?" he called.

"What do I do now?" he asked the window.

"Nothing," Remy answered. "It's done. There's nothing to do."

Guillaume turned. "I made a deal with my wife that she would cease abusing our son, and she did not honor her end of that deal, and I'm to do nothing?"

"It was over forty years ago and she's dying."

Guillaume jutted his chin forward and clipped, "I don't care if it was a hundred years ago, *she promised she'd stop hurting you.*"

Well...

Fuck.

"I forgot how much the children love beignets," Guillaume suddenly declared. "I'm going to Café Du Monde to get some for them."

It was arguable, but Melisande's beignets might be better than CDM's.

Remy didn't argue it.

It was not arguable, but the first morning at the family home in New Orleans, they'd all want the House. It was the second morning they went to CDM for beignets.

He didn't mention that either.

He said firmly, "Please be careful."

"*Mais bien sûr,*" Guillaume replied before striding from the room.

Remy looked down to his food, but he didn't eat it.

He then heard a noise in the kitchen, and even though his mind was fucked right the hell up with all that he'd just learned, he wasn't going to ask Melly to make the effort of cooking his breakfast and not eat it.

Therefore, he set about doing that.

She came back with a fresh pot of coffee, and about five minutes later, both his sons, faces and bodies slick with sweat, fresh glasses of juice they likely got from Melisande in hand, came in from the kitchen and parked themselves at the dining room table.

"There's no one here, so your personal assault in the form of sweat on the turn-of-the-century dining chairs is unoffensive," Remy noted.

Yves slugged back juice.

Sabre said, "Whatever. Who has chairs at a dining room table you practically have to wear a tux to sit in?"

Remy skirted that and asked, "Run good?"

"Hear me now, hold me to it later, I will never live anywhere with humidity *in my life*," Yves declared.

"Word, bro," Sah agreed.

"Maybe drink your juice and go take a shower?" Remy suggested.

"You okay?" Sah asked, watching him closely.

"I'm fine," Remy lied.

"You down here by yourself?" Yves asked, his gaze sliding over the folded paper on the table.

"Your mom and sister are still sleeping." He turned his head to Yves. "I'm surprised you're not."

"Sabre dragged me out, telling me I should run it off rather than get up in Grandma's shit again."

"Though, that was *fucking epic*," Sah remarked, reaching to the coffee.

"Hear me now, don't hold me to it later, your brother is wise," Remy joked to Yves.

Both quirked grins at him.

Then Sabre's eyes returned to the paper.

They came back to his dad. "Was Pépé here?"

"He left to get you guys beignets."

"He give you shit about Yves?"

"No," Remy said and looked again at Yves. "He says homosexuality has been around since before recorded time, so it's entirely natural."

Yves didn't hide his surprise including enunciating it. "Whoa."

"He and I still would like you to lay off your grandmother," Remy went on.

"The marital affairs crack was not on," Yves clipped.

"She's a dying woman hiding behind her lipstick. You're a vital young man with your whole life ahead of you, and your mother was standing there looking like she was about to be called to film her next scene with Brad Pitt. Maybe cut her some slack?" Remy requested.

"You're totally hotter than Brad Pitt, Dad," Yves told him.

"I'll take that as an informed opinion," Remy quipped.

Yves busted out laughing.

"What else did you and Pépé talk about?" Sabre butted in.

Remy leveled his eyes on his oldest boy who he saw was unamused.

He regarded him a beat before he asked back, "When'd you get so fucking smart?"

"He knows we have the House the first day. Why's he getting beignets?" Sabre pressed on.

Yeah.

Fucking smart.

"He told me something I didn't know. That we'd left Mom four times in his efforts to get her to stop doing what she was doing. I remember being in France with him, and Mom wasn't with us. I was just too young to know why we were there. All my life, we went there often, so it wasn't entirely out of the norm. Though, I do remember going to school there for a couple of months when I was in first grade, which was not normal. The final time was a couple of years later. The last straw and he made that clear. She promised she'd stop. Then I told him something he didn't know, she didn't stop. He was understandably pissed and he's taking a drive to cool off."

"He...took you away?" Yves asked.

Remy reached toward the coffee pot to give himself a refill. "Apparently."

"Well, damn," Yves muttered.

"Do you believe him?" Sabre queried.

Having filled his cup, Remy put the pot back. "I remember explicitly being in France. And with this brought to mind, I remember my grandparents being there and being pretty damned attentive. Uncle Luc and Aunt Francesca coming to visit frequently. I also know I have an affinity with Uncle Luc, and in some senses Aunt Francesca, because we're family and they're great, but also because Uncle Luc had little patience with my mother. Aunt Francesca just avoided her, though she made a point not to avoid me. When Mom was around, they'd take me on a lot of excursions, pointedly leaving her behind. But Uncle Luc..."

He shook his head, caught the fact both his sons were watching closely and listening to every word, allowed himself a private moment to let it settle what great fucking kids they both were, then he carried on.

"Looking back, he actively disliked her and would shit-talk her, doing this to her face. Mostly in French, which she knows a little of, but never became fluent since Dad translated for her all the time. But I knew what he was saying."

"Always liked that guy," Yves murmured.

"How do you feel about all that?" Sabre inquired.

Before Remy ate one of his last oysters, he said, "I need to think on it."

"He loves you, Dad," Sabre said.

Remy swallowed and paid even more attention to his son.

"I know he does," he replied.

"No, I think that was why I was so pissed at him," Sabre said. "Because, you know, he looks at you sometimes and his chest gets all puffed out. And it's like...like...if I look at the sidelines after I make a goal or I see you after I've made an important pass, that's how you're looking at me. And I thought that was all bullshit with Pépé, because you can't love someone and let them..."

Sabre didn't finish.

So Remy said, "I know."

"But, you know, if he took you away. If he thought...I don't know. He loves her too. Like, a lot. But he left her and that kinda freaks me out because she's always been a pain, and he puts up with it. But he left her. For you."

He did.

Four times.

"And he always remembers we like beignets," Yves said quietly. "It's tradition. First day, the House. And second day, Pépé takes us to CDM."

"Tradition," Sabre agreed. "Because he knows we love beignets."

Remy looked to the window.

"Stop talking about it, Sah," Yves muttered.

He glanced between them and assured, "I'm all right."

"Sure?" Yves asked.

Remy smiled and nodded at his last born.

"Maybe it'll get to, like, feeling good to know he, like...*tried*," Sabre suggested.

"Jesus, Sah, *stop talking about it*," Yves clipped.

"I'm fine, and yes, maybe it will, Sabre," Remy said.

"I'll shut up now," Sabre replied, sitting back with his coffee.

"I'll give fifty dollars to either or both of you if you can manage to shower and dress in clean clothes that don't smell like a locker room before Melly comes back with your breakfast," Remy challenged.

Yves's chair almost tipped over, and Sabre didn't spill a drop of the coffee he took with him as his sons bolted from the table.

Then Remy sat with the remains of his own breakfast and coffee and stared at the window with his great-grandmother's unseeing eyes gazing at the back of his head.

And he gave himself a minute to sit with the profound idea that, yes.

He tried.

CHAPTER 20
Time Is Running Out

Wyn

My husband sat on the bed, and I stood between his spread knees wearing a robe, makeup done, with my hair wet and slicked back with product already applied, waiting to be blown out, and I listened to him tell me about his eventful time at the breakfast table.

I did this making note not to let Remy loose on his own again in this fucking house.

He had his hands on my hips and his eyes on my stomach.

I had my hands on his shoulders and my gaze locked to his face.

"What I don't get," he said when he was finished with the rundown and finally lifted his face to me, "was why he didn't tell me."

"I'm not sure how you say to a little boy, 'We're leaving your mother because she hurts you,'" I replied. "It's more like you're consumed with the thought, 'I have to get my child away from danger,' and then get him away from that danger."

"We have kids, Wyn, and at eight years old, they were all mature enough to understand something like, 'if they hurt you again, no matter what, you tell me, and I'll make it stop.' He said he left it to the housekeepers to report. I've been thinking on it, and she must have figured that out. After we came back from that last time in France, she never did anything dramatic, except the concussion, and she drove me to the hospital herself after that. Unless it was just a tantrum that didn't involve anything physical, it was no longer loud. It wasn't bloody. There were no broken bones. She was hiding it. She knew, if he knew, she was done. She'd lose us both. And it was fucked-up love, but she loved me. That said, she worshipped him. I'm not sure she'd survive without him. And by that I mean, she'd make that so if she lost him."

"Like, take her life?" I whispered.

He nodded.

I was still whispering when I said, "Remy."

"Seriously, Wyn, what kind of *deal* do you make with your wife to stop her from abusing your child? What—?"

He stopped talking and we both stilled when we heard the words shouted from several rooms down the hall.

"*You lied to me!*"

Nothing and then more from Guillaume.

"*That was not what you promised! We went together. Je n'étais pas là alors t'as juste décidée d'arrêter?*"

And now Colette, in a shriek.

"*Speak English when you're shouting at me!*"

"*Bon sang! You've been married to a Frenchman for fifty-four years!*"

"He said," Remy translated quietly, "I wasn't here, you just quit?"

"Quit what?" I asked a question he couldn't know the answer to.

More from Guillaume.

"*Finalement, fait-moi l'honneur d'apprendre ma langue!*"

"Finally, do me the honor of learning my language," Remy murmured.

"*Speak English!*" Colette shouted.

Guillaume acquiesced.

"*You were supposed to stop! You were supposed to continue to attend sessions! And for both, you did not!*"

"*Things were fine!*"

The next was bellowed so loud, it was a wonder the walls didn't shake.

"*THEY WERE NOT!*"

After that, a door slammed, heavy footfalls could be heard in the hall then on the stairs, and Remy and I were left staring at each other.

I broke our silence with a silly quip.

"I'm thinking his drive didn't help."

Remy smiled.

Then he fell forward and buried his face in my stomach.

I smoothed his hair back.

I gave him a second, then I guessed, "Sessions? Do you think he meant counseling?"

He took his face out of my stomach and looked up at me. "Probably."

"That was the deal," I deduced. "It wasn't just the housekeepers keeping an eye on things. He'd gone with her, but when he wasn't around, she was supposed to keep going, and she didn't."

Remy picked it up. "And as far as he knew, nothing else happened, so he thought she was better. Then after a few years, I put a stop to it myself."

I turned my head and looked at the wall, beyond which, at the end of the hall, was the master suite.

"She'd act up when he was with his women."

Remy saying that made me look down at him again.

"I won't defend cheating, but that's his issue, honey. It's no excuse for what she did," I noted gently.

"I need to find him, make sure he's okay," he said. "Definitely not getting back in his car."

I nodded.

He stood and I didn't move because he was pressed against me.

I tipped my head back, and quickly, because I knew he'd be keen to get away, I rolled up on my toes.

I meant to kiss him, but he kissed me.

Then he left the room to see to his dad.

———

"PLOT TWIST," Noel said in my ear.

I was out on the front veranda sitting on a thick black-and-white striped cushion that didn't do much to make comfortable the gorgeous but practically unusable wrought iron chair.

If this was my house, I'd have wicker out front. It would be pretty, fitting and comfortable (I'd also have ferns, they were softer and more welcoming).

But the wrought iron was definitely more aesthetic.

Which was apropos with Colette Gastineau.

It looked beautiful, proper.

But it was unyielding, and in various locations, it dug into your skin.

"Yes," I agreed to Noel.

Obviously, I'd told him everything.

"What's happening now?" he asked.

"Now, Remy spoke with his dad. The boys and him are off somewhere with Guillaume. I've no idea what they're doing, but they're doing it keeping him from her and waiting for my call. Manon is getting ready. When she is, they're swinging by to pick us up and we're all going into town to do some shopping and get some lunch."

"And Colette?"

"We're under strict instructions from Guillaume that Colette needs to 'rest' today. Apparently, they've planned some sort of special dinner tonight, which was why Guillaume requested we pack something non-casual to wear."

Noel chuckled, saying through it, "Like you'd ever go anywhere without at least one *non-casual* outfit to wear."

He was so right about that.

He lost his humor and went on, "Be careful, Wyn. The wicked witch of the south is on her back foot, and it's dangerous to corner a witch."

"This is why Remy is also not here. It was my idea they go somewhere. I'm here, covering Manon on the home front."

"God, I hate it for Remy that this trip to visit his dying mother is akin to going to war."

It didn't need to be said I hated it too.

Since I did, I took us out of that discussion and into a much better one about wedding flowers (due to the season the event was occurring, but also because they were my favorites, I'd decided all white roses with some ever-greens) when I heard a noise at the front door.

I looked that way, expecting it to be Manon.

But it was Colette.

"I need to go," I broke into what Noel was saying about the addition of eucalyptus.

"Everything okay?" he asked.

I just managed to say, "Colette," before she was out the door.

"Right, keep me briefed. Love your face, love your family, you'll get through this. Bye."

And then Noel was gone.

Colette approached.

She was in red slacks. A black turtleneck. A silk scarf in reds, creams and yellows, which if I was not mistaken, was Prada knotted at the base of her throat and draped her shoulders. Black and cream Chanel ballerina flats. The sheath of her hair shimmered with health. And today, full makeup.

That said, seeing her standing and without the froth of scarf and long duster, it was much more obvious she'd lost weight. If she hadn't donned her usual mask and armor, she would appear frail.

"Good morning, Wyn," she greeted as she glided to the tiny table where I sat and lowered herself to the cushion of the chair across from me.

She matched the color palette.

"Good morning, Colette," I replied.

"The house is rather quiet," she noted with the iron will of a woman who knew all in it heard her shrieking at her husband an hour before but was intent to ignore it. "Where has everyone gone?"

"The men are out doing man things. Manon is getting ready," I answered.

"At ten in the morning?"

"It's eight our time."

"Ah." She looked to the street even as she noted, "I'm pleased to see you're wearing your wedding rings even if you and my son are no longer married."

I wasn't about to mention our upcoming re-nuptials.

If Remy wanted them to know, Remy would tell them.

Though I did think it safe to say, "Remy asked me to put them back on."

"Well, it's lovely you cared to see to his feelings on that."

Don't bite, Wyn.

But I bit.

"Once we were back together, I would have done it myself. He just got there first in asking."

She turned to me. "Of course, you love him so very deeply."

Okay.

I tried.

But I wasn't going to do this with her. Be her target when there was no one else at whom to aim her venom.

"Colette—"

"You need to talk to my son, and he needs to talk to his father."

Oh hell no.

I wasn't going to battle for her either.

I opened my mouth again.

But she said, "Remy's misdeeds are not on his father's shoulders."

I closed my mouth because I had no idea what she meant by that.

"Guillaume has been living three years in agony," she went on. "I'll not die, knowing my husband shoulders a burden that isn't his."

It was truth I spoke when I said, "I'm sorry, I'm not sure what you're talking about."

Her gaze pierced mine. "I'm sorry, I'm quite sure you do."

Okay.

I wasn't going to play a guessing game with this woman either.

"Perhaps we can agree not to get involved in each other's marriages," I suggested.

"I can't agree to that, considering my son left his beloved wife because he's mostly *his father's* son," she retorted.

Although she was right about that (in some ways), I felt my brows rise, indicating my bemusement.

"Men need to do these kinds of things," she continued. "I'm happy you came to realize that."

"Do...*what* kind of things?"

"You don't want me to say it."

"Actually, since I don't know what you're going to say, I do."

Colette arched a cunning brow. "He moved that woman in with him, didn't he?"

According to Remy, they hadn't spoken in three years.

How did she know that?

"How do you know about that?" I asked through stiff lips.

"Remy was a cerebral boy, cultured. He preferred drawing or playing piano to catting about with his friends. But when he did make a friend, he made that friend for life. And some of his friends have parents who are *our* friends."

Wonderful.

This meant Remy told Beau or Jason about Myrna, and one of those two idiots told their folks.

"We were divorced," I reminded her.

"And she was not his before? Or another one, perhaps?"

Oh my God.

"Remy wasn't cheating on me."

"That's what I say to myself, dear."

Right.

I didn't live her life, as much as she wanted me to.

I was also done.

I stood and looked down at her. "My husband wasn't cheating on me, Colette. And our marriage is none of your business. Now, truly, I am sorry about the state of things with you. So please, take this as honest and heartfelt when I say, don't make this visit ugly. Make it about something else. And *really*, you need to make it about something else. You have five people who've come to visit you who'll have nothing but memories soon. I'd suggest giving them good ones."

With that, I started to move in front of her to get to the door.

I could hang with Manon in her room as she finished getting ready, the better to nag her to hurry so we could all get away from that house and this woman.

"He adores you, you know," Colette noted as I passed.

I didn't break stride as I said, "I know."

"I'm not talking about Remy. I'm talking about Guillaume."

That stopped me and I turned back. "I know that too."

"So of course, he blames himself. It eats at him like acid."

"He blames himself for what?"

"For Remy leaving you for another woman." She fluttered a hand with perfectly peaked nails painted an unblemished buff. "The apple doesn't fall and all of that."

"Guillaume thinks...?" I couldn't finish that.

Because I now knew what Guillaume thought.

He thought Remy had done what Guillaume had always done and that's why we ended.

And because he loved his son, and me, and our children, our family, it had tortured him that was the example he'd set.

When it wasn't that.

It was Colette.

And she loved her husband.

So in her way, she'd come out to speak to me so I would go about ending that torture.

"It wasn't about another woman, Colette," I said softly.

"All right, dear," she murmured disbelievingly.

Because this was Remy's mother, and she should know, firmly, I repeated, "It wasn't about another woman. He suffered for you with that. So much, he'd never do that to me. We'd been divorced two years before he had another woman."

The skin beside her eye ticked.

That was all I'd give her on that.

But for her and Guillaume, I said, "I'll talk with Remy and encourage him to sit down with his dad."

"I love him, you realize, with my whole heart." She took a delicate breath and clarified, "Remy."

I slid my head to one side like I was relieving a muscle on the other, righted it and began to bid her adieu again.

"I know Remy has shared..." She couldn't say the words. "But I do love him."

"Colette, let's not talk about this."

"You think you know."

"I *do* know."

She turned on her cushion to fully face me. "Guillaume's family was very close. His parents thought he could do nothing wrong. He was the apple of their eye. The brightest star in their sky. I was very happy he had what I didn't. Your parents were lovely. I watched. I saw. They cherished you. Do you know the meaning of the word *cherish*?"

"Please, I don't—"

"Until I had Guillaume, I didn't have that. And even when I had Guillaume, I truly didn't have that. How could I give something I didn't have myself?"

"I'm acutely aware of your health, and I feel right now—"

"It was all I knew," she hissed.

"No," I retorted. "I'm looking at you now, and I know you knew better."

She opened her mouth.

But this time, I got there before her.

"We're done talking, Colette. If you have amends to make, they aren't to me. They're to my husband."

"My grandchildren—"

Ah yes.

Last night was not lost on her either.

"And to them as well," I carried on. "As I said before, but you didn't catch it, so I'll make myself clearer, you now have two and a half days to take care of important business. Honest to God, I hope you take advantage of them so maybe you'll get more than two and a half days. Because as hideous as it might be for you, no matter how you look at it, time is running out."

And with that, I left her looking perfect on her iron chair and dashed into the house and up to my daughter.

CHAPTER 21
Storm the Bastille

Wyn

"I want whatever the fuck is going to happen tonight like I want someone to tie me to a chair and pull my teeth out," Remy muttered to himself where he stood beside me in the bathroom, hip to the counter, arms crossed on his chest, watching me as I peered into the mirror, gliding lip stain on my lips.

I didn't have a chance to reply.

There was a knock on our door, we heard it crack open and Sabre call out, "You guys decent?"

"Yup," Remy called back, pushing from the basin and turning toward the door.

I looked into the bedroom to see my children march in.

And my heart actually fluttered with how magnificent they were.

Sabre was wearing gray slacks that fit him so perfectly, they looked tailored for him, a sparkling white shirt with a navy-blue vest over it, and black loafers with his skin showing at his ankles, so either no socks or likely (because his mother taught him better) footies.

Yves was in darker gray slacks with a black shirt, the cuffs rolled up to his elbows, and burnished leather dress boots.

And Manon was a vision in a flowing, mauve chiffon, long-sleeved maxi dress with a high, round neck. It was embroidered with big flowers in pink, purple and yellow with bold green stems and leaves. A dress I knew (because I'd bought it for her) had a full cutout back. Her lustrous hair was in a side pony.

Remy was in blue and gray. Blue slacks and a lightweight gray sweater, over which he wore a matching gray sports jacket.

I was in a currant-red, twist-front kimono dress that had dramatic sleeves, was delightfully slouchy around the middle and had a short hem that showed off my best asset: my long legs. My hair was smoothed up in a wide, velvety top knot. On my feet were Rene Caovilla gold, bejeweled, embroidered lace, sling-back pumps.

And yes.

If my family was going to war, I didn't care what it said about me, this was the armor I'd choose.

"Before you say it, we know we look like the fucking Kardashians," Yves grumbled. "Sah and I have already puked."

"I didn't puke. I'm killing it in these duds," Sabre replied.

I started laughing.

Manon moved forward and used the doorframe to lean into the bathroom. "And we have it figured out, Dad. If things get weird, I'm faking an epileptic seizure."

"And if Grandma gets mean, Yves is going to start talking about how big and buff Theo is," Sabre added.

"I can talk about that, for, like, three hours," Yves shared. "She's got some chops, but I think I can outlast her."

They were being so funny, and so fabulous, they took all my attention.

So it came as a surprise when Remy ordered roughly, "All of you, in here."

As I'd mentioned, the bathroom was heavenly.

However, it was not large.

But that wasn't the only reason we all huddled together when the kids wedged in with us.

Remy's long arms almost wrapped around us all, but considering Sabre's and Yves's were just as long, we were covered when Remy said, "Everything I live for is in my arms."

All kidding was now aside, Manon made a peep, and I held her eyes as I kept hold on my own emotions.

"I messed up, and you rode that wave with me," Remy carried on. "And I cannot express how much that means to me."

All right.

No.

He had to get beyond that.

I looked right at him.

"Honey—" I began.

"But right now," Remy spoke over me, "I have to remind you, your grandfather is losing the woman he loves, so I have to ask you to see to him. She might make it hard, but we've all learned things today, where what you just gave me is what we all have to give him. Soon, we're all he'll have left."

Manon had been briefed about the morning's revelations (though she, like us all, did not miss her grandparents fighting).

And I'd shared with Remy the conversation I had with his mother on the veranda.

"In other words, no fake epileptic seizures. You with me?" he asked.

"With you, Dad," Sabre said immediately.

"Totally," Manon chimed in.

"Always, Dad," Yves said.

"Right," Remy muttered on a squeeze of his arms that made us all squeeze ours. "So we don't look like we're prepared to storm the Bastille in Tom Ford and Stella McCartney—"

"This isn't Stella, Dad, it's..."

Manon didn't finish when Yves bumped her with a hip, which meant we all got a corresponding hip bump.

"How about we stagger our arrivals?" Remy's gaze swung between his sons, "But one of you escort Manon."

"I'm totally making a solo appearance. My outfit is rad, and I don't want Manon to steal my big entrance," Sabre declared.

"You sure you're not gay?" Yves razzed.

"I could be, with how hot I look," Sabre returned.

"Settled. Yves will go with Manon," Remy broke in. Then he moved in a way we all broke apart, but only to stop holding each other. We still stood close together in the bathroom because there was no room to move. "Now, your mom isn't ready so head out."

"You go first," Sabre said to Manon and Yves.

"*You* go first," Manon replied.

"I don't know if anyone is down there yet," Sah retorted. "You can't make an entrance when no one's there to see you enter."

"Oh my God, you're straight but you're still somehow gayer than me," Yves remarked.

"Dude, get an eyeful, I *am all that*," Sabre shot back.

"Men, shut the hell up and roll out," Remy ordered.

"Come on, Manon, the booze is down there," Yves muttered, grabbing his sister's hand and pulling her from the room, which worked for me—breathing space.

But Sabre clearly hadn't thought ahead to where the alcohol was and how he'd get some. I could see he was realizing his mistake as they walked away.

Our two youngest headed down, and Sabre went into our room and threw himself on our bed.

I turned back to the mirror to assess the stain and add gloss.

I did this with a side eye to Remy and teased, "You will note what's happened after you shared your gateway beer with our youngest."

"Is Manon of age yet?" he asked.

I shot him smug smile. "In Louisiana she is."

He grunted.

I got serious. "Are you going to be all right?"

"Trying to figure out how and when, but more how I say to my dad, 'You know, you fucking around on Mom wasn't the reason I blew up my marriage. At least, not the way you think it was. You inadvertently leaving me to take care of her was,'" he replied.

I finished with the gloss and turned to him. "How about I talk to him?"

"And say what?"

"I don't know, I'll figure it out when I talk to him."

"I've thought about it today, and with what Dad said, I want this visit to be about healing. At least for him and me."

I nodded. "That occurred to me with what you just asked of our kids."

"What I mean is, whatever is said should come from me."

He was right, and I gave him a small smile to share not only that, but that I'd stand down.

"He's been a mess all day," he noted.

Guillaume had.

To anyone else, he would seem no less dashing and confident.

But none of us (especially Remy) had missed he'd been quiet, withdrawn, and it hurt to look at him because his eyes often rested on Remy, and they were haunted.

"All of this is exacerbated by her illness," I noted and shifted closer to him. "And he's been confronted with something unbearably heavy in the midst of it. He's losing her, and he's justifiably furious with her. I can't even imagine. But one thing I know, baby, is the only balm for a hurt like that is love. And you and your dad might be feeling your way with that, but we have it in abundance, and it'll be all around him."

Before Remy could answer, Sabre was at the bathroom door.

"Heads up spoiler. I just watched Jason and Clare walk in the side door. And when did Nat become a knockout?"

"Shit," Remy whispered, and I wasn't sure why.

Mystery special dinner solved, Guillaume and Colette had organized a dinner party with their son's childhood friend.

He was close with Jason, I was close with Clare, and the kids had grown up with Nat.

Maybe he didn't want to pretend things were okay in a crowd, even with one of his oldest buddies.

Maybe he didn't want his son to make a move on his oldest friend's daughter.

Remy clarified with his next.

"Park the killer charm, son. Jason and I go way back. I don't need to talk him out of shooting you."

"I can't help it if they fall at my feet."

I smiled as I turned and tucked my dual tube stain and gloss in my small gold bag, along with the compact I'd already put in it, the lip liner, and mints, because this was New Orleans and Melly. Dinner was going to be amazing, but it might lead to unpleasant breath. It was a house party, so I'd take the bag with me, set it somewhere so I didn't have to carry it, but it'd be closer than running up the stairs for touch ups and breath duty.

"Sah," Remy warned.

"Right, right, I'll try to be less awesome. It'll be hard, but for you, I'll do it."

"Jesus," Remy murmured, but I could hear the amusement.

I turned back and asked, "So, do I get two escorts?"

And to that, I got two answers.

My husband: "Absolutely."

My son: "Totally."

CHAPTER 22
Mantle of Alpha Protector

Wyn

S abre sacrificed making his big entrance in order to be at his mother's side, and we arrived downstairs to find Manon, Yves and Guillaume mingling with not only Jason, Clare and Natalya, but also Beau, his wife Katy, and their two sons, Julien and Louis.

And I knew Sabre had only been trying to keep the tone light, but it couldn't be missed that he wasn't wrong about how he looked, or how a certain member of our ensemble had blossomed.

Therefore, when we arrived, Nat took one look at the young man, who, if memory served, she last saw as a boy of sixteen, and that look took in all of him and lingered. And I glanced at a girl I last saw when she was thirteen, who then had pale skin, freckles, chubby cheeks and dark hair, but now was a dead ringer for Anne Hathaway.

And an iffy night got iffier.

Because not only did we have that to contend with, Julien *and* Louis were eyeing Manon in a way that Yves *and* Sabre appeared to want to shove their teeth down their throats.

And Colette had not arrived.

Then again, no one stole Colette's thunder.

Not Sabre.

Definitely not me.

So as the adults became reacquainted, the young adults chose their battlegrounds, this even if Jules and Lou had always been thick as thieves with Sah and Yves, with Jules one year older than Sah, and Lou two years younger.

But Manon had grown up too.

And interestingly, it didn't escape Sabre's attention, Nat's chosen position was to make an impossible attempt to become one with the cream walls and bloused damask of the draperies.

Which of course (although years had passed, a woman never forgets such things) signals the scent to a predator.

And Sabre had an excellent sense of smell.

On this thought, I wandered with the martini he had shaken for me back to Guillaume and asked *sotto voce* to my father-in-law, "Do they still duel at dawn in New Orleans?"

To my delight, in his genteel way, he burst out laughing.

"*Ma chérie*," he started when he'd controlled his hilarity. "At least Sabre has a second if he should have to avenge Manon's honor. Poor Jason will have to turn to Beau. And Beau will be caught between Jason and Remy."

"Manon has a boyfriend," I assured him.

"Is Sabre not taken?"

I shook my head.

"He's about to be," Guillaume remarked.

I took a sip and watched my son leave the protection of his sister to his younger brother so he could approach a wary beauty who had no clue she was beautiful, then watched that beauty nearly knock over an etched glass urn as she sought escape.

"His mother and I wanted Remy to be around people he's comfortable with," Guillaume murmured into his sidecar. "What a lovely added bonus to the evening's entertainment."

I slid my gaze to Remy, who was focused not on Sabre, but on Jules and Lou checking out his daughter, but he felt my attention and he looked to me.

He shook his head in fatherly resignation.

I stifled a giggle with a sip of my martini.

Guillaume made an odd noise beside me, so I turned to him.

And my heart squeezed.

When he caught my eyes on him, he said, "Suffice it to say, I'm utterly delighted that whatever issues you were having have been ironed out."

"Suffice it to say, I would be delighted if my husband and his father did the same thing during this trip."

My words surprised him so much, at first, he didn't cover it.

Then he said, "We're all here for Colette."

"No," I refuted quietly. "We're all here for the both of you."

"I'm sure he's shared," he noted just as quietly (my guess, referring to what happened at the breakfast table), before taking another sip of his drink and finishing, "And I must apologize for my behavior earlier. It was vulgar." This definitely referred to him shouting at Colette.

"You're allowed to be human," I replied.

"Am I?" he again spoke into his drink.

Wow.

Damn.

Because...yes.

That was a good question.

One that surely every parent at some point in their lives asks themselves.

"I can't speak for Remy," I said carefully. "And he also doesn't want me to, but what I will do is encourage you to think on things, Guillaume."

He fixed his eyes on what I knew was nothing across the room and asked benignly, "And you don't think I have, now doing this for decades?"

"I think that the thoughts you've been centered on have blinded you to the fact your son is standing right there."

His body gave a mild jolt and his focus shifted to me.

So I kept talking.

"I also think you know your son. So you know, if he didn't care, not only would he be nowhere near here, his wife and his children wouldn't either. And that, Guillaume, is what you *should* be thinking about."

And with that, I moved closer, then in, kissed his cheek and walked away, catching my daughter's eyes.

She read me, turned and said something to Yves, and they both immediately made their way to their grandfather.

I approached Clare and Katy, who had formed a small knot because Remy, Beau and Jason were in their own.

"I hate you for those legs," Clare, who was petite, said.

"I hate her for that hair," Katy, who had great hair, said.

"We have to set aside our hate, sisters, because there's so much youthful testosterone flying around this room, things are bound to give, and someone might get their dress torn," I joked in reply, instead of what I normally would do. Find some way to shift the genre of words out of jovial envy, which included negativity that didn't hide talking yourself down, even if at the same time you were talking someone else up.

I had great legs and great hair.

Clare had a great ass, also great hair, and was sweet as sugar.

Katy had a great rack, further had great hair and an awesome edge.

We were all fabulous.

The word "hate" shouldn't come into that in any way.

But even if I'd chosen what I thought was a playful conversational gambit, I'd said the wrong thing.

Clare gave Katy a look then smiled tightly at me. "I need another drink. Do you?"

I shook my head and didn't point out her glass was half full.

She took off in the direction of Guillaume.

I turned to Katy. "Did I say something wrong?"

"Ah hell," she replied.

I'd said something wrong.

"What did I say?" I asked.

She visibly engaged in a mental battle before she came closer and shared, "Not my place, and you didn't know, and Clare gets that. You've also got great boys, but considering Sabre's not attempting to hide he's smitten, you need to know. Nat was assaulted."

My throat closed.

"I'm sure you remember, she used to be really outgoing, a total extrovert. But unsurprisingly, men scare the shit out of her now," Katy shared.

"Oh my God," I whispered, because I did remember that. I just thought she grew up, Sabre grew up, and even if you were outgoing, you could get shy around someone you were attracted to.

"Yeah," she agreed. "Jason lost his fucking mind. Beau had to sleep over at his house a couple of nights because Clare was worried he'd do something stupid. It was...a thing."

"When did this happen?" I whispered.

"A year ago."

"Does Remy know?"

She gave me a funny look, then it occurred to her Remy and I were not together a year ago, and she said, "I'm sure he does. Even if Remy is nearly a continent away, those guys act like they're still in high school."

Of course.

And in all that was happening, it wouldn't be on Remy's mind to say, "By the way, Nat was assaulted."

My gaze wandered to Sabre. "I need to talk to my son."

"I kinda think you don't," she said, and I looked back to her. "Sah's a good kid. He'd never, not ever, and she needs to remember there are guys like that. She also needs to remember she's beautiful and it's okay for men to think she is, and they're not all monsters. But more, for her to know there's good attention to attract, and she's funny and sweet and pretty, and it's healthy to attract it. But I also think maybe you should, because if Jason clues in, the night could get testy. He tries to act like things are normal, but he's always been protective."

I nodded.

Her eyes went beyond me, and she murmured, "Oh boy, prepare to curtsy."

I turned and watched Colette swan in wearing a forties style green dress with a keyhole neckline and dotted lace Dior kitten heels with the signature side ribbon.

It was simple, but as women like her were wont to do, she made it fabulous.

And then, it actually hurt to further watch no one give a damn she'd arrived.

On the one hand, you couldn't act alternately queenly and cattily to everyone you knew for years and expect them to continue to kiss your feet. That kind of crown always got tarnished and people learned to avoid the strike of claws.

On the other hand, this was her home, her party, and the woman had cancer eating away her life.

So I shot a look to Sabre, but I should have known.

Before my son caught it, Remy was approaching his mom.

"I cannot tell you how glad we are that you guys are back together," Katy said, and I tore my attention from my husband escorting his mother to her husband, grandchildren and the drinks cabinet. "And I mean no offense, Beau would be ticked if Remy came to town and he didn't see him and all of you. And I missed you like crazy. It's about time you all came back. But what gives with the formal invitation? We all knew it was just a matter of time before you guys sorted it out. Is it a thing with the older generation to throw a soiree when a couple is reunited?"

"First, Phoenix is lovely in December, the perfect place for a family Christmas away from home, where you also might attend the fabulous remarriage of your friends on Christmas Eve," I hinted. She grinned, and then I gave her some more news. "But Remy has also been estranged from his parents, and they're trying to make amends, so this is about them giving him a 'comfortable' night with his buds."

"Only Colette would think to force me into a pair of heels as a 'comfortable' night' with Remy's buds."

"She also has terminal cancer."

"Holy shit," Katy whispered, her gaze racing to Colette.

I nodded even as I lifted my martini to take a sip before I went on, "So I figure this is a kind of a last hurrah, though for her sake, I hope she has more of them before she gets..." I didn't finish.

"Yeah," Katy agreed.

Clare approached and immediately said, "I'm so sorry, Wyn, I made you feel weird. It's just—"

"I shared, babe, it's cool," Katy muttered.

Clare looked relieved.

"I'm the one who needs to apologize. I put my foot right in my mouth," I said.

"You didn't know," Clare replied.

"I didn't, and you must know, I hate that for all of you," I returned.

She nodded with a mumbled, "Thanks, sweets."

"This reminds me, I need to have a word with my eldest," I noted.

Clare caught my hand so I didn't move away. "You really didn't know. It's just..."

"I have a daughter, honey, so I don't know, but if anything happened..."

Neither of us concluded our statements.

Both of us got it.

And not only didn't I want to think on it in regard to my daughter, I really didn't want her to think on it any further in regard to hers. But more, I suspected she wanted to think on it much, much less.

I squeezed her hand, let it go, and even though I wanted to, I didn't hug her or anything that might signal to Nat we were talking about it. Instead, I smiled at them both and then turned away and took another fortifying sip as I made my way to Sabre.

Apparently, during my discussion with Katy, a détente had formed, because he was chatting with Julien.

"Can I steal my son?" I asked Jules.

"Sure, Wyn," Julien replied, then he took off in the direction of where Manon, Yves and Lou were now together and talking.

"You want me to save Dad from Grandma?" Sabre asked.

"I want you to steer clear of Natalya."

It was then I realized with the way that got his back up, he really *was* smitten.

"She's a friend, Mom."

"You be absolutely appropriate with this information, Sabre," I demanded quietly. "But she had some trouble a year ago and it's made her timid around boys."

"What kind of—?"

He blinked his eyes slowly before they moved through the room to land on Nat.

Then I watched, both proud and frustrated, as my son firmly shrugged on the mantle of alpha protector.

All right.

Maybe there were times when Remy had been too good of a teacher.

"Sabre," I said warningly.

He jerked his attention to me.

"You mean some guy hurt her?" he demanded.

"It's none of our business, you just need to—"

"She's always been hilarious. Like one of the guys. She was fun to have around, even when she was a little kid. And tonight, she hasn't said dick...*to anybody*."

"Sah—"

"So some fuck *fucked with her*?" he growled.

Oh boy.

"*Sabre*," I said low, but sharp.

"What are you guys whispering about?" Manon asked, bellying up to us, dragging her younger brother and her father with her.

I glanced and saw that Katy, Beau and Guillaume were now attending Colette.

My attention rushed back to the second family huddle of the night when Sabre announced, "Some fuck attacked Nat."

"*Sabre*," I hissed. "What did I say about appropriate?"

"Oh my God," Manon breathed.

"Are you shitting me?" Yves's voice was kind of loud.

"Children," I snapped.

"Shut it down. *Immediately*," Remy rumbled, and as always happened when he used that tone, they shut it down. *Immediately*. "Sah, back off. Manon, you see to that. Yves, keep your brother in line. Now, we're not whispering about this. *Mingle*."

And with that, he took my hand and pulled me away.

"Did you know?" I asked out of the side of my mouth as we went.

"Beau told me. Jason lost it. Beau thought I might need to fly out. But Clare impressed on Jason that Nat needed her father, so he needed to get his head out of his ass. It didn't happen to him, it happened to Nat. Honest to Christ, I don't know how he did it because I felt his pain, but he got his head out of his ass."

"How bad was it?" I asked.

"Bad," he answered.

Damn.

I did not look at Natalya.

I watched Sabre and Yves huddle with the younger guys.

And then I watched Manon go for casual as she approached Natalya.

"You could have given us a heads up," I chided.

"How could I know Sabre would be interested? She's like a sister to him."

"But she isn't a sister. She's a young woman who looks like Anne Hathaway."

"She was pretty when she was little too, and he didn't notice," Remy pointed out.

"When a boy's sixteen, and a girl is thirteen, you don't notice. When a guy's twenty-two and a young woman is nineteen, they notice."

"My bad," he grunted his concession because he knew all this even better than me.

"How's your mom?"

"It was a blow when no one fainted at her beauty when she arrived, but she's Mom. She survived it."

"How are you?"

"I'd rather we were all in the courtyard at Bacchanal, drinking wine and shooting the shit with live music happening. But it's good to see them however it happens."

"Your mom and dad wanted you to have a comfortable night with friends."

"Well, they delivered, if we can manage to stop Sah and Yves from rallying Jules and Lou to tear apart New Orleans to find the guy who did what he did to Nat. Bonus"—he looked down at me—"you in that dress."

"You like?" I asked coquettishly, swishing my hips.

"I love everything I see."

I frowned severely. "Stop. We can't nip upstairs. You'd mess up my hair."

"Not if I'm on my knees."

That made my knees get weak, but I powered through it and retorted, "My intention was to be on mine."

"Yeah," he agreed. "That would mess up your hair."

Indeed.

He was far too dominant when it came to, well...everything. Especially that. He'd find it impossible not to touch my head when I went down on him.

Though, as a challenge...

"Miss the guys," he said, taking me from my intriguing thoughts. "Haven't seen them since I met them for their fantasy football kickoff in Vegas a couple of years ago. But I hope this thing ends early."

"It won't," I warned.

"Good you're a night owl."

"You are *so* lucky."

"Don't I know."

God, I loved this man.

I tipped my head farther back.

And Remy accepted my invitation.

He lifted his head to Beau, who remarked, "Maybe we should take a break, babe. Get the magic back."

Clearly, along with Katy, they'd gotten close while we were talking.

Remy stiffened at my side.

Katy slapped Beau in the gut. "God, you're a dufus. And *hello*. They were always all over each other." She looked to us. "Pardon my husband. He has the social skills of a panda. All play, no brain."

"Why is it hot when she insults me?" Beau asked Remy.

"Because she's right and a smart woman is attractive?" Remy asked Beau.

"Right, that's why," Beau muttered.

They laughed with each other.

Katy and I laughed with them.

But while I was doing it, my gaze wandered to Guillaume and Colette.

I wished it wouldn't have.

Not because Guillaume looked content and even happy that his son was having a good time.

But because Colette did too.

CHAPTER 23

The Moon

Remy

I t was the end of the night and Remy was pissed off.

Because their friends had left and the family were all in the mural room having one last drink before heading to bed, and that family included his mom, which was not why he was pissed.

He was pissed because that family didn't include Sabre.

After dinner, when the younger crowd all disappeared from the dining table to hang in the games room, Sabre had come to Remy to ask for the keys to the rental. And since he'd been palling around with Jules and Lou, Remy gave them to him, thinking this was NOLA, they were young, it was Friday night, clearly they were going into town.

At his age, that was what he would do.

But no.

Before they left, Clare, with hope in her voice, and Jason, with a storm in his eyes, had informed them Sah was "escorting Nat home."

That was the last thing Remy thought Sah would do.

Because that was the only thing he told him *not* to do.

"Remy," Wyn murmured from beside him on the couch, squeezing his hand where he held hers on his thigh. "Relax."

"I told him," he murmured back.

"Remy."

She said his name in a way he stopped scowling at the rug and turned his gaze to her.

"You raised that man, what do you think is going to happen?" she asked.

Shit.

He tried to make himself relax.

"I've looked them up, and I want us to take a ghost tour tomorrow night," Manon said into the room. "You wanna go Pépé?"

"I don't know, *ma belle*," his dad replied hesitantly. "With the game, it'll be a long day."

Beau had scored them some tickets, so they were going to Tulane's home game with a tailgate before that.

Guillaume nor Colette was going to the game, but they were going to the tailgate.

"Have you ever been on one?" Manon asked her grandfather.

"Of course not," Colette scoffed, openly insulted by the very thought her husband would do anything so common.

Wyn's fingers around his tightened.

"Why not?" Manon shot back.

"Tourists do that, darling," Guillaume intervened with a gentle smile. "And we're not tourists."

"I'm going to do everything everywhere I am, even if I live there," Manon declared. "If I end up in New York, I'm going to see the Rockettes at Christmas. If I end up in London, I'm going to that studio where they filmed Harry Potter. If I end up in Sydney, I'm going to learn every inch of the opera house."

"Are we ever going to see you?" Wyn teased.

"Totally, since I'll be all those places working for you as your scout," she replied cheekily. Then she turned back to her grandfather. "Pépé, you should go with us. Grandma, if you're not up to it, I understand. But you should come, Pépé. It'll be fun, you'll get to be with us, and you'll have new anecdotes to tell during dinner parties."

"I'll think about it, *mon bijou*," Guillaume replied.

"I must know about this young man you're seeing," Colette butted in, this aimed at Yves.

Remy got tense again.

"What do you wanna know, Grandma?" Yves asked cautiously.

"I'm not sure I want to know anything," she replied. "Except I want *you* to know you should sample life's delights. You seem enthralled with this person, but you're only seventeen. You can't possibly know if you're truly enthralled if you haven't been enthralled with someone else."

Yves smiled at her, and it was genuine. "We aren't getting married or anything. I'm in high school."

"Are you enthralled with him?" Colette asked.

"He's pretty enthralling," Yves muttered.

"Listen to your grandmother, Yves. You're an extortionately attractive young man. You're only going to get more handsome. Look at your father."

Remy's fingers twitched in Wyn's.

"And do what your father did," she went on. "Enjoy yourself, but do not settle. Wait for the right one."

The room went completely silent.

Colette, pretending not to know she'd dropped the bomb of uttering her first public acknowledgement that she approved of Wyn for Remy, turned to Guillaume who was sitting in an armchair across from where she was in another. "You should go with them tomorrow night, my love. I'm not up to it, but the children need to get back to school. This visit is short. You should make the most of it."

"I shall go," he murmured, not looking at her.

The guests were gone, appearances no longer needed to be kept. He wasn't being cruel or rude, but Remy's father also was not having it. And saying throwaway things that were nevertheless kind about Wyn weren't going to crack the wall he was building between them.

His mother knew when she was stymied, so she turned to Manon.

Remy got tense again.

"At dinner, you spoke of someone you're seeing," she noted.

"Yeah, Benji," Manon confirmed carefully.

"What does he do?" Colette inquired.

"He's a graduate student, studying forestry."

"What can a man do with such a degree?" Colette demanded to know.

"A lot, but it doesn't matter what he does," Manon retorted. "I know what I'm going to do. I'm going to follow in my mom's footsteps, and it's gonna be righteous."

"Smart girl," Colette sniffed, sending another ripple of surprise through the room. "Stick to that path and do not follow your grandmother's. Don't get me wrong, the happiest day of my life will always be when I first saw your grandfather. It was also the luckiest day. He was perfect for me. But before that, I wiled time away when I should have been making my mark. Learning about *me*. Take it from your grandmama, Manon. Know who you truly are before you ever give yourself to somebody. Or more importantly, create a family."

At his age, his father's jaw was not as firm as it used to be, but it was so solid right then, none of the grenades his mother was launching were going to shake it loose.

Colette scooted to the end of her seat and looked to her son.

Fantastic.

He was next.

"Did you enjoy tonight, Remy?" she inquired.

"Yeah, Mom. It's always great spending time with the crew. Thanks for organizing it," Remy replied.

"My pleasure," she said quietly then let him off the hook, or purposefully didn't bait him on it, and looked back to Guillaume. "I'm tired, darling."

Guillaume sipped his port and replied, "Then I'll see you when I go upstairs."

Colette's face froze, and Remy caught Manon giving wide eyes to her mother.

But he turned to his son. "How about you walk your grandmother upstairs?"

"Sure," Yves readily agreed, popping up from his chair. He walked to Colette, offered his arm, and with exaggerated gallantry, did a small bow and said, "My lady."

His mother sat on the edge of her seat, staring up at her grandson, and Remy felt his chest tighten as her upper lip began to quiver.

She rallied, wrapped her fingers around his arm and replied, "Kind sir."

"I'm gonna stay up there after I see to Grandma. After being dragged out of bed this morning then dragged through New Orleans, I need to hit the sack," Yves announced as he helped his grandmother out of her chair and started them to the door.

And again, as Wyn said something to their son, Remy was tense.

She was trying to hide it, but his mom was going slowly, looked stiff, and a night she could easily face and then go to their club and have a nightcap after, had clearly tired her out.

"'Night, everyone. Thanks for a fun party, Pépé," Yves called.

"*Ravi que ça t'aie plu*, Yves," Guillaume returned.

(I'm so glad you enjoyed it.)

"Welp!" Manon cried after they left the room, gracefully moving from lounging on her hip on the floor in front of the fireplace to her knees. "Even though no one dragged me out of bed at oh dark thirty to take a run, I'm going to go up too. You don't look this fantastic without good sleep. It was a great night, Pépé. You're the best."

Like her mother would do, she had no issue moving from any position to the next, even in that long dress, which was what she did, taking her feet.

She then went right to her grandfather to kiss his cheek, and Remy felt Guillaume's enraptured expression in the back of his throat before their daughter came to her mom and dad to do the same thing.

"Hold up, honey, I'm going to call it a night too," Wyn declared before Manon disappeared.

He began to move, turning to her, starting, "I'll—"

"No, you won't," she said under her breath, her eyes darting to Guillaume and back to Remy.

He sighed, accepted her kiss and watched her after she rose from beside him go to Guillaume and bend to peck his father's cheek.

"Good night, gents," she called on her way out, linked arms with their girl and smiled largely at the men. "I'll see you both at breakfast. Stuffed full of beignets. I missed the House this morning and I'm all over it tomorrow."

She gave an elegant wave, and with their daughter, disappeared out the door.

Remy turned to his father. "Another drink?"

Guillaume looked him right in the eye. "I know what you're doing, and it is far from your job to make me feel better, *fiston*."

"I didn't leave Wyn for another woman," Remy announced.

Not smooth, but Guillaume shut his mouth so fast, Remy could convince himself he heard his teeth clatter.

"I can't deny I had buried some issues about how I grew up, they affected me and our marriage to the point I did something mindless and stupid. But it wasn't about another woman."

"But...we had heard you were living with someone, and you told me yourself there was someone else."

Remy nodded. "Yes. My mindless stupidity lasted three years and Myrna was a part of that. I regret it for a variety of reasons. She felt there could be something more, even if I was clear I didn't feel the same. I was so deep in my head, I didn't realize she'd never let that idea go. It got messy. That's on her, but it's also on me. She asked to move in, I shouldn't have said yes. Allowing her to move in was a statement I didn't mean to make. And now I see how she could misinterpret it."

It took a beat before Guillaume asked, "Do you know now why you said yes?"

Remy lifted and dropped his chin. "Yes and no. I know I was lonely. I was lost. I knew in my gut I'd fucked up, but that was buried so deep, it didn't occur to me to sort my shit. But I never should have involved yet another person in that. I'd already hurt my family, I didn't need to drag someone else into it. So I don't exactly understand why I did that last. I just know it's over."

"You seem to have a handle on all of this now," Guillaume noted.

Remy shrugged. "Someone said something that hurt Wyn. She came to a family meeting, and I saw she'd been crying. Things got a lot clearer after that."

Guillaume turned his attention to his glass and smiled into his port. "*J'imagine que oui.*"

(I imagine they did.)

He took a sip and asked his son, "Who hurt Wyn?"

"One of her friends. Not a nice woman. Hated me even before I left Wyn, and she let Wyn know it."

Guillaume's brows shot together. "Hated you? But why?"

"She had a lot of reasons, and she shared those with Wyn too."

"Of course, Wyn stopped this madness," Guillaume said with surety.

To that, Remy shook his head. "No, she just bitched to me about what the woman would say."

Guillaume tensed in his chair. "Why on earth would she do that?"

"Because she thought I hung the moon. And because of that, she thought I could take people talking shit about me. It was me being a goddamn idiot that proved to my wife I'm human."

"You hang the moon, Remy."

Remy went solid.

"For her, for your children...for me," Guillaume carried on.

"Dad—"

"Do you not think you do?" Guillaume demanded.

"I know I don't. No one does."

"You do."

"Dad—"

Remy's body gave a jolt as his father abruptly surged to his feet. "*You do.*"

Surprised—and worried—by his father's reaction, Remy murmured, "Please, sit down, Dad."

"When a parent hurts you, the only thing you can think is what you did wrong to deserve it."

Right.

There it was.

"Dad, sit and let me get you another port."

Guillaume sat, but he said, "It's important you know this."

"I'm not perfect."

"You are to me. To Wyn. To your children."

"Not anymore to Wyn or the kids. I broke our family apart."

"Then you fixed it," Guillaume retorted. "Perfection isn't *perfect*, Remy. *Mon Dieu*. There's perfection in righting a wrong. There's perfection in taking an incorrect turn and finding yourself on an unexpected but beautiful journey. Even if there's pain along that journey, if it takes you where you're supposed to be, it makes it no less perfect. The woman who sat at your side, spending half the dinner leaning into you thinks you light the night sky. The children who act as sentries for you know no other world but that one because that is all you gave to them." He shook his head. "You've always been so hard on yourself. Now, I know why."

Quietly, Remy rebuked, "Neither of us can blame her for everything."

"We can't?" Guillaume asked.

"Dad, she's not going to be with us much longer."

"I don't wish to talk about your mother," Guillaume decreed.

Remy's lips thinned.

Even if he didn't want to talk about Colette, his dad wasn't done with their last subject.

"Has it occurred to you that in messing up, as you say, you gave your children permission to do the same? There's also perfection in understanding you don't always need to be perfect," Guillaume asserted.

Remy studied his father a beat because this was absolutely a point to consider.

But not about himself.

He then reminded him, "I hurt all of them."

"It's impossible to live without hurt, Remy," Guillaume rejoined. "Surely you of all people know that. You learned it early enough."

And that was self-recriminating.

But he had no shot at a response.

At that point, Sabre strolled in, greeting, "Hey. You guys are still up."

Guillaume and Remy looked to Sah, but it was Remy who spoke.

"Love you, but, son, I expressly told you not to go there with Nat."

Sabre's face got hard as Guillaume inquired, "Why on earth would you do that?"

"She's having a tough time of it lately," Remy told his dad.

"I'm sure I've not met a single woman who does not find time less tough when a handsome man pays her attention."

"There are times when that's the case," Remy replied.

"*Ridicule*," Guillaume returned.

"There are *times*, Dad," Remy stated.

And it took another beat before Guillaume's face paled.

Then his gaze moved to Sabre. "You handled her with care, *fiston*?"

"Yeah, Pépé," Sabre assured.

"Now that you got her home, lay off," Remy ordered.

"Gonna be hard, since I think I talked her into transferring to U of A next semester," Sabre retorted.

Jesus Christ.

"Sah, why would you do that?" Remy demanded.

"Because she needs someone looking after her."

"You're there for a semester and then you're gone, Sah. She's in her freshman year."

"Then Yves will be there next year."

"What if he goes to ASU to stay close to Theo?"

"If he goes to ASU, I'm never talking to his ass again. But Nat needs to get away from this place."

"That'll take her away from her family, Sabre," Guillaume pointed out.

"Yeah. And it'll also take her away from Loyola, where the guy who raped her also goes," Remy fired back.

Guillaume made a pained noise.

Remy was stunned.

"She told you that?" he queried.

"Yeah," Sabre grunted.

"Why is he still—?" Remy started.

"Listen, Dad, it's hers. It's all hers. She gets to handle it how she wants. Okay?" Sabre clipped.

"How much did you guys talk?" Remy asked quietly.

"It took some work, but she opened up. I've known her since we were little. It's no surprise."

Maybe not, but his son had to be half miracle worker to get the shy girl who'd been there that night to open up about what had happened to her.

"If you like her—" Remy began.

"You know, she's been raped," Sabre bit out. "It's not like she's dirty or unfit or broken forever or anything."

"I absolutely know that, Sah. And I see you're feeling this deeply. But you have two allies sitting in this room. Settle down," Remy growled.

Father and son stared at each other.

And then Sabre said, "I wanna find him and I wanna—"

"I know."

"I cannot believe that piece of trash is walking around campus like nothing happened."

"I can't believe that either. But like you said, it's hers."

"I think I might walk Manon to every one of her classes from now on and sleep in a tent outside her house."

Remy relaxed.

"How do you, like...let her be in the world?" Sabre asked.

"The same way I can let you be in the world," Remy answered. "I understand life is going to find ways to kick you in the face. But I know I raised good, strong, smart kids who will carry on. And if they can't, they know they can always come to me for help. The same thing you and I both know that Nat has."

"I want her to come to Arizona," Sabre declared.

"Because you like her?"

"Yeah, but not only. She needs to get away from this place. She needs a fresh start. But also just...*yeah*. She's gorgeous and she's sweet and she's Nat. And the Nat I took home tonight is not ever going to get there with me long distance. I'll always be the older brother who's safe to talk to when I don't wanna be that anymore. And that has to happen in Arizona."

"You could move to New Orleans," Guillaume put in smoothly.

"I can't do that and work for Dad, Pépé," Sabre replied.

"*Je vois*," Guillaume said, smiling a small smile before drinking the last of his port.

But as much as he loved Sabre and the words he just spoke, Remy was conflicted.

He wanted to work with his son at his firm.

He also wanted his kids to go off and explore.

Because when he did that, he'd met their mother.

And there was no escaping the fact Remy's mother was right.

He loved Nat and he hated what had happened to her.

But both of them were far too young to get too caught up in the emotions they were feeling right now. Because it was not lost on Remy that Sabre might feel like the big brother now, but that wasn't the way Nat looked at him.

"Go get yourself a drink, kid," he ordered.

"You want another one?" Sah asked.

"You too jazzed about Nat to go to bed?"

"Totally."

"Then sure," Remy answered. Even if what he wanted was to meet his wife in bed, he wanted more to have a drink with his son and talk things out so Sabre wouldn't invent ways to keep himself hyped up and angry and then find his way to Loyola's campus.

"Pépé?" Sabre asked, coming to get Remy's glass.

"I'm done for the night, *merci*, Sabre."

"Cool. Be back," Sabre muttered and walked out of the room.

And when he did, Guillaume stood.

"This is all for me," he announced.

"All right, Dad. Sleep well," Remy replied.

Guillaume nodded and walked to the door.

He stopped just beyond it, turned back to Remy, then looked to his side, down the hall to the front parlor where Sabre undoubtedly was at the drinks cabinet.

Then he looked back at Remy.

"Let him have this," he advised.

"They're too young," Remy refuted. "And she's fragile."

"Ah, but you see, life is moments. The French know this. The French know moments need to be lived. If you look too far in the future, Remy, you don't see what's before you." He tipped his head to the hall. "This is their time now. I never understood when people said youth is wasted on the young. Young people live in moments. It seems to me they know precisely what they're doing. Sabre and Natalya need their time now, Natalya most especially. But being young, they live the fact that nothing is forever. It's just *now*. And if it's right, if it's meant to be, the path will lead there. It always leads back to what's meant to be. You know that above all, no?"

Wyn was upstairs in bed, waiting for him.

So he, above all, knew that.

"You're right, Dad," Remy admitted.

That was when his father delivered his parting shot.

After another glance down the hall then back to Remy, he asked, "*Et mon fils,* you do not think you hang the moon?"

He made a *tsk* noise.

And vanished from sight.

CHAPTER 24
Perfect Boy

Wyn

I looked up from what I was doing with Remy's cock in my mouth, but I knew better.

My gaze going up that long body, encountering that flat stomach, that wide, slightly furred chest, that muscled neck, his stubbled jaw to find his eyes dark and on me.

Yes.

Always a mistake to look at Remy when I was sucking him off.

There was a flush to his cheekbones and absolutely a smolder in his gaze. But he and his big body were sprawled before me, head to the headboard, pillows under his shoulders, one long leg straight, the other bent and fallen to the side, like he was relaxed and just hanging out while I serviced his dick.

No matter how many times I'd done it, it always got to me.

And this was no exception.

I kept eye contact as I took him deep then sucked hard as I slid him out.

He smirked.

Really?

Time to play dirty.

This I did, sliding him back in and grasping his balls, giving them a little tug.

He grunted, then I found myself being dragged up his body. He rolled us.

Kicking one of my legs aside with his knee, he used his hips to aim and then glided inside.

Nice.

I huffed out a breath.

"We get nasty when there aren't five other people in the house, three of them my babies," he growled in my ear as he shifted gears from gliding to starting to fuck me.

Okay, was it hotter than all that had just transpired when my husband called his grown kids his "babies?"

Don't bother to answer.

I knew the answer.

It was yes.

"I think nasty got us two of those babies," I panted in his ear as my hands slid to his ass.

He lifted his head, going faster *and* harder, warning, "Wyn."

"Two houses, we need to double up on our sex box, baby," I told him.

Another growl, this one with no words, definitely fucking me now as he took my mouth and spiked his tongue inside.

I arched into him and dug my nails into his ass.

He began to slam into me.

Now we were talking.

He broke the kiss and stilled, I stilled, the house stilled when we heard Colette scream, "*Don't you dare think you'll move her into this house!*" Pause, probably for a reply from Guillaume before, "*Not even over my dead body! I'm leaving everything to Remy! My son will see to it that* cunt *will never step foot over the threshold.*"

The C-word?

Whoa.

A door slammed and I lifted my hand to Remy's jaw.

He began to focus on me, but his eyes went to the door when we heard more from Colette.

Except now it was coming from the hall.

"*Don't you walk away from me! I'm the bad guy? Me? They think* I'm *the villain of this story, when their precious grandpa* fucked everything that moved!"

Remy pulled out, rolled off, tossed the covers over me and grabbed his jeans.

Through this, Guillaume could be heard ordering, "Go back to your room."

To which Colette retorted, "It's *our* room, Guillaume, even if you've *far* from slept every night of our loving marriage by my side."

Remy was yanking up his jeans, and I was out of bed reaching for my robe.

"This is not the time," Guillaume declared.

"When's the time, my love? They're all here and I'm *dying*. Remy should know my express wishes about what to do after I die while you and your *whore* circle like *vultures*," Colette returned.

I was tugging the belt closed on my robe, and Remy was still pulling on a tee as he yanked open the door.

"Not here, not now," he commanded, stepping into the hall. "Mom, go back to your room. Dad, you and I will—"

"You and your father, you and your father, *you and your father!*" Colette screeched just as I arrived at Remy's back and pressed close.

Her gaze was on her son, and she was standing in the middle of the hall, barefoot, wearing a pink peignoir set, of all things.

"What about *me*, Remy?" she demanded. "As usual, you'll go off and console your father, but what about *me*? I'm the one who's *dying*."

"*Je m'en occupe*, Remy," Guillaume murmured.

I wasn't sure, but I thought he said, "I'll handle this."

"Dad—" Remy started.

"Listen to me, Remy," Colette ordered. "Listen closely to your mother. You do not let that Estelle anywhere near," she slapped a hand to her chest, "*my home*," she tugged at her embroidered robe, "*my things*. This is *your* home, your *grandfather's* home, your *great-grandfather's* home. Your *legacy*. And it should not be besmirched by his," she tossed her hand toward Guillaume, "*filth*. If you cannot promise me you'll do that, I'm leaving it all to *Yves*."

But Remy was stuck on something else she said, I could tell by the way I felt him holding his body.

"*On ira parler*," Guillaume said, what seemed like urgently, to Remy.

I knew part of that: We'll go talk.

"Estelle?" Remy asked incredulously.

And boom.

From the way he asked that, I remembered what Remy had told me last week.

That was his father's lover from years ago. The one he'd introduced Remy to.

She was still...?

They were still...?

Just as urgently from Guillaume, "*Laisse-moi t'expliquer. S'il te plait.*"

Definitely, let me explain. Please.

Remy looked to his mother. "Mom, go back to bed."

And I pressed closer to his back when Colette's face twisted and she shrieked, "*I knew it! You always take his side! You* never *loved me. You and your father, you and your father.* YOU AND YOUR FATHER!"

"Colette, calm down and go see to yourself," Guillaume ordered, approaching her.

But she stepped back, not taking her eyes off Remy, so I wrapped my arm around his belly and my heart sank a bit when I saw the other doors in the hall were open.

Not that they couldn't already hear, but our children were blatantly listening.

Listening to their father's life growing up performed in a drama in the hallway.

"And just like your father, off *fucking other women*, when your wife is at home *raising your children*," she accused.

Remy started to back up, I knew, to push me into our room as he called, "Kids, doors closed!"

"They should know, do you not agree?" Colette asked. Then shouted, "*Don't you walk away from me, Remy Jacques Gastineau!*"

"Mom, you need to—" Remy began.

"I need to what?' she demanded. Suddenly, she looked at me. "You!"

Remy pushed harder and I was in the room.

He was closing the door when she screamed, "*You let him leave! What kind of wife are you? You let him leave!*"

He turned to me.

I framed his face and ordered straightaway, "Honey, look at me."

"*Don't you touch me!*" Colette shrieked. "*She wears his rings! She let him go and she wears his rings! Don't you dare TOUCH ME!*"

Her voice had been going down the hall and then the door slammed again.

His mind was to that, I could see it, so I repeated, "Look at me, Remy."

We heard a loud bump.

And Remy was out the door, gone.

I raced after him.

"Back in your rooms," he snarled at our kids who were now in the hall.

He shot through the door at the other end, I went in after him and stopped dead.

Colette was standing holding a heavy glass orb in her hand.

With apparent difficulty, Guillaume was trying to pick himself up from the floor, at the same time holding his jaw.

Remy crouched by his dad, but he looked to his mom. "Did you hit him?"

She shook her hair and demanded coldly, "Get out of our room."

I dashed to Remy and Guillaume. Colette made a move toward me as I did, I skirted her easily, but suddenly Remy was there between her and me.

He yanked the orb out of her hand, and he was not gentle, but how he did it did not harm her, and she cried out like he'd assaulted her.

"Come with me to the kitchen," I whispered to Guillaume and his already swelling jaw. "We'll get some ice."

"He was hurting me," Colette claimed.

"Come with me, please," I repeated to Guillaume.

"Come on, Pépé." Sah was there, stronger than me, carefully helping his grandfather up.

"Oh, he's so *suave*. He's so *charming*. You're all under his spell," Colette mocked as Manon got close to Guillaume's other side and slipped an arm around him while he held his jaw. Sabre took his weight, and they started walking their grandfather to the door. "I know what that feels like. It's so very beautiful. Until he *betrays you*."

"Grandmama, let's talk, okay?" Yves, standing by his father, cutting her off from Guillaume, Sah, Manon and me, urged. "You can get dressed. We'll go out. Get some chicory coffee."

"He *touched me*, Yves," she pouted.

"I'll make some coffee, bring it up," Yves said.

"Melisande makes it perfectly," she sniffed.

"I'll go get some, bring it up," Yves pushed.

"My perfect boy," she half-whispered, the other half was a fawning coo.

My perfect boy.

A chill went down my spine, sending out shards of pain and freezing my blood in my veins.

She'd said that to Yves before.

When he was being good, catering to her crazy-ass needs, had she said that to Remy?

Good God.

Now I understood his driving need to be perfect if *this* was what he was up against.

This had been his life.

This had been his *childhood*.

I had no idea how I kept my feet because my heart had shattered.

"Son—" Remy started.

"Got this, Dad," Yves murmured.

"Son—"

Yves turned to his father. "Got it."

239

Unable to bury my need to get my husband away from her, I went to them, grabbed Remy's hand and tugged.

He looked down to me.

And the look on his face destroyed me.

Yes.

He'd tried to be her perfect boy.

Fuck.

It sucked she was dying because I wanted to *kill her*.

Colette spoke.

"I am so very sorry, Wyn, I don't know..." I turned to Colette, who was holding her robe together at her chest, gazing about as if dazed and she didn't know where she was, the wily, crazy, *bitchface* fox, "...what came over me."

I said nothing, just looked to my son as I pulled his father to the door.

"It's okay, Mom," Yves said. "I'll be right down to get some coffee."

I studied him.

I saw he had this.

"Be very careful," I urged.

He jutted his chin at me.

I nodded then yanked Remy out the door.

He barely got both feet in the hall before he again looked down at me, disengaged his hand from mine, and then, with his long-ass legs, he ate the distance to the stairs.

I ran after him.

I didn't catch up, but I was only a couple of steps behind when he hit the kitchen.

Manon was holding a dishtowel filled with ice to Guillaume's jaw. Sabre was prowling the kitchen like a cat. Guillaume was trying to pretend no one was there.

And Melisande was not messing about with putting a breakfast tray together.

Her face was tight with fury, but her movements were economical and practiced.

She caught Remy's eyes and didn't hesitate sharing, "She does this." Pause and, "Too damned often."

"Melly," Guillaume murmured.

"He's your son, he should know," Melisande retorted.

Guillaume shut up.

"I can calm her down," Melisande told Remy.

"You're safe with her?" Remy asked.

"She only does it to her husband," Melly spat.

"Yves is up there," Remy replied.

She nodded, picked up the tray and hustled out.

"I have this, *ma belle*," Guillaume said to Manon, trying to take the ice from her.

"I have it, Pépé," she assured.

"My girl—" Guillaume tried again.

"She won't leave your side, Dad. So don't try to make her," Remy rumbled.

I pressed my front to my husband's side and slid my arms around him.

He wrapped his arm around my shoulders.

"*Si bien*," Guillaume muttered. He lifted his gaze to Remy. "What can I say? I fell in love with her."

"Mom?" Remy asked.

Guillaume shrugged. "Both of them."

Both of them.

Colette and...

Estelle.

"And I met her...why?" Remy asked.

Guillaume's gaze drifted. "I was going to leave, you see. She had stopped... with you. At least I thought. But not with..." Guillaume didn't finish, but we all got the gist since Manon was icing his jaw.

He thought she'd stopped beating Remy.

But she had not stopped beating Guillaume.

"And she, the other, *my* other." He couldn't wring the fondness out of his tone when he referred to Estelle. "She loved me."

"And she didn't hit you with huge-ass glass marbles," Sabre growled.

"Sah," I said softly.

"So you took me to see her because...?" Remy prompted.

"I wanted to see if you liked her. We were all going to move to France."

"When I was there, you went back to the bedroom with her," Remy reminded him.

Our kids exchanged glances.

"Of course, she was upset," Guillaume said.

"What?" Remy asked.

"She made a special sundae for you, and you didn't seem to like it. She wanted you to like her. So very much, she fretted about it for days before I took you to meet her. I told her you liked ice cream, and she must have tried ten different sundaes before she settled on that one to make for you. She was upset when she thought you didn't like her. So I took her back to suggest she give you some time, it all doesn't happen just like that. Then I came out and we went home."

"I thought you were back there forever."

"You were young, everything feels like forever, especially if you're bored and have nothing to do. We were away perhaps ten minutes. If that long."

Remy looked out the kitchen window.

I held on to him even if my heart was breaking for Guillaume.

"Why didn't you leave?" Remy asked the window.

"I came to my senses."

Remy looked back at him.

"If I left, who would see to your mother?" Guillaume explained.

"Oh, Pépé," Manon whispered, still holding the ice to his jaw but putting her head to his shoulder.

"But Estelle...she's still in your life?" Remy pressed on.

"She loves me," Guillaume said softly.

"*Oh Pépé*," Manon moaned, still holding the ice, with her head on his shoulder, and now she turned into her granddad and slid an arm around him.

Remy stood motionless for a second.

Then he walked out the back door, down the stairs to the side of the house, and I followed him with Sah following me.

Remy stopped, transferred the orb he was still holding to his right hand, and with a brutal side-arm throw and deadly accuracy, he launched it into a bird bath, which broke apart on impact.

"I know you're ticked as shit, but that was rad," Sah remarked.

"He had a chance to be happy, and he took care of her," Remy said.

I got closer and murmured, "Honey."

"He had a chance to get away from this goddamn mess, and he stayed with her."

Sah got closer and said, "Dad."

Remy looked to his son. "Is his jaw broken?"

"Melisande, who by the way, is kick-fucking-ass, felt it a little bit while Manon was getting ice. She said it's okay. But seriously, Dad, that thing broke a concrete bird bath. We should get him to the hospital."

Remy nodded, turned on his bare foot and stalked to the door.

Sah went to follow him, but I caught his hand, "You go with them. Take Manon. I'm staying here with Yves."

And Colette.

"Don't get near that batty bitch," Sabre ordered.

"We'll be okay."

"Mom, I'm not going any-fucking-where until you promise me right now, you aren't gonna get anywhere near that crazy bitch."

Damn it.

I had a few things to get straight.
I stared at my son.
"I won't get near her," I promised.
He examined my face.
Then he turned on *his* bare foot and jogged after his dad.

CHAPTER 25
Part of the Family

Wyn

Needless to say, the tailgate party was out.

After they'd left to go to the hospital, I phoned Katy to explain why we wouldn't be joining them at the football game that day, and I did not hold back with this explanation.

I did this not only because Beau had gone out of his way to get us tickets and they should know why we weren't able to join them, but also because we didn't live in New Orleans, close to Colette and Guillaume.

And that scene, as hideous as it was, obviously was not unusual.

In other words, I was worried about Guillaume, and since we lived a continent away, we might need backups.

"I cannot believe my ears," Katy hissed after I explained that morning's goings-on (leaving out the Estelle part, but that was the only part I left out) and the fact Remy, Manon and Sabre were at the hospital with Guillaume.

"I couldn't believe mine either, or my eyes. I don't know how long they'll be, but I don't think anyone will be in the mood for football after they get back. I'm so sorry, Katy. It was very nice of Beau to—"

"Stop it, that's the last thing we'll be worried about today," Katy cut me off to say. "Are you still there? At the house?"

"Yes, with Yves, who's with his grandmother, settling her down."

I heard something out in the hall, so I went to the door of our bedroom where I'd vamoosed to put on some underwear (at least) and opened it to see Melly carrying an empty tray to the stairs.

She gave me a tight-lipped nod.

I returned it, she moved to the stairs, and I looked down the hall to see the door to Colette's room was closed.

I closed my own, and while this was happening, Katy asked, "Do you want me to come over? And Beau? He can come too. I can also call Jason. Does Remy need his boys?"

"I need to ask Remy about that, but I don't want to disturb him right now," I replied.

"Of course. Yes, of course," she muttered.

"I'll be in touch, but don't change your plans. I know that would upset Remy. Though, it might be an on-call situation for tonight."

"Beau loves football, Wyn, but he loves Remy more. So even if it's before that, we're there."

I loved that, obviously.

"Thanks, Katy. I'll keep you in the loop, all right?"

"All right, babe. Take care. And while Remy's not around, stay away from that woman." Her voice dropped when she finished, "Dear God. Poor Guillaume."

"I will. Thanks for listening."

"Anytime, and definitely let us know. Beau will be worried, yeah?"

I could tell by her voice, she would too.

"Yeah."

We said our goodbyes, and even though I was still in my robe, I walked downstairs, into the kitchen.

I barely made it into the room before Melly, at the sink doing some dishes, said, "He made me promise not to say anything."

I was sure he did.

I walked closer to her and grabbed a dishtowel.

"I told him he should call his son. She should get help," Melly went on. "He told me he didn't want anyone to know, specifically Remy. He said it was a personal thing. He defends her. Says she's high-strung. Her upbringing was difficult." She looked from the sink to me. "Her upbringing was difficult," she practically spat. "Like she's thirty and discovering herself. Not eighty and absolutely should know better."

I made a noise of assent.

"But I should have said something," she concluded.

"Well, we know now," I replied softly, no recrimination in my voice, because it wasn't her fault. They were her employers. But I could see by the line of her frame she was still tense. "And if Guillaume asked you not to, that made it very difficult for you. To be loyal to him and feel disloyal if you were to have shared."

"I know Estelle," she declared.

I took a mixing bowl from her, vaguely wondering what she'd made in it, and started drying it, all while gazing at her as my silent cue to go on.

"She fell, broke her wrist, found doing some things around the house difficult, and Mr. Gastineau was going over to help her quite a bit. Mrs. Gastineau figured it out and pitched her usual fits, and yes, that's plural. So he couldn't go. It tore him up. I heard him on the phone with her. I told him I'd go. And I did, a few days a week for about a month."

She'd been rubbing a wooden spoon under water for some time, and she stopped doing this not to rinse but to look at me, and kept talking.

"She's lovely. She's the complete antithesis of Mrs. Gastineau. We made friends. We decided to form a two-girl dinner club. We go out to dinner once a month together, she gets a pick, I get the next pick. She's been going to some of the restaurants for decades that she's taken me to, and everyone loves her. *Everyone* loves her, Wyn. Because she's that kind of lady."

"Okay," I said softly, having no idea what else to say and somewhat preoccupied with how heavy my heart was at hearing what Melly had to say about Estelle.

"He needs to move from here, move in with her. I can take care of Mrs. Gastineau. He needs to get out of here."

I knew what to say to *that*.

Or at least what to ask.

And my voice was pitched high in concern when I asked, "How often does this happen?"

Melly shook her head, realized what she was doing with the spoon, rinsed it and handed it to me. "Not a lot, and still too much. It's the shouting. The slamming doors. The ugly words hurled at him." She looked at me again. "Was she always like this?"

"She's never been a warm woman, not even to the kids, though she didn't hide her love for Guillaume, so no, it's never been like this. I've actually never heard them fight like they did yesterday, and definitely not today."

She gave a curt nod. "There's all kinds of abuse, I'm sure you know. She hits him and pushes him and scratches him. But the things she *says* to him. It's awful, Wyn. I completely understand why he's with Estelle. What I don't understand is why he stays with Mrs. Gastineau."

"Is she...appropriate with you?" I asked carefully.

"She thinks I'm her ally, and I'll admit, I make it so she does. I don't agree with her when she complains about Mr. Gastineau, but I nod and make sounds that she might interpret as that. I do it hoping, if she gets it out with me, she'll be nicer to him. Or hoping he'll see I can take care of her, handle her, and he can find some happiness."

She straightened from the sink, turned fully to me and kept going before I could say anything.

"You know, he isn't going to be around forever either. Estelle is younger than him. She isn't, like, some arm candy type of person. She's in her late sixties. But she has time...*they* could have time to *be happy*. Because one thing I know, she's given up half her life to be with him, having him and not having him, because she loves him more than I've ever seen anyone love anybody, except for how much Remy loves you."

Except for how much Remy loves you.

Estelle loved Guillaume how Remy loved me.

My heart, which I had not yet had the time to bandage together, hurt even more at hearing that.

"And just to be clear, I'll stay on," she continued. "I helped nurse her through the last cancer situation. I'll help this time. She trusts me. She likes me. I'll never let her think differently. So *you* can trust me. You and Remy. But Mr. Gastineau..."

She hesitated, then forged on.

"It's getting worse. And it'll get even *more* so. And maybe in a world where things are cut and dried, you can say what he's done, having two ladies he loves, is the wrong thing. But it isn't. In this instance, it isn't. Because...yes, Mrs. Gastineau needs someone just like him to love her despite who she is. And Mr. Gastineau needs someone just like Estelle, who loves him for all that he is."

I felt the tears welling up, and as Melly watched me, I saw them well up in her too.

To try to put her at ease, my voice slightly husky, I said, "Obviously, we're going to have to deal with this while we're here. And I will one hundred percent keep you informed. But I thank you, for me, but also for Remy. I thank you for how you've cared for them. *Both* of them. This has to have been a real trial for you, and it means more than I can say that you stuck by them. Truly, Melly, you have our gratitude. From the bottom of our hearts."

She gave me a jerky head nod, swallowed and grabbed a dishtowel, muttering, "Do you want some breakfast?"

I allowed the change in conversation and asked, "What did you make?"

"There's fresh biscuits and gravy, or waffles."

"Maybe we should move here and help out," I mumbled.

She cracked a grin at that, which brought me at least a little relief.

247

"I'm going to go for a waffle," I decided. "But I'm going to check on Yves and get dressed first. Okay?"

She nodded.

I moved to the door.

I didn't move through it, turning back when Melly called my name.

"I knew it wouldn't last," she said.

"What?" I asked, tensing for more information about Guillaume, Colette and Estelle.

"Remy's and your breakup."

A gust of air escaped my lips.

"You're his life," she went on. "I worried for him a lot. So did his dad, even Mrs. Gastineau. He can breathe without you, but he can't *breathe* without you. Do you know what I mean?"

I nodded, having trouble breathing myself.

"You feel the same way," she said. "So we all worried about you too, I think, even Mrs. Gastineau."

"It's been hell," I replied softly.

"I'm so happy it's over."

"Me too, honey," I said with feeling. "Me too."

"Yves will want the biscuits," she declared.

She knew us so well.

Part of the family.

"I'll make sure there's plenty left for Sabre and Remy too. And a waffle. For Manon," she finished.

Yes.

Perfect.

I smiled at her.

Part of the family.

CHAPTER 26
Soit Dit en Passant

Remy

When he drove into the back drive of the graceful, oppressively beautiful mansion that was his childhood home and stopped, having given the kids the plan while the staff were assessing his father at the hospital, Remy had barely put the car into park before both Manon and Sah peeled out.

Remy turned immediately to his father in the passenger seat.

"Hang on a second, Dad," he said.

Guillaume had his hand on the door handle ready to step out, but he twisted to Remy, still holding the ice pack they gave him at the hospital on his face. No broken bones, which with that orb and at his age was a miracle. But they told him to keep that pack on as long as he could take it.

And apparently, his father had developed a high threshold for pain, because it had to be cold as fuck, but he hadn't stopped icing it since he sat in the kitchen with Manon.

Remy felt his lips thin.

Guillaume looked to the back of the Denali, noticed the kids were long gone, and his eyes darted to Remy.

"Son—"

"I'd like to ask Sah to bunk with Yves for the rest of our trip. Wyn and I'll move into my old room. And we'll move you into the guest suite."

Guillaume took the pack from his face and turned fully to his son.

"Remy, please—"

"I'm not telling you to do that, I'm asking you to think on it. And when I say that, I mean *please* consider it."

"Your mother and I have been together for a very long time, *fiston*," Guillaume said quietly.

"She's not too old, or too sick, to learn there are consequences to her actions," Remy replied.

A warmth swept into his father's face, along with a sadness, and Remy's stomach plummeted.

"It is who we are, Remy," Guillaume whispered.

"By protecting her, she took you from me," Remy announced.

Guillaume's body ticked.

"I want you back," Remy decreed.

Wet hit is father's eyes, sparkling there, and that was when Remy's throat closed.

He had to clear it before he went on, "We'll move her to Phoenix. We'll look after her. We'll make sure she has company. Is comfortable. She won't be alone at her end, I promise you that, Dad. I vow that to you. You can come visit. You can be with her when her time draws near. In the meantime, you find happiness in your life. And I want to meet Estelle again before we leave. I want Wyn to meet her. If she's up to it, the kids. And I want us seeing each other more. I want my children to get to know their grandfather. Their *real* grandfather. Not who you had to be because of the way she is."

It took a second and some clearing of his own throat before Guillaume responded.

"You must know that, although these things you say are most beautiful, I cannot abandon your mother this way. Not now."

"And I can't leave you to what's happening in that house," Remy retorted.

"Today was bad. She's distraught. Not herself. She's dying, Remy."

"It's a goddamn miracle she didn't do worse damage, Dad," Remy shot back. "I threw that sphere at a bird bath and the concrete broke apart. If she'd hit you two inches up, caught you on your temple..."

He couldn't finish.

"As I said, today was bad, Remy. I'm usually far more careful so she can't do such damage."

Wrong thing to say.

And Remy communicated that in the only way he could, considering he was so angry he wasn't able to speak, so he growled.

"Son, I'll be fine," Guillaume assured.

"I'm not leaving you to that," Remy repeated.

His dad shook his head. "You have to go back to your life. Reuniting it with your wife. Your concern touches me, *fiston*, but the dramatics of this are not the norm. I will be fine. She will be fine. *It all* will be fine."

"Then we're coming back far more often."

Guillaume's lips tipped up and he replied, "I won't argue about that."

Remy held his father's gaze a moment, debating how far to push this and deciding not to push it any further because odds were he'd get nowhere, and more importantly his father had definitely had enough that morning when it came to his mom.

Instead, he'd push for something else.

"And Estelle?" he asked.

Before Guillaume could stop it, his eyes lit with excitement, but his mouth said, "I don't think your mother—"

"This isn't about Mom. This is about the woman you love."

And then, Remy watched in shock as his father's upper lip trembled.

He'd never seen his dad betray that type of emotion.

Not once.

Not in fifty-four years.

It took a moment for him to lock it down before he replied, "I will call her."

"Good," Remy grunted.

"The children too?" Guillaume inquired. "Are you sure?"

"I am absolutely sure I want my kids to meet the woman who has loved my father for years."

Guillaume began to look doubtful. "Perhaps you should talk to Wyn about this first."

At that, Remy pulled his phone out of his back pocket, opened up his texts, and before he read them out loud, he said, "From Wyn. First, 'Melly needs a raise.' Then, 'And we're adopting her, even if it's unofficially.' After that, 'We need to talk about meeting Estelle, honey.' And then, 'I'm pretty sure Manon and Sah will track her down and introduce themselves before we leave if we don't see to it.'" He looked again to his dad. "Is that enough?"

"I love you with my whole soul."

Remy's head jerked like he'd been punched in the face.

But Guillaume was not finished.

"We are losing your mother, but I will be happy when I slip away, because I know I made a son who is the man I wanted to be."

"Stop, Dad," Remy said, his voice hoarse.

His father didn't stop.

"I was not faithful, to either of them. I cannot tell you how much I fretted that I'd bragged of that to you, and you took it in and became me, and that is why you lost Wyn."

"It isn't, Papa, I told you that," Remy whispered.

"I know you know this, Remy, you have children, but please, understand it coming from me to you right now. I don't need to be happy. I just need to know you are."

"For fuck's sake," Remy croaked, reaching long and catching his dad behind his neck, pulling the man to him, and then wrapping both arms around him.

Guillaume's arms went around Remy too.

They hugged and held on, and it took some effort for Remy to get his shit together. He felt the same coming from his father.

But when they were both breathing easier, carefully, Remy let him go.

Guillaume ducked his head as he pulled out his handkerchief.

Remy did not hide it as he rubbed the wet from his cheeks.

"I'm hungry, and I'm sure Melly has deftly switched breakfast to brunch. It isn't quite as easy to make it lunch. So we must get inside," his father shared.

Remy nodded, sniffed sharply and then got out of the car.

That was a lot. It meant the world. He was keen to tell Wyn about it.

But he should have known he and his dad couldn't have it without his mother fucking it up.

She did this by sitting at the dining room table with the rest of his family, like nothing was amiss, like he hadn't just had his father's face X-rayed because she'd very nearly crushed his jaw.

And she did it by stating the minute Guillaume and Remy strolled into the room, "*Finally*. I've asked them all to show some manners and wait for you. But we're *famished*."

Remy stood stone-still.

Guillaume shifted closer to him.

Wyn began to rise from her chair at the table.

Sabre's face turned red.

Manon went pale.

Yves placed both hands palm down on the table like he needed that control, or he didn't know what his hands would do.

And then Remy turned to his father, gently tugged the ice pack from his fingers, but it was not gentle when he tossed it on the table.

It slid across, upending the Waterford saltshaker, skittering the pepper, smearing the butter, glancing off the coffee pot and coming to a stop about a foot from his mother's place setting.

"We were at the hospital, Mom, so Dad could get an X-ray on his jaw after you attacked him, and when we return, that's what you have to say?" Remy asked with lethal calm.

She, too, slightly paled, but she also opened her mouth.

"Your father is—"

That was when it broke.

Years...

Years of holding it together tenuously. It just...

Snapped.

"*Shut the fuck up!*" Remy roared.

Colette bounced back in her chair, her hand coming to her Hermès-scarved neck.

Wyn got up from her seat.

"Remy," Guillaume murmured, getting even closer as the door to the kitchen opened and Melly came into the room.

"He wants to be with you to your end," Remy told her. "Right now, that's his call. It won't be if what happened yesterday *or* today *ever* happens again, Mom. I mean the physical abuse *and* the verbal abuse. The shouting. The foul shit that spews from your mouth. Definitely you hitting him with *anything*, even if it's just your hand. If it happens again, I'm flying out, I'm collecting you, I'm taking you back to Phoenix, putting you in an apartment, and then waiting for you to die."

"Honey," Wyn said urgently, and just as urgently making her way to him. "Let's step outside."

He glanced at his wife and said, "No." Then he looked back to his mother.

"I will not have you talk to me this way in my own home," Colette declared.

"It's my home too, Mom, as well as Dad's, and I won't have you pulverizing his bones in it," he shot back.

Colette stood, slowly, regally, and shook her head in a feminine way to get the hair away from her face before she stated, "I believe you need to call the airlines and see if you can be on an earlier flight."

"I believe that's not your call," Remy retorted.

Colette looked to his father.

"Guillaume."

It was a demand.

Handle this.

"*Je vais bien,*" Guillaume replied.

(I'm fine.)

She knew what those words meant, and she glared at her husband.

"*Soit dit en passant*," Guillaume kept going.

(By the way.)

"And I have not seen my family for three years, my love, and we have only one day left with them. Therefore, I am not going to send them home now," he continued. "So if you cannot be civil to Remy, perhaps Melly can bring you a tray in the mural room where you can eat."

"Civil...*to Remy?*" she asked. "Your son just raised his voice to me."

Guillaume didn't reply.

Not verbally.

He moved to his chair, pulled it out, looking at Melly, and he said, "I'm sorry for the delay, *ma chérie*. But we're ready for brunch now."

Sabre reached out and righted the saltshaker.

Manon used her napkin to wipe up the butter.

Melly disappeared into the kitchen.

"Do you need more ice for your jaw, Pépé?" Yves asked.

"I'm fine, Yves, but thank you," Guillaume answered, snapping his napkin in front of him and placing it on his lap.

Colette stood through all of this, glaring at her husband.

Wyn took Remy's hand and led him to his place at the table, the only person in a middle seat. Yves and Sabre flanked Colette, Manon and Wyn flanked his father.

"Pour me a cup of coffee, will you, Sah?" Remy asked.

Sabre reached for the pot as Remy slid his cup and saucer toward his son.

"I cannot—" Colette began, cut herself off when Melly appeared, and then demanded, "I'll have a tray *in my bedroom*, Melisande. *At your earliest convenience.*"

She then stormed out of the room.

Guillaume seemed tense and couldn't hide his concern, but he didn't watch her go.

"So, Pépé, the tailgate is out and probably the ghost tour too, so we decided we're doing a *Star Wars* movie marathon, and you gotta tell us where we're starting. Did you see the originals?" Sabre asked.

"No, Sabre, I—" Guillaume began.

Manon leaned into her grandfather, exclaiming, "That's *impossible*, Pépé! You haven't met Luke, Han, Leia and Chewie?" She then turned her attention to her brothers and declared, "Ohmigod, now we have, like *twenty hours* of movies to watch."

"Maybe we should do some select *Star Trek*," Yves suggested.

"Maybe we should just boil it down to *Galaxy Quest* and then get dudded up and go to one of Emeril's restaurants for dinner," Sabre suggested.

"I vote that one," Wyn put in.

"Did you bring another dudded-up outfit to wear?" Yves asked his brother.

"Am I my mother's son?" Sabre asked in return.

"You are but that doesn't mean you listen to me," Wyn stated.

"I do when you talk about looking hot," Sabre shot back.

Wyn laughed.

So did Manon.

Yves grinned broadly.

But Remy looked to his father.

He was smiling at Sabre, his face maybe not relaxed but the humor was genuine.

He also felt his son's eyes, so his focus shifted to Remy.

"What do you say, Dad? A sci-fi spoof and see if we can get in at the Delmonico?" Remy asked.

"The Delmonico, Remy? There's no way we can get a reservation at this late date," Wyn said.

"*Ne t'en fais pas*, I will find us a booking somewhere we will all enjoy," Guillaume assured as Melly returned, arms laden with food.

"Damn, Melly, why didn't you say you were bringing in a trough?" Sabre clipped, jumping from his chair and moving to help her.

"It *is* my job, Sah," she replied as he took the massive bowl of sausage gravy from her.

"This weighs a ton and I'm about to shove my whole face in it," Sabre said, staring down at the bowl.

"If you do that, Sabre Gastineau, I'm never cooking for you again," Melly warned.

Sah jolted, muttering, "Right," and he put the bowl on the table.

That was when Remy heard a chuckle from his dad.

He again looked that way.

And again, saw his father's face not exactly relaxed.

But the humor was absolutely genuine.

Remy would take it for now.

Because it was good.

And because he had no choice.

CHAPTER 27
Not Going Anywhere

Remy

"I don't know if this is a good idea," Wyn murmured, staring at the doorway leading to the hall that led to the stairs, which Remy would be climbing in a few minutes in order to have a conversation with his mother.

The kids were camped out in the family room with Guillaume, setting up to watch *Galaxy Quest*.

But Wyn had taken him aside to share fully her conversation with Melly, and although Remy didn't want to adopt her, he did decide to broach the subject with his father to feel out some other way to share their gratitude for her loyalty.

Now, he'd had his conversation with his dad.

He needed to have one with his mother, something he'd just told his wife.

But the look on Wyn's face screamed she wasn't a fan of this idea.

"Baby," he murmured.

"She's not going to change, no matter what you say," Wyn noted.

"She's dying," he stated, point blank.

Wyn's lips stretched down before she caught herself in the grimace and wiped it clean.

"I can't leave here without at least making an attempt with her at some kind of...*something*," he asserted, not very clearly, but it was the best he had because he didn't know what he was looking for from his mother, he just knew he had to try. "I also can't leave here without making it perfectly clear that what occurred this weekend cannot carry on. She's dying, he's losing her, she has to get her head out of her ass and make the time they have left something *not this*."

"You kind of made that clear earlier, honey," Wyn noted.

"I did and I didn't. I was over-emotional, ranting and had just thrown an ice pack. That isn't going to penetrate. And it's important that particular message penetrates."

"You'll get no argument from me on that," she mumbled.

"I—" he stopped talking when an alert sounded on his phone that he'd never heard before.

Puzzled, he pulled it out and stared in surprise at the notification.

It was from the app for the alarm on the house.

Not his house.

Their house.

The home he shared with Wyn, where she now lived.

He'd never deleted the app from his phone, and she'd clearly never updated the account to have him kicked off.

"What is it?" she asked when he opened the notification.

The back bedroom window sensor had been tripped.

The back bedroom being the master.

Her room.

Their room.

"Does the house alarm still go to the police?" he asked.

"Why?" she asked in return.

Shit, fuck.

They did not need something else to worry about.

He looked to her. "Apparently, I'm still an authorized user on the alarm, baby," he said, turning the screen of his phone to her.

Her eyes dropped to it and widened just as his phone rang.

It was not a known number, but considering what was happening, he took the call.

"Is this Mr. Remy Gastineau?" the caller asked.

Yep, not only did she not change the account, he was still first point of contact.

"It is," he confirmed.

"Can you please give me the verbal password for your home alarm?"

Fuck.

"Scrum."

"Thank you. We have a sensor breach on a back window in your home, Mr.

257

Gastineau, and the code has not been entered to stop the alarm. Is this you, or would you like us to dispatch police?"

"What does 'sensor breach' mean?" he asked.

"While the alarm is set, someone has either opened that window, or broken it," the rep answered.

"We're out of town. Send the police," he ordered.

"We'll see to that immediately, Mr. Gastineau. Please stay available for any calls."

"Thanks," he replied, and they rang off.

"Sensor breach?" Wyn asked, moving closer to him.

"She said either someone opened the window, or broke it," he told her, debating calling his friend Bill on a college football Saturday for something that might be nothing.

"Fabulous," Wyn mumbled.

"It'll be okay, she's sending the police," he told her, then, thinking about her jewelry, much of which he'd given to her, and he wasn't a man who skimped on presents for his wife, he said, "Please tell me you put a wall safe in that new closet of yours."

"Of course I did."

"And you didn't leave it open."

She didn't stop her eye roll. "Of course I didn't."

"And you locked anything valuable in it."

"Darling," she drawled, and he knew she was losing patience with his questions, so he felt his lips quirk because she was cute when she got uppity, and Remy definitely could use a dose of her cute *and* her uppity right now. "I'm not an idiot, but I also have tens of thousands of dollars of purses and shoes on display in that closet, and no...none of those are locked away in a safe."

His smile died.

"Locked behind a door?" he asked.

She shook her head.

"Wyn," he growled. "Seriously?"

"We have an alarm," she retorted.

"And we're out of town for four days, but even if you were at work, that closet should be shut and locked as another line of defense against intruders."

"If I did that and I came home, as I invariably do, and I went to my fabulous bathroom, which I also do, switch on the light, something I further do, and all of its lush opulence is presented to me in its full glory as a stunning visual of the fruits of my various labors, which it always is, it wouldn't be if I closed the door to the closet."

"Do you need that visual more than you need the things that make that visual the visual?" he demanded.

Her face scrunched and she fired back, "What's the point of having an alarm if it takes away my visual?"

Shit.

He'd forgotten how she could be damned adorable and totally fucking annoying at the same time.

"I cannot believe we're having this conversation," he replied.

"Yo," Yves called from the doorway. "You guys gonna park it with us and watch the movie, or are you gonna stand in here for an hour and chat?"

"There's been a breach at the house," Remy told him.

"Remy!" Wyn snapped, obviously not feeling the sharing of this news with their son, which would no doubt lead to the sharing of it with all their kids.

But Remy, for once, had no mind to his wife.

He was staring at his boy.

"Yves," he said, firm and clear, Remy's tone meaning Yves needed to communicate what was behind that freaked-out look on his face.

"Which house?" Yves asked.

"Mine. Ours. The family house...our first one. *Whatever*," Wyn babbled. "It doesn't matter. Nothing to worry about. The police are on their way."

"Our house." Yves was talking like he wasn't doing it to them.

"Yves." This time, his son's name out of Remy's mouth was a warning.

Yves focused on his dad. "Do you know where this breach was?"

"The back bedroom," Remy told him.

"Mom's room?"

Um.

No.

Remy did not like that.

Therefore, he was back to growling. "Yes. What—?"

Remy didn't finish as Wyn cut him off to repeat, "It's nothing to worry about. The police are on their way to check it out."

But he watched his son look down the hall, then Yves walked fully into the parlor and requested, "Mom, can I talk with Dad for a second alone?"

He liked that even less.

And when Remy looked to Wyn, he saw she'd cottoned on to Yves's behavior and was now regarding her son with squinting eyes.

"Why would you need to do that?" she asked.

Yves adjusted his request "Or, maybe, can you go get Sah for me? Then stay in the family room?"

Now it was Wyn who was sharing a warning with her, "Yves."

"Please, Mom, don't ask. Can you just please go get Sah and let us talk to Dad for a sec?" Yves pleaded.

And it was a plea because he was definitely troubled about something, and it wasn't just the fact that there might be a break-in.

It was something else.

Or something...*more*.

"Honey, just go," Remy urged. When Wyn looked up at him, he promised low, "I'll tell you. You know I'll tell you."

She studied his face, but she did know he'd tell her.

So she nodded, gave their son a look, then walked out.

Yves came farther into the room, and Remy waited until he saw Wyn disappear into the family room before he said to his son, "I'm not going to like this, am I?"

Yves looked to his dad and pressed his lips together.

Movement in the hall had Remy's attention returning there, and he saw Sabre not sauntering, but hustling to the parlor.

Fucking shit.

Sabre closed the door behind him and asked Yves immediately, "Someone broke into our house?"

"Sabre, me. You're talking to me," Remy demanded.

Sah looked to Remy.

"What the fuck is going on?" Remy asked.

"Okay, Dad, uh, you see, well...the thing is that it all kinda..." Sabre didn't finish and turned to Yves again. "Did you call Theo? I mean, is he on top of shit?"

Before Yves could reply, Remy stated, "If you let your friends use our home while we're away to—"

Sabre cut him off.

"No, it's Myrna."

Remy felt his torso lurch.

"Okay, see, the day you, like, shared about Grandma," Sabre said fast, "before Manon and me left Tucson, she was waiting outside my last class for me."

Remy didn't move a muscle.

"Dad," Sabre was now talking very softly, "I hate that today, with all the shit that's going down—"

"If you delay another fucking minute in telling me what the fuck is going on, Sah, I swear to God..."

Remy let that hang.

Sabre quickly began talking again.

"She told me she needed to talk, and she spewed a load of lies at me, Dad. Total lies. Whacked lies. Like, *unhinged*."

After he pointed his face to the ceiling, Remy drew in a deep breath.

"Obviously," Sah continued, "I didn't believe her, I told her that and told her to back off."

Remy returned his attention to his son and asked the question that might least have the result of him tearing the room apart.

"What does Theo have to do with this?"

Yves joined the conversation.

"After you told us about your, uh...history, Sah told me what went down. Theo was there and we decided that we were going to give you a breather with the Myrna crap, so you could deal with the Grandma crap. And she said some stuff to Sah that had us thinking she was kinda...*stalking* you. So, while I kept an eye on Mom and Sah kept an eye on Manon, Theo was going to keep an eye on...other things."

The reason both Sabre and Yves went shopping with Wyn and Manon last weekend.

Remy didn't know whether to hug his boys or shout at them.

He did neither.

He asked, "What did she say that made you think she's stalking me?"

"She knew Mom had been to your house," Sabre told him.

Remy breathed carefully and deeply.

"Can I call Theo to see if...you know, he's noticed anything?" Yves inquired carefully.

"Yes, you can. Then you tell him to stop doing whatever it is you talked him into doing," Remy replied.

"He volunteered, Dad," Yves shared, and this was proudly.

Theo was a good guy.

He was still a young guy, and it was clear Remy had underestimated just how fucked up Myrna was.

That knowledge settled hard and hot in his gut in a way it was going to linger and fester as anger turned to worry.

Because now, she might be breaking into and thus invading Wyn's space.

"Call Theo," Remy ordered. "But again, tell him to stand down. I'm phoning Bill."

Yves nodded and stepped to the window.

Remy took in Sabre's expression, which told him that Sah was feeling that hot, hard feeling too, before he pulled up Bill's contact.

But then something occurred to him, and he asked Sah, "How did she know where to find you on campus?"

Sabre shrugged. "I didn't ask. She started piling on you and it was total bullshit, so I ended it quick and got away from her."

"What did she pile on me?"

Sabre's head moved like he had a crick in his neck.

Shit.

"What'd she say, Sah?" Remy asked quietly.

Sah took a second, then he shared, "She said you got her pregnant, told her to abort the baby, got ticked when she wouldn't and threw her out. Including dumping all her stuff in the pool."

And again, Remy was rendered motionless.

"I didn't believe her from the beginning, Dad," Sabre assured swiftly. "I knew she was totally lying even before she kept talking, and it was obvious she was totally lying."

Goddamn shit.

They were here and he had no choice but to take this forward.

To get it behind them, Remy didn't delay.

"She tried to trap me by attempting to get pregnant," Remy disclosed.

"You are fuckin' shitting me," Sabre whispered, angry color coming to his cheeks.

Remy shook his head. "That's why we ended. Though, I would eventually have come to the understanding I'd made a mistake with your mom and moved us all where we needed to be. But Myrna precipitated that by playing a very nasty game."

"That fucking *bitch*," Sabre hissed.

"You need to stay calm, Sah," Remy warned. "And I need to call Bill. He and I have already had a conversation about this, but it seems it's escalating."

Remy paused when Yves rejoined them and gave his dad a nod that he'd taken care of things with Theo. Remy went on, encompassing them both with what he said next.

"I understand why you did what you did. Saying that, you shouldn't have done it. I needed to know this happened." He focused on Sabre. "I love you. To my soul, I love you, Sabre. And again, I understand why you kept this from me. But not only was it important for you to share it so I'd know the fullness of what's happening with Myrna, and this was crucial to understanding she was not going to go away gracefully, I'm your father. When anyone puts you in a position like that, I have to have that information so I can protect you, my son, my boy, my blood, as well as my family. Do you understand what I'm saying to you?"

Sabre nodded. "Yeah, Dad. I'm sorry."

"I want to be clear. You don't need to apologize. You did what you felt was right. You were trying to protect your family too. It's simply that, in this instance, you made a wrong move for the right reasons. Do you get that too?"

Sabre nodded again.

"Are you going to tell Mom?" Yves asked.

He didn't want to.

But he was going to.

Therefore, he nodded.

But he said, "We don't know if this break-in is Myrna. We don't even know if this is a break-in. But even if it doesn't have anything to do with Myrna, what you've told me she's already done, both your mother and Manon need to understand that Myrna is behaving erratically."

When both his sons gave indication they'd heard him, Remy made his first of two calls.

He was brief in explaining to Bill what had happened, mostly because Bill got the gist of it fast and wanted to get into his car and head over to the house.

After that, he asked his boys, "Can you both go to the family room, ask your mom to come back and stay in there with your sister and grandfather?"

He got more nods, his boys took off, and once they were well down the hall, Remy made his next call.

He was not surprised to get Myrna's voicemail.

"Sabre has shared that not only did you approach him after class, you gave indication to him that you're watching my house. This will be my last communication with you, Myrna. I'm reporting your behavior to the police. If anything else happens, I'll be petitioning for a restraining order. Now, I'll remind you this is done, we are done, and I'll encourage you to let it go. Please, move on with your life and let me move on with mine."

He was watching Wyn approach the room by the time he finished leaving the voicemail, and he hung up.

She closed the door behind her.

"Okay, tell me," she demanded, standing across the room from him.

He hated doing it, that feeling in his stomach intensifying, but he again didn't delay.

He told her what was happening.

After he was done, for a moment, she said nothing.

Then she asked, "Do you think whatever is happening at the house right now is her?"

He also hated that he had to say, "I think it's a good possibility."

Wyn didn't move from her position in front of the door, but she looked beyond him, toward a window. Though he knew she didn't see anything because she wasn't really looking.

She was reacting.

"Honey, I'm so fucking sorry—"

He didn't finish when her eyes shot back to him.

"You have no responsibility for this," she declared, her words short.

"I brought her into my life. My home. Our children's lives."

"When you did that, were you aware she had stalker tendencies?" Wyn asked.

His lips almost twitched at that, and he answered, "No."

"So how do you bear any responsibility for her actions?"

"You'd feel the same way I feel," he pointed out.

"Yes, I would. And when I told you I did, *you* would share very logically as well as resolutely that I bore no blame for another person's deranged actions," she retorted.

Remy had no reply to that.

Therefore, Wyn asked, "Why are you standing all the way over there?"

"Why are you standing where you are?" he returned.

She moved immediately to him.

And that hot feeling in his stomach lessened.

She put her hands on his shoulders and pressed down before she curled them around the sides of his neck and leaned into him.

Remy slid his arms around her and pulled her closer.

"We'll get through this," she said softly.

"All right," he muttered.

She gave him a squeeze. "We will."

And again, he was not thrilled he had to remind her, "She tracked down Sah."

"Our son isn't ten and unable to handle himself. He handled himself and her. Yves knows. We'll share with Manon." Remy's gut wrenched at that. Wyn carried on, "They'll stay alert, and we'll be careful to keep communication open. She'll move on."

"If she's broken into your house—"

"Then we'll press charges."

"Baby—"

Her expression tightened. "She means nothing to me, and what you two had is over. Regardless that she wishes to mean something to me, albeit something negative, and stay in your life, even if it's an unhealthy way, we won't let her. This will be communicated to her one way or another. And that's it, Remy. The end."

"You think it'll be that easy?" he asked.

"If we make it that easy, yes," Wyn answered.

Remy allowed his gaze to move over his wife's face.

He noted her eyes were more green than brown.

She was pissed.

But she was also in his arms and not going anywhere.

"Then that's what we'll make it be," he agreed.

It was slightly forced, but at hearing his words, she smiled.

Remy then said something else he detested saying.

"Let's get this over with, get all the kids in here, talk to them, including Manon."

"Your dad?"

"You told Sah when you went to get him, did you do it in a way Dad and Manon heard?"

"No, Guillaume and Manon were setting up his Disney Plus. He doesn't already have it. Apparently, neither he nor Colette watch much TV, which is pretty admirable. But I digress. They didn't hear."

Getting that answer, Remy shook his head. "Then no. I don't want him worrying about this. Can you figure something out to keep him occupied, or stay with him while I talk with the kids?"

Wyn nodded, rolled up on her toes and touched her mouth firmly to his.

"I'll be right back," she said as she rolled away.

He let her go.

He'd find out that it wouldn't just be "it." It wouldn't simply be "the end." Not after he talked to the kids, and when they were on their way to the family room to carry on with their plans, he got a call from Bill.

The break-in was Myrna. The police caught her in Wyn's closet.

By the time they got there, she'd filled three garbage bags with Wyn's shoes and purses, what she intended to do with them, she had not yet shared.

Bill asked what Remy wanted him to do.

Remy told Bill to press charges.

Bill assured Remy he'd see to that and then said, "Be with your mom and dad, with Wyn, the kids. You'll be home Monday. That's soon enough to deal with this woman's shit."

And seeing his father's eyes come to him with concern, not a stupid man by any means, so he knew something was up, Remy pasted a smile on his face and decided to take that advice.

CHAPTER 28
Bunny Boiling

Wyn

"This is so fun. It's like Cock and Snacktails without the cocktails or snacks, or being physically together and with *me* in attendance. And I never get to go to Cock and Snacktails," Manon gushed at the computer screen where Kara, Bernice and Noel each had their own squares, and Manon and I were sharing one.

Guillaume had gotten us a booking for dinner. It was late, but it was Herbsaint, a restaurant I'd been wanting to try for a long time.

We were supposed to be getting ready, but Manon shanghaied me into this Zoom meeting to talk to the crew about what to do about Colette in the very little time we had left to do anything about Colette.

Manon was staunchly ignoring what was happening with Myrna. At the time Remy shared, she said only, "She didn't hide her bitch very well, but apparently she did hide her psycho *super* well."

Remy appeared destroyed that this was affecting me and the kids, so I'd given her a look and she shut her mouth.

And that was all the attention she gave it, outwardly. I'd have to take her temperature about that later.

Remy had updated me (but not the kids) that the break-in was, indeed, Myrna and that she'd been preparing to do something with some of my babies. What, we might never know. Though I was thinking that there was going to be a number of listings on The RealReal, because I wasn't sure I'd be able to enjoy anything that woman touched.

I also wasn't sharing the brunt of my feelings about this with Remy.

I wanted to be so adjusted I could just set it aside as her damage and move on with what we were dealing with at the present, and much more positively, Remy's and my reconciliation.

But the woman had broken into *my home*.

She'd touched *my things*.

I wasn't sure anyone was *that* adjusted.

But that was for another time.

Now, it was about the drama with Colette.

"Love you, but it's sex night with Reed and I have some shaving to do. What's up?" Kara started us off.

"You have a sex night?" Noel asked.

"Life happens during the week. Things get postponed," Kara replied. "This can get out of hand. Momma needs her orgasms, and not just quickie self-induced ones in the shower, which, by the way, always irritate Reed. Somewhere along the way, he's claimed dominion over my orgasms. He acts like a big baby every time I give one to myself. So we decided a few years ago, Saturdays were sex nights, no excuses, non-negotiable. And thus, Saturday nights are *the best* nights of the week."

"Does the sex box come out?" Noel queried.

"Sometimes. And sometimes I play nurse and he plays doctor," Kara told him. "But tonight, I've decided he's been a naughty boy. He just doesn't know it...yet."

"I never thought I'd worship a woman any more than I worship Wyn, but Wyn's got competition," Noel declared.

"Since I already know about Kara and Reed's sex night, can we talk about why we're all on this Zoom?" Bernice pressed. "It isn't Cor and my sex night, but I've just decided it's going to be, so do you mind if we get things grooving?"

I knew without her saying Cor was never a naughty boy.

But Bernice could be a naughty girl.

"God, I love you women," Noel murmured.

"Grandma hit Pépé in the face with a huge-ass glass marble and we thought she might have broken his jaw, so we had to take him to the hospital," Manon shared as I watched the variety of reactions from my friends, eyes getting big, faces growing pale, brows rising to hairlines. "And apparently, this is a thing. She's like...a husband beater."

"Holy shit," Kara whispered.

"So, like, Dad wants to talk to her and whatever," Manon continued. "But Mom and I think he should just be done with her, and we should concentrate on Estelle, Pépé's girlfriend."

"His...*what?*" Bernice asked.

"Apparently, Guillaume has had a wife and a long-term mistress," I shared. "And by that, I mean Estelle has been in his life for decades. Remy even met her when he was a child."

After a moment of stunned silence, Noel remarked, "I will say this kind of thing is absolutely *delicious* when you're watching people wearing Nolan Miller acting it out on television. It doesn't seem half as fun on a Saturday Zoom call when you're talking with people you care about."

Bernice smiled.

Kara laughed.

I thought Noel could say that again.

"What do you mean, Remy wants to talk to her?" Bernice asked, thankfully swinging this conversation back to Colette.

"I don't know, and he doesn't either," I told them. "But I think he thinks he can get her to stop abusing Guillaume."

"He thinks he can, or he hopes he can?" Kara inquired.

"Hopes," I clarified. "This is...a situation. It's not a one-off. I...I don't want him to..." I didn't know what I didn't want him to do.

Get anywhere near Colette?

Check.

Give her any more of his time?

Check.

Give her any more of his emotion?

And again.

Check.

"I wish we could just take Pépé and go," Manon said.

I did too.

"Are you thinking of meeting this Estelle?" Bernice asked.

"Totally," Manon answered.

I just nodded.

"Okay, that seems a little weird to me," Bernice admitted.

"You're not alone," Kara replied.

"He loves her. She loves him too. They were supposed to take Dad and ride off into the sunset *years ago*," Manon told them. "But Grandma got in the way by being...*Grandma*."

No one spoke as they digested that.

So I did.

"Colette is a lost cause, and this would be a waste of time and emotion for Remy. She's also dying, and the fact that this will be a waste of time and emotion for him is one of the last memories he'll make with her."

"She *is* his mother, Wyn," Bernice noted.

I did not point out I very much knew that, however much I didn't like it.

"Your mom is your mom," Bernice went on. "No matter how much some of them don't deserve it, and Colette sounds like she really doesn't deserve it, you never give up on them. Remy will never think this is a waste of time or emotion, even if nothing comes of it, and the memory he'll have is that he tried. He needs to do this, his way, when he's ready, and all *you* can do is be there for him when it's over."

With that, I was reminded why I loved Cock and Snacktails nights so much.

My friends were *life*.

"Damn, that's some wisdom right there," Manon whispered reverently. "Can I come to Cock and Snacktails from now on?"

And that was life too, watching my daughter soak in the knowledge of her elders, respecting it rather than fighting against it.

To her question, simultaneously, she got three yeses and one no, the no being me, but only because she was at school and didn't need to be driving up ad hoc every time a C&S was called.

Thus, she gave me big eyes and gasped, "*Mother!*"

"Until you graduate," I added. "Though, you can come if you're home."

Her face cleared and she grinned. "Oh, okay then."

There were smiles on the other *Brady Bunch* blocks of the Zoom call, but even in their small squares, I could see concern in their eyes for the maelstrom we were facing here in NOLA.

"We'll be okay," I assured them.

"And we'll be here," Kara replied.

Yes, my friends were *life*.

We didn't dally after that seeing as it was sex night for Kara, a spontaneous sex night for Bernice, and Manon and I had to get ready for dinner. So we all went our separate ways.

I had my face close to the bathroom mirror, ass tilted, wearing panties and a bra and perfecting the tail of my winged eyeliner when Remy propped himself by his shoulder in the doorway to the bathroom.

I turned my head toward him.

He'd already changed for dinner, wearing tan pants and a black button-down that was given the full tuck, making the casual combo that slight bit more formal, which was needed for dinner.

But his broad shoulders, muscular thighs and thick hair, which had been tamed by running his fingers through it, gave his look that super dose of sex appeal.

He was beautiful. He might not be perfect, but he was pretty damned close to it.

And he was mine.

I took firm hold on that knowledge before I spoke.

"Where have you been?" I asked gently.

"Hanging with Dad. Having a chat with Melly. Talking to Bill about what's next with Myrna. Leaving a message for Lisa to source a bird bath to replace the one I broke today."

That was Remy, never really one to be idle or let things slide.

"Okay."

"And making some decisions."

Oh boy.

I turned fully to him, his eyes swept the length of me, and really, I had no idea how I'd convinced myself my husband had stopped being attracted to me. We'd had a heavy few weeks, the last few days the heaviest, and still, the expression on his face right in that moment shouted that was a lie.

"Honey," I called when he seemed stuck in the act of staring at my hips.

His eyes lifted to mine.

"I'm going to talk to Mom, and when we get back home, I'm going to talk to Myrna."

I decided not to say anything, and not only because I didn't know what to say.

"With Mom, I don't know how that's going to happen, or what I want from it, but it has to happen," he declared.

"Yes," I agreed.

"With Myrna, I hold some responsibility for what she's doing, and she needs to hear that."

Oh hell no.

I straightened and opened my mouth, but before I could say anything, Remy went on.

"I can use what happened to me in my childhood as an excuse. I can do that with what I did to our marriage. I can do it with how I treated Myrna. But Wyn, baby, how can I sit down with my mother and talk to her about who she is to me, what she did to me, what she's still doing to Dad, knowing a long time ago she knew it was wrong, and she didn't find some way to stop herself from hurting people she loved. And in the now, when she's dying, find some way to reach out to us and assume culpability for how she fucked up her entire family's life, and not assume culpability for what I'd done in mine?"

He had a point there.

He wasn't finished.

"I never loved Myrna, but she's a human being with feelings, and actions speak. I let her move in. I might not have made promises, but I did have a relationship with her, and I can understand how she expected that to grow because that's what happens."

"In some instances," I retorted. "In others, it doesn't. People break up, Remy. And when they do, they don't stalk the other person's child or break into his wife's house."

"I'm not excusing what she's done. I'm copping to my part in it."

Why did he have to be so mature?

Well, two could play that game.

"You're right, actions do speak, as do words," I returned. "You made no verbal promises to her. On top of that, you told me you didn't ask her to move in, she asked, and you let her because she was in a jam. And in the end, you didn't ever *really* let her move in. All of those things say something, she just didn't want to hear it."

"Would you want a man who didn't take responsibility for hurting another person? Whatever that person did, however that person behaved, would you want a man who didn't assess his part in the situation and admit he fucked up too?" he asked.

Damn it.

"No," I muttered.

His lips twitched.

They stopped doing that, and softly, he said, "Everyone talks about the bunny boiling. But no one says dick about the married man who started a relationship with a woman when he had no business doing it. I'm not excusing bunny boiling either. But this narrative has to shift, and we both know it. And I don't want to be a part of that narrative not shifting."

"Sometimes it's hateful how wonderful you are," I announced.

He grinned and replied, "Say that looking hot in black underwear when you're over here."

"There's three feet of space between us and you have longer legs," I pointed out.

Remy didn't take time to consider my statement, nor did he reply.

He just erased the space, and I was glad I hadn't done my lipstick, because the kiss he laid on me would have meant I'd have to do it again.

———

REMY and I were lying in our bed that night, in the dark, on our backs, both of us staring at the ceiling, and we were holding hands.

"Well, that sucked," he said.

He wasn't talking about the food, the ambience, or the company of that evening.

He was talking about the mood and how all of us tried to pretend it wasn't as shitty as it actually was.

"Yes," I agreed. "But this won't last forever. We'll get past it."

He blew out a deep sigh.

"So, you know, you being adult and accountable is making me realize I'm not."

That made him turn to me, still holding my hand, but he reached out and rested his other on my belly.

"You're entitled to be pissed at Myrna for being a pain in the ass," he noted, then reminded me, "You didn't do anything to her."

"No, I mean with Bea."

The air grew dense around us.

"I can't hide behind my posse with this," I told him. "I need to face her. Me. Personally. She's been the worst with you. I care about her. She's my friend. But you're my husband. She should know she's been hurtful, she's still being it, and I should listen to whatever she has to say about why she does it."

"I never thought I'd say this in my life, especially after today, but now I'm not looking forward to either of us leaving here and going home."

That made me turn to him, slide close, press closer and repeat, "We'll get past it."

He circled me with his arms and grunted, "Yeah."

"We're together and I love you."

He pulled me deeper into his body and his grunt of, "Yeah," was sweet this time.

We snuggled.

Neither of us found it easy to fall asleep.

But eventually, we did, which was good.

Because we had one more day in New Orleans, and there was no way around it.

It wasn't going to be a good one.

CHAPTER 29

Never Change

Remy

The next morning, the family sat for breakfast with his dad, but not his mom, Melly pulling out all the stops, (yes, even more fantastic than The House or her biscuits and gravy). But as they lingered over coffee and mimosas that were very easy on the OJ, Remy excused himself.

He did this to find his mother.

He didn't have to go far.

After he set his dishes in the sink, he caught Melly coming in from outside. She took one look at him and shared, "She's in the garden."

Remy nodded, gave her a grin he knew was weak, she returned the same, and he headed out.

He did this only to stop dead when he saw his mother sitting among the lush greenery, large urns tumbling with flora, elegant statuary dotted around, an understated fountain tinkling.

She had a peach pashmina wrapped around her shoulders over a honey-colored turtleneck, even though the temperature was already over seventy degrees. She was holding a delicate coffee cup by the saucer, fingers of her other hand to the curve of the handle of the cup, dipping her head to take a sip.

What froze him was not only the fact Colette had to be wrapped up like that, sitting in the sun in her garden, which was a likely indication of not only her being perpetually underweight, but of her illness.

It was also the fact that the last time he'd seen his grandmother, she was in that same position, in that same garden, but it was the afternoon, it was summer, even hotter, she was still wearing a shawl because of illness (and being underweight). And she was drinking sweet tea.

If memory served, she passed peacefully in her sleep within weeks of that visit.

But she was peaceful because she'd been drugged, seeing as she, too, had died of breast cancer.

Remy's Grandma Lucette had adored him in a sticky sweet way that never failed to make him uncomfortable.

It also never failed to rile his mother to the point of consequences for Remy when she had the opportunity to mete them.

Considering the fact Lucette lived with them until Remy was four, this had not had a positive effect on Remy's youngest years. Guillaume then moved her to an elegant bungalow five miles away, and it hadn't gotten better, it was just brought on for different reasons.

Nevertheless, this conditioning left him with a confusing feeling of relief when his grandmother died when he was nineteen.

He understood now, as an adult, that Lucette's fawning love had to be a smack in the face to Colette.

Having no love from her mother, watching him get it had to hurt.

What he didn't understand was why she took her hurt and used it to make him feel the same.

There was all of this on his mind.

And there was more.

Including the fact that moment was the first time Remy had truly faced the fact his mother was dying.

While he and his family had been there, she'd been the worst version of herself. The one he knew but his family had just met. And even though he was aware of her condition, her behavior had masked it.

In that moment, he knew the woman in the garden was dying.

His mother was dying.

And he was not feeling relief, but what he was feeling was nevertheless confusing.

Colette didn't turn her head to look at him when she took him out of his thoughts by calling, "Was it you or Sabre who broke my bird bath?"

Melly wouldn't share, nor would his dad, so she probably found the glass sphere in the yard, or she'd been looking out the window when he'd done it.

Remy came unstuck and moved to her.

He didn't answer until he'd folded himself onto the thick, pear-green pad of a heavy, black wrought iron chair at her side.

It was wide-seated and comfortable for him.

She looked almost childlike perched on hers, so thin, you could fit three of her on that seat.

"It was me," he told her.

"I assume you'll replace it," she remarked.

He would have started the conversation by asking after the fact she was dressed like it was chilly, going on to inquire if she was feeling all right, ending with if she needed anything before he got to the meat of their discussion.

Regrettably, his mother had a knack for conversational introductions that were supremely aggravating.

"I've sent an email to Lisa, she'll take care of it," he assured.

After, with great care, resting her china cup and saucer on the table beside her, Colette finally turned her head to Remy.

"What would you do if Wyn cheated on you?" she demanded to know, a hint of belligerence in her tone.

So they weren't going to ease into it.

Fine.

He'd roll with that.

"I wouldn't attempt to break her jaw with a paperweight," he returned.

She sniffed, looked away, and murmured, "Of course not. You're a man. Men can't get away with that kind of thing anymore."

Jesus Christ.

"Are you trying to upset me?" Remy asked.

She turned again to him, but before she could say anything, he spoke.

"I left the five people I love most in all this world sitting at a table together, an unusual circumstance, in order to have an important conversation with you, and you lead with giving me shit about your bird bath and saying hideous things about domestic violence?"

"So I'm not one of the people you love most in the world?" she queried.

He'd opened himself up to that one.

He skirted it.

"You chose not to have breakfast with us, and here I am."

Her eyes flashed with irritation that he'd deftly sidestepped her first parry.

"You can't blame me for putting my shield up," she retorted. "Of course I'd be defensive. Your visit hasn't exactly been loving."

"Yes, I can blame you because you're my mother. You should never need a shield with me. And I could say the same to you about how this visit has gone, times four, because my wife and children have endured it along with me."

Her gaze turned hard.

But he kept at her.

275

"And the reason you need a shield is not because of something I did, but rather, the opposite."

"I love your father with everything I am," she shot back.

"Which begs the question, Mom, of *why you'd hurt him*."

He took a deep breath, and when she didn't answer, he lowered it on her.

"And me."

She looked away.

Right...

No.

"We need to discuss this. We leave tomorrow, and as I've already made you aware, I'm not crazy about the idea of leaving Dad with you." It took him a moment before he could finish what he wanted to say, but he did it. "And I deserve some answers."

"You can't possibly understand. Wyn worships you. You've always been her su..." She cut herself off from what she was about to say, fidgeted with the fringe of her pashmina, and instead said, "From the moment you met her, you became her world. She'd never do anything like that to you."

Remy might not, until recently, have understood how highly his wife regarded him, but he'd never once worried she'd step out on him.

So what Colette said was true.

He couldn't possibly understand.

But they both knew that was a weak excuse.

Or did they?

"Mom," he said carefully, "I don't condone Dad's cheating, but it isn't okay what you do to him, and it really was not okay what you did to me."

She grew silent.

Remy didn't let it go. "I'm out here because I'd like to understand."

"I'm dying, Remy. This may be the last time you see me breathing, and this is what you want to discuss?" Her head whipped in his direction. "Really? *This* is the only private moment I've had with *my only child* during your visit, perhaps your *final* visit, and *this* is what you bring up?"

"This may be the last time *you* see *me* too," he returned.

"Yes, exactly," she spat, leaning slightly his way, a look on her face that made his insides twist, he was so familiar with it and that long-remembered terror of what it might bring. "And I'd *much* prefer to discuss something else."

He kept a lock on the fact he was getting pissed, but he didn't give in to her demands.

"Right, then let me share that for the last three years, Dad has been kicking his own ass because he thought he was the reason I tanked my marriage, when in fact that reason was you."

She gasped, her eyes getting huge.

"Would you rather discuss that?" he pushed. "Because, like I needed to be perfect for you... No, that isn't right. Like you needed me to be perfect for you, you needed me to be everything for you, and I lived with that so long, I absorbed it. Which meant I also needed to be perfect for Wyn. To be everything for her. And when it came clear she didn't need me for everything, she could make her own money, she could contribute to our family, our lives, she was a success on my level, I couldn't deal with it. I didn't know who to be if I wasn't taking care of her. I didn't know *how* to be."

"I will never understand why she went back to work when she didn't have to," Colette muttered.

Christ, she never changed.

"Damn it, Mom. Are you serious?" he bit out.

She tilted her gaze to the sky. "I cannot *believe* you're being this cruel to me in my final days."

For fuck's sake.

Remy took a calming breath and slowly released it, before he urged, "Please, Mom, for the love of me, of Dad, of your grandchildren, your family, the legacy you're leaving, stop the fucking drama and *talk to me.* I'm sitting here because *I want to understand.*"

Her eyes sliced to him, and she snapped, "Watch your mouth around your mother."

Remy stared at her.

Then he sighed, sat back and gazed at an urn overflowing with some dense foliage that was green as well as purple. He had no idea what it was, but he was proud as hell that Sah could walk out and tell him.

"After your performance yesterday morning, I've decided I'm changing my will. I'm leaving everything to Yves," she announced.

"Fine," Remy replied.

"I know you think it isn't much, but no matter how dire our straits became, Mother closely guarded the Cormier jewels. They're worth hundreds of thousands of dollars. And there are other heirlooms that do not belong to your father. Sculpture. Paintings."

"Mom, I make a shit ton of money. I have a waiting list that's two years long for clients to get the opportunity to access my personal designs. I employ thirty people. I have a wife who loves me enough to forgive me for doing something unforgiveable, and three smart, healthy, funny, kind, beautiful children. I'm rich. I couldn't care less about jewels and paintings."

"You're an artist, and you don't care about art?"

Remy dropped his head.

There it was.

She never changed.

This was going to be it.

This was going to be his last real conversation with his mom.

Fuck, he never should have walked out into that garden.

Then again, if he hadn't, he would have had yesterday's events as his final moments with his mother. This hadn't gone well, but at least it wasn't as bad as that.

The story of his relationship with his mom.

Since there was nothing for it, he lifted his head.

And to the urn, he used a tactic that had worked before. It hadn't worked perfectly, but it had worked.

"I've spoken with Melly. I'll be arranging to pay her an additional salary. I've asked her to keep a close eye and report to me not only if you ever harm Dad physically again, but if it verbally turns ugly as well. She's agreed to do this for us. She knows I'm informing you of this, and she's agreed to that as well. I'll also be asking Beau and Jason to drop in and make sure Dad is safe. You had all the chances you're going to get. The minute I hear you've harmed him, as I said yesterday, I'm flying out, collecting you, and you'll spend your final days in the desert with me and Wyn. This is not negotiable."

"You can't kidnap me, Remy."

No, he couldn't.

"If you refuse to come, I'll talk Dad into coming, and you'll die alone."

Silence followed that remark, so complete, he sensed she knew how serious he was about what he'd just said.

Good.

And they were done.

He stood and looked down at his mother who'd tipped her head back to look up at him, a dying woman with defiant eyes.

Her hair was perfect, as was her makeup, as was her outfit. She needed to put on about twenty pounds.

But she was beautiful.

She was eighty years old and dying, but still stunning.

For fifty-six years, she'd had an adoring husband, who was an inveterate philanderer.

But she'd traveled the world. She'd lived in the lap of luxury. She wore silks and furs as a matter of course. She had diamonds and she had pearls, and she had everything in between.

If she wanted it, it was given to her.

She also had a healthy son.

Wyn had always had exceptional, and expensive taste in clothes, even before it became her business.

Remy loved his wife and was interested in all she did, so he was aware that his mother was right then wearing approximately four thousand dollars in clothing, not including the makeup and jewelry. The latter probably tipped that scale at least another twenty K, perhaps just from her diamond watch.

She was wearing more than some people made in a year.

Colette's husband had cheated on her, but from the moment he came into her life, she hadn't had another care in the world that mattered.

She didn't worry about paying a mortgage or health insurance or feeding herself or her son. She'd never held a job. And she knew about her husband's serial infidelity, but it was her choice to stay with him.

She made that choice because of all of this.

There'd been bumps along the way that she'd handled very poorly, but that didn't change the facts.

She was a beautiful woman who'd lived a beautiful life.

"I'm going to remember you like this," he said quietly. "Not the empty part. Not the vicious part. Not the selfish part. Not the insensitive and heartless part. But how beautiful you are. How perfect you look sitting in this garden. That's what I'm going to remember, Mom."

He saw her lips quiver and then he saw her chin lift.

But she didn't say a word.

Because she was Colette Louise Cormier Gastineau.

And she would never change.

Remy bent and kissed her cheek.

Then he turned, and not looking back, he walked away.

He saw his father in the window of the conservatory, watching them, so instead of going in the back door he headed that way.

The door of the conservatory had closed behind him before Guillaume asked, "How is she?"

As he'd attempted to do at breakfast that morning, Remy tried not to let the deep discoloration at his father's jaw make his gut burn.

And as happened at breakfast that morning, he failed.

Which might have been why he answered, "Stubborn, dramatic and bitchy. In other words, the same as always."

Guillaume assumed a disappointed father's face as he admonished, "Remy."

He knew she couldn't hear them, so he knew it was safe to ask his next question, and this was because he was the man they raised in all the good and bad parts of how that happened.

"Have you spoken with Estelle?"

His father took a big breath and said, "Yes. And although she very much wishes to meet you, Wyn and the children, she respectfully declines to do so during this visit. She feels it should be about your mother."

And that spoke volumes about the woman Estelle was.

"It's her choice," Remy conceded. "But please consider bringing her out to visit as soon as you can. Wyn and the kids want to meet her, and your grandchildren deserve to see their grandfather happy for once."

A muscle ticked in his father's cheek.

But he let it go and shared, "Beau and Katy phoned. They'd like us to come over for a crawfish boil and football. Wyn and the children wish to go."

Remy nodded, relieved they all had something to look forward to. He reached and squeezed his father's arm before he let go and made to walk away.

"Remy," Guillaume called.

He stopped and looked at his dad.

"I won't be going to the boil, and it's likely your mother will also send her regrets."

Right.

It wouldn't do for anyone to see that huge bruise on his face or have the woman who gave it to him hanging around, making faces as people scarfed down crawfish, shrimp and potatoes, and gnawed on corn over a newspaper-strewn picnic table before they shoved Katy's famous bread pudding down their throats.

Remy wondered how many times his mother and father sent regrets for the same reason. He then decided not to think about it. If his ploy with his mother worked, that particular part of their lives was done.

"We won't stay long," Remy assured.

Guillaume nodded, and Remy was again about to leave in order to look for Wyn when his dad spoke again.

"If you could spare a few minutes, it'd mean a great deal to me if you would share what's been troubling you since yesterday, the part that isn't about your mother."

And...

Damn.

Two things had been cemented during this visit:

His mother had always been his mother...

And his father had always been his dad.

"There's a problem at home," Remy told him. "It's getting sorted, and I'll finish handling it when we get back."

"This problem would be?" Guillaume prompted.

Remy hesitated.

His mother had always been his mother, and as such, his attempt at trying to have an important and long overdue conversation with her had the results it had.

But his father had always been his dad, this visit had been the worst on him, and Remy had told Wyn that at the very least from their time in NOLA, he wanted to figure shit out with his father.

It was time to figure that shit out.

"The woman I was with between leaving Wyn and finding her again is causing problems. She's targeted Sah, and yesterday, she broke into our house and was caught by the police in Wyn's closet, filling garbage bags with her things."

The color drained from Guillaume's face.

"She was caught, Papa," Remy said gently. "I have a friend who's a cop who's helping out, and I have a plan for when I get home to deal with it."

He could see his father was getting angry now, not at Remy, at Myrna.

"That plan would be?" he asked.

"I'm going to speak to her. I'm going to accept the responsibility I hold in hurting her and not communicating well with her, and I'm going to ask her to leave us alone."

"Do you think this will work?" Guillaume queried with open disbelief. "I don't have to tell you her behavior is extreme, *fiston*."

"I've no idea. I just know it's the right thing to do."

"What did she do to Sabre?"

He wanted to share this less than the other, but he didn't hesitate before he gave it to his dad.

"Sah liked her, more than Manon and Yves, who both weren't big fans. She knew that, so she tracked him down and told him I got her pregnant and kicked her out because she wouldn't get an abortion, none of which, obviously, was true."

"*Mon Dieu!*"

Definitely pissed now.

"Dad, it's going to get handled one way or another."

Guillaume shook his head. "I do not understand what is becoming of this world."

Which meant none of his father's mistresses had behaved so badly, or they'd been easy to manage if they tried.

Remy didn't go there.

"Do you need anything from me?" Guillaume asked.

He shook his head. "No, Dad. But thank you."

Guillaume nodded.

Remy went for it.

"I chose poorly," he admitted.

Guillaume tilted his head, his gaze growing soft, and he replied, "*Fiston*, we, none of us know the demons that plague a soul. Their purpose is to stay hidden and wreak havoc on the ones who love their host the most. I think you and I, and Wyn, we all know this."

He clapped a hand on Remy's shoulder and left it there before he continued.

"Now you have glimpsed this woman's demons, and you've made the decision to treat her like she is as the rest of us are in one way or another, driven by invisible demons to do harm. And you intend to offer compassion." He squeezed Remy's shoulder. "Honestly, except for when I learned you and Wyn were reconciling, I've never been prouder. And, son, you have, over your years, given me many reasons to be proud."

Remy held his father's gaze, pushing aside the recent memory of his talk with his mother, pushing aside all the shit that was going down with Myrna, pushing aside how his family was getting dragged through it right along with him, and rooting himself in that moment.

Eyes locked to his boy, Guillaume knew the exact time to stop holding Remy by the shoulder and instead, tug his son into his arms and hold him a different way.

It was not lost on Remy that he'd held Sah in the exact same manner not too long ago when emotion had overwhelmed his boy.

It was just the first time in his life that he felt what Sah felt.

And fuck.

It was beautiful.

CHAPTER 30
Deserved Defeat

Wyn

"This is all kinds of fucked up."

That was Sabre.

"We'll leave before she'll even be up tomorrow, Sah."

And that was Yves.

"Yeah, because, unlike ninety-nine-point nine percent of grandparents *in the world*, she isn't going to deign to drag herself out of bed to say goodbye to her only son, daughter-in-law and grandchildren before we go and, you know, before she *dies*."

And that was my dramatic daughter.

"She's asked us to meet her in the mural room before she retires to bed, something we all understand is very likely the last time any of us will see her, so we're going to give your grandmother her wish and meet her in the mural room," I declared.

"Who says 'retires'?" Sah grumbled.

Colette did. Those were her words when she met us in the hall when we arrived back from taking Guillaume out for some gelato after we returned from the party at Beau and Katy's.

We'd lingered over gelato.

It was late.

We were leaving the next morning at eight to get to the airport.

She had incurable cancer.

She needed to get to bed and so did we.

"Up and at 'em," I prompted when none of my children moved.

They were lounging on Remy's and my bed where they'd thrown themselves after we trooped up with excuses of using the loo and freshening up before we met Colette, but instead, we all filed in here to have an impromptu family meeting.

However, even at my command, my kids didn't get up and at them. Since they were not paying me a lick of attention anymore, I turned to their father, who was standing at my side. He was also who all of them were watching.

He had his eyes to the bed, an expression on his face that made my heart leap into my throat.

"Remy?" I called.

He continued to stare at our kids, and I didn't know if he was lost in thought, or he was very much right there, seeing them vividly.

I curled my fingers around his and whispered, "Remy."

He didn't answer me.

He asked our children, "Do you know how fantastic you are?"

Oh God.

Well, that answered that.

He was seeing them vividly.

I pressed close to his side.

"Yeah, Dad," Manon answered swiftly.

"You're smart and funny and kind and loyal," Remy went on.

I started pumping his hand.

"And we got hella style from Mom." Sah tried to inject some levity.

"Like Dad isn't killin' it in the style department." Yves tried to help.

But Manon was reading the room.

"You're fantastic too, Daddy," she said.

Remy cleared his throat, squeezed my hand and announced, "I just want you to know that. Know I think it and know it's true. Don't ever forget it."

Manon looked to me.

Sabre didn't move his gaze from his dad.

Yves got up and gave his father a hug.

The kids didn't get the lowdown of Remy's conversations with his parents, but I did, so I wasn't surprised, even if I was moved, at what just happened.

Sometimes we assume people know we feel as we feel and think as we think. We hope our love, and the reason we feel it, is understood.

But in the end, sometimes we just need to say it.

Remy was going to go on living after he lost his mother not really knowing what she felt.

I understood entirely why he'd need to share what he'd just shared with his children.

There were two more hugs for Remy and the kids moved out.

But I recaptured his hand and held fast as he moved to follow them.

He looked back at me.

"You okay?" I asked a stupid question.

"I'm the happiest I've been in five years, and I'm coming apart. The polar opposite sensations are weird, but that's where I'm at."

I liked the honesty but wasn't thrilled about where he was at.

Which meant I was forced to do the only thing I could do.

I nodded and said, "I get it."

"And I'm proud," he continued.

I smiled at him. "We have great kids."

"No," he said. "I mean, yes, we do. What I meant was, I'm proud of myself. I stumbled along the way, but I broke the cycle." He jerked his head to the door. "They will never feel that tightness I felt when I saw Mom get mad this morning. And all their lives, they knew they were priorities. They knew their health and development and education and feelings were important."

"They knew they were loved," I whispered.

I watched his corded throat move as he swallowed.

Then he nodded.

I reached in and touched his lips with mine.

I didn't pull very far away when I said, "And so are you."

That was when Remy touched my lips with his.

We headed out, and I knew my husband was still experiencing polar opposite sensations.

I, on the other hand, was suffering only one.

This being tamping down murderous intentions as the words *that tightness I felt when I saw Mom get mad* bounced around in my brain.

It was no surprise the scene was set when we entered the mural room, the children already there, as was Guillaume.

As was Colette.

I saw immediately this swan song was not going to be playing for sympathy.

Oh no.

And I could have called it.

Colette was not going to go out like that.

Our last memory wasn't going to be that.

No, she sat in the middle of the sofa wearing sage velvet pajamas, edged at the hems and the sleeves of the matching robe in delicate dusty pink lace. Her

285

hair was pulled severely back at her nape, exposing for the first time how truly gaunt her face was. But nonetheless, she not only hadn't taken off her makeup, it looked like she'd refreshed it, so she still looked a version of stunning.

But the shocking red of her signature lipstick was gone, a nude pink in its stead, as one would do.

One didn't go to bed in shocking red unless it accompanied your ensemble.

Surrounding her were magnificently wrapped presents.

So we weren't going to be pushed to offer sympathy.

We were going to be reminded of what Colette thought we would be missing when she was gone.

Again, not a surprise that she didn't decide to speak to all of us one by one so she could tell us how much she loved us. Share her favorite memory we'd made. Explain how she treasured time spent with us. And then impart some nugget of wisdom we could call on in our futures to make a tough time easier, or a hard decision into a quick one, her lasting gift.

We were going to be given things that we would feel bad we didn't want because they reminded us of her, and since she'd given them to us in her current state, we would feel obliged to keep them anyway.

Pure Colette.

God, I wanted to scream in her face.

I didn't.

I sat in a chair, Remy perched on the arm of it, and I pointed out the obvious.

"We're all here, Colette."

"Yes," she said instantly. "And we'll start with you."

She picked up a somewhat wide, definitely long rectangular, jeweler-sized box wrapped in linen-colored paper and tied with a strip of a champagne satin. In the exorbitant bow were two perfect ivory roses.

I'd seen a lot of jewelry boxes in my time, but none that unique shape.

She held it out to me.

Remy got off the arm of my chair in order to fetch it.

He handed it to me, resumed his seat, and I saw the roses were real.

I unwrapped the parcel.

Inside was an ivory velvet box, and when I opened it, I saw a long strand of pearls resting in a cloud of alabaster silk.

"Those are my five times great grandmother's pearls," she proclaimed grandly.

Dear God.

She'd given me slave pearls.

I felt bile race up my throat as I stared at the necklace in horror.

"Every first Cormier woman has owned those pearls for the last one hundred and eighty-five years," she went on.

I swallowed difficultly, lifted my head, and croaked, "Thank you."

Sadly, it sounded not only sickened, but like a question.

Colette's brows drew together in confusion.

She powered through that and stated, "I hope you one day give them to Manon."

Pearls were not the most expensive luxury jewel you could buy, except these looked perfect. They shone because they'd been well cared for. Each pearl appeared perfectly matched to the others. The strand was very long, and the unnecessary clasp was extravagant and encrusted with diamonds, the better to show it off.

I'd gauge, depending on who made them, and the quality and carats of the diamonds, they were worth anywhere from $20,000 to $35,000. Maybe more.

I would, indeed, one day *very soon* give them to Manon.

And then she could decide what to do with them.

"I...this is so generous of you, Colette. Thank you again."

She dipped her chin to me, looked to her side, and put her hand on a wide, rectangular box that was so tall, it was resting on a slant from the floor against the couch.

"This is for you, Sabre."

It had no roses, and because genders had colors apparently, the satin ribbon was black.

He opened it, and when he glanced at what was inside, his expression was my feeling of five minutes before.

"That's your five times great grandfather's cavalry saber," she explained. "A saber for Sabre," she ended on a quip.

I looked to Guillaume, who was standing behind the couch, off to the side, not close, but also not far from Colette.

His lips were thin, and he was studying his wife with an expression I'd never seen him give her.

Distaste.

I was wrong.

This wasn't a swan song.

She was punishing us.

"You're giving me a Confederate sword?" Sabre asked, openly insulted.

"Sah, just take it," Manon murmured.

He ignored his sister.

"You know I'm a Yankee," he told his grandmother.

A hysterical giggle nearly escaped my mouth.

"I believe at the time Arizona was in the hands of the Spanish," Colette said, also openly insulted.

"I believe at *this* time being a Yankee is the state of an educated mind," Sabre fired back.

I pressed my lips together, doing it so I wouldn't let out a whoop.

"You cannot escape the fact you have Cormier blood," Colette snapped.

"Whatever. I can't take this on a plane," Sabre replied.

Guillaume entered the burgeoning fray smoothly, stating, "I'll keep it safe for you. Now, Colette, if you would carry on. They need to be up early, and it's late for you."

"I'm not certain I want to carry on," Colette retorted. "I'm handing them their legacy. It doesn't matter who lost that war. It still holds value, and it's part of this family's history. That saber is in pristine condition. It's worth thousands of dollars."

Sabre opened his mouth.

"Son," Remy said.

Sabre closed his mouth.

But he didn't reopen it to thank his grandmother.

She waited, which meant we all waited.

But my firstborn said nothing.

Colette sighed with irritation and turned to the seat beside her.

She held out a box wrapped like mine toward Manon. It was much smaller and only had one sweetheart rose.

"This isn't tainted," she spat.

Manon took it, opened it, and I could hear her swift intake of breath.

"Those are the earrings your grandfather gave me on our honeymoon. They're diamonds, radiant cut, nine carats total," she pronounced.

Now I understood Manon's breath. We'd all seen Colette wear those earrings over the years, and we'd seen it often.

We also knew she didn't wear them because they were magnificent (and they were), but because Guillaume had given them to her in the first blush of love and marriage.

Okay, maybe I was wrong. Maybe she wasn't punishing us. Maybe she felt this stuff genuinely had nostalgic family value, not to mention monetary value (even that saber), and she was trying to show she cared for us in her inept way.

I sensed this because Yves was the favorite, not Manon, and those earrings were worth quite a bit of money.

But they were priceless in terms of sentimental value.

And Colette wouldn't think the pearls she gave me, a necklace she wanted Manon to have, were slave pearls. She'd think of them only as Cormier pearls.

"I can't take these, Grandmama," Manon said softly.

The line of Colette's shoulders lightened, she smiled beneficently at Manon and replied, "I want you to."

Manon twisted her neck in order to look up to her dad, so I did too.

He nodded.

Manon turned again to Colette, holding the box in both hands to her chest. "Thank you. They...were given in love and...worn with love. I'll always remember that."

Colette's face warmed, and I was proud of my girl for pulling that off.

"Yves." Colette held out another box.

Yves got up to take it, sat back down, opened it, and then pulled out a gold pocket watch, allowing it to swing from its chain.

"That is a Breguet," Colette announced grandly. "It came over from *France* when your ancestors came here. Abraham-Louis Breguet is one of the finest watchmakers of all time. In fact, the watch he failed to finish for the queen, Marie Antoinette, before she was executed, is *the* most expensive watch in existence. That's"—she lifted a hand to point a finger at the gold dangling from the chain around Yves's finger—"not as grand, but considering how it appraised the last time we updated our insurance, it's nothing to sneeze at either."

I caught Guillaume and Sabre exchanging a glance that I read as Guillaume silently assuring my son, who had not been gifted a watch made by a royal watchmaker two hundred some years ago, that he would be taken care of by his grandfather.

Sabre didn't care. He'd never been a "things" kid. If he had the right cleats and an abundance of food, he was good.

Oh, and stylish clothes.

"Thank you, Grandmama. It's beautiful. It's also cool," Yves said.

My last born. Perfect.

I felt my lips tip up.

"And Remy," Colette began.

My lips flattened and my neck tightened.

"This is for you."

She held out a box to him.

Remy again left me to get it but came right back.

I craned my neck to see what it was, curling my fingers around his thigh for moral support as he opened it.

He set the box aside after he pulled out an eight by ten black and white photo that was framed in an exquisite silver frame.

It was a picture of a much younger Colette and Guillaume, both of them smiling happily, hugely, Colette in another frothy peignoir set, sitting in a hospital bed in the curve of Guillaume's loving arm.

She was cuddling baby Remy close to her bosom.

Tears stung my eyes.

"What is it?" Sabre demanded menacingly, ready to do battle, and because of his tone, my gaze darted up to Remy.

His eyes were shining too.

"So you will never forget you were loved," Colette declared.

My throat closed.

Remy looked to his mother and his voice was gruff when he said, "Thanks, Mom."

"You were," she said firmly. "And you are."

No one said a word or made a noise.

Until Remy broke the silence by repeating, "Thanks, Mom."

"Time for bed," Guillaume announced.

Thank God.

Remy started it, and we all followed suit.

He got up and moved to his mother. Cupping her jaw, he leaned in and kissed her other cheek.

When he pulled away, he looked in her eyes and requested, "Please get up with us to say goodbye."

"We'll see," she murmured, her gaze sliding from his.

We all followed suit with a cheek kiss for Colette, even Sabre and me, and then we collected our gifts and made our way out of the room and up the stairs, trooping right back into Remy's and my bedroom.

The kids resumed their positions on the bed.

Remy sat in the couch and pulled me into his lap.

"I'm not keeping that—" Sabre started.

Remy interrupted him.

"We'll have it appraised then put feelers out to history museums. Mom is right. That sword has significance. So does our family's history. Not good significance, but if we do not keep wide eyes and open ears to the lessons of our history, we won't learn from it. That sword doesn't signify righteous rebellion, it's an artifact of deserved defeat. As such, its existence is important, and we'll find somewhere it can exist and teach valuable lessons. Once we find that, we'll gift that sword, and your mom and I will give you the money it's worth for you to use as you wish as your inheritance from your grandmother."

"I don't need the money, Dad," Sabre said.

"We're still giving it to you," I replied.

"When you do, I'll be donating it," Sabre returned.

"And since it'll be yours, that will be your choice," Remy retorted.

Sabre didn't say anything further.

"You okay, Dad?" Manon asked.

"I'm fine, honey," Remy lied.

Since we all knew he did, we piled onto him (well, I was already on him, so our kids joined me), holding him close, showing him our love, and in so doing, giving it to each other.

I knew I'd never forget that particular Gastineau scrum.

I knew Remy wouldn't either.

OF NOTE...

Colette did not wake up early the next morning to say goodbye.

CHAPTER 31

Adulting

PART ONE

Wyn

"I can't help but think this is a bad idea." Noel's voice came from the speakers in my car.

"Simultaneous meets, and we're both done," I replied. "We can reconvene when we're finished, and it'll be behind us. No fretting about the next one coming."

It was the weekend following our return from New Orleans.

I was on my way to Bea's house to have a conversation.

Bill was at Remy's house because Myrna was heading over there to have a conversation with Remy.

She didn't know Bill was going to be there, but I demanded that Remy not meet with her alone. He saw the wisdom of this and not only didn't put up a fight, he thanked me for the idea.

Bill was going to hang in the guest suite, give them room.

But he'd be close, which made me feel better.

"No, that's the good part," Noel said. "What I mean is, talking to Bea by yourself."

"In the end, it's between her and me," I reminded him.

"That's debatable," he replied.

"She's the worst with Remy. Kara gave up on her long ago and really doesn't care whether their friendship continues or not. She's already decided to ghost her. And Bernice agrees that she has her own private things to say.

Further, it isn't cool, ganging up on her."

"Do you think she's considered for one second if *her* behavior is cool?" Noel asked, then went on before I could speak. "I'll answer that since the answer is obvious. No."

"It's the right thing to do."

"Correct," Noel agreed, surprising me. Then he explained, "But there are people who don't deserve the right thing because they haven't *earned* it."

"You still have to do the right thing, honey," I said quietly.

"Ugh," he groaned, which was his form of capitulation.

I changed the subject. "Let's talk about the wedding for a second."

"Right, let's, because I'm *way more annoyed* about that. Remy has given me carte blanche."

"Noel—" I began.

"No. You're nickel and diming things. You can't be wearing an Oscar de la Renta wedding dress and serving Costco champagne, for God's sake."

I hadn't suggested Costco.

However, what I'd suggested wasn't far off.

"I—"

"Wyn, this poor girl syndrome thing has to stop."

I blinked at the road.

Noel kept speaking.

"I'm not going to be stupid about things. You guys are rich but you're not billionaires. We're not talking ridiculous. But Remy said you couldn't have the wedding you wanted the first go 'round, so he wants you to have what you want this time. And that's not only what you're getting, it's also what you're letting him give to you."

Letting him give to you.

Letting Remy give it to me.

"I'm doing it again," I blurted.

"Tell me about it," he retorted.

"No, I mean pouring the wine back into the bottle."

"Sorry?"

"I have poor girl syndrome," I told him.

"Uh, I hate to be common, as you know, but there's no other response that fits as well as this one. No duh?" he asked. "We've only had this conversation fifty thousand times."

That was an exaggeration.

But that didn't make his statement untrue.

"It upsets Remy," I shared.

Noel finally cottoned on to how important this bent to the conversation was.

"He needs to feel like he's taking care of me," I went on.

"That's what you do for the people you love," Noel said carefully.

"It's more with him. I need to do better at not pouring the wine back in the bottle."

"First, gross. *Never* pour wine back into the bottle. But Wyn, what upsets him is not only that he wants to feel like he's taking care of you. It's that, since you haven't let that go, since you haven't settled into the life you two built together, a life that's impressive and by no means one where you have to horde wine or *anything*, it probably feels like he's failed at taking care of you all along."

Oh my *God*.

Yes.

This.

This was precisely what triggered my husband three years ago.

Noel was still talking.

"However, most importantly, although this is about him, it's also about you. We all can't blow every penny we earn, but you don't do that. Neither of you do. Not even close. But you splurge on a five-thousand-dollar bag without blinking, and don't use Ziplocs."

"That's about the environment," I fibbed.

It was, but it wasn't.

"Whatever. You know what I mean. Seriously, *pouring wine back into the bottle*?"

And...seriously.

That *was* gross.

"My parents worked very hard when I was growing up, and we still didn't have much."

"Okay, so you worked very hard as the next generation, and you have a lot more. Do you hold guilt about that?" Noel inquired.

"No. I don't think so."

"Is this bigger?" he asked, oddly eagerly. "Do I need to call a Cock and Snacktails?"

Eagerness explained.

The seal had been broken for Noel on that in a big way. I'd been home for four days, and he'd wanted to call three Cock and Snacktails, mostly about me talking to Bea by myself, but once it was because I postponed my mani-pedi (by *a day*), and he felt I needed a lecture from all my bestest friends on self-care.

He did this, by the way, while giving me a lecture about self-care.

"I think I need to be open about this with my husband, explore it with him, and ask him to work on it with me."

"I suppose that's a better idea," Noel mumbled.

"This means you have carte blanche, honey, within Remy's budget, that is," I pointed out in order to improve his mood.

"Oh my God, it does!" he replied. "I gotta go. I have calls to make. Byeeeee."

And then he was gone, and I was smiling at my windshield.

The smile didn't last long, primarily because, a few minutes later, I was pulling into Bea's driveway.

She made me stand at her door probably a full two minutes before she answered the doorbell, and for once, I was on time.

"Wyn," she greeted coolly, stepping out of the way.

"Hi, Bea," I greeted much more warmly, hoping to set a tone, or at least push back on hers so she'd fall into mine, and then both of us could find a way to get beyond where we were and learn to be better at what we were.

Friends.

I stepped inside.

She led me to the living room, turned and stated, "I'd offer you something to drink, but I'm not sure how this is going to go, and if you're here to be abusive to me, it isn't going to last long enough for it to be worth the effort."

Not a great start.

"I'm not going to be abusive, Bea, of course not."

"You haven't been very cool with me lately, Wyn, so you can understand my concern."

I had agreed to meet at her house to make her feel safe. Not on neutral ground, on her turf.

I gave her that.

And for years, she verbally tore apart my husband to my face, as well as his, and anyone else who would listen, and I'd let her.

Now, it was time to come to terms, and she was gaslighting me.

But I wasn't going to bite.

So I didn't.

"We have things we need to talk through," I told her.

"You're getting back with Remy," she surmised.

"No, I'm not. We're back. We're remarrying during the Christmas holiday. We just returned from New Orleans as a family because his mother is dying."

I stopped speaking because she rolled her eyes and shook her head at the same time, crossing her arms on her chest, and it came to me in that moment that we were both still standing.

She hadn't offered me a seat.

I'd been in that house more times than I could count, and she hadn't asked me to sit down.

Nor did she have a word to say about Colette's situation.

Now, she might not be Remy's biggest fan, but she didn't know Colette was like she was, and both Colette and Remy were human beings, so learning the mother of someone you knew was dying merited *something*.

However, it didn't get it.

Instead, she told the ceiling, "It's utterly ludicrous what women will put up with from a man so they'll feel some worth when they're already worthy."

"It isn't about feeling worth, it's about love. I love him, Bea."

She looked to me, not hiding the sneer in her lip.

I ignored that and forged ahead before she could say something else that was annoying.

"I also can't have you trash-talking him. Not to me, or to Remy, or to anybody."

Her eyes got big. "Trash-talking him?"

"Please don't pretend you don't know what I'm talking about," I said quietly.

Her face twisted. "God, he's got you wrapped around his dick again, doesn't he?"

I said nothing, just stared at my friend, feeling the bitterness emanating from her and hitting me like a thousand little spikes, leaving a thousand little wounds.

"You do know this is pathetic, don't you?" she demanded.

"No," I said, still quietly, this time my voice clogged with hurt. I saw Bea register that hurt, a flicker of something warmer and kinder in her gaze, but I kept going. "I know it isn't anything of the sort. I also know that I can't stand here any longer, and it guts me, utterly rips me to shreds to say that I think it's healthier for the both of us if we go on with our lives without each other in them."

"So you're picking Remy over me," she scoffed.

Dear God.

What was wrong with her?

"He *is* my husband, Bea," I pointed out.

"He left you. He *broke* you when he left."

"I was devastated, but I wasn't broken. We both know that. Please don't dramatize what happened to *me*. Not you. *Me*. I felt it. I lived through it. Not you. But I went to work. I continued to build my business. I took care of my home, my children, myself. I was hurt, torn up. I loved him. I missed him. I was painfully confused. I didn't get why he left. It preyed on my mind relentlessly. But I was *not* broken. Further, Remy and I discussed it. There were reasons he left."

"Yeah? What reasons?"

"I would hope you understand, considering how this conversation is going, why I feel that isn't any of your business. What's important is that they were significant, I know them now, I understand them, and we've worked through them."

"You know what pains me, Wyn?" she asked.

I'd come there wanting to understand what pained her.

I no longer felt that way.

I didn't get the chance to tell her not only didn't I know, I didn't want to know.

She told me.

"That I've spent so much time on you, and in the end, you're one of those women who'll do anything to keep a man in her life. All the show with your big business and your Hollywood clients, and when it all boils down, you're just the little woman."

I let the "little woman" thing go because that was pure bullshit and not worthy of comment.

"You've spent so much time on me?" I whispered.

"We've known each other years," she retorted.

"We have. But I'd like to understand. Have I been a project? Or has this been a friendship?"

"You know what I mean," she huffed.

"No, I don't. I wouldn't ask if I did."

"You need a man," she snapped.

"I don't need him, Bea. I want him. I love him. There is no weakness to a woman who wants a partner to share her life with."

"Men like that are dinosaurs."

I shouldn't ask.

I asked.

"Men like what?"

"Toxic men," she declared. "The kind who spread their legs far apart in an airplane seat because they need so much room for what they consider are their big balls, and they don't give that first fuck that they're invading *your* space. Space *you* are entitled to. Men like *that*."

Remy didn't do the man spread, at least not when he was sharing space on a couch or in a restaurant booth or on a plane, or, truthfully, *anywhere*.

But I wasn't going to share that.

I also wasn't going to defend my husband. I wasn't going to put energy into doing something that didn't need to be done, and something she wasn't entitled to have.

She'd known me for years. She'd also known Remy.

She knew this already.

However she wanted to view him was hers. The fact it wasn't the truth was something I now understood, I could talk to her until I was blue in the face, and it wouldn't change.

She'd made up her mind. For some reason, I right then realized I'd never get the chance to understand, it was ugly, twisted, wrong and harmful, but she'd done it and she was sticking to it.

To stick by her decision, hurting Remy was okay with her.

Worse, hurting me was too.

I'd reached out to her. I'd gotten into my car and come to her. I was standing in her living room. I was giving her my time. Everything I'd done was making it clear she meant something to me, and I wanted to do what I could to salvage a friendship with a person I cared about.

And she was cold to start, manipulative in the beginning and vicious from there.

Noel, damn the man, was his usual right.

She hadn't earned me standing right there.

But I did it and now it was time to leave.

"Thank you for all the kind things you've done for me and my kids, and all the lovely memories we've shared," I said, and gave her a sad smile, watching the animosity waver on her face as distress flashed in her eyes.

But I didn't hesitate.

I turned to leave.

I was out the door, foot on her welcome mat, pulling the door closed behind me, when it was tugged from my hold.

I looked back, hope blooming in my chest.

"You're going to regret it, going back to him," she warned.

The hope died.

"Try to be happy, Bea. I want that for you," I replied.

And then, without looking back, my heart feeling like a rock in my chest, I walked to my car, got in, started it up...

And I drove away.

CHAPTER 32

Adulting

PART TWO

Remy

"No, if you don't mind, let's talk here," Remy said as Myrna, who he'd just granted entry, started to walk to the family room.

Her step faltered. She looked at him where he stood, arm extended, indicating the living room, a room she didn't know was closer to Bill so Remy's friend could hear what was going on from behind the opened door you couldn't see from that space.

Noting her expression, he felt the same as he did when she immediately picked up his call after he'd connected with her to set this meeting. The same as when she'd immediately agreed to meet. The same as when he opened the door.

He felt uneasy at the hope in her gaze.

She moved down the steps to the living room and headed toward the couch.

"Would you like a drink?" he asked.

"I'm not sure, do I need one?" she asked in return.

"I don't know about you, but I do."

Her lips quirked, and he had the unsteadying sensation that she was calm and contented.

She thought she was getting what she wanted, what that was, Remy didn't know. He was simply concerned because whatever it was, it was likely she wasn't going to get it, and he'd learned the hard way that Myrna not getting what she wanted didn't go well for him and his family.

KRISTEN ASHLEY

"Wine? Vodka tonic?" he offered, not going to her usual, a margarita, because he wasn't going to put that kind of time into making it.

"Wine," she answered.

"I'll be back," he murmured.

There was a white opened in the fridge. Wyn had opened it the previous evening while he grilled chicken. Over dinner, they'd gotten involved in a discussion about household chores, this devolved into an argument, and they'd ended up fucking.

It had been superb.

In the end, he took her point about being too traditional about the gender divide in everyday life. But since neither of them did most of those things anymore (Wyn was now also using his laundry service), it was moot. Though, he promised to try to be more aware, and if he wasn't, receptive if she brought it up.

Since they'd fucked and talked themselves out, they'd then gone to sleep.

And didn't finish the bottle.

Remy poured wine into two glasses and returned.

Myrna was on the couch, right in the middle, like his mother had sat in hers the last time he saw her.

After giving her the glass, Remy moved across the space to sit on the piano bench.

He took a sip, waited for her to do the same, then he started it.

"I wanted to apologize."

She studied him closely, her eyes carefully shuttered.

"For what?" she queried cautiously, but curiously.

"For letting you move in. For leading you on. It wasn't my intention, but that doesn't mean it didn't happen. It's clear it did. I can understand how you felt there was more between us, because I was not communicating effectively with you. I can understand how you felt we had a future, because I hadn't made my feelings clear to you. I was checked out, I allowed things to go on too long, and considering your feelings for me, which I knew you had, that was unkind."

Now she was staring at him, shock unhidden.

"I don't like that you tracked down Sabre and lied to him about what happened between us. I don't like that you broke into Wyn's house and did whatever you tried to do. But I'm not telling you these things solely to get you to stop pulling shit on me and my family. Quite a bit has happened since we split, I've taken a hard look at what I've done, so I'm saying all of this because you deserve to hear it."

For a second, she sat there, frozen.

300

After that second was over, she lost it.

Completely.

Her crying was so bad, Remy had to get up and take the glass from her or it would have been on the floor.

He set it aside with his and approached her, but he didn't sit by her, he didn't touch her, he crouched in front of her.

He let her cry for a while, but when, instead of getting better, it got worse, and he saw Bill edge into the room, Remy knew he needed to address it.

He shook his head at Bill, who disappeared, then he turned to his ex.

"Myrna, what's going on?" he asked.

She was bent to her thighs, face in both hands, but at his words, she jerked back to sitting on the couch.

"I-I-I pulled that fucked-up shit with S-S-Sah be-because I was so p-p-pissed at you," she hitched out.

He'd figured that part out himself.

"Okay," Remy murmured.

She took in a breath that broke about five times.

Christ, he wasn't fond of her or her recent behavior, to say the least.

But he felt that.

"The m-m-minute he stalked away from m-me, God, he was so upset, so m-mad at m-me, I got in my c-car, drove home and thought,"—another broken breath and then a wail—"*what the fuck is wrong with me?*"

Remy didn't answer because that was also his question.

"I mean, I was acting like a crazy person!" she shouted, then shot out of the couch so fast, Remy had to lean back to miss her and almost landed on his ass.

Instead, he straightened and retreated. Not so far she'd feel snubbed, but Bill recommended he keep distance between them, and Remy was definitely listening to Bill.

She swiped at her cheeks and faced him.

"Okay, so...listen. You're gonna be mad, but just listen, okay?" she asked.

Remy braced but nodded.

"So, I was, like...you know..."

He didn't know but she didn't go on.

Then she exploded, "*Fuck!*"

He was growing concerned about her behavior. Myrna unstable, he'd learned, was not a good thing.

"Myrna, just tell me," he urged patiently. "What's gone down between us can't possibly get worse, unless you let it, so just say it. You're here for us to work this out. This is a safe place for you, I promise."

"I went part-time," she blurted.

His head jerked in confusion. "What?"

"Okay, this makes me sound bad, and I was in la-la land because I was crazy about you, though really, that's just excuse, but I'm blathering. It isn't debatable. You've got money."

Remy didn't speak.

She, lamentably, kept going.

"You weren't asking me to pay rent. You weren't asking me to contribute to the bills. I thought..."—she lifted her shoulders, dropped them—"I thought we were solid. I went part-time. I mean, work's a drag. Play is so much better. I took a pottery class. Did a lot of hiking and mountain biking. Hung at Lola's, drank coffee and read. I mean, I just, well...I kinda used it as a break."

"You didn't use *it*," he stated flatly. "You used me."

She sucked her lips between her teeth.

"You were supposed to be saving to get your own place," he reminded her.

She let her lips go and replied, "When you didn't, you know, push that or even really mention it again after I moved in..." When he opened his mouth, she quickly said, "At least not after the first few months, I thought...I mean, I figured..."

She trailed off.

So Remy finished for her.

"You decided to read our relationship how you needed to read it, and then you took advantage of it."

Softly she said, "I didn't do it to be mean or a mooch, I really was crazy about you, Remy."

Remy didn't trust himself to speak.

"The thing is, I knew before you knew. You know...about Wyn."

He spoke then.

"That I still loved her?"

Looking miserable, Myrna nodded.

"You kept going over to her house. Any excuse, you were over there. You'd come home, all amped up." Her lips tipped at the ends in a melancholy way. "I knew you, baby. I knew every inch of you. Every tone of your voice. Every smell you gave off. That amped up you were, it wasn't about being pissed, though you were telling yourself that. You needed to get laid. But,"—she drew in a huge breath—"even so, you never touched me after. Not when you got home, not for days. You missed her, you were like...*pining* for her, and I wouldn't do."

Fucking hell.

I wouldn't do.

Christ, he was an ass.

He sunk back down on the piano bench, muttering, "Jesus, Myrna."

"So, I panicked," she said. "I panicked because I loved you, and you loved her. I don't even know what the fuck was wrong with me. I tried to get pregnant when I knew you didn't want it. I guess being crazy about you made me crazy. Because I was acting *crazy*. And I panicked again when you got so mad about it and told me I had to leave. But that wasn't just because I was losing you. I got even crazier because we were over, and I didn't want that, and because I didn't have the money to go."

She sucked in a breath, and when Remy remained silent, she carried on.

"I asked to go back to full-time, but they gave that position to someone else, and they couldn't swing it for me. I needed to find a new job or another one to add to what I had, not to mention a deposit and first month's rent. But you didn't give me enough time."

"It wasn't my responsibility, considering you didn't tell me your employment had changed. If we were living together as you thought we were, as partners, this was something I was entitled to know. But regardless how we were living together, considering the fact I was footing the bill, I simply was entitled to know. Can you explain why you didn't do that?" Remy requested.

"Because I knew it would mean you'd make us end," she admitted. "I knew that would shake your shit, you'd reflect on that request, and know we weren't there, and then we'd be over. Obviously, I wasn't letting myself understand what was behind the shit I was pulling then, but upon reflection, I understand it now. I didn't want to face it, so I just rode the wave I was on, even knowing on some level I was headed for a wipeout."

She gave it a moment to allow that to sink in before she tried to joke.

"I can share with some authority that sitting in a jail cell for two days while you beg your really ticked-off mom to bail you out is a pretty hefty wipeout. And as you know, she liked you. So when I confessed to how jacked I'd been behaving, she wasn't doing cartwheels of joy at the adjusted child she'd raised."

She was being honest, and amusing, but all of this was eerily familiar.

Myrna was a thirty-nine-year-old woman who thought work was a drag, lied or held back important truths to get what she wanted, and threw tantrums and acted out when she didn't get it.

In other words, this all seemed too easy, so he wasn't ready to buy it.

"What did you come into this house thinking was going to happen?" he asked.

Now she appeared guilty, but she said nothing.

"It can't get worse, Myrna," he pointed out.

It probably could, but for fuck's sake. She'd tried to trap him with a child, stalked his son, broke into his home and used him for his money.

So she'd have to get creative to top all of that.

"I thought you'd make a deal with me. If I left you alone, you'd drop the charges."

Remy sighed.

She went to the couch, but she didn't sit in it like she owned the place this time. She rested her ass on the arm like she was ready to spring up again if he so demanded.

"You don't have to drop the charges. I have no priors. The lawyer Mom got me said if I plead guilty, he can swing a deal so I'll do community service and probably get a year's probation. It sucks, but I'll have a record. That said, it is what it is. I did it. If you can be a big enough person to say what you said to start all of this off, I can face the consequences of being a huge moron."

"Are you going to leave my family alone?" he asked.

She lifted a hand his way.

"You need to know, the last part, it wasn't about Wyn. After I did that thing to Sah I realized how fucked up I'd been behaving and refocused my energies."

She dropped her hand and made a self-deprecating face when she took in his skeptical expression.

"I needed money," she shared. "You know me and Mom don't get along all that great. Dad's a dick. I'm not going there. I'm living with her, it's not working for either of us, so I have to get out. I got another job, decent money, but now I'm hanging on by a thread, because they aren't real thrilled I worked for them for a few days then I had to call off because I'd been arrested for breaking and entering and attempted burglary."

She stopped speaking and bit her lip when she noticed that Remy wasn't responding to any of her attempts at humor, but she didn't give up.

She let go of her lip and forged on.

"I just knew Wyn had stuff. Expensive stuff. And I needed money. That part wasn't about hurting you or her. Honest to God. It was because I had to find some fast cash and I figured she'd be insured so what would it hurt?"

When he didn't say anything, she spoke again.

"Just so you know, sitting in that cell, I realized I was still in the dying throes of crazy, and you and Wyn wouldn't think the same way."

"We didn't. Neither did Sabre, Manon or Yves," he asserted.

She flinched.

She never got along with Manon, but she really liked Sabre, and tried her best with Yves.

He needed to wind this up.

"I wasn't being honest with myself, and you were caught up in that," he said.

Her face got soft. "Remy, did you miss me telling you about my near-fatal brush with being a moron?"

With her expression and her words, he was remembering what attracted him to her in the first place.

She could be sweet as well as funny.

"I knew you weren't into me," she admitted on a whisper.

"That doesn't absolve me." He did not whisper. "The idea of me getting back from Wyn's and you knowing where my head was at, it doesn't feel good I put you through that."

"But you didn't know where your head was at. I don't know why you two broke up, you never shared that with me, and that in itself...I mean, seriously, baby, you didn't ever give me anything important."

She let it sink in, how deep she'd dived into what they had, or more importantly what they did not, and then she continued.

"All I knew was, you were suffering for it. I fell in love with the wrong dude. I knew it. I didn't do anything about it. You liked me and wanted to spend time with me. You knew you couldn't give me anything more, even knowing I wanted it, and you didn't do anything about it. We both fucked up. We both admitted it. And now..."

She pulled in another breath, this one so big, her chest moved out, her shoulders went up, and he could see relief on her face when she let it out, before she concluded.

"And now we can both move on."

"I appreciate that, Myrna. But you need to move on understanding it's Wyn's decision about dropping the charges."

She shook her head. "I'm not asking you for that. I'm just saying, what's done is done between us. You don't have to worry about anything else from me. No matter what she decides. I'm done acting like an idiot over a guy. It's over."

It's over.

Could he believe it?

"I want to trust that," he said quietly.

"You can trust it," she said firmly.

Both of them sat in silence, staring at each other.

Myrna broke it.

"I fucked any chance of being buds with Sabre, haven't I?"

Oh yes, she'd categorically done that.

He nodded and gave it to her honestly. "Yes."

She shook her head morosely, looked at her lap and said, "God. Total moron."

Yes, she had been.

But she wasn't.

However, he wasn't going to convince her of that. Like he wasn't going to get into how she was in fact a thirty-nine-year-old woman who needed to keep a job, look after her finances, stop bumming off people, including her mother, and get her shit tight.

But he wasn't that person to her and never would be.

She raised her head, caught his gaze and said, "I'm sorry too. I appreciate you being the bigger person, laying things out like you did. But what I did was sheer lunacy. I can tell you, I knew it at the time I was doing it, I just couldn't seem to stop myself. But now, I see it, and honest to God, Remy, I'm really, really sorry about it. All of it."

It was then, finally, Remy felt for her.

"Demons," he said.

"What?" she asked.

"Demons," he repeated. "My dad told me we all have demons in us that push us to do things that hurt the ones we love most. I did it to Wyn. You did it to me. I know now how mine were born. And maybe...hopefully, knowing that means I can control them. I think, Myrna, maybe giving some time to figuring out how yours were born will help you get to that point too."

"Short journey straight to my dad being a narcissistic, asshole dick to me and my mom and my brother our whole lives," she declared.

He smiled.

"There you go. Maybe work on that?" he suggested.

She stood, but went to her wineglass, picked it up and took a healthy gulp.

She then put it back down and looked at him.

"There aren't many like you, baby," she told him.

"You'll find the one who can't live without you."

"Maybe." Another shrug. "Maybe not. I just gotta get to the place where I understand I'm good as I am. Because I really am. Good, I mean. I can take care of myself. I know how to use a drill. I know how to use a tire gauge. I'll be fine."

That might be the most mature thing he'd ever heard her say.

"You will," Remy agreed.

"Still, we had some fun, yeah?"

He gave her that.

"Yes, we did."

Then he made certain to maintain the boundaries they were establishing.

"And then we didn't."

"Right," she whispered, absolutely reading his message.

She picked up the wineglass again and threw back another big dose.

She set it down and returned her attention to him.

"Happy?" she asked.

He nodded.

"I'm glad," she replied, her look and tone sharing she was being genuine, before she pulled in one last visible breath and said, "See you on the flipside...or as will probably be better for us both...not."

She winked, it was supposed to be jaunty, but it failed.

She was sad and perhaps a little lost, and likely more than a little afraid.

But she didn't give him any of that straight out, she held it back.

He still felt for her.

But he didn't do anything about it.

Turning once to wave at him on the way, she left, and the door clicking closed behind her was one of the best sounds he'd ever heard in his life.

That might not be nice.

But one thing it absolutely was.

It was honest.

CHAPTER 33
Adulting
THE FINALE

Remy

"I'll drop the charges."

They were out by his pool, sitting next to each other in his armless chairs, a champagne bucket filled with ice, the martini shaker that still had half the double martini he'd stirred for Wyn in it on the table between them.

Remy was drinking a beer.

The sun was setting. The outside lights he had on a timer had already switched on. He'd left the wine room illuminated. It gave ambience, and it was a cool view.

And he'd just finished telling his wife about the surprising conversation he'd had with his ex.

"You don't have to do that, honey," he replied.

"She needs money. She clearly needs not to be further in the hole with her mother. Attorneys are expensive. We can all cut our losses and move on."

"That's big of you," he noted. "It's also unnecessary. She's ready to face up to her actions."

"Okay. But I think after your mother behaving like she did, and Bea behaving like she did, and neither of them willing to take even a step toward the center to find an impartial place to discuss things, Myrna going totally off the rails and having the wherewithal to drag herself back deserves to reap the rewards of demonstrating she has the capacity to be a decent human being."

Remy sucked back a pull from his beer in preparation.

He dropped the bottle to his knee, swallowed the brew, and asked after what had not yet been shared, "My guess is that means things didn't go well with Bea."

"I didn't time it, but I figure our conversation lasted five minutes. The last thing she said when my fabulous Valentino wedge was on her not-so-welcome mat as I was on my way out to my car, and out of our friendship, was not nice. So yes, I can confirm things didn't go well with Bea."

After saying that, she took a sip of her drink.

He watched her, and when she was done, he promised, "I can take it. You can tell me what she said."

"Well, this time, it wasn't all about you. It was about me and how weak a woman I am that I need you."

Right.

There was all that had been going on the last few weeks.

There was him knowing Wyn was off to talk to Bea that afternoon, at the same time he was waiting for Myrna to come over, which had been stressful as fuck.

There was his conversation with Myrna, one that ended on a hopeful note, but it didn't delete the fact that not only had she done all she'd done, he'd discovered she'd also used him for his money so she could take "a break" from being a responsible adult. And he still didn't trust her, so it remained to be seen if she'd do as promised and leave them alone.

But none of that was the reason he took a breath to control his fury.

And failed at controlling his fury.

"*That fucking cunt!*" he roared.

Wyn, twisted in her seat to face him, only grinned at his reaction and took another sip of her martini.

After that, she drawled, "God, you're hot when you get protective."

"I'm not finding anything funny," he growled. "That bitch is a goddamned bitch."

"I'm not being funny. You're undeniably hot when you get like this."

"Wyn," he warned.

She kept grinning.

Remy kept being angry.

"I wanna prove that piece of shit right, flip the neanderthal switch and demand you have nothing to do with that woman again, but it's your choice. I will state, however, that I will be very displeased if you have anything to do with that woman again."

"Don't worry about that, baby," she replied, the humor leaving her expression. "The bridge has been burned. There's no rebuilding it."

Shit.

He needed to get a handle on it. She'd lost a friend that day.

"Honey," he murmured.

"It's okay," she said, but everything about her screamed it was not.

"Come here," he ordered.

She moved from her seat to squeeze into his with him.

He held her close, and she rested her head on his shoulder.

"I thought," she told the pool, "Bea loves me. I thought today would be tough on you. That Myrna was a deranged stalker and we had to gird our loins for more of her shenanigans. I thought Bea would see reason, meet me in the middle, discuss things like the adults we are, and even if she still held some animosity toward you, she'd shield me from it, because not doing so hurt me. I thought she loved me enough to do that, because I loved her enough to reach out and try to find middle ground. I thought I'd come away with my friend, and right now, I'd be comforting you." Not moving her head from his shoulder, she took another sip before she concluded, "I thought wrong."

"I was thinking the same."

She sighed.

"Gird our loins?" he teased.

She twisted to set her glass down on the table behind her, turned back and slapped him in his abs.

He chuckled.

She retrieved her drink.

"I'm sad," she admitted. "But even so, if one of us had to come out a loser, I'm glad it was me. Myrna was freaking me out."

He didn't want her to be a loser, ever.

And he wasn't going to share, but he didn't think she was one.

He detested Bea, didn't trust her one bit, and he was glad she was out of both of their lives.

It was selfish, but it was the truth.

And he was also pleased his experience meant they were hopefully going to be free of Myrna's bullshit. Because it pissed him off it freaked out Wyn and their kids, and he'd worried what was already damned extreme would only get worse.

"I'm just glad it's over," he said.

"Yes," she agreed.

"Have you told Noel and the girls?" he asked.

"I wanted to debrief with you first."

"They're probably worried."

"Kara isn't. It's sex night for her and Reed."

He laughed, even if mostly that knowledge made him feel slightly ill. He didn't need to know that much about Kara and Reed, or anyone.

But he had this back, all that was her, including her sharing all that went on with her friends...*their* friends.

He'd missed Kara. And Bernice.

And it was good he had this back.

"You should probably tell her anyway," he said. "At least send a text. But I know Bernice and Noel are probably stressed out, so you need to see to that, baby."

She heaved another sigh, kissed his jaw, then rose from the chair, holding her glass, a long column of grace in crisp white jeans, an over-sized, gray boyfriend shirt French tucked and silver Valentino wedges.

His wife.

A fashion plate.

Always stunning.

She stopped a few feet from him and turned back.

"Do you know how she tracked Sah down at school?" she asked.

He shook his head. "We didn't go there. I can contact her again and find out."

"No," she quickly replied. "We'll let that be a mystery for the ages."

She seemed genuinely unconcerned, so Remy let it go.

For his part, he'd thought about it, and he'd remembered Sah had left his class schedule on the kitchen counter, where it had remained for a week before his housecleaner had moved it to Sabre's bedroom. It would not be a surprise if Myrna read it, just out of curiosity.

Though it seemed farfetched Myrna would have memorized it enough to know how to find him on any given day. But it was an explanation that made sense, and between that, and those two kicking back on occasion, when Sabre could have talked about his classes, he figured she was no supersleuth. Something stuck, and she'd followed that lead.

And that was that.

Wyn moved to the house to get her phone, and Remy alternately watched her legs and ass as she did it.

She disappeared, and since he had his phone in his pocket, he took that opportunity to call his dad.

It wasn't a long call, but it was a disturbing one.

Guillaume tried to be positive, but Melly was also now reporting in, and

Remy knew that it seemed Colette had been holding on for Remy and his family's visit.

Now, even if it had only been a few days, the news was it seemed she was declining rapidly.

Remy knew it helped his father hearing from his son.

In the end, Guillaume didn't offer to pass the phone to Colette, and Remy didn't ask, which was probably a relief for them both.

It was even darker now, so Remy moved to the firepit across the way where it sat between some loungers. He lit it, contemplating what they'd have for dinner, thinking some takeout would be a good idea, when he realized that Wyn hadn't returned.

He looked to the house, seeing one lamp in the living room lit, but not seeing her there. The rest of the house, save the wine room, was dark.

He moved that way.

She was nowhere to be found, until he commenced a full search, and discovered her in his walk-in closet.

The minute he appeared, she turned to him and said, "Darling, this is dire."

He burst out laughing.

He had a lot of clothes, because he did what he did and it included having a lot of meetings, not to mention she was his wife, and finally, he just liked clothes.

Still, it was only half full.

But it was a galley walk-in, long, but close, and very dark.

She lifted both hands in front of her, pressed them out and asked, "Can we blow out this wall, do a *wee* expansion of the bathroom, give you your own closet, and build an oasis for me?"

Remy stopped breathing.

She kept talking.

"And by that I mean I want a full vanity and room for expansion. I'm already at my limit with my closet, which was not good forward-thinking on my part."

He had to push it out, so it was guttural when he inquired, "You want to move here?"

She turned fully to him. "Your kitchen, it's cool, but a negative." She whirled a hand at her side. "This. A disaster. But your outdoor space, pool, wine cellar and the guest suite are all positives. You also have more bedrooms and I like the sunken living room and bedroom. Mine, or our old house," she quickly amended when she caught the look coming over his face. "The kitchen, memories, and my closet, which I'm growing out of. But,"—she flipped out both hands—"we're all in a new chapter in our own ways. The kids off to do their thing, you and I starting over. I might want to do some painting and a bit of redecorating. It's all very *bachelor*. It doesn't have to scream that a woman lives here, but some cosmopolitan neutrality wouldn't hurt."

"You can do whatever the fuck you want," he said.

"It's going to cost a lot and I expect you not only to design the addition," she parried. "But also be involved with the redecorating."

Like he'd allow it any other way.

"She lived here," he reminded her.

"She stayed with you," she amended. "It's always been yours. However, I fully intend to make it ours."

Remy neither moved nor spoke, he didn't trust himself to.

If he did, they'd be fucking on the floor in his closet, and he wasn't sure his cleaner vacuumed in there regularly.

"I have poor girl syndrome," she announced.

He felt his brows come together. "Sorry, what?"

"That's what Noel calls it. Sure, I recognize I now have money. I'm comfortable. I treat myself. I live well. But it surfaces in weird ways. It makes me do strange things that don't make sense. Like I'm totally okay buying expensive crabcakes for the kids because they love them, but I balk at lobster rolls, when everyone loves those too. But just the word 'lobster' triggers something in me, and that something holds me back. Like I was fighting Noel about the kind of champagne we'd serve at the wedding. I'm spending fifteen thousand dollars on a dress I'll wear once and serving our guests champagne that cost seven dollars a bottle."

"I already overrode your decision on that, baby," he murmured.

He was mildly surprised that admission caused her to smile and walk to him.

She put both her hands to his chest, and he wrapped both his arms around her.

"What I'm getting at is that what you, and Noel I'll add, have been trying to explain to me for a while, I finally understand it. I don't know how to stop doing it. But I think it'd be a good idea if we had some kind of safe word. Like when it happens, you say 'syndrome,' I'll come into the moment, and we can maybe take a time out and explore why I regressed to that place."

"That works for me."

"If we do that, my hope is I'll work my way beyond it, and eventually it'll go away. But even if it doesn't, we'll both be aware of it, rather than just you, so it won't cause harm."

Fuck.

Fuck.

But he loved her.

"Sounds good," he grunted.

Her eyes moved over his face before they caught his. "You gave me a beautiful life, Remy. From the moment I met you."

"Wyn," he groaned, dropping his forehead to hers.

"I'm sorry. It's like a tic. Me doing that, making you feel like you weren't giving me that kind of life."

"You have nothing to apologize for."

"I never, ever wanted you to feel like you weren't giving me everything I needed, Remy. Everything I needed and much, much more. Because you did, you do, and you do it in a way I know you always will."

"I just want you to be happy."

"One thing's for certain, you always gave me that. Even when we fought."

That made him smile.

"I love fighting with you."

She started giggling. "Honey, I know. You pick fights so we'll fuck."

He started moving backward, toward the bathroom, which would lead them toward the bed.

And he asked, "What would piss you off right about now?"

She stopped giggling and burst out laughing.

He loved that sound.

So he decided not to piss her off, and instead, listen to it.

But when she was done, he didn't delay.

He dragged his wife to bed.

Epilogue

COME RAIN OR COME SHINE

Remy's phone rang.

We both immediately woke, if not fresh, certainly alert, even though that night we'd tested what our fifty-something bodies could do in my big tub, and I was pleased to say we'd bested that challenge splendidly.

But when we were done, we'd fallen into bed, exhausted.

Remy had moved back into our old place because he hadn't delayed in drafting plans for what we were going to do to our new place. Work began two weeks ago, which was only a week after I'd told him I wanted to move in.

Normally, neither of us kept our phones by the bed.

Lately, Remy was keeping his phone by the bed.

"Dad," he answered, and I could tell he was trying to keep the sleep out of his tone, but he didn't quite succeed.

My heart sank and I looked at the time.

It was five in the morning.

I suspected Guillaume hadn't failed to calculate the time change.

Instead, I suspected he'd waited as long as he could to give us as much sleep as he could before he called.

"We're coming," Remy said, paused, then more firmly stated, "*On s'en vient*, Papa."

I threw back the covers and got out of bed.

I was washing my hands after using the bathroom when Remy was off the phone and coming toward me.

"I'll go wake Yves," he said.

"I'll call Manon."

He nodded. "When I'm done with Yves, I'll call Sah."

I nodded.

And while I talked with my daughter, I pulled out my husband's and my luggage.

I SAT in the waiting room with my children.

I supposed it wasn't a surprise she refused to see them, considering she hadn't refused to see me, and she looked like hell.

She wanted me in first, without Remy, and I wasn't certain why, even now, because she'd looked at me, reached out a hand, I took it, she squeezed weakly and said, "Thank you for coming," like I was in a receiving line.

She'd then let me go, turned to Melly, who was in the room with us, along with Guillaume, and she said, "Help me with my lipstick, cher."

When Melly moved to do as asked, her attention went to Guillaume.

"I want my son."

And I was dismissed.

Remy was now in there with Guillaume. Melly had gone to get coffees.

I was worried sick, literally nauseous, wondering what was happening in that room.

Manon sat close to my side, her head to my shoulder. We were holding hands.

Yves was sprawled in a chair, legs stretched out, ankles crossed, eyes on Sah, who was pacing.

Remy walked in.

When he did, we all perked up.

Then, without a word, seeing the look on his face, we all moved and took him in our arms.

"SHE WAS RIDDLED with it when we were here."

Remy was whispering in the dark.

"Yes," I whispered in return.

"Will of steel to hide the pain she was in."

"Yes."

We were face to face, body to body, snug in each other's arms.

"She died with perfect lipstick."

316

I didn't exactly know why, but that made me smile.

"Yes."

"He's struggling. He's still pissed at her with what she did to me. Feeling guilt about what he did to her, about not knowing what had happened to me. Probably feeling relief that it's finally over, not only her pain, also the madness of their lives, then feeling guilt about that too. But he loved her."

That was for certain.

"Yes. He very much loved her."

Remy said no more.

I gave it some time, then I squeezed him and asked, "What are you feeling?"

"I'm glad her pain is gone."

I waited, but that was all he said.

I closed my eyes tight, agonized that was all he felt at his mother's death.

I opened them and asked, "What did she say when you were in there?"

"She told me I was handsome."

I waited again, but that apparently was it.

"That's it?" I prompted.

"And she asked Dad and me to hold her hands. We held her hands. She looked at me. She looked at Dad. She closed her eyes. And after a while, the nurse said she was gone."

Oh God.

"I felt it, though," he said softly. "When it happened. Before the nurse told us, I knew. You can feel it, baby. When life ends."

I pushed closer.

Remy stroked my back.

"Sleep, Wynnie."

"Okay, my love."

I agreed, but I didn't sleep.

Neither did he.

Though eventually I did.

But he did not.

IT HAPPENED AFTER THE FUNERAL.

Incidentally, at said funeral, Manon and I both wore big hats.

And red lipstick.

We were back at the house, the mass of people (Colette would have been gratified) who'd come after the internment were slowly fading away. Remy was playing the piano and had been for some time. A stroke of genius, because he could nod to people, they could murmur their condolences, but for the most part, he was left alone to lose his thoughts in the notes.

Melly found me and asked for a moment of privacy.

I gave it to her.

When I did, she gave me a wide, flat, black velvet box. No adornment. No wrapping.

"She said it would speak for itself," Melly told me.

Then she left.

I lifted the top of the box.

A thick cream envelope fell out, drifting to the floor.

But I was struck by what was inside, on a bed of stark black silk, an exquisite diamond necklace made of round, pear and marquise diamonds in a timeless design.

I'd seen that necklace before in a photo.

I bent to retrieve the envelope, set the box aside, and opened it, sliding the card from within.

The handwriting was cramped and wavy.

Pained.

And it said:

Wyn,
I wore this at my wedding.
I wish to invite you to wear it to yours.
Thank you for loving him in a way I did not.
Yours, Colette

I didn't want to share it with Remy.

But I needed to share it with Remy.

So once we had our own privacy, I did.

He stared at the note a long time.

And then finally, held safe in my arms, my husband shed tears for his dead mother.

I PLACED the frame among the others on the piano.

There were many.

Since all the kids played as well, Remy had bought his own grand for his house and left this one here for them to use, which meant now we had two.

I didn't play, they both looked the same to me, so I'd let him pick which one he used when we combined houses.

The other one, we could put in storage and give to whichever kid settled in a place they could take it if they wanted.

"Okay?" I asked, looking at my husband.

Remy was watching me.

When I asked my question, he came forward and moved the frame holding the photo of his parents, delighted with their newborn son, from where I'd buried it among candid rugby shots, Christmas buffoonery and fun on my parents' farm.

He put it pride of place, on the outside.

The first one you'd see.

"Just for a while, baby," he murmured. "When it hurts less, we'll move it."

"It can be there forever, if that's what you want," I told him.

He was staring down at the picture.

"I wish that happiness could have followed them for the next fifty-four years," he said, his voice faraway.

And he meant it for them, not what that would mean for him, but that was what he would have wanted for his parents.

"Well, it didn't," I replied gently. "But that little boy felt their love and happiness enough in that moment, he recreated it, gave it to another family, and so far, they've had it for decades, and they treasure it. So all was not lost."

He looked down at me, his expression not faraway.

He was lost in unhappy memories.

But that didn't mean I missed the love shining there for me.

This time, I knew exactly what my Remy needed.

"Play," I whispered.

He bent and touched his mouth to mine.

Then he sat at the piano bench.

I went to the kitchen and poured us each a glass of red. I grabbed my book.

I returned to him, set his glass on the piano, curled into the couch, opened my book, but I didn't read.

Remy played "Nuvole Bianche."

I sat with him, and silently, for all he'd never had, for all Guillaume and Colette let slip through their fingers, I wept.

Guillaume was as I'd never seen him before.

Nervous.

It was cute.

However, she was an absolute mess.

That was, she was until Manon cried, "Oh my *God!* I love your top." Then rushed her, grabbed both her hands, leaned in and kissed her cheek, popping back to say, "Hey, I'm Manon, and I'm *so glad* to meet you."

Then Sabre drawled, "Seriously, the men in this family have good taste in women. This bodes well for me."

To which Manon added, "And the women have good taste in men, so you're covered too, Yves."

She'd then latched on to Benji, who I quite liked, but Remy detested.

Sabre performed his greetings. Yves did too. Theo and Benji were introduced.

The nerves came back but quickly melted away when Remy went in and gave out hugs.

I played cleanup, smiled into their eyes, then looked around and asked, "Right, who wants sundaes?"

At my words, Estelle dropped her head to hide her very pretty face at the same time she dug into her purse for a hankie.

"Come on, Miss Estelle, you have to come to my room," Manon demanded. "That's where Mom's hiding her wedding gown. You have to see it. It's *divine*. Dad and the boys can make the sundaes while we oo and ah over it."

And with that, Estelle was claimed, dragged to Manon's room, and I trailed behind, leaving the men to make the sundaes.

The first time, we danced to "Something" by the Beatles.

Remy had insisted.

This time, we danced to "Come Rain or Come Shine" by Ray Charles.

Because again, Remy insisted.

The drifting white feathers that adorned my skirt flirted with the black of his tuxedo trousers.

The diamonds at my throat twinkled in the light.

I couldn't say I was a great dancer, but Remy was an excellent lead.

His mother taught him that.

In his arms, on that dance floor, with everyone we loved looking on, especially our children, if you'd asked me three years ago if it would have been worth what we went through to get to that moment, I would have said, *hell no.*

I still wasn't sure living those years without the man in my arms was a pain I'd ever be happy to have experienced.

I would say that every couple should have another wedding ceremony decades down the line.

The dress. The cake. The dancing.

The vows.

The beauty.

All of it.

Have it again at a time when you could appreciate it. When you knew how much work it would be, and how much joy there would be, and how many fights were going to happen, and how much laughter you'd share, and how crucial it was to have someone at your side when times got tough, and how deep love had the capacity to grow, and how never ending that capacity was.

I loved weddings.

I'd never been so happy as I'd been on my first wedding day, and no matter what anyone thought, that included the exquisite joy I felt on the birth of all three of my children.

Except for that day.

Except for right then.

In that moment.

With Remy.

I was the happiest I'd ever been.

Because we had our life, our kids, our memories, each other, and the capacity for the depth of our love to grow.

Never ending.

Then it happened.

We danced by where Guillaume and Estelle were sitting, both watching us with rapt attention, though Guillaume's was more rapt.

Yes, she'd come to Phoenix in order to be in attendance.

Remy had insisted.

And as we danced, I heard her say to Guillaume, "My God, honey. They're perfect together."

I smiled at my husband.

His return was a smirk.

And I knew one thing for certain in this crazy world.

She was right.

The End

Acknowledgments

Huge shout outs and hugs to Amanda at Pixel Mischief Design for creating the fantastic cover for this book and Kelly Brown, my editor, for keeping my shit tight. An especially big hug goes out to Camsi Ouellet-Roy for making sure Guillaume's and Remy's French was correct.

Love and gratitude to Liz and Donna, my read-along cheerleaders who buoy me while I'm writing so I'm not totally alone in my lair.

And as ever and always, thank you to my readers for giving my stories your time and loyalty.

Learn more about Kristen Ashley's
River Rain Series.

Starting with the first book,
After the Climb

Welcome to River Rain

After the Climb
River Rain Series #1

They were the Three Amigos: Duncan Holloway, Imogen Swan and Corey Szabo. Two young boys with difficult lives at home banding together with a cool girl who didn't mind mucking through the mud on their hikes.

They grew up to be Duncan Holloway, activist, CEO and face of the popular River Rain outdoor stores, Imogen Swan, award-winning actress and America's sweetheart, and Corey Szabo, ruthless tech billionaire.

Rich and very famous, they would learn the devastating knowledge of how the selfish acts of one would affect all their lives.

And the lives of those they loved.

Start the River Rain series with After the Climb, the story of Duncan and Imogen navigating their way back to each other, decades after a fierce betrayal.

And introduce yourself to their families, who will have their stories told when River Rain continues.

After the Climb

PROLOGUE

The Meet

Corey

Forty-four years ago...

He stood beside Duncan and watched her go.

And as he watched her flounce away, all mad because Duncan was being a jerk, he knew he could watch her forever.

But she was walking away. They didn't have forever. He knew that because, even though she was way down the creek before she made that turn into the woods, it seemed like it was all of a sudden that she was gone.

That was when he looked to his side and up, at Duncan.

Yeah, up.

Because Duncan was taller than him.

It wasn't just being tall.

Duncan was a lot more "ers" than him.

And when Corey's eyes got to Duncan's head, he saw his best friend was still staring at the spot where she last was, like she was still there.

And Dun's face was all weird.

Corey knew that weird.

He *felt* that weird.

Deep in his chest.

Like it'd been there all his life, even if he'd never felt it before.

It was a good weird.

Corey didn't get it, but maybe it was the best weird ever.

No.

Duncan couldn't feel that same thing.

Not for *her*.

Not for her.

"Why'd you have to do that?" Corey grumbled.

Dun didn't even look at him when he replied, "I don't know. I don't know."

He didn't have to say it twice.

Why did he say it twice?

And why did he keep watching that place where she'd gone?

"She's just a girl," Corey muttered.

That was when Duncan finally looked at him.

And he knew.

They both knew.

Imogen wasn't *just a girl*.

And she never would be.

AFTER THE CLIMB IS AVAILABLE NOW!

About the Author

Kristen Ashley is the *New York Times* bestselling author of over eighty romance novels including the *Rock Chick, Colorado Mountain, Dream Man, Chaos, Unfinished Heroes, The 'Burg, Magdalene, Fantasyland, The Three, Ghost and Reincarnation, The Rising, Dream Team, Moonlight and Motor Oil, River Rain, Wild West MC, Misted Pines* and *Honey* series along with several stand-alone novels. She's a hybrid author, publishing titles both independently and traditionally, her books have been translated in fourteen languages and she's sold over five million books.

Kristen's novel, *Law Man*, won the *RT Book Reviews* Reviewer's Choice Award for best Romantic Suspense, her independently published title *Hold On* was nominated for *RT Book Reviews* best Independent Contemporary Romance and her traditionally published title *Breathe* was nominated for best Contemporary Romance. Kristen's titles *Motorcycle Man, The Will*, and *Ride Steady* (which won the Reader's Choice award from *Romance Reviews*) all made the final rounds for Goodreads Choice Awards in the Romance category.

Kristen, born in Gary and raised in Brownsburg, Indiana, is a fourth-generation graduate of Purdue University. Since, she's lived in Denver, the West Country of England, and she now resides in Phoenix. She worked as a charity executive for eighteen years prior to beginning her independent publishing career. She now writes full-time.

Although romance is her genre, the prevailing themes running through all of Kristen's novels are friendship, family and a strong sisterhood. To this end, and as a way to thank her readers for their support, Kristen has created the Rock Chick Nation, a series of programs that are designed to give back to her readers and promote a strong female community.

The mission of the Rock Chick Nation is to live your best life, be true to your true self, recognize your beauty, and take your sister's back whether they're at your side as friends and family or if they're thousands of miles away and you don't know who they are.

The programs of the RC Nation include Rock Chick Rendezvous, weekends Kristen organizes full of parties and get-togethers to bring the sisterhood together, Rock Chick Recharges, evenings Kristen arranges for women who have been nominated to receive a special night, and Rock Chick Rewards, an ongoing program that raises funds for nonprofit women's organizations Kristen's readers nominate. Kristen's Rock Chick Rewards have donated hundreds of thousands of dollars to charity and this number continues to rise.

You can read more about Kristen, her titles and the Rock Chick Nation at KristenAshley.net.

facebook.com/kristenashleybooks

twitter.com/KristenAshley68

instagram.com/kristenashleybooks

pinterest.com/KristenAshleyBooks

goodreads.com/kristenashleybooks

bookbub.com/authors/kristen-ashley

Also by Kristen Ashley

Rock Chick Series:

Rock Chick

Rock Chick Rescue

Rock Chick Redemption

Rock Chick Renegade

Rock Chick Revenge

Rock Chick Reckoning

Rock Chick Regret

Rock Chick Revolution

Rock Chick Reawakening

Rock Chick Reborn

The 'Burg Series:

For You

At Peace

Golden Trail

Games of the Heart

The Promise

Hold On

The Chaos Series:

Own the Wind

Fire Inside

Ride Steady

Walk Through Fire

A Christmas to Remember

Rough Ride

Wild Like the Wind

Free

Wild Fire

Wild Wind

The Colorado Mountain Series:

The Gamble

Sweet Dreams

Lady Luck

Breathe

Jagged

Kaleidoscope

Bounty

Dream Man Series:

Mystery Man

Wild Man

Law Man

Motorcycle Man

Quiet Man

Dream Team Series:

Dream Maker

Dream Chaser

Dream Bites Cookbook

Dream Spinner

Dream Keeper

The Fantasyland Series:

Wildest Dreams

The Golden Dynasty

Fantastical

Broken Dove

Midnight Soul

The Dawn of the End
The Rising

The River Rain Series:
After the Climb
After the Climb Special Edition
Chasing Serenity
Taking the Leap
Making the Match
Fighting the Pull

The Three Series:
Until the Sun Falls from the Sky
With Everything I Am
Wild and Free

The Unfinished Hero Series:
Knight
Creed
Raid
Deacon
Sebring

Wild West MC Series:
Still Standing
Smoke and Steel

Other Titles by Kristen Ashley:
Heaven and Hell
Play It Safe
Three Wishes
Complicated
Loose Ends

Fast Lane
Perfect Together
Too Good To Be True

CPSIA information can be obtained
at www.ICGtesting.com
Printed in the USA
LVHW042104160623
750008LV00002B/5